Family Drama

Rebecca Fallon

Family Drama

Rebecca Fallon

b

THE BOROUGH PRESS

The Borough Press
An imprint of HarperCollins*Publishers* Ltd
1 London Bridge Street
London SE1 9GF

www.harpercollins.co.uk

HarperCollins*Publishers*
Macken House, 39/40 Mayor Street Upper
Dublin 1, D01 C9W8, Ireland

First published by HarperCollins*Publishers* 2026
1

A catalogue record for this book is available from the British Library

HB ISBN: 978-0-00-873830-3
TPB ISBN: 978-0-00-873831-0

This novel is entirely a work of fiction.
The names, characters and incidents portrayed in it are
the work of the author's imagination. Any resemblance to
actual persons, living or dead, events or localities is entirely coincidental.

Set in Adobe Garamond Pro by HarperCollins*Publishers* India

Printed and bound in the UK using 100% Renewable
Electricity at CPI Group (UK) Ltd

This book contains FSC™ certified paper and other controlled
sources to ensure responsible forest management.

For more information visit: www.harpercollins.co.uk/green

for my family, with love
and M.C. always

1997

Bear right on Argilla Road, past Douglas Orchards, down the hill. Wrought-iron gates mark the Ingram estate (est. 1928) on the left. Turn a sharp corner and the trees out your window peel away, revealing the shoreline. Of course, you can't see the sand in the winter; snow blankets the beach and the marshes, thick and inevitable and heavy. So drive slowly, and follow the caravan of cars toward the ocean.

On the beach, amid the cloud of dark winter coats, you'll see a pair of twins standing small and bereft, their neon parkas incongruous against the sea. They are waiting for their mother to arrive. The air is punishing and the crowd is silent. A small, ancient-looking vessel splashes to shore, *ELYSIUM* painted in large green letters on the starboard side. The crewmen jump off and heave the boat onto the beach; an unusual arrangement, but the captain made an exception for the Bliss family. The young men loiter on the damp sand.

At last she comes, at her leisure, wearing thick make-up and her wedding-day earrings, her car churning up sand and snow. The crewmen shiver as they remove her from the back of the hearse.

"Sebastian, Viola, come along!"

The twins are lifted now, up onto the back of the boat, and they're pushing off – tear-streaked relatives and friends growing smaller and darker as the beach recedes.

It's only on board that the twins realize their mother is not in a box, but a bag. "It's cotton," their father explains, "so she can return to the earth." Is there earth under the water? They wonder. The material reminds them of a guitar case, like their mother is an instrument. They glance at their father, perturbed. He's looking at the sky.

The water is choppy and rain begins to spit against their faces. The bag is still. When they have passed the point where they can see the land, the engines thrum to a stop and everyone gathers at the bow. A shriveled man in a dark suit says a few words. A wonderful person, wasn't she? Strong, courageous in her work as she was in the battle for life. A true New England woman. This, the year of Our Lord, nineteen-hundred and ninety-seven. It's hard to hear him against the crashing surf.

Time for a last look. The zipper on the bag riffles halfway over their mother's body and catches like a broken fly. Nothing in the universe has ever sounded so morbid. The twins stare as the wrinkled man fails to jam it down, catching again and again at the same warped tooth, and settles for crudely spreading the synthetic flaps apart with out-stretched arms to reveal their mother's face, a mask in an expression she has never worn. Their father is crying.

From the hold of the ship, the crew produces four cannonballs, wrought iron, heavier than both twins combined. Their father and the captain lower the weights into the bag. Small flowers are pressed into the twins' small hands, *throw them into the sea*. Someone plays an endless, somber note on a trumpet, and their mother – indelicately – is thrown over the side of the ship.

A bell is rung eight times. The engine skips a beat as it turns back to shore, leaving in its wake a pair of shipwrecked hearts.

Aunt Sadie bulges against the cheap material of her funeral dress, the only black clothing she has ever voluntarily purchased. The nylon rubs against the floral embroidery of the chaise longue in the dining room, and Viola understands instinctively that these are fabrics that do not belong together. She and Sebastian are sitting underneath the din-ing-room table, watching the throng of suit trousers and stockings that have entered their house to eat their food and say nice things about their mother. Most of them are unknown to Viola, and so she fixates on Sadie, whose voice carries across the room, unmuffled by the tiny cocktail sausages that she is shoving into her mouth two at a time.

"They're addictive," she is shouting. "I'm stress eating."

Sebastian sprawls out long-ways under the mahogany table, belly down and transfixed by the details of a coloring book that Sadie brought along for him. He is lost in the stripes of a tiger hunkering between the low leaves of a paper jungle. Occasionally he kicks back his legs (still clad in small suit trousers) onto Viola's lap. For her present, she had received a doll that apparently practices aerobics. The doll is like a Barbie but, importantly, is not a Barbie, so there is no point. *Her hair is dark, like yours.* The not-Barbie's smile is hollow. The not-Barbie is as pointless as the million tiny grains of sand that have been tracked into the house on the bottoms of people's shoes. Viola is calculating how long it will take to undo. Even now, on the inside of her Mary Janes, she can feel where sand got in, where it is rubbing against her tights.

"We should go to the zoo," Sebastian says. He is blending green and blue wax with his index finger on the rainforest fronds. The gaps under his fingernails are crusting with rainbow sludge.

"I thought animals have diseases." They were going to get a dog before her mother got sick, and now she's glad they didn't. She shifts onto her side and takes Sebastian's idle hand in hers, begins methodically excavating the wax. His hand is limp and compliant.

"Yes," he says gravely. "They can make fur grow all over your body."

"Even in your mouth?" Over the past few months, Viola has developed an aversion to all possible carriers of illness. The reason for this is uncomplicated. She avoids: handshakes, the kitchen trash, large still bodies of water. Sebastian, though messy, is exempt from her precautions because he is more or less an extension of herself. And he reminds her not to worry.

"Yes, even in your nose and all over your eyes." He reaches up and pops the metal barrette out of her hair and tosses the curtain in front of her eyes. "Like a rug."

"I'm a rug-a-saurus," she says, laughing her musical machine-gun laugh. Sebastian pokes her in the stomach and she convulses into sharp tickled elbows and knees. He can't help following her into hysterics, loud and hiccupping, and it sounds like a pair of legs is joining in the laughter until they realize that the noise is actually a loud sob and they remember that their mother is dead. From the floor, Viola can see a pair of tearful silk trousers being comforted by a wide pair of slacks and led away.

"You don't have to touch them if you don't want to, Lola."

"What?"

"The animals."

Lola is the leftover product of a fat baby tongue that found the three pretentious syllables of her name too complicated. He is the only one who calls her that now. She pushes her hair back and watches as he returns, with a sense of deep purpose, to his coloring book. It is critical that neither of them dies, but in the event that they had to, she would rather they did it together. The idea of living without him makes her sick.

"It's horrible," Sadie is saying now, in as hushed a voice as she can force. "It's just not what she would have wanted."

Sebastian pulls himself forward and Viola follows his attention. If they lean out through the chairs, they can see Sadie is addressing a long pair of nude pantyhose that resolve in sand-flecked heels leaning against the table. Her face is a mess of runny make-up, dark smudges covering the pouches under her eyes. She is holding, under one arm, a framed photograph of her sister, Viola's mother. Her legs are splayed wide and unladylike.

"You want a spot on the earth that people can go to," Sadie continues, her voice rising. "You want to belong to somewhere."

The slacks cut back in front of Sadie (pardon me, excuse me) and Sadie shifts onto her haunches. All around the room, snatches of her mother are traded between strangers, the currency of grief:

"It's so unfair. Isn't it? Just desperately—"

4

"So young, so much talent"

"One of Salem's bright lights"

"And her looks – I mean, before she lost them, she was—"

"I am not saying I believe in ghosts," Sadie erupts, "I don't believe in ghosts. I'm just saying, there's a way of doing things, you know, you put someone to rest."

At that moment, she catches sight of them, tilts herself to inspect the little faces huddled under the table. A clump of black eye paint has smeared over the puggish upturn of her nose. She is looking at Viola like she would like to devour her.

"Come here, sweetheart."

There cannot be any doubt that Sadie is a contaminated person. Viola can see it in the purple stains crusting on the dry parts of her lips and smell it in the sour belly-breath escaping toward her. Sadie reaches out her fat, desperate hands. Viola looks to her brother, pleading him to render her invisible, breathing short, panicked breaths.

Don't make me.

Sebastian rolls his eyes and allows her to scuttle behind him.

"Viola!" Sadie despairs. Sebastian, unafraid of his aunt, crawls to her outstretched arms, and Sadie wraps him in a deep embrace. "That's a good boy," she says. "Your mommy loved you so much. Do you know that?"

He beams at her as she takes another long slug of wine, places the empty glass on the windowsill. Her hand flaps at the room, everyone in it. "This is too sad."

In an awkward galumphing motion, Sadie is on her feet, Sebastian tucked under her arm like a football, giggling. She groans, strains to hold him; he is unwieldy now at seven. His head hangs under the table like a bat.

"Come on, you."

He waves to Viola as he bobs away, out of the room. And she is alone.

*

5

"Sorry we can't stay," Dan Dunning says, leaving behind a Tupperware of something produced by his thoughtful, accomplished, very alive wife. He pats Al on the shoulder. "The sitter will be waiting."

"Thanks for coming."

"Let's do lunch sometime. At the club. I've got a China trip coming up, but we'll work around it." Dan is always going to China. And now he waves goodbye in the way he has always waved goodbye, pressing his lips tight together as if there is something more he wants to say. He closes the door, taking with him the linger of Al's school days, pressed collared shirts and sharp graphite, the safety of a time before.

Al squeezes the Tupperware into the refrigerator with the others. The house is full of strangers now. So many people who saw his wife from other angles, transformed her into different things. Friends from Salem, from Burbank. Bohemian like her, dramatic. Their intimacies frighten him, the way they look at each other with such feeling, and erupt in sobs and warbling anecdotes, as if it is all too much to be contained. As he is closing the refrigerator door, one of them places her hand on his arm and just looks at him, sincere and intense, as though she can communicate with her eyes alone. He doesn't know her. Who is she to have all this sadness roaring just beneath the skin? Someone his wife brushed up against for a moment? He nods and looks away, willing her to leave, hostage to her feeling. His own pain is certain and deep. Susan's absence is already a horrible fact of himself, a motionless mark.

"You just hope it isn't hereditary, don't you," one of them is saying. "Poor sweetheart."

Why do they have to drag his daughter into it? Isn't it enough to mourn one person today? It occurs to him that he hasn't seen his children in at least an hour. Is that an instinct he should have, to check on them? *How am I going to do it?*

It's not like he hasn't been alone with them. Susan was often gone for long stretches when she was filming *Life and Times*, the second most popular soap in the country. Merrily, Sadie reminded him of the fact just a few hours ago, arriving at the beach with a large box of home recordings. No official videos were available, and she'd offered him her collection like a box of rare gemstones. *I'll need them back,* she said. *But watch them, it'll be good for you.* As if he could bear to play back all the hours she spent pretending to be someone else. Choosing a different life.

No, Al is no stranger to early weekday wake-ups, packing lunches, getting them showered and dressed and onto a bus. But he always had one eye on Friday night, when she would arrive home heroic and exhausted and scoop them up into her arms. She was a natural parent.

If he had known, then, how little time there was, he'd like to think he would have handled it differently. Convinced her, earlier and more forcefully, to spend every one of her precious hours with them. The idea of the family moving out there, though discussed, had been inconceivable. His work, his everything was here. *Don't feel guilty, not now.* She would have grown out of it, with time, settled into the gentle currents of motherhood. He's convinced of that, isn't he? Now she'd never prove him wrong.

She would have hated that.

He has been staring at the microwave for an indeterminate period of time when a hand connects with the area between his shoulder blades and a man is asking him a question.

"What?"

"I said, have you got a lighter, pal?"

"No. I mean, I have matches."

"No. No, it's fine, actually, I'm trying to quit. I've already quit actually. If anyone asks, this conversation never happened."

The man is familiar but unplaceable, and Al watches him cast around the kitchen like he's lost something.

"Looking for something?"

"Me? No, no. Just looking."

He's handsome, the man, angular, young, speaks with an unexpected brogue. *What is a Scottish man doing in my house?* His shoes are nice, polished. Completely inappropriate for the weather. The man is peering at the outside of the refrigerator, the magnets, the abundance of photographs.

"Ah," the man says. "It's you."

"Sorry?"

"You're the husband."

Al looks at him blankly. The man sets his whiskey on the table and opens the refrigerator, begins to root around through the many home-made meals that ooze and chill in plastic prisons.

"Hope you have an appetite."

It's the smile that jogs his memory, roguish but genuine. He'd been on the show with Susan, played one of her boyfriends or something like that. Maybe his voice was different. Al can't remember. He has only watched a few episodes anyway – how was he supposed to stand watching his wife with other men? How was he supposed to congratu-late her? Everyone always told him, you have to separate the character from the actor. But it was her, wasn't it? Doing those things? They had never had a successful conversation about it, the things she needed to do. Ignoring it made the relationship work. It allowed him to forget.

"It'll go quickly. The food, that is. Well, maybe everything will go quickly."

"Everything?"

"Maybe not. Sorry, I shouldn't presume. I shouldn't make presump-tions about your appetite. Or your sense of time, really."

"Life and time."

"Quite." The man removes something from the refrigerator, closes the door, points at him. "You're funny. She never said you were funny."

Al is unsteadied by the asymmetry of the conversation. He had never heard Susan mention this man, and now he is slipping out of the room, taking with him memories that Al will never unlock.

"I hope it goes at your preferred pace."

"What?"

"All of it. Life."

8

He wants to shout after him, but doesn't know what to say. He feels the sudden crushing sensation of his wife's inaccessibility. That perhaps he never knew her at all.

The halls are swinging back and forth. Sebastian's face is red with the blood and the laughter rushing into it, as Sadie flies him into the living room and onto his mother's chair, which – perhaps instinctively – no one has sat in, wide arms and faded florals.

A few people are sitting in the other chairs though, older peaked faces, looking openly at him and his aunt. His silvery bird-like grandmother cranes toward the fireplace where a few crusty logs are giving up their forms.

This is the old people room, he thinks. He can smell their oldness on their clothes, their breath. It feels unfair that they should be warming themselves in here, so almost dead, when his mother had been – until recently – so very alive.

"Where is your father?" his grandmother asks him. He shrugs, without looking at her face. He hates when his grandmother is in charge, which is a lot recently. She shouted at him earlier for throwing his wet coat on the floor. The room takes on the stillness of a waiting room.

"We're going to play a little music, all right?" Sadie announces, though it isn't really a question, she is already thumbing through the reams of plastic CD cases that clutter the stereo alcove. "Jazz, jazz, jazz," she grumbles dismissively. "Where is your mom's stuff?"

Sebastian points to a basket on the floor, and Sadie crouches and plucks out a case with a blonde woman's face on it, lasers shooting out of the sides of her head.

"Faster Than the Speed of Night," she grins. "There she is."

The old people look uncertain. Their quiet has been disrupted. Sebastian watches his aunt with a new reverence. *She doesn't care – she really doesn't care.*

"Honey, will you dim the lights?"

A few piano notes crinkle out of the speakers.

"I'm not sure—" his grandmother begins.

"It was her favorite," Sadie says with sisterly authority. She holds out her hand to Sebastian and he goes to her and spins into her arms as the ballad begins, and Bonnie Tyler begins to sing: searching, ascendant, eclipsing.

Sadie is lifting and swinging him, commanding as she skids him through her legs and sings, TURN AROUND, BRIGHT EYES, her own eyes shining with the woman who isn't there, happy-sad, pulling joy out of a desperate vortex, and yes – he feels for the first time since she left – magic might still be possible.

Without Sebastian, the underside of the table is no longer of interest, but Viola has no desire to follow her aunt. Something about Sadie is not put together properly, a part of her brain probably or something inside her that makes her weird. Bodies are full of insides – it's gross when you think about it.

Her father is not in the kitchen, amid the throng of her mother's friends from work, tattooed and emotive, their faces smudged with make-up, even some of the men. *Where is her dad?* If he isn't careful, they might take over the house.

She ignores the dark-painted nails that claw at her hair as she pushes through them, as though she is a dog or a cat, passive. The conversation that she had with her mother – not their last, but their last alone – is tumbling through her mind. *Love is the most important thing,* she was saying, pressing hard into the back of her palm with a finger that was surprisingly strong and urgent. *Love, love,* was coming out of her horrible mouth, dry around the edges, and she had felt ashamed of this alien creature, hairless and wrinkling prematurely, her beautiful face naked of eyebrows and eyelashes. Ashamed also of her own fear, her inability to feel love toward the thing her mother had become. She hates thinking about her now – even the happiest memories are painted in the nauseous colors of sickness. *You can't catch it,* her father had said, *not in that way.*

Sebastian had been braver. He had kissed the strange soft skin of her skull. It didn't matter to him; boys are made differently, out of tougher things. Even if they look the same, if they have the same flushed and fleshy cheeks, the same downy hair on their arms, their insides are different.

Outside the window, a bright snow swallows the house, luminous under the moon, thickening over the driveway. Viola places her small, pale hands on her stomach, prods softly with her fingers, feeling for that invisible organ. A strange name, she thinks: you-ter-us. She finds nothing except her taut skin, but that doesn't mean it isn't there. The thought of it makes her sick.

As music that she recognizes as her mother's begins to spill from the living room, she leans close to the wall and pushes through the bodies to the front door, the gold knob chill in her fingers. Cold air hits her like a seawall. Under the orange glow of the porch light is the back of a man (not her father), sitting in a dark coat, snow dusting his shiny leather shoes. Next to him is a jar of dill pickles, and he plucks one out and eats it, staring out at the cars disappearing under the snow.

"We're going to have a hard time getting out of here," he says, and his voice is like a voice she has only ever heard in the movies, a somewhere-else voice. Soft. Refined. When he turns to see her, he looks surprised, as though he were expecting someone else. "Oh," he says. He reaches into the jar next to him. "Pickle?"

Viola shakes her head, but walks over to get a better look at him. Kind brown eyes, a thin face, hair tucked behind his ears.

"Don't blame you," he says, crunching into another. "They're intense." He wrinkles his nose.

"Then why are you eating them?"

"I'm trying to quit smoking. Someone said this was a good idea."

"It doesn't seem like the same thing."

He grins. "You're not wrong."

She bends and sits next to him.

"So what do you do, then?" he asks.

What does she do? She's never really thought about it. She eats breakfast, rides her bike, reads books. She plays in the snow, watches the sun set. It's hard to put it into words.

"You know, are you a lawyer, or a banker? You strike me as a lawyer. Thoughtful, analytical sort. Stickler for rules."

"I'm seven."

"Well, I'm twenty-seven. It's not a contest."

What is this pickle-man playing at? "Who are you?"

"Orson." He holds out his hand. "Sorry. Rude of me. I should have said."

"Viola." She eyes him mischievously. She's seen lawyers on TV. They wear suits and briefcases. It doesn't seem very difficult to her. "I am a lawyer, actually."

"I thought as much. Well, I hope you're on the good side."

She nods, though she isn't sure what the good side is. She hopes she's on the good side too. Will she have to get a suit?

Snow is falling on their knees now. Through the low orange light in the living room, she can see bodies starting to pool in, music splashing out through the glass window.

"That your brother?" Orson asks, nodding at Sebastian who is spinning around, laughing in the melee of adults jumping into the room.

Viola nods.

"He's a good dancer."

"I guess so." She hadn't really thought about it before, that dancing was something you could be good at. "I'm a good dancer too," she asserts, even though she isn't sure any more what qualifies one to be good at anything.

"Is that right." He screws the lid back on the pickle jar. "That's the way with lawyers, I've heard. They all wanted to be dancers."

"I'm a lawyer and a dancer."

"Well, that's very American of you."

She looks at Orson, his long hair, his funny, asymmetrical smile. She feels the urge to hug him, to curl up into his lap, but it would be strange, wouldn't it? She doesn't know him at all, really. But he's the first grown-up today to speak to her like a person, a real person instead of a sad child. She's tired of everyone expecting her to be useless.

"Viola, would you do me a quick favor?"

Anything.

"Can you smell my breath and make sure it doesn't smell like pickles?"

His nose brushes her nose, her face, his face, his cold skin, his breath, steaming in the frozen air, sour but not unpleasant, his eyes, her little eyes. "Smells okay to me," she says.

"You're a star. Come on, I've always wanted to dance with a professional."

He stands up and reaches for her hand. Headlights bob slowly up the driveway and catch on the porch beams, on the white, cold backs of their hands, on the forgotten, empty pickle jar, everything touched becoming more important by the touching, becoming extraordinary.

Al sits with the engine on, staring through the fogging windshield at the house that he bought almost ten years ago (before the kids, before the cancer) with romantic notions of restoration and a return to simpler times. In hindsight, it was an overzealous expenditure of the little that had been left to him in his father's will. 168 Argilla is one of the First Homes of Aldwych and a small round plaque by the door reads 1720. It is built in the New England colonial style, which is to say that the nine windows on the timber façade are straight-forward and shutter-less, its roof tilts at a sharp forty-five degrees, and every aspect of its bearing promises simplicity.

He had romanticized it. The idea of owning a bit of history, the challenge of constantly renewing the past into the present, the collapsing sense of time, the trace elements of prior inhabitants. Not that he believes in ghosts, just the impressions people make on a place.

Of course, it was all for Susan. She was the kind of woman who deserved somewhere special. No chain-link fences, no neighbors to hear if you shouted. She had taken to the project; sewing new curtains for the kids' room, picking out paint colors. Putting her stamp on things. It is strange to think of her now, just another individual who used to live here, a name that appears on one census and not the next. He itemizes the work that needs doing: dredging the gutters, sealing the leak in the roof that appeared last month. He wonders whether he can handle it alone.

Sue. Suze. Susie-Q. Susannah in the Morning. Mom. How many thousand ways she was with him, in different moods, in different moments. How many dictionaries of their private language had been lost to time. He's not entirely sure how he found himself sitting here burning gas, but it was the only place he could go. Perhaps he thought he'd find her out here, that his version of her might be less suffocated by theirs.

Was it love at first sight? People call it coming home, talk about it with nostalgia. But all he can remember is seeing (for the first time) not his past but his future. The man he might have been with a woman like her, a woman who feared nothing, certainly not the rules, and certainly not him. When he was with her, none of it mattered; all of the academic jargon stuffed in his brain gave way to laughter, to easy feeling, desire. At least it was that way at the start. For some reason, now, the start is clearer than the end. She loved him too, immediately, he is sure of that – or he was sure, at the time. Now the certainty is eroding under his inability to confirm that love was the reason she got into his car that first time, the reason she kissed him. Why else, if not for love, would she have done such a thing? *Did you know even then, Susie, that there was only one way for us? Or were you just in a mood?* Desolate questions. What he would give to know what she was thinking. His mind seeks absolutes and absolution, definitive confirmation that it all meant something.

On reflection, he never truly became the man he hoped to be with her: bold and uninhibited. Everything soft and safety-seeking won out, didn't it? *If I had more of her time,* he thinks. He sighs heavily, mourning, also, himself.

Through the low glow of the windows, the bodies of strangers are passing, congregating in heavy flocks. Exchanging Susans that never belonged to him. That never will. In the boot of his car, Sadie's tapes sit, meticulously labelled with air dates and episode numbers, a record of the woman his wife was without him. The scale is hard to ignore.

They agreed the show wasn't suitable for the children. Now, without the counterbalance of her, it might never be. It might only disrupt their certainty of who she was, her love for them. Oh, why has it fallen to him to explain this part of her he could not understand himself?

You can't dwell on the bad times, his mother said yesterday. He had been staring at bags of superfluous medical supplies when she came patting his back. Both of them were thinking about his father, who fell away piece by piece, who forgot first their birthdays then their names. He wasn't himself at the end, though it was hard to say definitively when he lost himself.

I suppose not, he said, and his mother had taken the bags down to the basement, where he would never need to look at them.

Only later he wondered whether she had been thinking of the other bad times, the shouting matches and his sister's departure. She ran off to the Catskills twenty years ago, married a ranger, became a recluse. Maybe she didn't mean the dying, but all the living you didn't want to carry; the fights and wrong decisions, the pain of loving someone who would not choose you. Was that how his mother got by? Scrubbing the record clean?

In a bright moment, it dawns on him: beyond the tapes, there is no evidence of Susan's other life. No box sets or billboards, no plane tickets or memorabilia. All the ghosts will disappear after tonight. The children will hardly remember it, the pain of lost time. And who in good conscience would remind them?

Could it be that simple to unwrite all their mistakes?

He's allowed, isn't he, to toy with the idea. After all, he's been through a lot.

Al blasts warm air onto the windshield, wipes off the dusty layer of snow, throws the car into reverse and slips into town.

Aldwych, Massachusetts is named for London's oldest port, from which ancestral Blisses set sail to exchange tea for beaver pelts. Out the window, you can see the slow-moving panorama of muddy-banked streets. Proctor, Masconomo, Agawam names crossing Puritans on every corner. Flashes of cold marsh threaten to submerge the town, and older buildings hang precipitously over wooden docks, crying out for fortification. On Market Street, a cavalcade of antique stores spew out old rocking chairs and lawn ornaments, the figurehead of an old boat. The children cannot yet judge the value of these things and are mystified by them – worthless or priceless objects, created for purposes that no longer seem necessary. It's up to him to show them what matters. To preserve what is beautiful.

He drives toward the beach, then thinks better of it and veers up Ingram Hill. The sky is deep and close and bare branches ache toward it, and he climbs until he reaches the dark, vacant summit. When he steps out of the car, cold air shreds his lungs. From the boot, he lifts the heavy box of tapes, shifts it over his hip.

They had come up here two years ago with the kids, sheathed in snow suits which they have already outgrown, the new snow hip-deep. Sue kept picking them up and swinging them forward to help them progress, while he dragged the two bright plastic sleds which skittered along the thin crust on top of the snow, bumping into each other and dashing apart.

"We should get a toboggan," he had said. He had the most wonderful toboggan when he was a kid. Beautiful. A Flexible Flyer. Curved mahogany, steel runners. It took real tactics to steer through powder.

As they reached the crest at the front of the mansion, Susan had turned around with an impish smile on her face. "We used to scoot down hills on trashcan lids. It's how I lost my first tooth."

The twins had gazed over the steep edge recklessly, with unshakeable faith in their snowsuits. Their mother planted herself on the orange sled and took Sebastian on her lap, curling up her little legs so he could sit between them. Al had done the same for Viola in the purple sled, only his legs were less containable and he'd had to dig his feet into the snow. *It'll give us a better kick-off.*

"Three, two, one!" Sebastian shouted, and off they'd gone, careening. It was a perfect sensation. Looking down the hill now, Al recalls the almost unbearable joy of racing forward, bouncing against his daughter and the purple plastic, his wife and son a blaze of orange meters ahead. It was the kind of joy that is so in pursuit of itself, that arrives at you with such speed and concentration that it cannot but bring with it a deep dread of the moment where it will inevitably end, where you will have to ask yourself whether joy like that will ever be possible again. That end might have arrived with a sudden scream, the orange sled in the air, flying away from the ground – a jump! someone built a jump! Al banked left to avoid the danger, but somehow, the orange sled landed, its riders squealing and hooting at how high they had gone, how fast. They pulled to a stop and collapsed at the bottom of the big hill, flopped into the snow, Sebastian a heap in Susan's arms.

"I think we all need to do that again," she said.

His heart had thudded in his ears, and here it thudded now, terrified even in certainty.

That was the only mother they ever needed.

The backside of the hill drops away sharply, a rocky face falling for forty feet into dead leaves and ice. Al toes over to the darkened precipice, clutching the box.

It's the quiet histories that get forgotten, silenced by the roar of spectacular drama. Their love was a quiet, steady thing. Somehow, he has become its sole keeper. Its greatest threat is in his arms. Why shouldn't he be – just once – reckless with the archive?

Blood throbs back into his cold hands. For so long now, life has just happened to him. Decisions removed from his control. No longer.

A small shelf of snow slips away under his foot.

Now.

NOW.

The box tumbles clumsily over the drop, cassettes plunging into the snow, a smattering of grave plots.

Now you've done it, says the Susan in his mind.

But it's over now, and for the best, yes? Yes – he can feel it lifting, her separate life, so many happy memories making their way back into the light. His fault or her fault, the whole fault-finding mission be damned. Quickly he treks back to the car, their faces flooding his mind, remembering the party spinning on at his house.

Wonder if they've noticed by now. Wonder if they'll ever notice.

Raucous bodies pile into the room, squeezing out the older people, the fire snapping and music playing, everyone knows the words. Sebastian is passed around like party dip, waving his hands, wiggling his hips and feeling for all the world that his mother is there.

The music dissipates the terrible splash of her body, conjures her the way she was before. His mother (the most beautiful woman in the world), hair sprawling, holding their hands on the first day of kindergarten, kissing him on the cheek, baking muffins on a Sunday morning, driving them to the beach on a summer's afternoon. Digging an enormous hole in the sand, burying all but his head. His mother, glorious in sunglasses, glorious in the summer sun. *Isn't that her!* – there in the corner, bending and laughing and gone again.

Sadie, the mistress of ceremonies, switches in Blondie, switches in Madonna. "Now this is more like it," she says, her eyes leaking black tracks into her dimples. A conspiracy is shared between them. Together they have revived her, shook life back into a dead room. "Don't forget her," Sadie says, insistent against the bouncy guitar. *Don't forget that she was like this.* Sebastian nods as the imperative lights inside him.

He feels Viola enter the room before he sees her, holding the hand of a strange man, shimmying along, spellbound. They find each other in the pulse of bodies, and a circle clears around them as they link hands and swing, hanging against each other's gravity. *Faster, faster!*

Everyone dizzy and delighted, the innocence of them! The necessary weight of her, the counterbalance. He pulls back, she pulls against him, and together as the music gives way, they let go, their love unraveled across the room.

A hush descends. His father, framed in the door, radiating a new firmness.

"Time to go, Sadie," he says.

"Don't be an ass," she hisses. Without another word, she stomps out of the house. The room is a deflated balloon. One, two at a time, the others make their excuses and depart.

"Do you want to play something?" Sebastian asks when his eyes have stopped staring at the door that his aunt left through. "Or watch TV?"

But Lola is gone too.

Outside, the driveway is roaring with engines of cars warming up, ice leaking away from the windshields, the more intrepid mourners attacking the situation with shovels and scrapers.

"Orson!"

His legs are dangling out of the passenger seat of a red car, and he is brushing snow off his bare feet, shaking them like they are electric. She doesn't know what she planned to say to him, but couldn't handle the thought of him disappearing into the night. Her imaginings have already been painted in Disney pastels; she knows a prince when she meets one.

"Well, hello. Are you coming with me?"

Everything feels possible. *Yes*, she wants to say. *Yes, I'm coming with you.*

"Where are you going?"

"California. Heard of it?"

She nods her head. It was a place her mother went. "Are you coming back?"

"Come on, get out of the snow," he says, reaching out to her and scooping her onto the seat beside him. When he pushes a button, a jazz clarinet dances out of the car speakers. Heat is blasting out of the dashboard, and he takes her hands in his and presses them toward the airstream. "It's much too cold here."

"You just don't know how to dress for it. It's not so bad if you know what to wear."

"Is that right?"

"Shoes are good for a start."

"Well, in California you don't need shoes," he says. "They're really more for decoration."

The heat is blowing hard against the skin of her hands. On the dashboard, a tiny woman in a hula skirt is standing still, waiting to lurch into life. "Can I come with you?" Viola asks.

"I'm afraid that wouldn't be a very good decision for you," he says. "You see, California is crawling with lawyers. You'd be better off carving out a niche. Like Borneo. Or The Gambia."

Snow is falling against the window, and the darkness outside of the car expands like deep space. Her own ignorance presents itself as an imperative, the world demanding to be understood. *What is Borneo? What is The Gambia?* Orson can tell her.

"Will you come back?"

Orson sighs, scrunches his leg up on the seat so that he is facing her. The hot air on her hands is reassuring, even as Orson's eyebrow is bending with some emotion she cannot place.

"Probably not, no. Which is a shame. More so for me than for you; you, madam, are destined to forget me. It's the beauty of being a young person; you forget anyone who doesn't matter. Or if you do remember me, it certainly won't be as any kind of full being. But that's fine. I'll happily carry on as a blur of color, occupying a wee back corner of your mind."

I love you, she wants to say. *Don't leave.* He cracks the door open and places her out into the snow.

"Have a wonderful life," he says.

The engine jumps and he is swinging away from her, already lost, the world becoming ordinary again.

Sebastian is backlit in the doorway. "Where were you?"

From the kitchen is the sound of the suck and pop of lids, the scraping of food off of porcelain, and the creaking of floorboards. Her face is wet with tears.

"It's okay," Sebastian says. "I miss her too."

How can she correct him?

Al's daughter floats toward him in the kitchen, and joins in the ballet of clearing napkins, glasses, trays of half-eaten cheese. The house feels colder than it ever has. He runs his hands under the hot tap, rubbing a sponge over a silver platter, and wills himself to think of warm and pleasant things that have come before, that – if he can only concentrate hard enough – will come again. Fishing boats. Tan lines. The Beach Boys, hot pavement, Florida oranges, the air inside a car that's been left in the sun. The day he met Susan.

1983

It is so hot she could die.

Sweat pricks the backs of Susan's knees, unbearable under her puritanical woolen skirts. You don't realize it, watching her onstage, how intolerable it is under the fat beams of stage-light. How an amateur would struggle to maintain character on a day like today. But at twenty-one, nothing about Susan is amateur. Even as you fan yourself with the flimsy matinee program and beg your eyelids to stay open against the torpid air, she enchants you with her conviction, her delivery, and – yes – her beauty. *Her looks don't belong here*, you might think, but then, people have been thinking that for years.

Now, backstage and desperate, she unlaces her blouse, hikes her three skirts up to her thighs. Two weeks ago, the air conditioning unit at the Courthouse Witch Museum in Salem gave up the ghost, and July is unrelenting. Eyes closed, Susan whispers lines under her breath:

I am innocent of a witch.

She takes the washcloth from her make-up bag, wipes the damp backsides of her knees, the nape of her neck. Her brain cells are melting. *How is anyone supposed to work like this?* If this show – this role – were not inscribed into her muscles, she couldn't do it. But after three years, Bridget Bishop – the first Salem woman hung for no good reason – fits Susan like a second skin. The sting of every slur, every false accusation, the raw rub of the noose on her neck are as familiar as her daily walk to the museum. Susan isn't well, hasn't been well for some time. How can anyone be well under these conditions, when daily you are murdered for being different. But that's the job: making

22

every moment feel like the first, staying awake to all that pain. It's like keeping a wound open that is trying to heal.

In the corner, a fan beats ineffectively, not even loud enough to mask the familiar lumbering footsteps outside the greenroom.

"Bourke?" Susan calls.

The director cracks opens the door, sticks through a snubby non-committal nose. "He's coming today."

"Are you sure?"

Bourke sighs. Every day, he has promised that someone will come to fix the air conditioner. This is just one of many ways that he has disappointed her.

"And Bourke," she says, "there's a kid asleep in the front row."

To be clear: she doesn't blame the child. They can't help themselves, kids, being honest. The problem is the look on Bourke's face now, the absence of concern.

"The heat is getting to everyone, I think," he says.

Behind the door, his fingers must be scrabbling at his shirt pocket, frantic for a cigarette. *Why do I know that?* she wonders. *It's pathetic.*

"Isn't it bad luck for me to be back here?" Bourke asks. He's teasing her. *Don't.* It is bad enough, being the only one around here who cares about theatrical superstition. Who treats their world seriously. Yes, it *is* bad luck for the director to interrupt the cast in the middle of a performance, but some things are more important than luck. Integrity, for example. Taking pride in your work. Keeping the audience awake. And to think: she once believed this man to be an agent of destiny.

After her final performance at Salem High, Bourke had emerged from the outpouring of parents and siblings and classmates, shook her hand, praised her craftmanship, offered her a job. In that moment, everything was confirmed; she had been chosen in the way she always imagined she would be – her talents too bright to ignore. Naively she clutched his compliments, jumped blindly into the production, told everyone – including herself – that she was saving up for Broadway's bright lights. Reassured her friends, as they swept off toward their own city dreams, that she wouldn't be far behind.

The reality, which revealed itself after months of half-assed rehearsals and uninspired direction, was that Bourke was a lazy bastard. He hadn't strolled farther than a few blocks to find his next Bridget.

The little money she makes here never lingers. It disappears behind bars and into her mother's pocket and the empty hat of the homeless woman on the corner by the fire station. On clothes that call out to her, satin and leather and stonewashed denim that jump off the racks, that demand to be worn. Clothes that feel like a way out. On new ballet shoes for her sister. Who else is going to buy them?

As Bourke begins to close the door, a tide rises within her.

"I'm going to try the new thing," she says.

The door swings all the way open, revealing the entirety of Bourke, a man in his late forties with half-moon glasses and a full-moon stomach. The stale coffee smell of him drifts over the threshold.

"Susan," he says. "We talked about this."

Yesterday in rehearsal, Susan had come on stage in running eyeliner and electric, damn-it-all hair. She never thought she'd still be here, three years later, but if there is a reason, it is Bridget Bishop. Bridget, staring down the gallows, is no bonnet-wearing sad sack. Bridget is wildfire and protest songs. Bridget is resistance. They are nothing if not in this together.

Bourke had not agreed.

"The audience is bored," she says. "You can't just read out the transcript."

"And you can't just make up history," he says. "Cosmetics were banned. Loose hair was banned."

"It's called artistic license," she says, tipping dangerously toward insurrection. Susan isn't normally the type of person to question authority. In general, she trusts easily, believes what she sees on TV. But Bourke has lost her respect. Yes, he may know about history, but she knows far more about art, which is to say, telling the truth. And the truth is not a fact, it's something you feel in your bones.

24

"I am serious, Susan," he says. "This is a museum. Not somebody's basement."

She can't stop herself from rolling her eyes. *Christ, he would be one of them,* she thinks. Or maybe Bridget thinks it.

"Do we have a problem?"

She is too angry to look at him, trains her eyes on the dusty tile floor. "No."

He turns and walks down the hall, leaving the door open, as if to say, 'I'm watching.'

A groan escapes her. *Is no one else interested in being alive?* Focus, now, return to the preparation. Take the anger, use it. Her demise is coming. *I am innocent of a witch,* she whispers, the words becoming incantation. Susan doesn't have a process, or at least, she's not sure what other people are talking about when they refer to it. All she ever does is allow herself to feel things, to understand without language a life beyond her own. She wants to live a thousand lives, to be a thousand people – this, more than fame or money or anything is the imperative. To transform so well that other people believe it. That it becomes the truth. So imagine it was you: arriving at death row, young and unready, to find that no one will save you. Not the church, not your mother. Not Goldie Hawn or Kim Basinger or any of the other saints to whom you pray. Not Bourke, not the well-intentioned nerds who complete the cast, not Mary and Angie and Bernie and everyone you know who went to New York. There will be no more nights of dancing or talking about the future, or getting up to no good in this run-down town. *No one came for Bridget Bishop. Who would come for you?*

When she blinks wet lashes and looks up to the mirror, a man is staring at her from the doorway.

This isn't unusual. Men stare. They comment wolfishly on her body outside Boston bars. She tells them what she thinks. Generally, it's that they should go to hell, but sometimes she surprises herself, asks for their name. They never expect it. But the truth she senses instinctively, looking at this man (his glasses, his general air of competence), is that he is here to save her from the heat.

"Oh thank God," she says. "It's just over there." She points at the defunct unit in the top corner of the room.

"Sorry?" he says blankly.

"The air conditioning?" She looks again. Is he dumb? Maybe he isn't really standing there at all. Maybe he is a mirage. Maybe the heat really is getting to everyone.

"Doesn't seem to be working very well," he says. He smiles. He wipes his brow.

Oh no. What is that phrase? *To a hammer, everything looks like a nail.*

"Please tell me you are here to fix that thing."

"Afraid not."

Dear God, she thinks. *Has it come to this?* Strangers permeating the doorframe, the charade of dressing-room sanctity revealed for the joke it is, the never-ending suffering of heat under her bonnet, under these too-many clothes, and all of it for what? Some regional re-enactment run by Salem's smallest museum? Once again, she has blinded herself with hope, seen what she wanted to see. Maybe she is just a bad judge of character. Her hands are untying her bonnet, dropping it onto the floor, raking through her hair.

Fuck it, she thinks. It's too hot to behave.

Somewhere in another dimension, the man is talking, explaining he is looking for some materials here in the museum. An assistant who had begun to help him has disappeared. "I think the head archivist is on holiday," he sighs. But the man does not exist in Bridget's world. Bridget licks three coats of mascara onto her lashes, pouring water from a flask onto her fingers and rubbing her eyelids until she can feel it streaking. She is thinking about injustice. She is preparing herself for a final fight. *I am innocent as the child unborn.*

Pointing to the fan, he clears his throat and says, loudly: "I didn't know they had those in the sixteen-nineties."

Susan squints, witch interrupted. *Can't he see she is working?* She inhales, takes him in. He is a man who requires a second look: his height is disguised by a bookish slouch, his steady blue eyes by thick, old-fashioned frames. There is a seriousness about his haircut, his crisp button-down, but he gives himself away with a cheeky, lopsided smile, a single, handsome dimple.

He thinks he's clever.

"Witchcraft."

"Makes sense," he nods. He holds her gaze, does not take her hint to leave. After a moment, he asks, gently: "Are you okay?"

Of course not. I am going to die. Bridget would say it, if she were responding, but this man is clearly concerned about Susan, her face smudgy and undone, flush with heat and emotion.

"I'm going to be fired." She realizes it only as she says it.

"Is there anything—" he starts. And then: "I'm sorry."

"Don't be. It will be worth it," she says with precarious mania. "It's better than sleepwalking through life."

He looks at her unblinking, inhaling as if he has something to say. What can he possibly say? She could laugh. He must have no idea. He does not leave. Instead, steadily, he crosses into the greenroom, as though searching for some way to comfort her. Can't he see, she doesn't need comfort? She has never been more powerful than on this precipice.

Nevertheless, he points his aquiline nose up at the machine, taps it twice with the flat of his palm.

"In my professional opinion, it's dead. Chuck it."

"And what kind of a professional would that be?"

"Well, I'm trying to become a doctor."

"So medically, it's dead."

"Oh, I didn't mean a medical doctor, obviously. Who needs them when the witches around here are so good?"

She laughs. Forgives, despite herself, the intrusion.

"I'm more of a history doctor," he continues, "or working on it. So, I guess I'm a professional in what does and doesn't need saving."

If you asked her, Susan would tell you that she doesn't have a type. She would also tell you that she hasn't been in love, but this she is less sure about. She finds it difficult not to fall, with sudden intensity, for the men she dates – it's too simple to imagine herself becoming the type of woman they would love in return. She does not see this as a fault. If anything, it's this capacity (she tells herself) that makes her such a convincing scene partner – the ability to find the lovable in everyone. The only point of consistency is unfamiliarity. In men she is looking for something she has not yet discovered, something she cannot find in herself.

So, this history doctor intrigues her. He is old, but not so old – not yet thirty by her estimation. He is looking at her with the assurance of someone who knows what he wants.

In the corner, a small black-and-white TV runs a feed from the stage. She has time.

"So what about me?" she asks.

"Sorry?"

"Do I need saving?"

He takes her in, the drama of her face.

"Something tells me you'll be all right."

A summer intern emerges, apologizes; he was unable to locate the documents, he tells the man. "You'd be better off returning next week, when the proper help might be available."

The man looks almost delighted by this outcome, stealing a last glance at Susan as he follows the assistant down the hall. Maybe she'll see him again. Maybe not. Either way, it does not matter, because here it comes now, the walk to her doom. Grasp at them, all the fleeting joys of life, every moment that you made a difference, that you didn't spend regretting. If she is sure of one thing, it is that she wants to live. She wants to see and feel and burn and wonder and love. She wants to say yes to all the world. When the boys come to drag her out, she resists harder than ever, her heels scuffing the stage, enchantment and anger radiating through her, the whole cast looking at her as though she might actually be a witch.

"Any final words?"

The tears are close to the surface now, instinctual. Here come the shallow – shallower – inhales like a sharpened pencil, liquid lead in her lungs. *You want a witch? Fine. Have me.* As she gives over to the carnal howl, the child in the front row stirs, opens his eyes.

BLACKOUT. The crowd on their feet. Adrenaline propels her through the greenroom, out of her costume, past Bourke (*Susan!*), out of the Courthouse. She can feel him chasing her, stray words perforating the applause still resounding in her mind.

"We talked about this—"

"A responsibility to portray factually accurate—"

"If I can't trust you—"

In the sweltering parking lot, she turns to face him. "So what?" she begins.

"I have to ask myself," he says, his brow knitting in concern. "If you really want this job."

Of course, being Bourke, he is trying to make it her decision. *You wanted this,* she reminds herself, *stand your ground.* But outside the showroom, the demands of the twentieth century are roaring awake. They'd have to pay her severance, wouldn't they? *How far would that go in New York?* She could find an apartment, something would come through, right? Her bravery is faltering under the material facts of her life. Stupid Susan, swept up in her own need to matter. You can't be important if you can't afford to live.

"I take this job very seriously," she begins, which is true.

"I'm not sure you do," Bourke says, his voice thin and pedantic. "The job is re-enactment. The job is accuracy. The job is trusting me."

The job is fucking boring. She needs to leave. But how?

A hand on her shoulder. That man again, the one with the glasses.

"That was great," he is saying. "You were terrific."

Why is he still here? He must have watched the show. He must have waited for her. A steadying thought. No one ever waits for her.

"Thanks," she manages.

"Are you the director?" the man asks, turning his attention. "I'm Alcott Bliss, I'm sure my name has come up."

Bourke is blank, blinking. Susan can practically see the frantic search in some mental filing cabinet for the name (Bliss, Alcott). He plasters on a smile, extends a hand. "Of course. Thank you for coming."

The man stands up straighter, adjusts his glasses. *Should she know about him?* He catches her with the quickest dart of the eye. *No*, the slow revelation. *He is trying to help me.*

"Well, as you probably suspected, I'm here from the board assessment committee. And we look at the value of all of the programming here at the museum. Well, I just have to say, I'm sure you are aware, but, there was talk of winding down this production."

Bourke's eyes are like saucers. As much as she hates the intervention, *oh*, this is what it feels like to have the upper hand! She has grasped his angle, keeping her face steady.

"N-no," Bourke stammers. "I wasn't aware—"

"Oh dear. Sorry to cause alarm, because you really ought not to fear – I must say, after the performance of Miss – ah—"

"Byrne."

"Miss Byrne, truly, I can only make the highest recommendation. Really sets it apart from what the other museums are doing, really brought it to life."

"Oh, well. You know it's always wonderful . . . Obviously, we have a . . . An innovative approach here . . ."

"Well, the direction naturally deserves much credit."

"He's a genius," Susan says, biting back sarcasm. She holds Bourke's gaze. He regards her like a fish on a hook.

"Well, thank you, Mr Bliss. It's been good to meet you." Warily, his eye softens. "I'll see you tomorrow, Susan."

Bourke retreats. *Catch and release.* Relief, regret, her swollen throat.

"I almost didn't recognize you," Alcott says, studying her cut-off jeans, her exposed navel, her sequin scrunchie, as though he expected something else, as though the discrepancy has impressed him. He is beaming ear to ear, high on his success.

"I thought we agreed I didn't need saving."

"You looked like you needed help."

"Thanks."

"I didn't mean it in a bad way."

"What could possibly be good about needing help?"

"Look, I'm sorry. I said you'd be all right, didn't I? Can I take you home?"

"I don't want to go home." Her unspent anger is turning to petulance. Home is a cage, and all his good intentions have damned her back to it.

"Well then, come for a drive."

It isn't a question. His face is set, like he has already read the script. Like he himself has written it.

Did she leave Bridget at the door? In the half-hung rumple on the costume rack? Or is she still here, making the decision for her, guiding the instinct that says: *go on, live!* Maybe it is the heat, or the rush, or the light sweep of his hair, or the way that he is looking at her, like he would chase her to the end of the earth. Is she the type of person to get in a stranger's car? Is that even a type of person, or does it all just depend on the moment?

"Fine," she says.

"I should warn you," he says brightly, "I'm Ted Bundy."

"I thought your name was Alcott?"

He laughs, as though she has made a joke, as if they have both been joking, but then sees the blankness on her face. "Al, actually," he says, holding open the passenger door as she climbs in.

Salem leaves them, the municipal red brick giving way to low, unloved shopping strips and the drearier outlying neighborhood where Susan grew up. Where Susan still lives in a dilapidated neo-colonial surrounded by a chain-link fence. *Is that her mother, out by the mailbox?* Who knows – who cares – they are rushing off north, over the bridge and up the wooded coastline.

"So," he begins. "How long have you been a witch?"

"Three years," she says. She focuses on the unfamiliar branches and low stone walls rushing by. Inside herself she surrenders to the situation, the relief of someone else taking control. *You didn't want to quit,* she tells herself. *Not like that. Not without a plan.* She just gets carried away sometimes. But the houses growing broad and secluded around her rub it in; she lacks the financial means to be reckless. Like it or not, he saved her from herself.

"It must be hard, a role like that."

"Gotta collect a lot of toadstools," she says. "Snakeskins, that sort of thing."

He laughs, loud and surprisingly high with a note of astonishment, as though he has never encountered a woman with a sense of humor. When did she last make anyone laugh like that? In profile, she can only see the coyer half of his smile, its hint of dissatisfaction, its reserve. It's not the first time she's taken a chance on an older man. The pleasant smell of him infuses the car, starchy with an undertone of sweat. She settles into the ease of mutual interest.

"So," she asks, "how long have you been a liar?"

"I'm not a liar!" he says with mock affront. When she looks at him, his eyes are dancing. "Well, at least, I try not to make a habit of it. I only lie on behalf of pretty girls. Or, you know, for the greater good."

"The greater good?"

"Yeah, sure. I would lie to save my family."

"What kind of a situation would require you to do something like that?"

"I don't know. If they were in trouble with the law or something."

"Is that very likely?"

"No. White collar, maybe. But they're far more plausible victims. Ransom-paying types."

"I see."

"Though my sister ran away about ten years ago, so who knows. Maybe she was fleeing the scene of a crime. Or just, you know. My parents."

He says it as though he expects her to laugh, but something makes her feel sorry for him. His hand rests easily on the gearshift, and she closes her eyes.

"I've always thought, not that this will make you feel any better, but I really think nobody leaves unless it's really, really for the best."

He waits, he watches the road. He does not rush her. Is it strange to feel so comfortable? *Does he know that tone in a man's voice?*

"My dad," she adds. "Every day he stuck around was a living hell. You never knew what you were going to come home to."

He only hit her twice. Once when she returned late from Angie's house. Another time when he had just come out of the shower. Barefoot, towel dripping. Some vocal exercises just out of her mouth. Me-may-mah-mo-moo. *Can we not have a moment of quiet in this fucking house?* Most of the time it wasn't physical. Most of the time he loved to see her act. She could always hear his laugh from the audience, a loud barrel-roll, like he wanted her to know he was watching. But it could turn on a knife's edge. If you weren't listening to him. If he felt insulted.

"Well, one thing you should know about me is I'm predictable as sin." Al smiles. Refuses to look at her with pity. "Your mom still around?"

"Barely."

"Is she not well?"

It has been several years since she spoke about her mother in the present tense. Someone capable of acting and reacting. Of opinion, of argument. "She's glazed as Jell-O," she explains. "She only ever talks about things that happened decades ago. There is no point trying to get her to see you. And I'm here trying to keep my sister organized and our whole weird ship afloat, which – to be honest – isn't my strong suit. So be careful what you wish for, if you want a family who needs you."

"So, you wouldn't lie for them."

"I guess it would depend what the lie is."

"How so?"

"Well, there are just certain things that I would never lie about."

"Like what?"

"Like . . . something fundamental about myself . . ." She presses her lips together, desperate to say something clever. It disturbs her slightly that she can't think of anything she wouldn't be willing to change. But adaptability is freedom, isn't it? "Or something I cared about," she offers. "Like . . . human rights?"

"Well, I find that surprising, considering you're paid to lie."

"Acting isn't lying."

"Well, what's the difference?"

"Well, good acting is all about being sincere. Emotionally."

"Sincere even when you're not being honest."

"You're getting too hung up on this honesty thing. Everyone knows it's a character. Obviously, I wasn't actually born in like, the seventeen-hundreds."

"Sixteen-hundreds."

"That's what I meant."

"I just don't get where the one thing ends and the other thing begins. How do you know what's you and what's not you?"

"Well, that's where all the fun is, isn't it?"

"I'll have to take your word for it." He grins. They pass a low brick public school, dense pines, a large boulder. "Is it frustrating for it always to be the same outcome? Every time, guilty?"

"You have to play it like it's the first time. Like anything could happen."

"But on some level, you must know. That must be hard to ignore."

"Well, I don't want to get stuck, if that's what you mean."

He nods. "I hear you. I wouldn't want to get stuck in the 1690s either. Hadn't even invented the spinning jenny yet." He says it like she is supposed to get it, like anyone else would. *Who is Jenny? Why is she spinning?* No, he has mistaken her, formed some false idea, watching her play at somebody else. As she begins to wonder whether this was a mistake, he says softly: "But you don't strike me as the type of person who would want to leave in the wrong way."

She considers his silhouette, his steady gaze, the light flickering against the far side of his face, and a soft wonder settles over her, that he has looked at her and seen some fundamental goodness. "No," she says. "I'm not." She drums her fingers on her bare leg. "Can we play some music?" She reaches for the radio button before he can answer. Low, brooding strings jump from the speakers.

"Put on what you like," he says, so she scans to the Top 40. A minute passes before he asks, "Who is this?"

"Are you joking?"

"No."

"It's Annie Lennox," she says. "Don't you watch MTV?"

"I don't have a TV."

In the backseat of the car is a pile of clothing and a toppled stack of books. "Do you live in here?" she asks gently.

"No!" He laughs. "I'm just taking some things to dry clean."

"You can afford to get things dry cleaned, but you can't afford a TV?"

"I didn't say I couldn't afford it." He is shaking his head, bemused. "We just never had one growing up. So I guess I never got in the habit. My dad hated it – television was everything wrong with America, he would say. It's making us depraved. Ruining democracy. Like people would stop thinking for themselves. Betsy – my sister – she couldn't stand it." The house was quiet, he says, except for classical FM and their ill-tempered beagle. "At school, though, we had a color TV. We all watched westerns. And *I Dream of Jeannie*."

"That was a good show."

"We were all in love with her. But I never liked how everyone talked about the characters like they knew them, like they were more real than people in real life. I don't know, I started to think maybe there was something to it, that maybe television does numb people."

His soft shirtsleeves, his steady wrist. *What type of man finds dry cleaning more essential than television?* Still, she always looks in at the shop on Canal Street, all those garments sheathed in plastic like a morgue. She thinks of her underwear drying on top of the radiator. Maybe one day she will take her things down there. After all, this is America. Never rule anything out.

"Where are you taking me?"

"Well," he says. "There's a place around here. It's just the most peaceful spot. You can swim, can't you? You seem like a swimmer."

She starts to laugh, smacked with the whole situation. "Sure."

"Good," he says. "But I have to confess I'm lost."

"Lost!"

"In fact, I'm turning around."

"We could go somewhere else."

"No," he says definitively. "The problem is, once you've been to the most beautiful place on earth, it's very difficult to settle for anything else. But I haven't been since I was a kid. So, bear with me."

It is impossible after that not to see his face layered with earlier, more vulnerable versions of itself. Impossible not to feel tenderly toward him as he tries to re-chart a route through the landscape of his memory, at first tentatively and then with agitated force, like he's trying to push an earring through a closed-up piercing. But eventually he finds the way, a dirt road slipping off through an embrace of elm trees. As the shade draws cool relief over their faces, she feels the romance in his stubbornness, his insistence on beauty.

Al has always been told he was clever, but never has he felt more pleased with himself as right now, having written them into this moment, created just the right mood, the sun hitting the treetops of this quiet, sublime world, the lick of water against the reservoir rim, the birds whooping and the humidity glistening. And even for all his planning, he couldn't have invented her.

The girl removes her shirt with the unselfconsciousness that must come with daily costume changes, and he averts his eyes politely, but not before absorbing the perfect white Renaissance breasts in a black bra, the tan lines of her summer clothes, the little hoop around her midriff where her belly button has seen the sun. She is Liz Taylor, green-eyed shiver beautiful. The world feels old and new and she feels old and new, like the prehistoric magma underneath the crust of this place has bubbled up and erupted through her. She is the most alive thing that he has ever seen. And here she is staring at him like they aren't both nearly naked. Like this is any ordinary day.

"It's deep enough?" she asks. The rocky lip of the quarry drops sheer ten feet from where they stand.

"Definitely deep enough," Al says. The woods are humming with heat. *How do you know what's you and not you?* Can he find some inner bohemian, sweep her off her feet? He removes his trousers and reveals a pair of white cotton briefs hugging pale, muscular thighs, tender hairs weakened by underexposure to the outside world. His hand, following an instinct of its own, reaches toward the left bulb of her lower back, urges her forward, fingertips picking up the moisture on her skin. She turns around and he stands back to paint her in his mind.

"What?"

"You are extraordinary," he says.

And he leans into her because it is the most natural thing to do, because he can see with perfect clarity a potential that she cannot possibly recognize in herself. For a moment her lips meet his, then he pulls back, a grin full of lightning, and runs and jumps off the overhang.

Hard smack on the bottom of his feet, water plunging up his nostrils and into his open mouth. When he re-emerges, he shouts as though he has only just learned to be wild, and she follows after him. One of her breasts bubbles out of her bra and she laughs and turns away and shoves it back in, his legs kicking vibrations into hers, a tumble of unseen waves passing between them as they tread through the thin, clinging fabrics, the miracles of life and living and the hazy air.

They kiss again on the dirt bank, his hands finding the back of her neck, her head tilting back reflexive. After a few minutes he laughs at the absurdity of having lost himself in all this. She can't be older than twenty-one.

"You could be anyone," he says.

"I am anyone," she laughs. "You, on the other hand, are someone."

*

When he takes her home, she asks him to drop her at the end of the street.

"Come on," he says. "It's late."

Her eyes are shining. All the heat is taken out of the air, and still he's hot with looking at her. Outside, something slams with a bang, and the air lingers with hot trash bags, with dogs that have gone too long without the rain. Crickets sing high and intense.

"Please. I'll just take you to your door."

She points to a house up ahead, a color he can't make out in the moonlight.

"This is the worst thing," she says, and smiles miserably, as though she's transforming back into another girl, as though the whole afternoon were just another part she was playing and this is the real backstage, the curtain rising on the peeling paint and people who are born and die in the same house.

"It doesn't have to be."

She studies him as though trying to understand his interest. Then, playfully, she takes an eye pencil out of her bag and writes her number on the back of his dry-cleaning slip.

Only the kitchen light is on. The mess is the usual mess, the paraphernalia of a house of unvisited women: shoes everywhere and coats slumped on the floor and last month's *Marie Claire* and a pile of sea glass on the coffee table for which no one has a plan. Everything is quiet, save for the hum of the oven, her little sister's socked feet slipping across the linoleum. The air is full of melting American cheese.

"Thought you weren't coming home," Sadie says.

"Just trying to keep you on your toes."

"Who were you with?"

"No one."

It's not that she was embarrassed by the house. Only, if you don't retain mystery, they won't call you again, and she does want him to call.

"Do you want one?" Sadie retrieves her sandwich, closing the oven door with the top of her foot. "Oh my God, look at you," she says, taking Susan in for the first time. "You're smiling."

"No I'm not," she says, but she is.

"Was that a boy?!"

"Shut up."

"Oh my God is he your boyfriend?"

"No." Something about Al needs protecting from Sadie, her inflexible opinions. Susan's sister raises her eyebrows, spins the Wonder Bread around in its plastic bag, waits for an answer.

"Did it rain today?" Susan asks. They talk about their mother in code.

"Stop trying to change the subject."

"I'm just asking."

Sadie wrinkles her nose. "A light drizzle."

"She upstairs?"

Sadie nods.

"Did she eat?"

Sadie shrugs. It would be useful if Susan's sister paid more attention. Their mother is always worse in the morning if she doesn't eat. A cat that Susan doesn't recognize pushes through the flap in the door. Sadie tears off a piece of bread to feed it.

"You shouldn't do that," Susan says.

"They're living creatures."

"I don't think they are supposed to have bread."

"It's a treat." She lays out two more slices of cheese on two more slices of bread, pops them in the oven. "So who is he? From around here?"

"No." To this, Sadie gives a knowing hum, as though Susan has said all she needs to know.

"How was dance?" Susan asks.

Sadie scowls. "I didn't get it." She shreds off a steaming corner of her sandwich, catching the drip of plastic cheese in her free hand.

"Oh no." Sadie has been talking about the fall recital for weeks now. A few years ago, a scout for the Boston Ballet had come and the soloist had been chosen as a background dancer in *The Nutcracker*.

"What happened?"

Sadie scuffs her foot on the floor like it doesn't matter. *Kick-ball-change.* "They gave it to that Winchester girl. Snobs. It's a fucking joke."

"Sorry, Sayd," she says. They probably are snobs, but the fact is, Sadie makes excuses for herself. *She needs to work harder,* Susan thinks. There's a woman on the Supreme Court. There's a woman in space. You can do just about anything in this country if you try. When Susan hugs her little sister, she stands on top of Sadie's toes, like she did when she was little. Sadie used to try to point them, tumble her off. Now she just stands passive.

"It doesn't matter," she says. "I'm going to quit anyway."

Anger like a tide, like freefall, pushing her away. "You can't quit."

"Why not?"

"I just bought you new shoes!"

Sadie crouches and stares into the oven and Susan wants to scream.

"It's not going anywhere," Sadie says. "Once you turn seventeen, that's it. If no one's noticed you by then, there's no point."

"Seventeen is too young to quit anything. And besides, you're not seventeen for two more months."

"I'm being realistic," she says. But the charge in her voice implies something bigger, as though her failure to hope is somehow Susan's failure to pave a route to happiness.

Sadie pulls the sandwich out of the oven, saws it in half, plops a triangle on a plate for Susan. They both bite into the orange, empty goo. *Sadie can feed herself,* Susan thinks. *She can take care of their mother.* On her half-empty plate, Sadie draws a ketchup frowny-face.

If I leave her, Susan wonders, *will we both fall apart?* In the reflection of the kitchen window, she catches her own face: another Susan, still out in the darkness.

1997

"Why don't we see Sadie anymore?" Sebastian asks.

Alcott Bliss and his two motherless children are standing in front of a thousand-pound pumpkin. Somewhere, someone is purchasing a rabbit, somewhere a man painted as a clown is falling into a tank of cold water. It's a Saturday, and the Aldwych Fair is heaving with all of New England: preps in chunky Land's End sweaters and mud-ready boots, hooded townies out for the day in their best or worst jeans.

He has done okay today, until now. He has dressed the children and convinced them to eat a large hasty omelet and counted to sixty while they brushed their teeth. He has got them into their fleeces and out of the house, away from the glowing red eye of the answering machine.

"Your aunt's been busy."

He has started unplugging the phone at night. If he doesn't, Sadie will just keep ringing and ringing.

"Is she mad at us?"

"Of course not, buddy."

"Then why does she sound mad?"

The problem is, Sadie won't stop asking about the tapes. Whether he'd watched them, whether they were helping. When he was going to return them. How could he explain: Al (the husband! the historian!) had destroyed a singular archive.

He could claim he lost his mind. It wouldn't be wrong; for so long, his mind had reverberated against Susie's. Now thoughts hang loose, unable to form against anything – anyone. How can they? The world is a steady stream of vacuous conversation, ghoulish euphemisms, small talk, sales calls – all of it maddening and insignificant. But he hadn't lost his mind. In many ways, it was the sanest thing he has ever done. Because what was it but a deranged fixation on some consecrated pieces of plastic? Those spools of film were not, and never would be, his wife.

Al puts his hand in his son's curly hair. "Your mother and Sadie grew up in a difficult house," he says. "Your mother was able to move past it, but Sadie had a harder time. Sometimes her emotions get the better of her."

"Is she okay?"

"Don't worry, Sebastian. We'll see her soon."

Al never wanted to become a liar, but deception has become a reflex. *Mom isn't sick, she's just tired. Mom isn't dying, she's just sick.* Maybe it started even earlier: *Mom doesn't want to be away from you.* And always implicit: *It's not my fault.* They won't be seeing Sadie soon. But no one need worry about that.

"It looks like an elephant," his son says, pointing at the pumpkin's pachydermic folds.

"Like an orange elephant," says his daughter. "Did you know, Dad, elephants never forget?"

At seven, Viola is a kind, unusual creature and seems to enjoy his company. As he enjoys hers – though she is becoming a conduit for Susan's intrusion. Every day, her mother's features ripen on her face. Her eyebrow, her collarbone. It's become confused – who belongs to whom, that sort of thing. Sticky-feeling.

He hugs them close as a band of teens pushes behind them. One boy shoves another one hard, upending a table of gourds. So many carefully cultivated specimens reel onto the floor and before Al can stop himself, he is bellowing "Hey!" in a bark that sounds like his father's, his arm is grabbing the boy's wrist.

"Pick those up."

Behind him, his children are trembling. With great composure he arranges his face, releases the wrist. When he turns back he is smiling and undangerous. *This is the job,* he repeats to himself. *To shield them.* Even (especially!) from his own ragged rage and anything that might provoke it.

In her last message, Sadie hissed: *She was going to leave you.*

Hug them close, never let them fear that they are not safe and loved.

Blinking, the Bliss family steps into the bright autumn sunshine. Pop songs battle cacophonous from rickety rollercoasters, fried batter barely covering the undertone of manure. As Al turns to consult a large map, his name slices through the wandering bodies. His son is shouting, legs in motion, bolting in the direction of – *who?* On his back, the terrible clap of a hand.

"Dan!"

A stampede of robust red-heads. Dan's wife grabs Al's arm for a quick squeeze, chasing her brood and his strays into the face-painting tent. Al faces his oldest friend, reluctant. In the last few months, neither has found the right way to reach out.

"It's good to see you, pal."

"What are the odds?"

"You're looking really well," Dan says emphatically, registering (Al surmises) the fact that he is dressed and upright. Al refrains from strangling him. He understands: they both want it to be true. But however well he might be faking it, he is not well. No one says his wife's name anymore. And Dan, who hardly knew her, who certainly did not love her, will not be the one to bring her back.

Al smiles. Fills his mind with other things: the stock market, an ancient technique for making red dye. Illuminated manuscripts. Space travel. Pasts and futures that reach beyond her. "You too, my friend," he says.

"Ahoy, mate!" Viola bounds up to them, face smeared with thick black paint, delighted with her eyepatch and moustache. She ties her hair into a beard underneath her chin.

"Ahoy sailor!" How sweetly she places her hands on her hips, cocks her head, plays the part. "Are we sailing the high seas today?"

"Ahoy!" she says again, her conviction greater than her pirate vocabulary.

"Aha!" Dan says. "Another actress in the family!"

His daughter blushes and beams and darkness wells inside him. Please, God. Not again. It's too soon to consider, to entertain dreams of departure, of becoming anything other than his sweet child. No more invented worlds where he doesn't exist, no more sharing, not yet, she's only seven years old and still his – his only – only his! His hands tingle, begging to offer her something else to belong to. He only has himself.

"I don't think so." He smiles benignly enough. "Wealth management, maybe. Buried treasure, it's a good start."

Dan chuckles, looks to his scrambling children. "Lunch soon?"

Over Dan's shoulder, his wife is reaching into a large bag, procuring a tidy plastic pack of Kleenex. She is wiping the snot and rubbing lip balm onto her littlest, while talking to the middle ones about their evening plan. She is watching the oldest, who is shooting a horse with a water gun. She is probably thinking about how to have a conversation about guns and violence and fairground games. She is probably thinking about how to adjust all of their meals to their liking, how to stop them from hitting each other and make sure all their homework gets done in time for tomorrow. Watching her feels like watching a future he once believed in, as familiar as if he had occupied it.

His pockets are empty except for Viola's over-stretched hair elastic and his own wallet.

"Sure," he says. "Let's do lunch."

As Dan departs, Sebastian bounds over, wielding a large stick like a sword. "Ahoy!"

"Ahoy!" Viola says, picking up her own smaller stick and raising it *en garde*.

"Enough!" Al snaps. "You're going to hurt somebody!"

Shocked, Viola drops the branch. Because it is the only thing he can do, Al resumes wandering through the grounds, unsure where he is leading. When he gathers the energy to turn back, his daughter is brooding, beard falling out, eyepatch smudged, untouched by the music of the carousel. She looks at him and asks—

"Was Mom in the movies?"

Her father looks at her sternly, as though she has broken a promise. Why does she feel so wrong? Wasn't her mother an actress? Or maybe she was a fortune teller. Her mother is receding in her mind like the ocean, something so big she can hardly get her head around it. When she picks it up it disappears into droplets.

"No, Vi. She did some acting, but it was only TV. They don't make recordings of TV."

"They don't?"

"Afraid not. Mommy lived with us, remember?"

She is tired of her mother being dead. Nothing ever changes about it. For a while, she expected her to walk back through the door, that death might be somewhere like California. But every day that passes makes it clearer: there will be no coming back.

As far as she can remember, her mother was mostly not there. She was never allowed to look at her, not on the television and not behind the closed door of her room. The strongest imprint is a sense of waiting, cold glass pressed up against her nose and a certain terror. Some facts seem important, and she clutches them like playing cards. Her mother was allergic to stone fruits. She doesn't know what a stone fruit is, but it doesn't sound very good. Her mother wore beautiful scarves on her head. Her mother grew up in Salem, which is where witches came from. But the sound of her voice?

"I can't even remember her."

When a person dies, can their memories die too? A terrible, tremulous thought.

Her father squats, eye-level. He takes both of her hands firmly between his and says:

"We all came here together, remember?"

The landscape of the fair breathes life into the story. She was there at the petting zoo, in her soft brown sweater, placing animal feed into their tiny hands. And wasn't she there, swinging Viola by the arms as they waited in line for the tiny train? Didn't she buy them each a candy apple, Sebastian's dipped in sprinkles? Didn't they all learn to square dance? The vision catches like a lit candle, flickers like a dream. Yes, her mother might have been just there, with sparkles in her eyes and color in her cheeks. The thought of it carries her away.

"She was the queen of the fair," he says. "She got to ride on the pumpkin float. She awarded the prize for best bovine. Everybody loved her."

"Did she wear a crown?"

"Absolutely. Don't you remember?"

She doesn't remember. But he is looking at her like she needs to make it true.

"I think so," she says.

"But she couldn't go last year," Sebastian says. "She was sick."

"I meant the year before," his father says.

"She didn't come the year before."

"Sure she did."

"I remember. She cried because she couldn't come."

Her brother faces her father, flushed and indignant. The moment ripples out into other moments. Sebastian picks up his sword stick and smacks it on the ground until it shatters into pieces.

"OK, Sebastian," he says. "You're right. It was just pretend."

As they race back to the house, the world rips away, open rolling fields and fences, thickets of houses and mailboxes, all of it too fast to make an impression. And the front passenger seat is still empty.

1986

Susan flings her arms around a man she has never met. She holds him for a lifetime of a moment, and the two of them sway together as though they have done this a thousand times, as though they are remembering a long-gone slow dance from their youth.

"Are you okay?" she asks softly.

"Sure," he says. They pull away and she searches his great green eyes, runs a hand over his tanned and shapely arms.

"Is this just a one-time thing?" she asks. The words bubble out of her mouth as though they are her own words, as though they have always been hers, as though she means every one of them.

"No," he says. "Well, I don't know. I'll have to talk to Sharon."

Tears well up, but she doesn't release them. "Sure," she says.

"You know I love you, right?"

She nods. She presses the back of his hand. "I know." Her eyes follow him out of the door. "Merry Christmas," she says softly, as though there is no one else in the room, as though she is as alone now as she will ever be.

A smattering of applause from behind a plastic table.

"That was lovely, Susan."

Now she smiles, relieved – charmed, even – and registers the three faces illuminated by the top floor window of the Burbank studio. Two men and a woman. Mark Flowers: the producer, small mouth and large tinted frames. Rip McFee: a writer, mullet, dimples. Shona Sussman: casting director, Texas accent, swiveling back and forth on her chair.

For Susan, it is almost too easy to become an ingénue again. The transition is a wading into water. She slipped into it at thirty-thousand feet,

47

pouring out a small bottle of wine and watching America present itself, green patchwork fields and silver cities. She offers it now to the starry, searching faces across from her, that heady mix of hope and potential.

"We have a few more people to see today," Shona says tentatively. "But as I said on the phone, I'm looking for that person who just sets me on fire." She cracks a bright giveaway grin.

"Why don't we meet later for a drink," Mark says. "To talk next steps."

Susan is beaming, repeating the name of a place on Sunset Strip.

Even as she crosses the holding pen full of similarly dressed women, all gossiping or muttering lines or sitting silently while they wait for their call, she knows she is set apart. The only trick will be convincing Al.

He never stopped calling her. Without coyness or any of the wait-by-the-phone assholery she was used to, he asked for her time. They drove out to the mountains, camped under the stars. Both of them carried the same native injury, a disappointment in the people who raised them, a deficiency of love. These were wrongs he was determined not to repeat. When they met babies, Al spoke to them so seriously, and it made her lust for him, his solid sense of self.

Late at night, he practiced his lectures with her. Though she could hardly follow the jargon, she coached his presentation: *slow down, talk from your stomach, look at my face*. He improved. The Harvard undergraduates started calling him Blister, which he said he hated, but she could see he really loved. He'd never had a nickname before.

As the romantic spontaneity subsided, he began to reveal his habits. He studied religiously from nine in the morning to noon, and then wrote in the afternoon from one to six, permitting no disturbance. On Sundays, he drove to visit his mother in Rockport up on Cape Ann, always bearing flowers and an excuse to leave. He took Susan to his favorite sandwich bar, where all of the options were named after poets and everyone behind the counter greeted him with the warmth of a regular; he had been coming since it opened twenty years ago. She began to see that Boston had shaped him intimately, and he held an almost mystical understanding of its layers. He populated the harbor with billowing ghost ships, extracted hidden spires and domes from the sheet glass and concrete. Everywhere they went, he pointed out the ancient haunts of intellectuals and politicians, talked about their interests and ideas as though they were as alive in the world as anyone else.

Susan didn't have a savings account. She didn't have a car. He gave her one of the small black notebooks he used to manage his own finances, and drew a line down the middle of the page: one side represented what would come in, the other what would come out.

"I'm so bad at this."

"Don't worry, anyone can learn this stuff. And anyway, you won't need to worry about it forever." He smiled and she smiled back, understanding this as an expression of faith in her eventual earnings, in her raw talent. Deploying his large, polite vocabulary, he drafted her resignation from the re-enactment show.

One Saturday morning, he arrived at her mother's house to pack her things into his trunk. Susan was wearing a cardigan he had bought her, clean and white, and walked out of the house decisively. She had hoped for more fanfare, but Sadie did not come down. And her mother, moving things aimlessly around in the small front yard, simply held up her soiled hands in lieu of a hug. "I guess that's it then," she said. When Susan closed the car door behind her, she put a hand over her face and exhaled endlessly.

She did not cry until they arrived at his apartment and she saw that he had shifted the bed, emptied out a set of drawers for her clothing. In the corner of the living room was a shiny, black television. He smiled his handsome, lopsided smile and she was overwhelmed.

"Why are you being so nice?" she sobbed.

"One day, I'm going to need you to be nice to me," he said. "When you're a star of the stage and you can have anyone in the world."

At night, after he'd indulged her in an hour of MTV, her hand rested limp against the warmth of his back and she felt – for the first time that she could remember – carefree.

But the problem was: in Boston there were no auditions. Or at least not enough to keep her busy. In six months, she landed only a single moisturizer commercial. She wasn't right for anything. Student gigs wouldn't have her, and the few professional troupes passed her over. Al started leaving clippings on the kitchen table: a role at Plymouth Plantation, a voiceover for an audio textbook, a radio spot for a local mortgage supplier. She could not bring herself to apply.

"How about teaching?" he suggested one day. "You're so good with kids."

The proposal crushed her more than she could possibly say. It was not unreasonable. She had contributed nothing to the rent. And she could see it came from his own earnest love of classrooms. He adored his students: their intelligent questions, the reflection of his efforts in their thoughts. But his casualness made her question whether he had truly believed in her success in the first place. She felt herself changing into an uncertain creature – estranged, for the first time, from her dreams.

Each day, relief arrived in familiar cymbals, those chords, the regular voices of Cedardale, USA, a disaster-prone town in middle America.

This is *LIFE AND TIMES*.

Susan fell headfirst into the stories, a tangle of mysteries and romances, cryptic calls to a local radio station, a small-town matriarch interfering with her son's chosen match. All sense of her failure vanished. After every show, she called Sadie to debrief. It was a way to talk without talking about themselves. She became dependent upon it. When a dentist appointment caused her to miss a critical episode, she spent the evening despondent, mushing her lobster bisque at the Seaport restaurant where Al brought her for dinner.

"Explain it to me," Al said. "It's just so melodramatic."

"You're dismissing it because of the packaging."

"And the stories."

"Okay, but – every day you just never know what you're going to see. People are always ascending and descending. No one's position in life is fixed."

"So it's about social mobility?"

"No, it's – the potential."

"The potential to . . . discover a long-lost twin?"

He laughed unconvinced, and frustration welled inside her. *I'm being inarticulate*, she thought. But fundamentally, he did not understand the need to escape reality.

It was Sadie who saw the casting call at the back of a fan magazine. "If you don't go for it, I'll kill you," she said.

So, Susan sent her headshot to Los Angeles. She told herself it was an exercise, that they would never look at her, that her experience in film was limited to the moisturizer commercial. Assuming it impossible made it easier to avoid the disturbing incompatibility of her desires.

When the call came asking her to audition, it felt like a fantasy. Like that ancient dream of being chosen – at last – was coming to life. In her hand, the receiver trembled with delicious beginnings. The tentative, sensual unknown.

"Are you sure you'll be okay out on your own?"

"Don't look so worried."

"I'm just saying, the homicide rate is a serious concern."

He was pacing and she could tell something else was bothering him. For Al, the unknown was full of demons.

"Why don't you come," she suggested. "Be my bodyguard."

"That's a good idea." He said it so gently that she felt within her a dangerous reprieve: the hope she really could have everything she wanted.

"She's a good girl gone bad." Susan is tipsy, radiating wonder and a terrible ecstasy on the lawn in front of the seaside hotel. "Knows the streets a little too well. Troubled. Vengeful. Wheedling secrets out of smitten johns. I just honestly can't believe it, Al, I can't believe they want me."

Al's heart is beating in his throat. His dream is liquid in his fingertips, threatening to slip away.

"Susie," he manages, "who wouldn't want you?"

All day he had wandered Los Angeles's vapid modernity and hideous perfume of gasoline and marijuana, wondering whether this was just a test. If it was, he couldn't blame her; Susie grew up in a home where love was an uncertain thing. She required a grand gesture.

So, he had flown on the horrible, turbulent plane and bought the hotel room with the romantic view and the dinner tonight which she hardly ate (so nervous was she to meet that man – Mark? Mack?) because he knew he needed to communicate to her, powerfully, his devotion. His pocket is heavy with the weight of his intentions, the string of words which were now—

"Let's get married."

None of it matters. Not the job offer or the strange ocean crashing into the night or the other guests who may or may not be watching from their windows. He is thinking only how much he needs her, this woman who makes him feel essential and unlike himself. He digs his hand into his pocket and pulls out an expensive, velvet box.

Susan drops to a squat on the ground, clutching her face. "Oh God," she says. She looks at the large yellow diamond, which he had chosen for its sparkle, because it made him think of her and them together, because it was not obvious but it was beautiful. Her face is open, an orchestra of feeling.

"You're right, I should be down on one knee," he says, kneeling nervously into the wet grass.

She pulls her hand away from her face. "You would move here?"

The box sits in his hand like a dead animal. He is trying to fix his face, to look reasonable and supportive, but how would that possibly work? This is a town of typecasting. Every hedonist here – new agers, punk rockers, surf bums – eyes him like he's a square. Next month he will turn thirty, and somehow, he has passed the point of reinvention. He knows what he is: a scholar who has staked his reputation on colonial America. How could he live here, bereft of museums or primary sources, lost for the ideals that founded this country: efficiency, thrift, intellect. He can imagine the glassy-eyed coeds mooning up at him, resentfully fulfilling a requirement, the deep training of his mind lost in an academic wasteland. How could he be confronted with it daily and maintain his sense of worth? It stung him beyond admission, that she could want something so far from him.

"You don't want to keep going for more roles? You know you don't have to jump at the first opportunity, Susie. You could do anything you set your mind to. You could be . . . Lady Macbeth."

"I could still be Lady Macbeth!"

"I just think. People see you in a certain way . . ."

What is he doing? There will be no talking her out of this. Framing it as an ultimatum will only agitate her. She is rocking onto the balls of her feet, grappling.

"That's not the point," he says. "The point is, this assistant professor role is tenure-track. It's not like they just hand these things out. I can't just leave."

"Right," she says. "No, of course not. But maybe eventually—"

"Sure, Susie, we can talk about it—"

"You know because at some point we'll want a family."

"You are going to be such a gorgeous mother."

"And you are going to be a very paranoid but ultimately loveable father."

"Susie?"

"Yes?"

"You haven't said yes."

If you look very closely, history is not a straight line. It is full of the punctures of accident, plagues and coincidence. But if you zoom out, it is more or less straight. Tending toward advancement, toward civilizations civilizing, toward people living longer and better and more enlightened lives.

"Yes," she says.

"Yes?"

"Yes."

He slips the ring from its bed and places it onto her long, beautiful finger.

2004

You can hardly call this music, the garble of noise emerging fitful from the pre-teens itching to break free from this: the last day before summer vacation. On the horizon are elastic days, new flirtations, the promise of bikinis and parties and other people's cars, of mixtapes and MSN messenger, a wild and terrifying world without structure. But until then, it's one last rehearsal, all together now, as we play the *Star Wars* Theme.

Through the mess, Viola can hear herself clearly. Her fingers move across the strings in pure expression, feelings gaining pitch and clarity, reaching for wordless perfection. She glances up at Mrs Crick as her right hand moves in time, as her left beckons for more sound.

Keep it up, honeybunch, her father says. *That cello will pay for college.* At the end of the day, she knows it's only an instrument. A means to an end. It cannot be her life.

She pulls the curved body against her chiffon dress, aware of the thinness of the fabric. She had wanted to look nice. You are supposed to leave everyone with a good memory of you before the summer starts. *Dress like someone might take your picture.* That was Molly McInerny's advice, though Molly isn't even here today – she had to leave early for some family reunion in Canada, which they both agreed was stupid. The upshot was Viola had to decide without consultation what was photo-worthy and now she cannot help but feel like she's overdone it.

Take the pearl bracelet, a birthday gift from her mother, received last week. These tokens arrive annually: a stationary set, crisp black shoes. Books: Dickens, Austen, Brontë. Opening them makes her sad. How many years had she prepared for? It was awful, thinking of her picking them out, planning for time they never had, guessing at their interests. She understands her mother worked hard to become sophisticated. She didn't grow up with much, her father always said. If anything, the bracelet is too nice, as though her mother were compensating.

They're obviously from Dad, Sebastian said, throwing his tennis racquet under his bed.

Not obviously, she sighed. Still, it would be nice to have proof. A letter or something. It would be nice to read her mother's words. Oh, what did it matter anyway, whether the presents are from her mother or her father? They wanted the same thing, her parents. They were soul mates.

Her brother has it out for her father these days. They fight about everything: the failed tests, the late arrivals home, the mouthing off, the too-loud music – it's all the same. *No, you can't draw on your walls. Yes, you have to go to tutoring.* Constantly she is forced to play the peacekeeper. To 'help him' with his homework, to smooth out his edges. It's exhausting.

As the song concludes, Mrs Crick holds up her arms. "I release you."

Into the hall. She hates this part, the dysfunction of limbs buffeting carelessly toward their next destination, the tongues pressing against other tongues against the bashed metal lockers that hang semi-open, or fully open, or closed but not locked, or locked with the padlock turned three times for safety, a spectrum of giving a fuck that places Viola at the squarest end. She is conscious of her arms brushing against people, a new attention. Her fluttering dress. Her brother's voice: *Is it summer yet?* All day, she's heard him calling rambunctious to Zach Papadopoulos. *Is it summer yet? Let me check . . .*

At thirteen, the twins share no classes. The only place where their names are found together is the signature-covered banner at the end of the hall: ALDWYCH CLASS OF 2009. Their handwriting is identical. But in the throng, twinness is protection. When her brother throws his arm over her shoulder, she is home.

"Remember," she says. "Other bus today."

He groans. On Thursdays, they go to their grandmother's house, which means getting the bus to the train station, riding it out to her cobbled seaside village at the end of the line. It takes forever. Last time, they arrived to find her asleep on the couch, having forgotten the day of the week. Her dad keeps trying to encourage her to talk to her grandmother about 'girl stuff', which never gets much further than 'What are we going to do about your hair?' Mostly they sit around having borderline too-old iced tea and watching tennis. Sebastian flops around like a bored fish.

"Yeah, about that," Sebastian says. "Let's not."

"Dude."

"Come on, Lola. Let's go to the beach."

"No."

"Why not?"

"I don't like the beach." She shouldn't have to explain. It's the people who will be there and the half-naked charade of conversation about anything other than who has tits or a boyfriend or whose mother is dead in the sea.

"How about the movies?" he suggests.

"Don't tempt me." Viola loves it, the quiet space with nothing ahead of her but the story, the arc of it, the inevitable resolution of lovers or heroes or justice restored. Her fantasies outstrip the offerings of their small-town world. And at four o'clock, Orson Grey will be starring in a delectable French romance. Gradually, he has transformed from acquaintance to fantasy, become the sole interest of her heart. But no: it is her responsibility to be the good one.

"No. Dad will be pissed."

"Do I look like I care?"

"You're so annoying."

"You're so boring," he tells her.

"OooOOoooh," Zach Papadopoulos says, colliding, pushing them both away from the river of bodies. "Someone's fancy today."

"Go away, Zach."

"Make me."

His hand, warm on her arm. His sweatshirt reeks of everything he has smoked in the last few months. The dog, the twins call him. An untrained Newfoundland. Always hanging around.

"Sit," Sebastian says. "Lie down."

"Roll over," Viola grins, raising an eyebrow as Zach spins in a circle. "Good boy."

Sebastian chuckles. Zach starts barking and lunges tongue-first for her ear. She screams and throws herself back against the lockers.

"Cut it out, dude." Sebastian kicks his friend hard in the shin.

"Aah!" Zach reaches to his leg, a lick of slobber now coating his chin. "Asshole."

"I'll see you at the bus," she is calling, and the hallway opens up, vaulting into the gymnasium. A short set of stairs, a familiar rhythm. After school, this is where she comes to leave herself behind. In the last year, she has begun to run harder and faster, to approach her body like a hard, perfectible thing.

But not now, not in gym class. Now is only a sham of an hour. In the changing room, the other girls are already in various states of undress, tying up oversized shirts with hair elastics to grant a peek of their bellybuttons, rolling up their Soffe shorts one, two, three times. Viola understands they are playing a game: to be noticed and worthy and attractive without ever standing out. It is a herd game, the game of prey. She could have tried harder, earlier, to blend in. But she has never quite been sure how.

As she steps out of her flats, Lisa DePaulo turns. "You're smuggling peas," she says, under the pretense of kind advice.

A hush befalls the tittering gaggle. Viola looks down at herself, the assertive nipples of her otherwise flat chest puffing through the delicate fabric of her dress. She doesn't own a bra.

Her neck grows hot, she runs to the toilet stall. Her eyes are stinging, and when she can hear the girls evacuating, she allows herself a single, stupid sob.

Why did no one tell her it was time to buy a bra?

She sits on the lid of the toilet, indulgently imagining her death: spontaneous combustion in a bathroom cubicle. *First Cello in the Youth Symphony Orchestra*, her obituary would read, *First place in the under-fourteen's cross-country regionals. Honor roll. Beloved sister. Never left America. Never fell in love.*

And then she pulls herself together. For the final hour of eighth grade, she tosses half-hearted dodgeballs and checks the minute hand of the clock every thirty seconds until Finally! The blessed bell. The flood of sneakers, squeaking, backpacks swinging over shoulders, papers shoveled into the recycling bin. Goodbye Lisa DePaulo! Goodbye gym class! Backpack covering her chest, Viola makes her way to the bus, still wearing her gym clothes.

In the parking lot, slouching sweetly, is her brother.

"Screw it," she says, breathless. "Let's go to the movies."

He pumps his fist in the air, wiggles a little dance. "What about Grandma?" he asks.

Together, they imagine her asleep in front of the French Open. They imagine her forgetting them entirely.

"She's getting old." Viola sighs.

"She's always been old," Sebastian says.

In her mind's eye is her father, his concerns and mislaid expectations. She does not want to betray his trust. But life is calling.

1986

In the Logan Airport departures terminal two days after their wedding, Susan touches Al's face and says confidently: "We can do this."

"You'll be careful," he says.

"I'll be careful."

"You'll look both ways when you cross the street."

"I won't cross any streets."

"You won't get abducted."

"I'll do my best."

The ceremony was a small, rushed affair at the registry office, which disappointed both of their mothers but made Al and Susan giddy. *People are going to think you've gotten into trouble, Al,* his mother said, and they both laughed about it afterwards. Screw her. Let them think that! He booked a too-big hotel room, a white duvet smattered with rose petals. And as he helped her out of her dress, pressing his lips to her temple, his able hands easing the spinal buttons out of their loops, she was filled with the knowledge of herself as an unbearably selfish person.

"And if anyone . . ." he starts now, "If you're not comfortable with anything, you can always just say no."

"I know," she says, smiling bravely. *It's daytime,* Mark Flowers explained, *so everything will be tasteful.* But she's no fool. If you don't say yes in this business, there are a hundred other girls who will.

"And call me."

"I love you," she says.

"I love you," he repeats. Do any other words have such hold over the present tense?

But the steaming California tarmac dissipates all thoughts of Al. A production assistant whisks her off to Rodeo Drive to pick out clothes for her character, Margie. She had discussed the wardrobe beforehand with Sadie: black. Leather and lace. Madonna meets . . . Minnesota.

Maybe you'll get to kiss Richard Matlock! Sadie had squealed. *Or Ali Alvarez, oh my God.*

Susan had rolled her eyes and impishly said, *Maybe.* She thinks of her sister as she thumbs blouses at Giorgio, her heart wild with initiation, with the unwritten. Her life opens up onto a parallel infinity.

That evening, a courier arrives at her motel to drop off the script for the next day, and a piece of that infinity breaks off and becomes concrete. Susan tears open the parcel, scans for Margie. There: entering the bar, a cousin from out of town. She inhales the scene, counts twenty lines – not bad for an hour episode. Everything is suggestive; a whisper in her ear, a hand on her thigh. With sudden terror, it hits her: this will be televised. Al and seven million other Americans will sit by while she is manhandled, will judge her with the same ease that she has always judged the characters.

It's not a betrayal, she tells herself. *It's your job.* But she worries he won't see it for what it is. That it will wound him.

In the morning, a taxi takes her to the studio. She says her name and is allowed inside. A cavernous complex unfolds, both familiar and strange. So many well-worn rooms clustered on top of each other, home to so many heartbreaks and heated arguments. It's loud already, with a roar of machinery and industry and voices calling this world into being, and here she is, part of it. All around her, people rush past paying no notice, until a harried-looking assistant director spots her, confirms her name.

"Thanks for reminding me," Susan says. "I had almost forgotten who I was."

The woman looks her over as though this isn't the first time she has dealt with amnesia on set. "One of the directors will be over to chat," she says, but fifteen minutes pass and no one comes. In fact, no one is acknowledging Susan at all. She's sure she is supposed to be doing something, getting make-up or a studio tour, but the whole place feels like a well-oiled machine in no need of a spare cog. She flips through the script again, trying to look like she's in the right place, to dispel the onset of doubt.

"I hear you're the prostitute."

"Sorry?"

She nearly doesn't recognize him because of the accent, rounded and Celtic, but looking at his face (brooding, angular) she places him as the barman, Joe.

"You're going to be shagging Glen over there, aren't you?" he says, pointing at the rugged older man in an eye-patch.

"One-Eye Stokes, you mean?"

"Sorry, was that a spoiler? I was drinking with the writers last night, they may have slipped some intel."

Across the room Glen folds and unfolds his hand, which she once watched him wrap merciless around a woman's neck. Susan inhales sharply.

"No, it's fine," she says bravely, though the thought of his rough, creased skin on her body is not simple to swallow. "I've always wanted to sleep with a killer."

"Don't worry," the barman says. "He's a sweetheart. Not one for the ladies, anyway."

Funny how you can get a fixed notion about someone. How little it takes to dispel it. When she looks at Glen again, he smiles gently in a way that One-Eye never would and she is rushed with tenderness, a wonder at how much of his life he has had to spend acting, in one way or another. Strange how many hours she has spent with these people to find she hardly knows them. The bartender, for instance, is young, but not nearly as young as he looks on screen. Twenty-one maybe. A few years younger than Sadie.

"Anyway, congratulations on being cast and all. I swear they only picked me because I could actually make a drink, unlike anyone else they got in. I mean, they are willing to forgive my horrific accent."

"Oh come on. It's not so bad."

"Well thanks very much," he says, putting it on, a drawling almost-Texan twang. There's room for improvement, but she doesn't need to say so. "By the way," he asks. "Have you got any cigarettes? These Los Angeles types are so holy about things."

She does. She shouldn't, but she does. Picked them up at the airport in a fit of nerves. It's a blessing to give one away. They have to be gone before she goes back to Al on Friday.

"Ach, what a pal!" he says, tucking it behind his ear. "I hope they don't kill you off or anything. That's always the worst, you make a new friend around here and the next day they're force-fed a poisoned donut and stuffed into an armoire."

"Jesus."

"Doesn't mean you can't come back though. Why Nancy over there has been killed about five times," he says, pointing to the show's grande dame, preening into a compact mirror. "Wardrobe down that way," he gestures. "They don't give you much of a manual, so, you know. If you need any help."

"You'll trade tips for cigarettes?"

He smiles, cheeky and boyish, and turns toward the stage door. "I'm easily bought."

Three hours later, she has transformed into Margie, hair piled high, eyes shadowed green, the will to misbehave gaining ground inside her. ROLLING in three – two – One-Eye Stokes has put his mask on too, is sidling up to her and slipping his hand onto her thigh, rumpling her thin synthetic skirt. She is too deep now to think about the space between skirt and thigh, between herself and the character, about Al or anyone else, about how she will be seen and whether she will be loved. The lines are coming out of her as though they have always been in her.

MARGIE
I won't tell if you don't.

2004

Hollywood Hits is easy enough to get to, if you hop in the back of Zach's sister's car. The high school girls seem unfazed, happy to spend the afternoon shoplifting temporary tattoos from Wet Seal and eating sticky orange chicken from the food court. There's nothing particularly appealing about Casey Papadopoulos and her friend Daria, but their overwrought mixtape and deep analysis of senior boys is a small price to pay for the destination.

"Don't you guys want to go to the beach?" Casey asks, eyeing them in the rearview.

"Apparently not," says Sebastian.

"I don't get it," says Zach. "Why are we going to a movie when we can just watch TV?"

"Film is art, television is furniture," Viola says. She heard that somewhere.

"What does that even mean?" Sebastian asks.

Obviously, he wouldn't understand. He still watches cartoons. She shouldn't have to explain: films are vehicles for humanity. They elevate understanding, take you to unimaginable places. They are recorded and packaged and available to rent forever and ever from Blockbuster; the recording confers its own importance. Television is cardboard. It is cheap microwave dinners. It is designed to disappear.

She chooses the simpler argument: "The actors are better."

"It's that one with Orson Grey, right?" Casey asks. "That like, oldy-timey one?"

"Lola, you are obsessed," Sebastian says.

"Shut up."

"What's it called again?" Daria asks.

"*Malentendu.*" Orson plays an aspiring novelist whose poor command of the language and proclivity for mishap lands him in the custody of a beautiful prison warden, played by Juliette Binoche. She will watch this film as closely as she has watched all of his films, as closely as she has followed his narrowly avoided marriages and (happy!) breakups. Their imaginary relationship has blossomed in the margins of her life. The waiting room of the dentist's office, for instance, where she flips through trash magazines, imagining her face next to his. Her name scribbled one hundred times in the pages of a notebook, Viola Grey (gray-violet, a whole spectrum of color and light emerging from the possibility). In the same notebook, she has written forty pages of a fictional saga in which she is sometimes his wife and sometimes the wife of the misunderstood Bond villain he plays on screen. As it turns out, Doctor Meltdown is actually very tender, and receptive to her feminine updates to his volcanic lair. It is childish, but she picks at her crush like Sebastian picks at the skin next to his fingernails.

"Sounds lame," Zach says.

"Well, it's not."

"He was in that show with your mom, right?" In the rearview mirror, Casey's eyes are bright.

"How do you know that?" Sebastian asks.

"Well our mom used to watch it. Like all the time."

"Don't be awkward, Casey," Zach warns.

"What! It's true. She's obsessed, like you guys are like these celebrity children."

"She was only on it a few times I think," Viola says.

"Not the way my mom talks about it."

"Really?" Sebastian is watching the back of Casey's head with intensity, and Viola can see an idea lodging into his mind, can see it is going to become a problem. Her problem, probably. "We've never seen it. I didn't think it was that big."

The thought of her mother's acting fills Viola with dread: other people experiencing her, owning a piece of her that Viola will never know – better not to think about it. Casey is just exaggerating to be nice. Most people do. When it comes to dead people, everyone is always smarter or kinder or more successful than they were in real life.

Besides, if she had been really famous, they would have gone out to Los Angeles, lived glamorous lives. They would have known Orson, really. But, being sensible, her mother must have realized it was impossible to make it out there. She stayed home and took them on field trips and learned how to hit a tennis ball. Some are born great, some achieve greatness, and some die before they get the chance.

"No, it was like, a big deal. Like, back then. I mean, I'm really sorry, like for your loss and everything. It's like, really sad. That she passed."

". . . Music the great communi-ca-tah, use two sticks to make it in the nay-cha . . ."

Zach is reaching to turn up the Chili Peppers, committed to changing the conversation through chaos. But it's not enough to lift the fog that has descended, the strangeness of their mother's name in someone else's mouth, in someone else's living room.

Sebastian is looking at his knees. Viola can feel the racing of his mind.

At the ticket counter, tingling, she hands over $8.50 in exchange for two hours and twenty minutes with the love of her life. Hurry into screen seven, scramble for seats in the back row! As the lights dim there is nothing else to think about, not the couple sucking on each other's faces or Zach Papadopoulos's thick scent or the empty candy wrappers on the floor or whether your grandmother has noticed your absence. The title card falls and the romance begins.

Paris, the thirties. Viola is absorbed by the direct address, the searching look in Orson's eyes that seems only ever to call out to her.

The warden is slipping Orson pages of the newspaper to read. She is also, as it turns out, a romantic, and understands that man cannot live on bread (or in this case, beef stroganoff) alone. Viola can no longer tell if the look of wry gratitude that Orson is giving the warden is the same as the look he gave her on the night of the funeral. As she looks around at all the faces basking in the great projected light of him, she feels an almost-jealousy, a rupture of the illusion that he is hers alone. *I'm the only one who actually knows him*, she thinks, a memory of dashboard heat blasting onto her hands. Even as a child, he saw her clearly – someone to be taken seriously. No: despite his miraculous rise to fame, despite all the world thinking they own him, he has always been her secret friend.

Orson scrawls a poem on the back of the newspaper. *Maybe I should learn French,* she thinks. *Maybe I should cut my hair short like Juliette Binoche.*

"Honh Honh Honh." Zach is applying a bad French accent to Orson's moving mouth. "You very pretty lady, let me show you ma baguette."

"Shut it!"

In the light of a full moon, the warden opens the cell to Orson's room and removes her trousers. As she watches, Viola awakens to Orson as a man with cheekbones like cut gems, a man who looks good with his shirt off. Though the air conditioner is aggressive, a pleasant warmth enters her body. Around them, parents who had underestimated the PG-13 rating are instructing their children to avert their eyes. Sebastian looks uncomfortable.

"Ooh! Make me a nice French bébé with a leetle moustache!" Zach whispers. Sebastian snorts so loudly that a man in front of them turns around and glares.

"I will kill you," she whispers.

In blessed silence, Juliette opens the window to a new morning. Viola imagines herself living in this beautiful way, autumn sunshine hitting the terrace of her European apartment, a book at a thirty-degree angle to the table, a tiny coffee in an exquisite ceramic mug. A pastry. A man, sitting across from her, unspeaking but glowing in mutual presence, each of them thinking profound, essential thoughts. Clean. Perfect.

*

"Dad, was Mom, like, a celebrity?"

The question is a non-question, unanswerable. Al's son is helping himself to seconds, tearing up bread into small pieces and mopping up barbecue juice. He'd been talking about high school, how different it was going to be, how they should start by impressing their teachers with the summer reading. *Everything counts*, he'd been saying, but he hadn't counted on this.

"Well, there are gradations of celebrities."

"OK, but like. Would people call her that?"

"Some people, maybe. But it would be an overstatement." To him, she was Susan. And now she is no one. Seven years have made her a figment to them, a voiceless, smiling woman in family photographs. He has simplified her into a person who existed solely for them. What is he afraid of? The door to another reality, the invitation to imbalance.

"Can we watch her show anywhere?"

"You know, Seb, it was really just a few episodes. I'm not sure there are copies. Soaps, they never had that sort of thing."

No, he can't admit to it; not to the tapes, not to any of it. He used to worry that they would hate her for all the time she denied them. But now he worries that they might hate him instead.

"How's Grandma?" he asks.

"Oh," says Viola. "She's good."

1989

"I saw your wife yesterday."

All around, the laughter of women – white women drunk on white wine – ripples over the manicured golf course of Anopsia country club, where, at the eighteenth hole, Mr and Mrs Dunning are celebrating their son's engagement. Behind, the Club House rises majestic: an alabaster estate girded by a large wrap-around porch. Bodies move impressionistic, pastel blurs of familiar and almost-familiar faces, and everything is perfect except for the missing space where Susan should be, the vacant area between Al's breastbone and his hip, his empty back pocket where, when she's happy, she sometimes slips her hand. She was supposed to be here by now. Her flight was supposed to get in around noon, and she was just supposed to be an hour or two late, but now it's been three and everyone's tipsy and loose under the afternoon sun, finding excuses to say the things they'd been wanting to say for hours.

Maybe she was delayed, Al thinks, *or maybe the plane crashed*. He's started having bad dreams after seeing pictures of the smoldering fuselage in Sioux City. *Stop*, he tells himself, *it could be a million things*. She probably stopped to get a milkshake or can't decide what to wear. Despite the increase in her filming trips, Al is still unused to her absence. He has come to rely on her in so many unanticipated ways; her coffee is stronger and deeper, she fills the kitchen with fresh, juicy fruit, which he never thinks to buy but always reaches for when it's there. She makes him laugh so hard he forgets himself – small tragedies become a source of silliness: their evil downstairs neighbor, the slow demise of his car. She rescues him from his tendency to ruminate. Skillfully, she handles the rodent problem, somehow catching them without killing them using only empty rolls of toilet paper. When she is gone, he resorts shamefully to the traps. Their corpses sicken him, and he has to hold his breath while taking them to the dumpster. *It's going to be haunted by mice ghosts in here!* she cries, when he confesses. *Well, I guess you should never leave,* he jokes, though really he couldn't be more serious, because how else is he supposed to convey the discomfort of situations like this, in which Sloane Roberts is swilling her lemonade and looking at him side-long, setting him up to be the butt of a joke. *I saw your wife yesterday.*

"Tell her I say hello." He's learned this much: get ahead of the punchline. If you laugh at yourself first, you seem in control. And the joke of his wife's absence has become common enough among his friends that he can smell it from a mile off. He smiles now as though he's in on it, as though the insinuation isn't pissing him off.

"She was on the TV," Sloane says knowingly. Al can feel the skin of his neck flushing, a few beers threatening to give him away. He hasn't watched an episode in months. He's begun to flick through channels while she's away, hoping to catch her, hoping he won't. Only once in a blue moon does Susan sit him down to watch one together. And even she'll admit that watching them makes her squirm: the strange hyper-awareness of her own voice, the back of her head. The dissonance, perhaps, between the wife on the couch and the woman in the scene.

Resting against Sloane's engorged bosom, a four-month-old infant wipes its face against her chest, threatens to wake.

"Hang on, is that what you've been doing all day, left to your own devices? Watching soaps?" Her husband Rod Roberts, an investment banker by birth, feigns shock. "I thought we were going for partner!"

"Well, I just stumbled across it when I was looking for the news . . ." Sloane colors with embarrassment. God forbid anyone at Arrow and Munch discover their senior associate has succumbed to the intellectual poverty of daytime television. *Come on.* It's one thing to think it, but another to insinuate it so nakedly. "Anyway," Sloane deflects, "she gave me quite a shock."

"Did she?"

"I assume you've seen it."

"Of course." Sloane raises a litigious eyebrow and Al is filled with the childhood queasiness of having missed something important, of being the last to watch the latest Western or hear about a girl he liked dating someone else. He thinks back to the scenes that Susan showed him: would he describe them as shocking? She testified in a kidnapping case, manipulated a shopkeeper. But the smirk on Sloane's face suggests something else. He is sick with unknowing, with needing and not wanting to know what the hell she is talking about.

"Well, it's spicy stuff!"

Nightmare images: other men, her skin, her mouth, their promise (to have, to hold) – how, how is Susie being discussed like a thing for public consumption when he has only ever known her as his most private friend? A person of bedtimes and mornings, of soft conversations and furtive weekend escapades. A person who writes him bright postcards with pictures of beaches and bridges, who dwells in his most vivid imaginings of the future, a someday mother, someday grandmother. Capable of anything – this is the gift and the curse of her. *Spicy stuff.* It's a good thing she isn't here because God knows what he's supposed to do with all this anger that's keeping him from finding anything polite or funny to say, freezing up the whole charmed moment.

A gentle voice pipes up. "Well, I just think it's great that you let your wife get along with her career. Some men can be so controlling." Angelic, petite Tillie Summers shoots a silly look at Rod, who shakes a fist at her, and everyone laughs even though they all know she's really referring to her own husband. Al laughs too, relieved for a break in the tension, and smiles at Tillie gratefully.

"Well, she's very talented," Al adds, a closing remark, because it's the one thing he knows to be true.

By the time Susan arrives, most of the partygoers have left, and all that remains of the hors d'oeuvres are pastry flakes and drooling pots of dip.

This is bad news. Susan is starving. The plane had been delayed by two hours and by the time she made her way through arrivals and into a cab back to the apartment, she was so tired that she sat down in the shower and nearly fell asleep. She might have forgone the whole engagement party had there not been a part of her that so missed Al, that needed his clean smell and warm arms, that would feel like it was still in permanent motion until she arrived at the stable point of him. Besides, he would worry if she didn't show. So she covered her hands in sticky volumizing product and ran them through her hair and called another cab to take her to the club.

Scavenging for something worth eating in the apartment (no apples, only an overripe banana), she discovered in the cereal cupboard a small half-decapitated mouse, its tiny teeth poking over its lower lip. Her appetite vanished. Only now, alighting at the club does she remember again her horrible hunger, her stomach disintegrating from the inside out.

"Fashionably late," one of Al's friends calls as she crosses the green to the vestigial party, the stragglers practicing their swings with invisible clubs, women trying to wrap up conversations. She is aware of their gaze, her trail of California stardust as she cuts across the rippling lawn wearing a pink dress with puff sleeves, a costume that is almost but not quite right, the slit in the thigh slightly higher than appropriate for a place like this, for people like these. They don't see much of Al's friends, for reasons that she can't quite grasp. *Most of them are snobs*, Al says, which Susan thinks is funny because a lot of people would say the same about him, being an academic and all. Still, they all seem smart and good at what they do, so why shouldn't they watch her with interest, a woman who has also proven to be good at what she does?

"Sorry," she says, explaining how they sat on the runway for an hour and the pilot had joked that he was also trying to get home for dinner because his wife was making cream pie, which had been amusing at the time but was somehow hilarious when she retold it now to this crowd of boozed-up preps looking for anything to keep the party going. And all the while she is looking at Al, reaching for his hand which he loans for a brief squeeze, the touch of his normalcy almost breaking her before he retracts, hardly making eye contact, hardly managing a smile at her story. She is filled with guilt at leaving him here so long on his own with all of these couples, for the minutes she wasted in the shower and sitting on the edge of the bed in a towel and changing from one dress to another. How she resents all the people preventing her from collapsing into him, cajoling him into forgiveness. *Fine*, she thinks, steeling herself toward the only other means of winning him over: a charm offensive.

Susan suppresses her hunger and sets about being delightful, making everyone laugh as she points out Rod's new tie and Dan's new almost-married-man handshake. She compliments the blonde, Tillie, on the coordination of her dress and her shoes. She takes the baby off Sloane, who looks relieved, and she smiles and glitters while she talks to it. It reaches its pudgy hands up to claw her face and she meets them with kisses.

"Tick tock," someone says, and they all laugh knowingly, including Susan, even though having children is the last thing on her mind, not when life is just getting started. But still, the Blessed Madonna act is melting away Al's sulk, so she keeps talking to the baby about every- thing it has yet to do in the world.

"Someday, you can ride in a hot air balloon," she says. "And drive a car really fast down the highway. And go swimming in the ocean and talk to cute boys."

"And if you're lucky, you can even be a hooker on TV."

"Rod!" Sloane exclaims. "Sorry, Susan—"

"No, no, he's right of course. I do consider myself lucky."

She smiles at Rod like she's in on it, like this is the kind of thing good friends tease each other about, not daring to look at Al whose mortification is radiating dire waves. Remember when he defended her? His silence makes her feel as though she's lost something. *It would only make it worse if he agitates*, she tells herself. She doesn't need saving. Smiling, she hands back the baby and moves closer to him – close enough to feel the static between them without touching – until, at the first possible moment, they can agree it's time to leave.

2008

Sebastian is trying to throw himself over a high, metal bar, his body arching in the unnatural way he has been told to arch it, head back, legs swinging up high. *You have to abandon your intuition*, the coach said as he walked the high jumpers through the technique, though really Sebastian has already abandoned it, it was gone the moment he donned the mesh uniform for the Aldwych Midnight Riders – a team name which was meant to invoke Paul Revere, but has been reduced to the orgasmic humiliation of organized sport. So jump, though it makes no sense, contort yourself into someone you are not. Watch as Lola runs laps around you. And when the coach is distracted, you can lie on the thick red mats and chat to girls.

"Bliss, let's go."

It's almost the end of the practice. It has to be. His brain is leaking pointless information and his body has stretched beyond itself. It would be nice, wouldn't it, to go roll up a lumpy joint, fishbowl the car, forget all the bullshit everyone has tried to cram into his head today. The tangle of quadratic equations and neutrons and *el subjuntivo*.

But no – he promised his dad: he has to try.

Call it a lost bet. Having rejected all extracurriculars beyond "chillin", Sebastian explained to his father that none of it mattered; his plan was to become an artist.

And what does that look like? Al had asked.

Sebastian had gestured to himself. His long hair in a greasy bun, his chipped black nail polish. He didn't have an answer beyond the feeling inside him. Being an artist is about living in a certain way.

73

About seeing as much as making things. Often, Sebastian feels he is watching the world through an alien camera, aware of a complacency that others hide behind.

His father sighed. *Seb, you know, very few people get to make a living being an artist. The tough fact of life is that the winners play it safe. They don't dick around in study hall, they don't mess with drugs. They study hard and show up to extracurriculars, and gradually, through facts, they grow to understand the world.*

Bullshit, he said. *I understand the world.* And with gusto, he threw himself at applications for summer programs, photographed his work from art class, mailed in forms to museums and universities.

Not a single yes. Ironically, what the artist had failed to see clearly was himself. Sebastian lacked technique. Maybe he lacked talent. But worst of all, he felt he had disappointed his mother. In his underwear drawer he collects her: strands of what might be her hair, old bottles of pills, a faded, woven keyring with her initials on it. A necklace with black stones, a silk scarf. It's stupid, an effort to gain access to something: the worlds she was interested in, the way she liked to feel. His memories are a profusion of finger paintings, confetti cut with novelty scissors. She was always determined to make something, even if it was only a mess.

Maybe he had mistaken her for a star. Maybe Casey was wrong all those years ago, or humoring them. Maybe she never made it big after all. He began to feel ashamed, using his mother as an excuse for wanting more than the life on offer.

Enough, he thought, *of playing the same old part, the fuck-up twin.* As bleak as it is, his father might be right.

Slowly he walks to his mark, stretching his arms to the sky, telling himself that this is good for him. Materially, of course, it has been. Cleaning up his act has invited prizes: an increase in his weekly allowance, muscle on his lanky frame. More time with Lola, on the field, in the car after practice, around the kitchen table at night doing homework. Even a new note of recognition in his father's voice – or if not recognition, tentative relief. It is almost enough to trick him into thinking he enjoys this. The fact remains: every fiber of him rebels at the nonsense of jumping, the endless, pointless repetition, the obsession with every gained centimeter. Last night he spent an hour watching videos of pros online, trying to mesmerize himself into submission. Their bodies alarmed him, carved out by this bizarre aspiration, their legs overlong, their asses comically flat. Contortion had made them monstrous.

"Come on, kid, let's see it."

He exhales. Somehow his body begins to move. Hop, skip, jog, accelerate, bending knee and twisting and throwing himself into the – shit (*fuck!*) shrieking pain rippling up his (agh!) – he felt it when he went over, bar clattering into his back, his ankle the new center of his body, his hands clutching it, his back on the edge of the mat, and he can tell even with his eyes shut that Lola – two hundred meters away – is aware of him, is coming.

"Elevate it." She moves him onto the grass, offering her knee as a surface while the coach calls for ice.

"I twisted it."

"You were tired."

Her face, though flushed from hours of exertion, is calm and focused. Gently, she unties his shoe, slips it as lightly as possible off his foot. She tilts his heel as though she can feel where it hurts, how far is too far. Directly she fires off instructions to the group that has surrounded him. "Get his backpack, the green one. Ask Zoe for an Advil. Tell Coach I have to go." She wraps gauze around the ice pack that has materialized, studies his face as though it will tell her how much he is broken.

"You're going to have to drive," he says.

"I know."

Last month they pooled their money (mostly hers) to buy a beat-up Corolla, a manual, the interiors so sticky and disintegrating they call it Sugar Baby. They both refer to it as "their" car, but really it's Sebastian's. He's the better driver, more at ease with the flow of the road. Every morning, he carries them to and from school. Generally, it's his favorite part of the day. They listen to talk radio. The world flows through them, a young black senator from Chicago, a peace agreement in Darfur. If the twins share anything it is this: an understanding that the world is an unstable place, that anything can be taken away from you at any time.

She lifts the keys from the front pocket of his backpack and he hops to the car, leaning heavily on her shoulder. She tugs hard at the passenger door while he balances on one foot.

"How long do you think I can play this up for?"

"A week, maybe."

"Damn. Is that it?"

He turns the radio on and she turns it off. "No distractions."

"Fine. By the way, it's been sticking between second and third."

"I won't need third."

Lola reverses like a geriatric, then begins to drive, leaning up close to the wheel, back straight as a board.

"This is honestly the least efficient ambulance I have ever been in."

"You've never been in an ambulance."

"Exactly."

"But if you want to, I'll amputate your damn foot."

"Yeah, yeah."

"Don't push it, I'll do it," she says. "I cut open a sheep eyeball in Bio yesterday."

The pebbled driveway judders his leg and he moans dramatically. She opens the door for him, helps him out of the car. He doesn't make it past the living room before sinking into an armchair. Lola fetches the ottoman, sets a pillow under his ankle. The ice pack has gone warm, and his ankle swells against the gauze.

"We might have a squeezy thingy downstairs," he says.

"A compression bandage?"

"That's the one. With all the medical stuff. In the basement."

He saw it, didn't he? When he was rooting around a while ago, looking for the Christmas presents that his father claimed were from his mother every year. It's where they would be, if they were really from her. He'd found nothing but junk. Cartons of dusty electrical appliances: old lamps and fans that don't seem to work, withered baggies of wingnuts and niche-looking metal fixings. A box of unwrapped medical supplies: bandages and syringes and sanitizers that had failed to save his mother's life.

Sebastian closes his eyes, listens to Lola's subterranean rooting. Pain shoots up his calf. *See, I told you*, his body seems to say. *This was a bad idea*. At least it's a half-decent excuse for skipping homework tonight. And skipping practice tomorrow. The week opens up in front of him, unencumbered. Beneath him, a noise.

"What?"

"I can't find it."

He heaves himself up, hobbles to the top of the stairs. "It was in a cardboard box."

"Is it this?"

He scoots down the stairs on his ass, holding his leg out in front of him. The box is large and well-packaged, a California address label cut through.

Inside him, something leaps.

"Open it."

The bandage is forgotten. Together, greedily, they unpack it: two faded sundresses, a broken pair of plastic sunglasses, a crumpled receipt, a dog-eared Danielle Steel novel, a loyalty card for a café in Burbank with four stamps on it, two loose headshots (one smiling, one serious), a folding silver frame holding each of them as infants (one smiling, one serious), a card for a Los Angeles taxi driver, and a thick stack of scripts for *Life and Times*.

"Holy shit."

There are dozens of them. There might be a hundred. Thick, marked-up scripts, a tower of days of her life, her name and thoughts and ideas in fanciful blue fountain pen and yellow highlighter, and *My God, this is proof. She was a real actress*. His mind is barely catching up to the implication as he flips through pages hunting for MARGIE LUDLOW. She is there, entering CUP O'SUNSHINE café. She is there in the margins, doodling a mug of coffee with steam rising out of it, sweet and distracted and familiar. *What is my intention?* she writes, and inside him something swells, threatens to overwhelm him, an overpowering righteousness at having found her.

"She was a star." Joy like far-off fireworks. With terrible clarity, the universe rearranges itself: his father never wanted him to know the scale of this. "He hid her from us."

"Who? Dad?" Lola looks pale. "I'm sure there's a reason."

"Lola, you can't be serious."

Above them, the sound of the front door. His father's heavy footsteps. The enemy among their ranks. *Fuck him*, Sebastian thinks. He will come back tomorrow. Think what more there could be! Yes! He did come from somewhere, from someone, from a person who felt and lived the way she wanted. He knew her, he has always known her, he can know her again.

Awkwardly, he grips the railing, hops back up to the light.

"Are you coming?" he calls to Lola, lingering.

"In a minute," she says.

Deftly, she had slipped the parcel of images behind her, trying to keep her hands still, not sure she could trust what she'd seen. Her brother, thumbing through scripts, in thrall of his own revelations, had not noticed their removal, had pawed through the haul as though it was complete. But now, alone, she retrieves a series of photographs of her mother's bare body.

The woman in the photos is laughing. Staring sulky at camera. Rolling curves of hip and breast, dark hair cascading. Clavicle and neck. She is wearing nothing but a necklace. She is wearing nothing at all. She is beautiful and complete but also shocking. Wrong. There is too much of her. *Oh God.* Viola's stomach, sick with a horrible knowing, with un-knowing, with suspicion and wrong-doing, with heritable dirtiness. *Who took these photos? Who were they for? Did she ever . . . Was she . . .* What? Unfaithful? Obscene?

Inside her, an origin story fractures. Refuses to reform.

1989

Late nights, blue lights, everyone smiling, coked, shaking the week off their shoulders, recovering from their plotlines. You have to become no one again, to disrobe from the character completely, before you can step back into yourself. Everyone is here tonight at the Whiskey-A-Go-Go: Mark Flowers, Rip McFee, even Shona was around earlier. Orson is talking to the girl behind the bar, showing her how he shakes a cocktail. Maybe it's the line she did an hour ago, but Susan cannot help feeling that everyone here loves her. That all of them believe in her, that she is a part of their glittering universe. Sometimes she feels like she is living in a glorious end state, as though the world – America! – has become its final freest form. *Is it fair to be so happy?*

Rip is handing her a margarita, sidling in next to her. "I owe you one."

Today, Susan was attacked by a dog during an attempted bank robbery. The heist was Rip's brainchild, and all the most desperate characters were swept up in it. It took all of Susan's willpower to keep breathing as the animal experts trained the dog to jump up on her, to let it push her back playfully, allow it to lap her face with its wet, leathery tongue. Her throat is still sore from screaming.

"Maybe next time you could send her to a fancy hotel or something. You know. A pedicure."

"I'll see what I can do," he laughs. She likes Rip, always has. He takes her seriously. And this storyline is big for him; they're hunting for a new showrunner and all of the writers are trying to show their stuff.

"You know, Susie," he says. "There are some big conversations about you right now."

"Is that so."

Margie has had a controversial reception. The fans are waiting for her to reap her deserts; after all, she's broken up two marriages, orchestrated an arrest under false pretenses, and slept with almost every man in town.

"Some people want to see you dead."

"Some people?"

He nods at the other writers smoking by the window. "It's not you obviously. There's just a feeling about the moral center of the show."

A pit forms in Susan's stomach, a fragile, disposable thing.

"Where do you see her going?" Rip asks. He looks at her and his eyes are kind, interested. No one has asked her this before. She has always understood her job: to take what she's given, to make it the best it can be.

"I think she deserves love."

Rip nods at this, sips his drink. "Who, then?"

"Why choose. Maybe it's a mystery."

"A secret admirer?"

They riff. Susan is brimming, ideas tap-dancing, unshackled out of relief or maybe . . . intuition? It feels enough like it, organic the way acting is, only this time she's shifting the order of things, stepping into new power.

"Maybe he's a serial killer?" she suggests. "Nice big storyline for you."

"That's real big," says Rip. "Showrunner big."

"Maybe we only see his gloved hand. Max in costumes keeps saying he wants to do more gloves."

"Gloves for Max."

"And get Orson involved. A suspect or something. That boy needs a break."

Rip's lip curls up into a smile.

"What. I'm talking with my hands, aren't I?"

"No, no. You're just a generous person, Susie."

"How do you mean?"

"I ask you how we can save your career and you just want to make space for everyone else."

She wrinkles her nose. "Sorry, I wasn't trying to – to overstep—"

Mark Flowers is at her other side. "I won't let them kill you, Susie," he says close in her ear. "And if they do, I'll give you a spin-off." And then, in a blink, he is spinning her off, onto the dance floor, laughter erupting from her whole face, her nostrils, her eyes lined with electric blue. He grabs her by the waist and picks her up, twirling her round and in the midst of all the stardust she cannot help but feel like a terrible person.

When Mark sets her down, his hand wanders lower, around to her ass. Smiling she shifts it back up. It's the sort of thing you have to get used to, hands like water on you in this city. She waves her own left, ringed hand at him, and Mark mimes looking around the room.

"I don't see any husband," he says.

Susan smiles as though it's all a big joke, as if they're all playing along, her stomach prickling with sickness, the need to extricate. *It's make-believe*, she thinks, *it's fairy dust*. She aches for Al, the solid object of his devotion. The distance crests in a sudden nausea. Putting on her best cheap laugh, she topples to the bar and drapes herself on Orson's shoulder. "Time for me to go," she pouts.

Orson pouts back at her. She knows he hates weekends, that he still feels lonely in this city, that he changes his accent just to be understood sometimes, that he'll spend long hours at the beach with his Walkman, listening to tape cassettes from his childhood.

"See you Monday?"

She nods. She knows none of them can understand why she's doing this, the back-and-forth double-life.

"Good luck," Orson says. Does he imagine her time with Al to be more difficult than it is, because of how she complains to him? It's not that she tries to misrepresent life at home, but she has to vent to someone. When she cannot get through to him. When she has to cancel plans. When they fight. Orson hugs her, kissing her cheek, his scent becoming known to her, sending her out into the bruise-colored night.

Are you sure you trust these people?

She had told Al on the phone last night about the dog, felt like she'd given him an excuse to air his misgivings.

Yes. I mean, they're professionals. I don't know.

You sound scared.

I am scared.

Tell them you don't want to do it.

I want to do it.

Agh. Suze. I just worry about you. You say yes to everything.

Sometimes she feels like she is becoming two different people, the woman out here (expansive, celestial) and the woman at home (protected, held). Perhaps she needs both of these things. Perhaps it is okay to need both.

I don't want you to worry, she said. *You sound like your mom when you worry.*

Well, then don't tell me these worrying things.

So, I should pretend like they're not happening?

No, just. Make them not happen.

Now we are into wishful thinking.

Oh, good, my favorite. Come home.

I can't. She couldn't bring it up again. The conversation only makes both of them sad, and they have become careful not to let it ruin the short sweetness of their moments. Goodbye has developed a new pain in repetition, the dull awareness of acclimation.

Outside, the streetlights are dancing over beetle-wing cars, none of them taxis. Maybe she should think about herself more. Margie would. Only the problem is, her interests only ever get her into trouble – they've brought her here, on the teetering edge of this star-strung set-piece city, three thousand miles away from the man who is her husband. The rising wail of Sunset, the smash of music and loud, late-night laughter is dulled by the drone of something bigger. The heavy inevitable reckoning with what she wants, what she *really* wants. She cannot avoid the costs of her interests.

2008

The clock by Sebastian's bed reads four in the afternoon. On his desk is a mess of unfinished homework. Doodles grow like fungus in the margins: geometric mazes and rocket ships and sea creatures. Crumpled efforts at essays stud the floor amid the cairns of dirty clothes and unpaired sneakers. But Sebastian is not there. And Sugar Baby is not in the driveway.

If you're looking for him, follow the scent of his deadly tail pipe out of Aldwych, toward the city. You'll hit the main road that passes over the Essex Bridge and drops into Salem. Keep to the backroads, away from the witch kitsch and ambling tourists, and you'll find him cruising a shabby side street, staking out a pale blue house.

His ankle is still throbbing from yesterday, complaining every time he taps the gas, so it's a relief to slow down. The house doesn't have a number, but the mailbox does, along with a crudely painted assembly of kittens clambering out of a basket. He hasn't seen Sadie in a decade, but she was right there in the phone book. Vaguely, he remembers the voicemails, a franticness he did not associate with adults.

They had a tough childhood, his father said once when he asked about her. *Your mother was better equipped to get out of it.*

But it doesn't look so bad, this house. Sure, it's smaller than his and a bit run down, but not unloved. There are gnomes in the front garden and an American flag. An old board that says *Welcome!* hangs from the gate in the low chain fence.

Sebastian pushes it open.

On the front porch, he stands before the weather-beaten screen door. Pop music plays inside. The sun is still high in the sky, and several miles away Lola is running around a track. A dog barks. He rings the bell.

The woman is shorter than he remembered, her blonde hair chopped in a puffy fringe on her forehead. She's wearing fuzzy leggings and a purple tank top.

"If you're selling knives, I'm sorry, I bought some from the kid yesterday," she says.

"Sadie," he says. "It's me."

His aunt looks him over and whispers under her breath, "Mary Mother of God." She wraps her arms around him.

"Come inside," she says. "I'm making coffee."

The walls are all papered: tiny rose bouquets and yellowing pastel stripes. The carpet exhales ash and citrus spray. In the living room, cat hair clings to everything. A black angora ball animates from underneath an armchair and slinks over to him, rubs against his calf. It is missing chunks of fur from the top of its head. Sebastian bends down to it.

"That's Nomar," Sadie says. "He's scrappy."

Boxes rise like buildings, a cityscape of old papers and photo frames and DVDs and small plastic containers. Abandoned gift baskets and stereo cables and Happy Meal toys. And everywhere, on every wall, is his mother. Upside-down and leotarded, head dangling off a sofa and pink satin slippers shot up into the air. Blood-spattered and nightgowned under a local newspaper caption reading *Salem Drama will be on Tomorrow and Tomorrow and Tomorrow.* Open-mouthed and diffident in red velvet, gesturing to a Christmas tree next to blonde and buoyant Sadie (laughing infectiously, sharp little nose thrown back like a mouse). In a smart white suit with shoulder pads, her arm thrown around her maid of honor.

"I've never seen this," Sebastian says.

"No shit, I bet it's the only copy. Where you been kiddo? Last time we spoke, you were obsessed with the rainforest, is that still your thing?"

"Not so much," he smiles.

When he looks at her eyes, they are rimmed red. "So to what do I owe this visit, business or pleasure?"

"Actually, Sadie, I was wondering – do you have any videos of my mom's show?"

Her face freezes.

"I gave them all to your dad."

Her nephew, sitting on her couch, his eyes dancing on the television in that way that Susie's used to, engrossed in the moment. That is the miracle of Sebastian: even as he breathes in the here and now, he is full of a world gone by. The layers of innocence and becoming are still so bright in his face that she can almost forget the years that Al robbed from her.

For a few months after Susie died, Sadie had been allowed (begrudgingly, she suspected) to take the children off of Al's hands. It wasn't much, a few Sunday afternoons. But each had been wonderful and urgent with the need to introduce them to their mother – the woman who had existed before Al, the parts of her that had been unchanged by him. They looked through old photo albums and she told them stories about the neighborhood growing up, the Halloween hijinks and the time they got chased by a dog after playing ding-dong-ditch and all the bonfires and sandcastles and Susie in all of it, the bravest of everyone, determined to do whatever it took to make something of herself. Susie inventing a not-so-secret club where they all had to eat dandelions. Susie in the school talent show, singing like Judy Garland, all the mothers crying. There was never enough time. After she'd dropped the twins off, she would think up all the things she had forgotten to say, write them down next to her bed. It agitated her, how little they knew.

One afternoon, she mentioned to Viola that her mother was an actress, that she had been on the television. That she was famous. Her little blank face was a shock. As though she didn't know a thing about where she came from. As though Al hadn't shown them all the tapes she'd meticulously recorded over years.

Maybe it's too emotional for him, she thought as generously as she could. After all, he hardly watched the show when Susie was alive – he couldn't handle it even then. But when he met her at the door, she suggested, gently: *It might be good for you to give them a play*. He'd smiled and thanked her, and closed the door in a way that gave her no assurance.

Of course, when he cut her off, Al did it like he was being clever, like Sadie was an idiot and incapable of detecting a pattern. After that day, the twins became permanently busy. Whenever she wanted to take them to dinner or a Sox game or drop by on their birthday, they were never short of commitments: band practice or swim practice or math practice. They were always practicing, though God knows what for. Why there isn't tax-paying practice or taking-shit-from-your-boss practice, she'll never be sure. With children, people are generally unrealistic.

What did I do? She begged him to tell her, but he only said: *It might be confusing for them. Being around you might make them upset.* Whatever that was supposed to mean, she had no idea. Did he think she might remind them of their mother? *Was that such a bad thing?* Or was her mere existence upsetting: a woman in her forties without a husband or any kind of life objective? Either way, it fucking pissed her off.

Sadie had disliked Al from the first day she met him. The rain was coming down heavy, spilling off into black puddles on the pavement. She was aware of the percussion of it, seventeen, practicing her footwork in the kitchen. Susie said she'd be back for dinner. Didn't say she'd be bringing anyone with her, especially not a man old enough to be Sadie's teacher and dressed like one in a suit jacket and foggy glasses. They burst through the door as though she wasn't supposed to exist.

"Oh!" Al said, seeing her in her leggings, startled but still hopping up and down, petite battement. "Gee, sorry, hi."

Susie, unfazed, introduced them. *Al, Sadie. Sadie, Al.* He started fussing with his shoes, shapely, expensive-looking leather ones, rubbing the wetness off his glasses and taking in the house. As he squatted to the floor to untie his lace, he nearly lost his balance, and grabbed onto the back of Susie's calf. She giggled.

"Sorry," Al said. "I'm making a mess."

"It's fine!" Susie said before moving to the sink, brushing past Sadie to wash a dish — something she had never done before unless under duress. Dishes were their mother's job if anyone's. But now Susie's hands cut through the soapy water, scrubbing and scrubbing.

He held his shoes, his toes curling underneath his feet in thin, argyle socks, assessing the uncontained pile that had accrued by the door: broken jelly shoes and single flip flops, dirty trainers.

"Do you have a bag?" he asked.

"A bag?"

"A plastic shopping bag. It's just, they're wet, I don't want to ruin—"

Susie turned off the sink and dried her hands. She fished a plastic bag out from under the sink and handed it to him, like this was a normal thing to do, and he placed his shoes into it so that they didn't come into contact with the other shoes.

Sadie felt a sudden desire to throw the sugar bowl on the floor.

It was easy to decide she didn't like him. That the relationship couldn't last.

Maybe it could have been different. If it hadn't been raining. If they had met in a park or a cinema. If she hadn't been interrupted. But it clouded her idea of him forever. She saw who he was and couldn't unsee it; a man who needed the world to comfort him, for its ugliness to be hidden away by other people.

So she decided to be ugly. For months after he stopped letting her come around, she left long, wine-fueled messages on his answering machine. Eventually he blocked her number. For years — she is now ashamed to say — she gave up trying to see them. *Maybe when they're older,* she thought. And now? It's as though no time has passed.

87

Sadie looks around. Over the years, the junk in her house has overtaken two corners of the living room and most of the staircase. The door to the spare room will not open all the way; clutter lines the walls and spills out of the closet – clothes that Sadie couldn't possibly fit into anymore jump off hangers, crawl out of large plastic containers.

And here, in the middle of all of her chaos, is her nephew, who wants to be nowhere else in the world. She should thank Al, really, for creating a plan that backfired so spectacularly. That's the thing about kids: tell them they can't have something, and they'll never want anything else.

"Where are they?"

Sebastian smells his father before he sees him, or at least the fruits of his labor. Chicken breasts sizzling on the stove top, an onion roughly chopped. Al is bathed in the smoke of it, a dish cloth thrown over his shoulder, his fogged glasses pushed up on top of his head. Stray capers. A gutted lemon.

"My day was great, thanks," Al says. "How have you been?"

"Where are Mom's video tapes?"

Al takes his glasses, rubs them with the dish cloth, places them back on his nose. He looks at Sebastian. His face is blank.

"The tapes that Sadie gave you? After the funeral? She said there were a hundred?"

"I don't have them."

"You don't have them?"

The chicken sizzles. Lola sticks her head in and asks, "Can I help?" No one responds.

"I gave them away," Al says.

"You gave them away?"

"What are we talking about?" Lola asks.

"Tapes. Of Mom."

"I'm sorry. I didn't think you'd be interested."

"You didn't think we'd be interested? Jesus, Dad, aren't you supposed to be a historian? Aren't you supposed to preserve things?"

"I don't think it's how she wanted you to see her."

Lola raises her eyebrows and her hands and skitters out of the room. Like this doesn't involve her too. Sebastian's voice is pumping in his chest.

"You gave them away. To where? To who?"

"I don't remember, Seb. I'm sorry. It was a long time ago."

"I don't believe you."

His father looks like he has been punched.

After that, Sebastian does not speak. He has no words. He waits for his plate and carries it up to his room. His mind rolls over everything his father has ever claimed about their mother. The Christmas presents, the moments she was around, moments he cannot remember, her happiness, here in this shitty little nothing town. He hid her career. He hid her sister. He hid her life.

Maybe he just couldn't stand that she existed beyond him. That she had any success outside his narrow little world of founding fathers and ancient documents and bone-dry essays that nobody reads. Maybe she showed him how little it mattered, trying to become Asshole Emeritus, all those patronizing nerds in turtlenecks. Or maybe there is something else, something more damning. Either way, Sebastian is going to find out.

In the morning he begs off school again. Ankle-related reasons. His father, who normally wouldn't tolerate this bullshit, says only: "If you must." Lola looks at him like she wants to say something but doesn't dare. When they leave, he makes a mug of instant coffee and disinters his mother's scripts.

On the living-room floor, he spreads them apart, arranges them chronologically. He follows his mother's movements through the dialogue, the marginalia. When she was pushed out of a taxi, she wrote: That asshole on Melrose Ave! And when she was nursing a child and crying to herself, she wrote: Sebastian, week three. *That's him!*

Everywhere, she's written names, none of which have to do with any of the characters. Women's names, but also men's: Rip. Mark. Glen. Orson – *Orson Grey!* What could it mean? Clearly, she was drawing from life, using the texture of California to inform Margie – fearless and reckless, good with being bad, taking whatever (whoever!) she wanted. The thought was a profound relief; that she had not spent all her short hours in his father's captivity, that she had experienced life in all its freedom and enormity, that she had maybe even loved other people. Margie, Susan, Susan, Margie, blurring into a single force of nature. His mother was an artist, a bombshell, a woman with the world in her hand. He turns another page. *Ali. Richard.*

Is she trying to tell him something?

This would all make more sense if he could see her in action. Or smoke a joint. But given he'll have to wait to score until school is out, he wanders to the kitchen, opens the drinks cabinet and sniffs an ancient bottle of Madeira. He could get drunk. He will get drunk. He is still only coming to understand the fluid fearlessness of alcohol, the way it moves through his body, clamoring for the arriving moment: *Now!* He pours his coffee into the sink and fills the mug with a heavy dollop. It tastes sweet and rotten and good.

The scripts paper the entire carpet, and as he meditates on the scale of them, an anger builds. Somehow, the most offensive thing is his father's insistence that she left no trace. Isn't that the point of being an artist – to leave a mark? He replays the conversation yesterday, Sadie's anguished hands running through her bangs over and over again. "Lots of people taped it," she moaned. "I just never made copies."

It's out there, he thinks. *Somewhere.*

His face, his cheekbones, the inside of his mouth tingle as he crosses the room and boots up the desktop.

Why has he never thought to do this before?

The machine hums to life unfathomably slowly, junked up with viruses. *It's LimeWire*, he tells Lola, blaming his music piracy, failing to mention his forays into the X-rated underbelly of the web. Videos take ages to download, but there's pleasure in anticipation. Knowing something magnificent and illicit is arriving. Awaiting the slow, tantalizing load of a tit.

Don't get distracted now, you're on a mission. A whir of a desperate fan, the monitor flickering blue, a chord announcing the dawn of information. Open a browser and type: SUSAN BLISS.

Nothing.

Crushing, horrible nothing.

SUSAN BLISS LIFE AND TIMES

Did you mean Susan Byrne?

An explosion. Sebastian's mother is everywhere, immortal, her headshot (how!) pinned to a forum page dedicated to Margie Ludlow. He gorges: the time she tried to kill herself by overdosing. The time she got in a knife fight with a pimp, carried a scar on her chest. So many strangers contain splinters of her! These are his people: LATfan4ever, burger_mama, daytimemuse.

Fuck. He tips the chair back, almost far enough to be dangerous. Into the dead of the house, he emits a stunned little laugh. He needs to call his aunt, to tell her: it's all here, it's waiting for us! How many years has he spent without a trace of her when all of this was here to be known?

Click through the jungle, the vast soapy universe, until you come across a link – a full episode! Sounds of a struggle. Men in torn suit jackets against a darkened backdrop. *Get up. Get up!* Melodramatic percussion, choral synthesizers. A heart being monitored from a hospital bed. A title card falls – this is: *LIFE AND TIMES.*

It's her, she's coming! A gun is removed from a man's back pocket, sirens blare to a conclusion and fade into the low tone of a cello. Enter his mother. *His mother!* Sparkling earrings, rosy cheeks, clothes clinging tightly. Look how she moves her mouth, how she leans to the side as she tells a joke. *His mother!* All of her, the fleshy pinkness of her arms, the lightness of her. *Her hair!* Long and dark, tumbling down past her shoulders. The bounty of it. The camera caresses her legs, her back. It grows dizzy on a prism of light refracting off of her earrings.

A young Orson Grey turns to combine a series of translucent liquids into a glass. The camera looks longways down the bar. His mother is reflected into a mirror, doubled. She is smiling a strange, coaxing smile.

His mother. In the overwhelming present tense, existing, now, here, existing and existing and existing. Maybe she has not actually died but just changed herself again, transformed into another character, living another life inside the internet.

He wants all of it.

Hours disappear. Sebastian searches involuntarily, urgently, sinking into the sound of her voice, pouring another Madeira and eating packet after packet of Fritos. The way people talk about soap operas, Sebastian assumed they would be trite. True, the sets are stagy and the dialogue isn't always polished, but the stories are brave, with real drama and controversy and his mother is fearless and free in all of them.

He follows along with the scripts, trying to piece together her thoughts in the margins with the actions on the screen. If he looks hard enough, he'll find it, the thing that brings everything together. By the time Lola comes home he is pacing like a nutjob, scripts strewn across every surface. She kicks off her shoes, pulls her hair out of her ponytail. "Jesus. You might want to pick this all up before Dad gets home."

"Or what?"

She shrugs. "Or you'll have to talk about it again."

"I want to talk about it."

"What could you possibly want to say?"

He spreads his arms across the mess of her. "Look!"

Lola looks. Her eyes are his eyes, the same pristine green, but somehow, she is looking without seeing. "The tapes made him sad, Seb," she says plainly.

"If he really missed her, he would have kept them."

"I don't think that's true, necessarily."

"Lola, he's hiding something."

In the background, their mother is talking to a man with slicked-back hair. Her hands are on her hips and she is facing away from the camera. She turns, and implores him not to leave her. Her lips are cherry red and her voice is fraught.

"I think you should ask yourself if that's something you really want to know."

He eyes her, his twin. Sees her seriousness. It's a look he knows well, Lola afraid of some nameless thing.

"Seb. Come on. Can we just talk about this when I'm back?"

Oh, right. He forgot: they're leaving him behind. Tonight, Lola and his father are lighting down the coast to look at universities well beyond his GPA. *What a bonding experience.* But he can see how bad she feels, so he simply says: "Whatever." Reluctantly, he stacks the papers, removes them to his room.

When his father comes home, he is humming: *Let's go fly a kite.* His father is not a man who hums. Nor is he a man who irons his shirts, but the iron was out on the table this morning, and his father's collar freshly pressed. *Is he that happy to ditch me?* When he sees Sebastian, he shifts, wary. "How was your day?" Al asks.

Sebastian can hardly speak through the anger in his chest at the unbelievable charade of all of this, but somehow, he manages: "Fine."

"Did you make any progress on that essay?"

"Some."

"I'm sorry there's not much in the way of leftovers. There's a frozen pizza in there, or I could leave you some cash for takeout?"

"I'll take the cash."

"Oh good, I was beginning to think you'd become monosyllabic."

Al smiles as though this is hilarious, and Sebastian imagines choking him.

"It's not too late, you know, if you want to come with us," Al says, and he looks almost sorry, as if a weekend with his favorite child isn't exactly what he wants.

"I'm good," Sebastian says. "Have fun being high-achievers."

The sun sinks and the pair of them set off. In the morning they will wake up in a small ivy-clad town and Sebastian will wake up here, with his mother.

NEW TOPIC: BACKSTAGE ROMANCES
user: cutandpaste
anyone no about any secret relationships behind the scenes
like with Susan Byrne in particular
curious cuz i have herd rumors
thx

1989

"What took you so long!"

Orson finds Susie scrunched into the end of the bar at Grady's in Burbank, one leg cocked up on a second stool. It's busier than normal, and he has to push his way through the throng that floods in on a Friday: grips and boom ops, brigades of production coordinators, actors and wannabes and disappointed autograph hunters and the people who work the studio canteen. Ever since Orson came to Los Angeles, the challenge has been sifting through them; figuring out who is import-ant, who is worth his time. Often, it's the people you least expect.

"I had to fight people off with my bare fists to defend this," she says, offering him the free seat. "Look at these battle wounds."

She shows him her un-bloodied hands, her long, elegant fingers.

"Ouch. Better get those taped up."

"The things I do for you." She slides him a single-malt whiskey, clinks her glass against his. "Cheers."

"My hero," he says. "Sorry, Mark wanted to talk about a storyline next week."

"Well, we all know what that's code for."

Flowers is notorious for his Friday afternoon "script sessions", which begin with a line of white powder and end sometime around four in the morning.

"The man is an animal."

"I don't know when he sleeps."

"He doesn't."

"I heard from Rip that he went four days last week without a wink."

"Jesus," he laughs. "Americans."

"Californians!"

Orson is ashamed to admit it to most people, but even after three years, the people here still bewilder him. For a start, everyone runs. If they aren't driving, they are running. Often they will drive quite a long way just to be able to run indoors in giant complexes with names like 24 Hour Fitness or The Jungle Gym. In the small town outside Glasgow where Orson grew up, people only ran when they were chasing or being chased. Or last call at the pub. So it's reassuring to have someone to hang out with who doesn't go in for jazzercize or step-aerobics or whatever godawful fitness trend they've cooked up this week. Susie makes sense to him. She drinks like she's coming up for air.

"Another?" she waves to the bartender. "Do you want one or have you already been riding the ski-slopes?"

"This is going to sound crazy, but he really did just want to talk," Orson says.

"God, imagine that. Must have been serious."

"Nah. Just this new serial-killer stuff. They want me to be a suspect, so. Have to be a bit more suspicious."

She raises an eyebrow like she can tell he's not giving her the full story. He's not, but he raises one back, to put her off the case. No need to tell her the awful thing Mark said. Rather have a drink and pretend it didn't happen.

"Do I know you?"

A woman (middle-aged, middle-American) is leaning on the bar, looking at Susie curiously, like an old friend.

"I don't think so," she says, smiling her winning smile and shaking her head. Susie is seven years older than Orson, but she's far less intimidating than the girls his own age around here with too-white teeth and terrifying abdomens. It's no wonder people just start talking to her.

"I'm sure we've met somewhere. Or maybe I've seen you." The woman squints. It's obvious now what's coming. If he had a magic pencil, he'd draw the lightbulb over her head himself. "I know! Margie!"

Susie beams, flattered, all generosity. "You're a fan?"

"Oh! I watch every day! It's very, very addicting. I'll arrange my day sometimes . . ." The woman natters on in the way that only Americans can, emphatically fawning, telling you things you already know. Even if a Scot had that many compliments in them, they wouldn't dare say them out loud. That's another thing he can't get over: people here are so vulnerable.

"Well, you probably recognize Orson," Susan says, trying to draw him back into the conversation, share the spotlight. But the woman looks at him blankly. "Joe? From behind the bar?"

"Of course! Gosh, you look so much smaller in real life! But maybe it's just that you're sitting down. A trick of the eye." *Well, fuck me then.* "Oh, I'm so sorry to ask, but would you mind awfully if I took a photo? It's for my daughter, see, we watch the show together every day."

From her giant backpack the woman procures a giant camera – everything really is bigger here – and before he can arrange his face, she's taken a shot.

"Enjoy your day," Susie says, delighted, waggling her fingers. As the woman slips away, she drops her jaw. "Oh my God."

"You're famous."

"We're famous!"

"She thought I was furniture."

"Don't be stupid. Everyone is going to be saying your name. Just be patient."

He sighs, puts his head on the countertop. "Patience is not my strong suit." This is why he came out here, isn't it? For a bite at the apple? But fuck, it's been a long week. It's been a long three years. Audition after useless audition, never any news from his pointless agent. Always, now he is telling himself: this is just a stepping stone. He won't get stuck making melodrama for housewives. Susie always acts like fame will just take care of itself, but Orson knows better. He's seen how it happens. It's why he's been buttering up the writers for more storylines, more airtime.

"Maybe this serial killer thing will be it for you. Your breakout."

"God, I hope so."

"Well, I hope not. Selfishly. As soon as the world discovers you, you're going to leave me."

"We're both going to leave, Susie. Don't you want to?"

Susie sips her drink, casts her eye around the bar, her eyes trailing the woman with the camera. "I used to think so. But now I'm not so sure. It's nice to have a long-term relationship."

"You mean, other than your husband?"

She sticks out her pink tongue. "I said long-term not long-distance."

He looks at her for a second, asking silently: *Are we going to go there?* Susie's husband is the drainpipe that all their conversations circle around. But for the moment, she swirls away, back to the here-and-now.

"I just want to do right by Margie, that's all. I still have so much to learn from her."

Orson smiles, because how can he not? For Susie, Margie is more than just a voice, a wardrobe, a posture. She is flesh and blood, a cause for crusade. A villain miscast and misunderstood, knocked again and again by life but endlessly brazen, endlessly resilient.

"You're such a pro, Susie. I've got more loyalty to my left shoe than I do to Joe."

"Well, Margie keeps me honest."

"Ironically. For a serial liar."

"Come on, are you really saying you don't love that? Knowing someone else so deeply that the sense of yourself slips away? Feeling what someone else feels? Wanting what they want? I'd do it for free."

No one on set is realer than Susie, no one works harder than she does. Yesterday morning at seven, Rip handed her thirty dreaded pink pages: last minute rewrites. Most people (Orson included) would have laid them out all over the floor of the set, pinned them to the wall, sneaking glances mid-take. But Susie went into a fugue state, somehow memorizing all of it before cameras started rolling. Afterwards, he got down on his knees and bowed to her. *If there's no eye contact, they don't buy it, kiddo,* she said. It's enough to make you feel like a fraud.

"I don't know," he says. "I guess I'm just not very 'method'. They're just roles to me. And I'm ready for the next one."

"One day. We should do a play together!"

"God, I don't know if I could get on a stage again," he says, "The audience, the pressure . . ."

"Well, at least with theatre it's all gone after the curtain comes down."

"That's even worse. Half the point of getting famous is being remembered."

"Aw, but Orson. I'll never forget you."

And when she looks at him, he can tell she means it, that this isn't just a bit. She's as real about this as she is about anything. *What did he do to deserve this?*

"Do you have to go home this weekend?"

She nods her head, pulls on the bags under her eyes. Shit, maybe Mark is right.

I'm worried about her, Flowers said earlier. *People aren't tuning in for her anymore. This flying is affecting her looks. She's supposed to look like you can fuck her from all directions.*

Mark grinned then like he had imagined it personally, like Orson was supposed to agree. It made him sick. But he bit his tongue, because more than anything, he needs Mark to like him.

"He's a lucky guy, your man," Orson says. "Married to a celebrity."

"Sometimes I'm not so sure."

If she knows what's good for her, she'll dump him, be out here full time. Talk to her. She trusts you.

The worst part is that Orson agrees. If Susie weren't flying all the time, she could be auditioning more. "Why doesn't he move out here?"

"He will. It's just not the right time for him, I guess. With the tenure stuff, and the college cycle. But when we have kids . . ."

"It seems like you're always the one compromising," he says softly.

She closes her eyes. Like opening them might give away the part of her that agrees. "I'm never compromising as long as I get to do this."

When she looks at him again, it's with a bright, clear conscience, a need to redirect. "What are your plans for the weekend, then?"

"Oh, me? Do nothing. Sit on the beach. Write some bad poems. Think about calling my parents, decide not to. Think about cooking, decide not to. Drive around Hollywood Hills, maybe break into a house, steal someone's identity."

"You're tragic."

"I know. Would you believe I haven't had a home-cooked meal since last Christmas?"

Susan nearly knocks her drink off the counter. "Orson!"

"I know."

"It's July!"

"I know."

"Jesus, kid. What are you doing tonight?"

"I thought we were going out—"

"No. Come on now. I'm coming to your house, I'm cooking for you."

She gulps down her second (third? fourth?) drink, grabs him by the hand, pulls through the crowd, quizzes him on his non-existent spice collection, asks whether she needs to buy olive oil. God, she's going to hate it, his dark, microscopic flat. There isn't a thing on the walls. But maybe this is good. Letting someone take care of him.

2008

On Sebastian's screen is a photograph, low-quality, both old and taken hastily, printed in a cheap publication. His mother, beaming. A young Orson Grey, confused. Like he doesn't want to be seen.

The caption reads: JUST FRIENDS? WE DON'T BUY IT!

The article is a jumble of words. No sign of husband / very cosy / enjoying / nothing serious / bold new / east coast / chemistry.

Holy shit. This is it. The answer! The secret his father has been hiding! She really had been free out there, reveling in her fame, playing and partying and sleeping with whoever she wanted! Sleeping with celebrities! God, it must have felt like the whole world was fruit at her fingertips. What a surprise that Al couldn't handle the idea of her with anyone else, the fullness of her life. It's clear now: she had not needed him – and Sebastian doesn't either.

The printer hums out warm pages, the image expanded to be unignorable. The craft box spills out onto the floor, sequins and pipe cleaners, construction paper and rainbow gel pens, materials of a glorious new reality. Life springs a new origin.

The car doors clunk closed, and they are on their way back, New Haven a disappearing gothic haze. Stone walls and students and locals and the smell of pizza dough and high monastic windows that Al can almost (but not quite) project his daughter into. How has time passed so quickly? Viola kicks off her shoes and throws her feet up on the dashboard and looks almost (but not quite) like her mother.

Turning homewards is a relief. Al can't leave Sebastian for too long, not in that state. It's too easy, these days, for his son to get into trouble. As they plunged south yesterday, even in the excitement of academic pilgrimage, Al had begun to feel the invisible limits of the car, which is to say the limits of himself, his ability to bear his daughter's distance. Pennsylvania is about as far as he'd suggest, New Jersey if (and only if) Princeton. Obviously, he'd prefer she chose Harvard, but kids have to branch out, don't they? Anyway, any Ivy would be a coup, and it's not unthinkable with her marks and her cello and her running. But faultless as she is – he can't help but carry with him a profound anxiety, which is the very plausible concern that she will reject him.

He drums his fingers on the steering wheel, clenches and unclenches his hands as he turns back onto the freeway.

"What did you think?" he asks.

"It's beautiful, obviously. And grand and magical."

Her thoughtful smile, her wrinkled brow. "I'm sensing a 'but'."

"I don't know, I can't explain it. There's a funny feeling there."

"How so?"

"Like it's pretending to be something other than what it is."

"And what is it?"

"It's pretending to be immortal."

He laughs out loud. "You don't think it is? One of the oldest universities in America?"

"Nothing American is immortal."

"News to me. I was planning on living forever."

He can feel her grin, the sun shifting over her ankles, his knuckles. The car fills with a superficial calm, a skin over the voice in his mind screaming: *Tell her now!*

He had thought he might say something last night at dinner, both of them enjoying fresh fish at a cosy, harborside nook, the sea only a smell and a calm lapping sound somewhere below them. But it had been impossible, looking at her. Sure, he could justify it as the savoring of a happy moment, but in his heart, he knew – *he knew* – it was cowardice. It would feel like telling Susan herself. Instead, they reviewed their favorite crime drama, the latest death in a bucolic British shire. They'd developed a habit of pausing halfway through episodes to hash it out.

It's the taxi driver, she'd insist.

It can't be, he would counter. *It's too obvious.*

Yes, he'd become reliant on television in the evenings, sacrificing his attention to the bright screen, quieting down his own thoughts. But mysteries hardly count as junk food, right? They keep the mind active. And period dramas have historical value. Maybe he is getting soft. But his daughter shares his love of sweet, cathartic resolutions, the pair of them as fitting as any detective duo; the opinionated stalwart and the precocious upstart. It's satisfying, premeditation, the idea that someone (even if a murderer) has planned out the when, where, and how of death.

"Heard from Sebastian?"

"No."

"Has he . . . Have you talked at all . . ."

"No."

It's embarrassing, relying on her like this. But he can't help but feel stability in this child, dependence on her judgment.

"It will be fine," she says. "He'll get over it."

She did not ask him to explain about the tapes. Perhaps she can picture it. Perhaps she understands the weight of the wife he never knew.

"He hasn't said anything about college stuff, has he?"

"Not really. He's been working harder."

"I noticed. It's good he's being realistic about the art."

"I just don't think school interests him. Not in an intrinsic way."

"Not like it interests you."

She looks out the window. Viola has never liked to be compared directly. She's sensitive about fairness.

"Would you want to stay close to him?"

"Like go to the same college?"

"I'm not suggesting that."

"No. I don't know." And between them sits the fat, silent fact that her brother also needs her. Without her, he might fall into an abyss.

"Viola, I need your help with something."

He exhales deeply and begins.

Last month, at Dan Dunning's anniversary party, he saw her again: Tillie Summers. Well, Tillie Hancock, since the separation. Her handshake came with a strange awakening, cauterised pathways sprouting new growths. She spoke about everything she was learning to do now that her husband was gone. For the first time, she figured out how to work the lawnmower. She lit the barbecue. After a storm downed power on the whole street, she finally discovered where the fuse box was. She started sleeping with a golf club under the bed. *My swing's improved*, she laughed, *I've been practicing in my sleep.* As she spoke, he observed the ways that she took care of herself: her tidy, manicured hands, the floral moisturizer that she rubbed into them almost unconsciously as she spoke. He had never understood the attraction before in carefulness, in precision.

Despite the unsubtle encouragement from Dan and his mother, Al has avoided dating. The thought of sitting across from a person and summarizing himself – a package of diplomas, offspring, and emotional baggage – is nauseating.

He wants someone who will understand intuitively how it felt to grow up in his world. To wander through the woods with a group of boys, parents caring too much and not enough, collective abandonment and resourcefulness. Someone who would understand these intangible moments forged him as much as anything else: losing his way, a small bridge collapsing behind him. The water was cold and the current strong in the middle, and Al remembered the strange recognition of his own power to alter an environment, of the very fact of a journey making it impossible to repeat.

And so with women. He could not take Tillie Hancock to the quarry and ask her to cast off her shirt. He could not kiss her suddenly, or propose something reckless – these ideas would not titillate her. He is too old for these moves anyways.

"I asked her to drop by tonight."

For a moment, the car is silent.

"Is that okay?"

"Dad!"

"Sorry—"

"No, it's wonderful?"

"Really?"

"I'm so proud of you!"

She touches her hand to his shoulder and he thinks of all of the hours and years he has put into this person, all of the car rides to orchestra practices, all of the balanced and unbalanced meals, the phone call from the nurse when Viola got her period and he had to buy her tampons and wasn't sure which ones were correct, and she was so mortified she didn't speak to him for a week – all of that was worth it for this moment of permission, this grace.

"So what was the favor?"

"Can you talk to your brother?"

Viola bites her upper lip. "Mm."

"Is that a yes?"

"You haven't given me much time."

"We'll be home in an hour."

But as they hit the city, traffic swells, hundreds of cars hitting the tunnels as Saturday night emits a gravitational pull. Al complains with increasing agitation about the endless construction, the tactical error in taking this highway rather than the other. By the time they arrive home, they are both exhausted and thirsty and desperate for a shower. And a sleek black car squats in the driveway.

"It's really nice to meet you," Tillie says. "I've heard so much about you."

Hanging from the antique mirror opposite the front door is Sebastian's masterpiece: the image from the forum enlarged over thirty sheets of paper, taped together, augmented with glitter, pipe cleaners, reflective stickers. In one of his mother's lipsticks, he had written the words: *Remember me?*

The blonde woman extends toward him a dainty, breakable arm.

"Sorry, you are—"

"Tillie. Didn't your dad—"

"No."

"Oh."

"Oh."

"I see."

Sebastian is reeling, full of Madeira and the fact of this woman, her connection to his father.

"So, you make art?" she says, gesturing at the image.

"Sometimes."

"I actually run a little gallery on Main Street, maybe you could come by."

He's seen those galleries, full of tragic, expressionless watercolors as bland as the people who buy them. They are places where art goes to die. Embarrassing. Embarrassing that she would consider him to be remotely interested.

Is this the type of woman his father wants?

His mother looks down on him with a conspiratorial laugh, and they are sharing in this, a gigantic joke, the brilliant coincidence of his timing. It's as though they were in it together, the two of them re-enchanting her, defending the house against this cookie-cutter Christmas-card country-club cockroach. How could anyone occupy the space Susan Byrne left behind?

"That's nice," he says, offering up his best patronizing smile. "I'll let you know if I lose my fucking mind."

The door swings open. For a moment, his father's face freezes. Then it folds away as he steps back outside, hiding a pain Sebastian did not know he could cause.

*

Shostakovich in E flat, frustration taking the form of a major key, impossible fingerings, sharp and grotesque. This is music for straightening your mind out, anger finding safe staccato expression. With her bow, Viola is screaming feeling without consequence.

Out of her window, Viola can see her brother stripping leaves off the trees bordering the marshes behind the yard. *Go, just go, have fun,* she had said to her father. *I'll take care of him.*

She holsters her bow and steps into the hallway to begin the painstaking process of un-taping her brother's "art". Her mother, Orson Grey. Her low-cut top, her enormous hair. The disturbing swell of her breasts. The look of her: out of control. The look of him: afraid.

It's stupid, she tells herself. *It's from some trashy magazine. He isn't like that. Whatever her mother may have been, Orson is no sleaze.*

What she feels for Orson Grey isn't love. You can't be in love with someone you don't know. She admires him that's all. She has read the article about how close he was with his grandmother. She has seen the photos of him with the baby bunny. In her bedside table, her mother's nudes remain hidden in a red folder, deceptively labelled SCIENCE. *He didn't take those photos,* she tells herself. *He's just not that person.*

She folds up the giant, decorated paparazzi image, slips the textured stack of it under her bed. Comparatively, it's an easier mess to clean up.

The darkness that comes earlier every day is already ribboning up the hickory trees that reach toward the last pink dashes of sky. Viola steps outside. "You okay?"

"I'm great," her brother says, peeling off a skein of bark, crumpling it in his hand. "Do you think we could give that woman a light food poisoning? Just bad enough so that she never comes back?"

"We have to give her a chance, Seb. She seems nice."

"God, Lola. A lobotomy seems nice."

What do you want from her? Does he expect all women to be like their mother? Unknowable, brimming with secrets? Is the problem that she's real?

"It's been ten years."

"Oh, you think Dad needs to 'get on with his life'."

"It wouldn't be the worst thing. For any of us."

He pulls at the bark and a large piece comes away in his hand. He picks it apart, crumbling away the fine layers.

"So, what do you think?"

"Of your little exhibition? I think you're nuts."

"The picture is real though."

"Bullshit, Seb. All those magazines are fake."

"You never believe me, Lola. Fuck it. I'm going to Toby's."

"Seb, don't be like that."

"Then come."

Toby Caruso's party. It's not her sort of thing. Nalgenes full of warm white wine, girls she can't stand, boys who frighten her. Normally, she would avoid it like a sinkhole. But her brother has been too alone for too long. Someone needs to take responsibility for him.

In the marshes, a bird is singing. These woods used to seem so thick, but it feels like the sea is creeping closer every day, erasing the known world. If she stands here long enough, can she keep the ground from falling away?

She squishes her face forward into a thin fish mouth. "Fine. But I'm not drinking, okay?"

"Fine."

"And don't abandon me," she says.

"I won't."

Two iPods plug into two separate speaker systems; if you stand on the staircase between the rooms you can hear the discord. But enter the downstairs bedroom, and behold the theatre of femininity: Viola unzips a sacred and mysterious bag bursting with powders and creams. Over the years they have been donated mostly by her father's estranged sister who lives in the Catskills, apologetically, as though no amount of lip liner could compensate for her maternal lacuna. Viola has never used them. Tonight, though, seems like as good a time as any. She pulls out a plastic case with a sea of shimmering blues, a small foam-tipped applicator. Molly was saying something recently about how your make-up should be different depending on your face shape. *What's my face shape?* She wonders. *How do I do this?*

She traces a tentative pencil around the rim of her eye.

My God, she would love to be loved.

Sebastian steeps himself in spray from a can that reads DARK TEMP-TATION. He puts on a shirt.

"Lola, let's go!"

They descend. Together they look good, almost as if they do this often. She's dressed almost identically, in jeans and one of his flannels. Her natural stride hits a cadence just faster than his, trained, muscular legs gliding, gliding ahead, shimmying into the peeling passenger seat. She seems nervous but excited, looks at him, big-eyed and trusting.

"Let's go, Sugar Baby," she says. He grins, turns up the radio loud.

Aldwych goes blue, a lazuline deepening into the Atlantic horizon, where it is already night. Together now, they listen to Arcade Fire, windows down, screaming the words into the almost summer night, transcendent. At a stoplight he looks over at her.

"Glad you're coming," he says.

Would he could freeze her now, just here, in the momentum before their grand entrance, his alone.

The mansion is packed with Coors Light, certainly more than Viola expected, and even as the twins arrive, some kids are pulling more out of the back of Toby's Jeep. *Who bought all of this?* T-Pain blares through the home speaker system. There are no neighbors close enough to hear.

Inside, people weave around Viola like an impediment, all of them losing control, heaving with the possibility of sex, the knife's edge of a good time. Party paraphernalia enters her sphere of gravity and rockets away – plastic cups, the occasional shot glass. Around her, she can feel the questioning eyes, the Aldwych contingent surprised to see her at an event like this.

Sebastian is already smoking a joint; how easily he blends with the music and the lights and the colors on the walls. Everywhere are family photos of a flawless foursome, blonde and white-teethed in crisp linens and boat shoes. She never thought to ask about where the parents are. How could she frame the question? *Nothing cool about paranoia.* But then again: Lisa's party got busted last month and the kids that didn't get away were taken to the police station. She screens the room, cataloguing escape routes: sliding doors to the garden, low kitchen window. If the sirens came, would she take Sebastian? Her hand twitches toward her brother.

"Lola! Want a beer?"

Sebastian flinches at the sound of her pet name in Zach's voice. Even to Viola it sounds wrong, too intimate. *Smile*, she thinks, *act normal.* And yet her heart is pounding blood, her rib cage fluttering with the impulse to run. She is passed a cup of liquid that she does not want.

"I'm fine."

"Yeah you are."

Zach glances over at her with alarming shyness, and she understands with sudden terror that he is trying to create an intimacy between them, a connection that does not include her brother. She clutches at the beer, everything slipping dangerously away.

"Come on," he says. "One won't kill you."

The party plunges deep into the heart of the house. Dread freezes her: this is *LIFE AND TIMES!* Cellars are for kidnapping, dirty cloths shoved into mouths, subterranean abandonment, life worse than death, skeletons, rats, stale waters, your mother's nudes. This one is dimly lit, and waves of electronica reverberate from the deep.

"Go," her brother says at her side. His breath stinks. She descends into a vast, cold space.

This basement is an ode to competition. Wood-paneled walls and trophies and tables: billiards, foosball, air hockey, ping pong. The room is trying to prove something: superiority, or masculinity.

"Jesus," she says under her breath to Sebastian.

"I know, right? Filthy." Filthy. He meant it in the cool way. Already, he is exhibiting the blur of a lost boy.

Behind them, heavy, sneakered feet drum down the stairs, boys pushing past crash on couches, making a show of hugging the girls, of play-fighting. She notices now, in this condensed space, how few girls there are, how very many boys. The beer is sliding down her untethered. The music batters a repetitive monotone. Where to stand? What to do with her hands, her body? She lingers on the edge of a conversation that PJ McPherson is having with some of the prep school boys she doesn't know, talking about a TV series that she hasn't watched, about a group of people who are stranded on an island that is trying to kill them, and she smiles and laughs even as they make references that she doesn't understand, says small meaningless things like *I've heard about it*, just to remain on the lip of the group, to try to connect in the way her brother connects.

Behind her, a voice is singing. Zach Papadopoulos is swaying on his feet, swinging a bottle of tequila, a reckless smile on his face. He puts his arms around the twins' shoulders.

"So, your dad's getting laid, huh?" he says.

"Don't be gross."

Somewhere outside of reality, someone is explaining a game, *focus now* on the rules of engagement. *You have to sit every other. Or like, as close to that as possible.* A ripple of titters and strategic glances as people jostle to get close to the objects of their hidden agendas.

What am I doing here?

"Actually," Sebastian says, "he's probably not even our dad."

"What the fuck."

"It's all there in the scripts, Lola. You should see all these other names. Our real dad could be anyone."

111

Sebastian cannot possibly share any shred of her reality. He is resident in some fun-house world. Of course they belong to their father! Look at the shape of their teeth, the straightness of their shoulders. Look at their hand gestures, the bend of their wrists. Were it not for her hair (and her eyes, and yes, her nose) she might consider herself Athena, springing fully formed from her father's head. His dry humor, his academic mind. His tendency to suppress his feelings, his selflessness, his discipline. But more than every genetic marker, he raised them.

"You don't know what you're talking about." Her cheeks are filling with a heat that might turn to tears. He is trying to take away the only parent they have.

"You'll see, I'll find him. If you think about it, we're not even supposed to be here."

In another universe, a bottle is spinning. The future is unravelling: her father, her brother, everyone spinning out from themselves, a family without gravity. *Just friends?* No. She raises the plastic cup to her mouth, sour amber liquid moving through her, fuzzy and quick. Behind her, Sebastian is ejecting onto an alien trajectory, placing an arm around Lisa DePaulo, slanting and tactile. Viola watches as the two of them stumble back up the stairs, and she is alone.

A nose slows to face her.

"Seb's sister – it's you."

Lisa is holding his hand and leading him beyond the lights that slant through the sliding kitchen doors. A breeze wafts through the cool night, carrying weed and firepit ash. Muffled voices, the downbeat of a bass, these things pass through him. It is quieter here, stranger; the party exists on another plane.

"You're like a little kangaroo," Lisa is saying as she reaches into his pocket to pull out one of the beers he snagged on their way out.

"Exactly," he says. Tonight she is wearing make-up and Sebastian finds her attractive in the ways that she intends to be found attractive:

mascaraed lashes, streaks of bleach highlighting her hair, piercing blue eyes. "Though I guess I'm a mama kangaroo," he says.

"What?"

"Only the moms have pouches, right?"

She shoves him cutely. "You're dumb. Come on."

They light out into the dark. He places a hand on her back, steers her around the side of the house. She responds to him easily; it is like pushing at an open door.

In a dark fold next to a coiled hose pipe, he's placing his hand on the wall next to her and closing his eyes and kissing her up against the house with tongue. Out here he can hear nothing but the ocean smashing the rocks below. Lisa's skin is the cool aquamarine of the glorious backlight shifting off of the pool. *I am alive,* he thinks as her lips pillow against his, as he opens his eyes to her closed ones, her face merging with his own, her hands tucking themselves into the pouch of his sweatshirt. *I am alive!*

But as the kissing continues, his mind slips away – wandering backwards and forwards, backwards to Lola, forwards to his new life, his new fantastical father. Maybe it isn't real, but is it so wrong to wish it were?

Wait, he tells himself as he leans his hips into her hips, *stay here!*

"Let's go in the pool," he says.

"What?"

He heard a story once from Sadie about his mother jumping in the pool at a party his father brought her to, the first and only one to do so. It was startling how vividly he had imagined the scene, despite having no details beyond the headline; not where it was or what she was wearing or what Al had done in response. In his mind it was summer. She would have been wearing a sundress, holding a cocktail, bored out of her mind. Impossible to know where this convergence of images had come from. But now, as he is peeling off his shirt and jeans and holding Lisa's hand and saying Ready? and diving into the water, he feels this vivid past meshing with the moment (Now!) like two images superimposed on each other, moving in perfect choreography.

*

Inside the closet is a single, full-length ski suit and a stack of board games. *Clue. Risk. Sorry.* And a tower of other boy games involving large military conquests, capturing and dominating. The faint smell of golden retriever.

For a minute it seems no one will come. Maybe this is her humiliation; no one wants to go in with her at all. That wouldn't be so bad, would it? Outside, whispered jostling and giggles. *Why is it taking so long?* She has finished the beer, and clarity is slipping away from her. She wonders whether time will pass differently in here, whether seven minutes will feel like seven years.

Finally, the door opens. A body crawls up next to her.

"Hi," Zach says.

Oh no.

The hot heft of his skin, the cheap beer fuming through his pores. *This is not where I want to be,* she thinks. He kneels close and she is aware of the size of him, how alone they are.

"Don't."

"Why not."

Calmly, he places one hot hand on her shoulder, fingers brushing unpleasantly against the back of her neck. Softly, uncertainly, he mumbles:

"You know you're prettier than your mom?"

It's a sudden kiss, and hot in the sense of temperature. He runs his hand down her back, and up, under her flannel and then his animal weight is pulling toward her and she jerks away sharply, allergic to his meaty hands, his drunk breath. Her throat constricts, every muscle electric and vile, retching feeling, seizing her—

"Fuck you."

She is pushing out back into the light and people are gasping and laughing, and she is thudding up the stairs, crying or not crying, blasting through the stale archaeological site of the kitchen (fossilizing half-finished beer cans) and the music is getting further and further away, and no one is coming after her.

"Sebastian!"

And there he is, his bare, dripping back, his hands and face and some other girl, water falling against itself, creating an oblivion around them.

Don't abandon me, she had said. Was it so hard for him to put her first? Or is it nothing for him to exchange one woman for another, to flatten her desires and fears into some inconsequential noise. *Fuck you too*, she thinks.

When he submerges, Lisa shouts, echoing into the dark. And Viola runs.

Sopping, Sebastian scrambles out of the pool, in search of a toilet or a towel or Lola. Ideally all three. He drags his shoulder along the steady exterior wall. He needs his sister to drive him home.

He isn't sure where Lisa is. She had jumped in, having taken off her sweatshirt to reveal a bright red bra, and the two of them kissed fumblingly in the water until she said she was cold. He remained for a moment, and he could see bodies passing through the kitchen, new lights turned on inside the house. The movements had a strange undertone, which he realizes is the absence of music.

He grabs his clothes, pulls on his jeans. The door is ajar, and Toby's mother is standing hands on hips, monitoring as people call their parents.

Dark, slippery pine-needle paths, the wide shoulder, the light of her phone dancing ahead of her. Viola knows every road in this town. Her shape becomes nothing, a rhythm, the slap of shoes on pavement and the steady heave of breath. Only once, she falls, destabilized by the new swing of her brain, shaving the skin of her knee. Her mind militarizes, commanded to action by beer and betrayal.

How did they get here?

The box. The scripts. The names in the margins, his psychoactive imagination. Dumbass Pandora. The problem is their mother, making her brother think that women are all vacant bodies, purpose-built for whatever men want to do with them. Sure, why not put it all out there, Seb? Doesn't the world need more doubt and conspiracy and empty sex? If everyone saw your sister like that?

No, it has to be undone, and like always it is up to her. She must release him from his own twisted mythology.

After twenty minutes, the house emerges from the woodland. Tillie's car is still in the drive, Al's is still out.

Good, she thinks. Because the last thing her father needs is another reminder of how much love can hurt.

Adrenaline pumps her up the stairs. Sebastian's door is open, the locker-room smell of him wafting into her face. Stumble over his detritus, thrust up a window. What we need is clean. Sanity. There. A messy, pored-over stack on the desk. Her knee stings distantly. She carries her mother's scripts to the living room.

The matches are on the mantelpiece. Strike one. Strike two.

She does not read the names written in the margins, she does not need to read them. The important thing is that her father never will, that their ambiguity will not cast new confusion onto the marriage he is only now, a decade later, recovering from. And maybe with time her brother will forget what or who he was looking for in here, stop wondering whether there was anything to be found. The flames kiss the pages as she drops them onto the plinth of the fireplace.

This is an act of kindness.

"I gotta go," Sebastian says to no one. Lisa is somewhere else, maybe with some other guy. It's not important. He finds his way to the gate (the gate!) the slanty, sideways, upside-down gate, incidental bodies opening like a sea in front of him as he crashes out into the night.

The keys are in his pocket.

He is newly aware, sitting in the driver's seat, of how wet his jeans are, and somehow in all of this, he has lost his shirt. He does not care.

As he drives home, he considers what he will say to his father.

I think you were fucking afraid of her. Something like that. *Because unlike you, she really knew how to live. Unlike you, she was somebody.* He will show him all the names in her scripts. And even if it's all bullshit, his own hopes getting away from him, at least maybe Al will admit it. That there are better ways to live.

Her brother, reeking of poor behavior, finds her in her room, pretending to read. She registers the simmer of his anger. *He doesn't know what's good for him,* she thinks. Gently, she places the book aside.

"Where did you put them?"

"Where did I put what?"

"You know what."

She holds open her palms in front of her, as if to say: there is nothing more to be done.

"Seb, they're gone. It's for the best. You're not thinking straight. Those names, none of it meant anything." She looks at his righteous, unbending eyes, certain that she is the only one still fighting for this family.

He swings at her face without thinking, as though she were not a separate being, as though the slapped cheek, the hand grasping out for stability were his cheek, his hand; as though she never stopped being the same as him.

Viola regains her composition. She breathes in and out. Her nose is full of iron. An engine is starting and tires are blistering against the gravel and something inside her is broken.

Good riddance, she thinks.

In the driveway is that woman's Subaru, black and unsuspecting. Any damage is good damage. *Pedal to the floor.* Metal smashing, the impact, his body crashing into the wheel, hitting the horn, the twisted-up smell of burnt rubber, irreparable damage.

Reverse, reverse.

The road is black as he drives directionless, turning right then left, then right, not caring where he ends up. Sugar Baby sputters, the front bumper dragging on the road. It doesn't matter. As the house, the car, all of it disappears behind him, the adrenaline begins to shake out of his body. He throws it in neutral just for the hell of it and rolls down a hill towards Little Neck, where a scant strip of sand faces Plum Island. He drives right onto the beach, why not. Maybe he'll never be able to get back. He stops meters from the water's edge.

In his glove compartment hides a matchbox and a mangled pocket Bible he uses to roll. In the backseat is a baggy with a nugget from Toby. The front fender is smoking. It's cold outside, and he feels slightly feverish, but crawls up onto the roof of the car anyway, stepping heavily on the bent hood. He lights up and puffs out into the dark sea.

It's peaceful out here. He lets the loneliness transport him, the weed soften his rage. Above, the stars shine darkly, alive or dead or illusion. When the anger drains, he is unprepared for the overwhelming grief, which cannot form tears in his eyes, but hollows out the sockets of his shoulders, the tissue of his ribs, every atom of his being.

Sebastian transcends Plum Island Sound. He is on the jug-handle moon, in the milky star fluid wiped across the sky. He is so far away that when his father's car rolls in behind him, he doesn't hear its punch on the gravel. It is only when he feels the familiar rough hand on his shoulder that he remembers the horrible pain of the world going on and on and on.

1990

The pain in Susan's breast is becoming familiar, a throbbing like a tide, now swelling, now receding, demanding her notice. She arranges herself into the airport toilet, navigating the geometry of her suitcase.

For a moment, a profound clarity arrives. She feels this often now, when she is caught between two places. And in the clarity comes a thought:

Please not yet.

But now, as she frees a stream of urine onto the Colorstick, the fluorescent lights shine painful on all the plot holes in her life. The wanting and not wanting.

It brightens an unmistakable blue.

Outside the stall, the squeak and clack of women's shoes. She breathes hard and tries to steady herself, staring at the grout between the tiles.

The taxi heads north out of Boston to Aldwych, an address that still feels unfamiliar when she speaks it, a town where large houses tuck behind woodlands and wildlife reserves. Al spotted the For Sale sign on a visit to his own mother nearby. He had fallen in love with it, he said on the phone, fervent about the project, the benefits of real countryside. It all felt so abstract to Susan, like the desire of an older person. *But Al is older*, she reminds herself, *six years older*. His friends are already leaving the city. Maybe soon, she will want it too: big empty rooms and the distant roar of the sea. When she was small, her mother would buy her oversized coats to grow into, so they would last longer. Besides, she was in Boston so seldom these days. It seemed a little cost to make him happy.

But now it feels comical, her life so foreign. New England autumn dances brilliant onto green grass. In the front yard her husband is

119

raking. California seems impossible: so many dazed and reckless nights, so many choices masquerading as obvious answers, as impulses without alternative. All of it leading her to this moment, this happening, this thing in her. *And now what?*

Everyone's heard the story: a girl on a soap gets pregnant and they dump her like an old mattress. A replacement comes in to film the next week. You can sue, of course, but everyone knows the rules: the studio can come up with a thousand reasons to fall out of love with you. There's nothing you can do.

Idiot, Margie says, somewhere in the back of her mind. *You did this.*

The taxi pulls into the driveway and her husband is opening her door, his lips finding the soft skin of her temple. Now he is moving to the trunk, paying the driver, lifting her suitcase like it's nothing, saying:

"God, I missed you. I'm thinking takeaway, just easy—"

Fleetingly, she wonders what it would cost her to get rid of it. Would she fragment into a million pieces? Would God or the universe prevent her from ever having a child again?

"Look, I bought some candy for the trick-or-treaters. Are KitKats too plain? I thought you might be in danger of eating them all if I got Milky Ways—"

Oh no. She wants this. She wants the tiny shoes and tire swings; she wants little fingers in her hair and a little voice asking her questions and singing sweet songs. She wants to make this man a father, a man who believed in her before there was anything to believe in. She wants to hear him singing nursery rhymes and giving the world structure, only she wants it for some future Susan, some Susan who has figured that world out herself. *Why must it be now?*

She lingers behind as they enter their new-old house, already teeming with the props of Al-and-Susan, photographs and candlesticks and kitchen utensils. They have just repainted the shutters. They have just hung a flag from the gable over the doorway. In her hand she is clutching the Colorstick.

"Al."

The fear must be written on her face, flowing through her, because he looks at her as though she has something terrible to say to him. She opens her palm. He plucks the test from her, studies it. Her heart beats in every part of her body, her fingertips, her ears.

"You're not serious," he says. "You're not serious."

She nods. His knees give way to a squat, and his hands clutch at his awestruck face, and his eyes cannot move from her eyes.

"Holy hell."

He is up, his arms around her, the smell of his chest consuming her. The world recedes to a dim concern. They are conjurers. They are voyagers bound for the unknown. She looks in his eyes and sees his readiness, his unvarnished love of her, and says:

"Al, I'm scared."

"Why are you scared?"

"I'm going to lose my job."

"And I'm going to get tenure. It will be fine."

She pulls away. "That's not the point."

"No," he says. "I understand that."

"I just don't know who I'll be if I'm not . . ."

"You'll be you. You're always you, Susie Q."

His eyebrows furrow. *He is worried about picking up the pieces of me,* she thinks. *He is not worried about my life.*

"We'll figure it out, Susie. You might feel differently. After."

An abrupt estrangement falls between them. She cannot blame him for expecting her to change. She has always been open to change. A *say yes* kind of girl. But what if this is it? If there are no more characters, no more stories? No more transformation. No thousand lives lived in a thousand ways. Oh, some rebel part of her is screaming that she will never feel differently after. That she will never want to stop.

"I might" are the words she says.

When he says *I love you,* he is talking about something distant from her. A simplified image of herself she allowed him to paint. Because she has not said: *I might not.*

Placing her hand in his, Susan follows him into the house.

121

2008

Al remembers a boy of seven years old, standing on a beach, eyes drowning in his first encounter with death. He remembers a boy of twelve, bringing home a report card that read: "Shows some promise, but limits himself." He remembers a boy, minutes old, heart rate plummeting, emerging for air from a cavity in the center of his wife.

The clock in the kitchen is ticking into the shrouded morning. Viola, who he discovered last night nursing a bloody nose, has not emerged from her bedroom. His son, who he found fucked and remorseless at the end of the beach road, is sitting across from him, pushing soggy marshmallow cereal around a bowl of gray milk. In an act of profound generosity, Al had saved the conversation for a soberer morning.

"What are we going to do, Seb?" he asks.

They towed Tillie's car. Sebastian's was still on the beach, a junkyard job. Tillie had been remarkable, waving her hand breezily, saying: *We'll figure it out later.* She watched the car disappear with the acceptance of a woman for whom destruction has become commonplace; who understood boys and their lack of regard for the material. But the house has taken on the charge of a warzone.

"You could ground me."

"Do we think that's sufficient? You hit your sister."

The dishwasher begins to beep and old anger is rising in his chest, a sense of cosmic injustice. He cannot stop the crescendo of the words: "Violence is unacceptable under this roof."

"So kick me out."

Defiant, like Susie, to the point of dangerous. It's arrogance, actually, obliviousness to the lives and needs of other people.

"Really. Where would you go?"

"I don't know. The city?"

"Oh yeah? What about school?"

"I don't have to go to school. Legally."

The dishwasher is still beeping and Al clicks it with his hand. A jet of steam cones toward the ceiling, fogging the window and his glasses, and Sebastian slurps his cereal. How did he end up with this child, hellbent on eliciting his anger, on injuring the women he cares for—

"Sure, Sebastian. You seem like you've learned everything you could possibly need to know. Go on, see what the world makes of you! Because here's how I see it: I leave for one night, and your rap sheet reads 'drugs, physical assault, a hit and run' . . . Am I missing anything else? Now's a good time to say."

His voice reverberates. Sebastian is wide-eyed.

He's beyond help, Viola said last night. She was leaning her head backwards over the bed with a Kleenex jammed up it, staring at the ceiling, her voice detached.

"No," Sebastian says. "That's it."

"Pretty frigging intelligent. You're going to be a hell of a hit."

Al had been raised to believe success was a linear march and any deviation led to ruin. Susan grew up with no structure at all, pursuing her intuition through failure and degradation and jobs she didn't want. What would he have told her at seventeen? *Don't do it.* Don't become the person you want to be. Where would that have left them? As his words hang in the air, he knows this is not the way to deal with this, that his son cannot be blamed for the wilderness he finds himself in. But without Susie he has no viable alternative. Al wipes the fog from his glasses on his t-shirt.

"Who is going to pay for Tillie's car?"

"I'll pay for it."

"It's not going to be cheap."

"It's fine," Sebastian says, in a way that isn't. "But I want to move in with Sadie."

Outside the window, the clouds are beginning to shift. When he calls Tillie afterwards, she sighs and says, "Boys require room to grow."

But Al has never known how to let people go.

Viola wakes to the loud chuckling sound of a car coming up the driveway. Sugar Baby is a mess, coughing up smoke, front bumper aslant, scratched up with black paint. Sebastian steps out and catches her eye through the window. They hover for a minute, unsure whether there is language enough for this, whether language is the right tool.

The bruise is fading on the bridge of her certifiably non-broken nose, the dark mark under her eye is covered up.

In a moment that demands embrace, Viola finds nothing. She feels the edges of herself, the point at which she will give up trying to keep everyone happy. Gravity is pulling her brother toward someone who isn't there, who won't catch him. As she closes the door, she is surprised to find there is nothing inside of her that wants to forgive him.

Al watches limply as his sister-in-law gathers his son out of the car. "Hey slugger. Come on in."

"Thank you for doing this," he says.

Al can tell Sadie is doing everything in her power not to say it out loud, not to weaponize the name of his wife, who would never have slipped up like this. They cannot be in a room together without conjuring Susan. A pain burrows between them that refuses to mend.

"Well, I'm sure it's better than his ending up on the street." She bites her lip as though this were sharper than she intended, but the implication – his inability to parent Susan's child – is felt.

He watches his son – his lanky frame disappearing inside of Sadie's house, not turning around, not glorifying the moment with so much as a wave. Susie used to leave like that, walking straight through security, set upon her destination, not looking back to see whether he was still standing there hoping that she would run back. Is there something broken about him, some manner that drives people away? He has only ever wanted simple, happy things, for a family to find the same goodness in the world that he has found. Is that such a crime?

When the door closes, he is still sitting in the driver's seat. If his wife were here now, would she run out after him? Would she find a way to say: *I love you?*

"Come on, kiddo," Sadie says, and Sebastian remembers his mother used to call him kiddo. Is there an age, a line in the sand, where you become too old to be a kiddo? "Mi casa es su casa."

The afternoon is spent cutting, sorting, pasting. Sadie is starting an event planning company and determined that mood boards will set her apart. Large clippings of flowers, spiky pop guitars, table settings, lipstick. *Better Homes and Gardens, Cosmopolitan, Boston Magazine,* some more than six years old and yellowing. Sebastian finds the process almost meditative, sifting through the magazines and waiting for an image to vibrate. *An upturned hand, a palm tree.*

At night, he settles into the bedroom that used to be his mother's childhood room, and clicks his way to the forum.

NEW TOPIC: EPISODE 5950 (1996)

They killed Margie off, apparently, after his mom got the cancer diagnosis. A practice run at death. Car crash: clean, pedestrian. The kind of death that could happen to anyone.

If he can't watch it tonight, he never will.

Now! Here she is, at the click of a button, in the passenger seat of a car racing down the highway, made up and dressed to the nines.

MARGIE
Slow down!

How did she make her eyes so wild?

Sirens wail in the background as the driver swerves through traffic. His mother twists to get a look out of the rear view.

```
            MARGIE
        It's not worth it!
```

In slow motion, a man steps out in front of them. The windshield, split-scattering into one hundred thousand pieces, the sucker punch of the airbag, and the barrel roll of the car: one – two – three – four flips, each one punctuated by metal slamming pavement. The slow, bloody turn of the driver, another woman, devastated, wailing at the curled-up body of the pedestrian. Orson Grey, his mouth moving over rising strings. The cop cars pull to a stop, cut the sirens. And then unbearable silence. A slow pan over guardrails wrenched spinal out of the earth. Her body lifted on a stretcher, lifeless but hardly scathed. An elegant garnet trickle.

Sebastian replays the scene multiple times, biting his tongue to stiff himself, hunting for the moment of impact. Someone had to decide when exactly she died. Didn't they? He flips through the comments below the video.

burger_mama: our angel has gone 2 heaven

Did it help to go through the motions of death? Maybe. But there's a difference between practicing and letting go.

He picks up and puts down his phone, wondering whether he can text Lola with some pretense, to ask: "Are you okay?" But he doesn't.

Later, they will remember it differently, who was the one to leave.

1997

Sebastian helped decorate his mom's new room with crayon drawings of dragons and trucks, and just now he is finishing a drawing of a monkey. He takes the tape off one of the cards someone gave her, cursive handwriting that he can't read that probably says *Get Well Soon*, and sticks the monkey on the wall by her bed. No one will notice about the card. His mom doesn't let anyone in except Sadie and doctors who look at her papers and change out the bag of yellow liquid behind her bed. It looks like pee but his father told him it was juice.

His mother is sleeping. She sleeps most of the time now. He doesn't understand, if she's just sleeping, why she wouldn't want to sleep in her own bed. This one is thin and uncomfortable, but it doesn't stop him from climbing up and sitting next to her hip. She is wearing her headwrap with the gold chain pattern on it, which has slipped loose a little bit, and he can see her naked scalp underneath. She let him touch it a few days ago, and it was clammy and soft. Lola hadn't liked it, had looked at their mother like she didn't know her, but Sebastian rubbed it like a crystal ball and it made his mother laugh.

He resists the urge to touch it now, but nestles himself against her. Her breath is wind blowing across a marsh. Even though she's sleeping, he can feel how desperately she wants to be with him. It's the reason he doesn't want to leave, even though today is Zach Papadopolous's birthday party at the roller rink, and he loves the roller rink. He hardly thinks about it now. It is very important to keep making crayon drawings for the wall. He is trying to use every color in his box of sixty-four, even though some of them are gross, and still has a few of them in his hand that he hasn't yet used. As he is sounding out a shade of green under his breath (ass-pair-uhh . . .) his mother's eyes drift open and she looks at him strangely, differently. As though she is also a child and lost.

"Did you see the monkey I made?"

"Where are they?" she asks.

"They're, um. I think they're coming," he says.

The words feel right, but the truth is, he doesn't know where they are. Lola keeps making excuses for why she doesn't want to be in here, and about five minutes or a million years ago, asked if she could get some chocolate milk. So she left with their father. Sebastian wanted to stay. He is afraid of what might happen if he leaves.

"Sebi," she says, "I'm going to sleep now. And I think you should go."

Shouldn't someone be here? He looks at the door. No one comes in. Not his father or Lola or Sadie or one of her friends or anyone else, not even a nurse, and he realizes that his mother is squeezing his hand because she is afraid.

None of this makes any sense. He always thought that dying would mean a great intensity, a scrabbling and then a moment where everything slows and dims, like Mufasa falling off the cliff and the world zooming backwards into a dust storm and everything terrible happening very far away.

"Do you want me to tell you a story?" he asks. Her hand is bent back, unnatural.

"Tell me about what you're going to do tomorrow."

"Well, there's school," he says, "and then after, if it's sunny, maybe Lola and I can go sledding. And then we are gonna have dinner and come back to see you."

"You'll be good to Lola, won't you? You'll help her?"

"I guess so. She's so annoying."

"She loves you. I love you too."

She squeezes him into her and breathes again in that raspy way and it really seems like it is taking a lot of work for her just to breathe, and also like someone else should be coming in any minute now, and she asks him, "What about the day after tomorrow?"

"Well, I guess it's school again and, um. It's a Tuesday so we have art class. And gym. Do you think Sadie will come over to babysit?

His mother does not respond. Her breath is farther and farther apart, and her chest has just about stopped going up and down, and maybe she is sleeping, and he puts his head in the soft spot under her armpit and he keeps talking: "And the day after that, I don't know, maybe it will be a snow day, and we won't have to go to school. If you put a spoon under your pillow, it will happen, if everyone does it. I'll bring one for you so you can do it too. And then we can come and hang out with you all day."

Afterwards, for weeks on end, he will not sleep an unbroken hour, in case he forgets to wake up.

When the doctor calls to Al, it is with more gravity than urgency. His name is the end of a sentence. Inside Susan's room, his son is nestled in the space between her breast and her armpit, talking to himself. At one point, it is possible that he was talking to her but now she is very obviously dead.

"Sebastian."

He didn't plan it this way. He hadn't planned for it to happen like this. He just left the room. He had only stepped out for a moment.

You don't seem like the type of person who would want to leave in the wrong way.

He looks at her body. He always thought there would be a last conversation. That it wouldn't be about walking with her to the bathroom. Or the choreography of their children, or the next round of scans or chemo. He had grown so used to it, the illness. *I know what to do,* he would think when she would start vomiting, and get the bag with her change of clothes and drive her to the care center, drink shitty coffee from the café, talk to her, wait, talk to the doctors, do what they said, know that she would feel worse and then better, administer increasingly powerful painkillers. And there was a kind of perverse happiness in this, in helping her, like they were sharing the project of their lives, united under the goal of saving her. He felt, for the first time since they had been married, like a team. Like he imagined a husband was supposed to feel.

She looks so small.

When they try to pull Sebastian off of her, his son starts screaming, asking where they are taking her, agitated that no one seems able to describe where she is going, and Al is holding him and he is kicking and it isn't fair.

"We weren't done talking," Sebastian says.

Until this moment (still looking at her body, assigning it a new word: corpse) he hadn't let go of the ending he imagined for them. Walks on the seaside, wrinkled hand holding wrinkled hand, a dog. A shared sense of the world. All the happy continuum of life. *When you get better*, he got used to saying, because it felt important for everyone, the project of hope, the fantasy of the future. It only occurs to him now how many conversations they never had. Like, how she should be buried. What she should wear. Who should be told.

He could collapse. But here they are, his wide-eyed children and he is the only thing standing between them and the end of the world.

2010

Viola walks down to the river, a cut-out shadow angling against stone. Even after a year, the limestone beauty of Cambridge has not ceased to affect her. She still wonders at the fact that she is here.

She knew it would be difficult for her father, her going. *Be careful,* he'd said. *Lots of murders over there, I hear.* Taxis hummed behind him, and she could see in the way he was leaning one hand on the car for support how her departure would shatter him. But looking around herself now, the choice feels inevitable. How could she not have been charmed by the Waugh and Forster of it, the stained-glass library light, the tall, wild stalks flourishing in hidden quads, the young ambitious bodies thirsting for knowledge and its distractions. At times she feels like she could stay here forever, wandering through a world of beautiful hypotheticals, growing closer to perfection, academia's controlled infinity.

"Oy oy."

Clapping her shoulder is her best friend Niamh in high-waisted jeans and septum piercing, her energy glowing like an LED light. They became friends out of the circumstance of adjacent rooms and inseparable out of a shared love of philosophy. At times, Viola feels she is taking an additional course in Niamh, learning how to write an essay on caffeine fumes and the remembered fragments of drunk conversation, how to conjure up the subtleties of intersectional feminism with an expertly raised eyebrow, how to correctly use the word *craic*.

"All right, stranger?" Viola ties her hair, long again and irrepressible, off of her neck and into a low ponytail, a piece falling to frame her mother's delicate nose, her thick-lashed eyes.

"Yeaaaaah," Niamh exhales. She pulls a pair of oversized sunglasses off her buzzed head and onto her nose, and they take off alongside the river. Niamh came back last night in a state, arguing with her latest boyfriend on the phone. She always returns from weekends in London with a new fling. Her lovers have been, in turn, French, Portuguese, Ghanaian, Belgian-Somali, and Glaswegian. *Cheapest way to take a world tour,* she says. Men or women, she doesn't exclude. She drops them as soon as they try to make her become anything she doesn't want to be.

Niamh loops her arm through Viola's and sighs. "Why can't people understand: debt is a battering ram. It's the principle of it. I just feel like relationships should be active. You shouldn't have to force anyone into being with you today based on how they were with you yesterday."

"I get that," she says. "But I think commitment is romantic. Is that lame?"

"I don't think there's anything unromantic about prioritizing your own interests – particularly if that interest is pleasure," Niamh says. "It's trying to control other people that kills the mood."

Viola thinks about this. "But I think promises have value. Otherwise, how else do you trust anybody? Or hold anybody accountable?"

Niamh laughs. "Anyone ever tell you you'd make a good lawyer?"

"Not in a while."

"You'd make a killing in contracts," she laughs.

Niamh, whose papers read with a casual brilliance, has no interest in besting her, or trying to show up her deficiencies, or even trying to change her mind – her manner is entirely sincere. She only insists on drawing Viola's attention to complexities she avoids looking at.

The river courses darkly, a cold continuum traversing out to the North Sea. They turn away, and the damp autumnal streets of Cambridge gather around them, cobbles and ancient walls.

"God I need to piss," Niamh says.

Viola lingers outside of an old Gothic church while Niamh runs in to use the toilet, thumbing through cheap cardstock prints of famous paintings.

"Anything good?" Niamh asks when she comes out.

Viola plucks out a grotesque, prancing Botero, its clownish fat rippling along behind it.

"Sexy."

"Get it, I dare you."

"Come on."

"I'll buy it for you. But you have to promise you'll hang it over your bed."

"Okay, fine." Viola feels impish, watching Niamh pay for the print in coins that still feel comically large in her hands.

"You have to tell all your lovers it's serious."

"Ha ha." They both know she doesn't have any of those. Niamh has a habit of poking around Viola's horrible virginity, a function of her pickiness, her quest for the ideal in all things.

Niamh pauses at a cork board and removes from her bag a stack of freshly printed pages advertising an experimental production of *The Bacchae* set in a techno rave.

"Rowan said if I put these up I could have free wine."

"Who's Rowan?"

"You know Rowan."

"Oh. That Rowan."

Rowan once walked in on Viola coming out of the shower on staircase seven, sopping and naked, and she had screamed (truly screamed), and his evening on mushrooms had taken a turn for the worse. Men were a rare sight at Sylvia's, their all-female college, let alone six-foot-tall men in fur coats. She found it difficult to forgive him.

"Oh, look, it's that guy," Niamh says, pointing at another flyer. "From that film."

"Who? Oh."

Of course, it's Orson Grey. She still watches all of his films, including the risqué psychodrama where he walked stark naked through a car wash in the dead of night. Hollywood seems unsure what to do with him these days, his heartthrob status passing with his youth. She's followed the turbulent relationship with the Armenian supermodel (off-again). Of course he still features in her imaginative landscape. Of course her breath catches in her throat when the camera zooms and the light hits his lip just so. Is it funny yet, the heft of her crush? Is she ready to surrender his memory to hopeless humor? No.

"I can't believe they keep asking these celebs to the Union," Niamh is complaining. "Absolute star-fuckers if you ask me. Have some genuine political discourse for Christ's sake."

A key turns inside of her, an engine igniting. *It's happening.* The cosmic approach she spent years imagining, as inevitable as it has always felt. The only obstacle is The Union: the beating political heart of the university, full of future cabinet ministers and technocrats, a place where loud voices carry and men (still, largely men) grow exercised about freedom of speech and rituals of debate. Generally, she avoids it. Its denizens are experiencing their time at university in an entirely different way; as though it were already behind them. As though they are simply steering their past selves from their lives beyond this city, using them as conduits for weightier mid-life aims. Does it make her equally guilty, the sensation she is having now, that everything she has done to get here has only been a prelude to this encounter?

After Niamh has finished stealing a pin from (and balling up) an advertisement for the Conservatives Association, they cruise toward their feminine enclave. Across the ancient green, buses are collecting frazzled tour groups. Darkness descends so early here, and if you don't look carefully, you might collide with a cyclist bearing some improbable object – a double bass, a Christmas tree.

"Pub?" Niamh asks. It's a sensible suggestion, under the dimming sky. But no. She needs to run, to think.

"I'll catch you later," Viola says. Legs activating already, carrying her through the porter's lodge, past the mail room slotted with personal pigeonholes, circling the manicured quad, skipping up staircase seven and into her room (reassuring thunk of the door), jeans, shirt stripped to the floor, her articulated ribs, her unprovocative breasts. And then it

134

begins: the binding of her chest, the fluorescent green shorts and top, hair pulled back tight now, curls coerced onto her scalp.

Quickly, into the park, past the tennis courts, over the familiar bridge, the rhythm of her own breath carrying her. The Cam, the distant turrets. The rushes bowing over to kiss the water, the familiar unfamiliar faces bleeding into each other, into the peripheral park, the falling darkness, families clearing out, pulling away. Consider, again, the value of a promise: an obligation created by an act of will, a sacrifice of freedom. The foundation of monogamy, trust, accountability. *That's romance, right?* Don't say it if you can't keep it – faithfulness is the bottom line. And don't stop moving when you get to the road in front of The Granta pub, not even if you see anyone you know, not even if the person you see is Orson Grey.

Orson Grey.

Standing outside chatting to a group of girls in the smoking area.

No, this is certainly not how you are meant to encounter him, sweating and unbodying, thinking in philosophical terms about the failings of your mother. It isn't your fault if you make eye contact, if you hold it for a moment too long, waiting ostensibly for the street in front of you to clear (it is already clear). Keep moving, don't look back, don't shatter the future just yet.

Six hours later she finds herself predictably with Niamh, at the afterparty for *The Bacchae*, exchanging gushy comments about the quality of everyone's performance for tiny – but crucially, free – plastic cups of wine.

"The whole cast was fit," Niamh marvels, "but maybe we'd all be more attractive if we just played characters written for us by someone extremely witty."

Orson. She had seen him in the flesh, a real man, distinct from the blur of characters he has played over the years.

"Cig?" Niamh is gesturing outside, where Rowan is smoking in his fur coat, still in full make-up.

"I'm good," she says, as though her smoking is a genuine possibility, as though today might be the day. Sweet that Niamh continues to ask. *Relationships should be active.* Nevertheless, she follows her out into the alley glowing purple and blue under paper lanterns and cheap strip lighting.

She is beautiful, Niamh, her downy head tucked under a bright red beanie, lips painted the deep purple of the night. On her arm a pale green bruise is blooming from a protest she went to last weekend over the Queen's Jubilee. Viola had seen the photos online of Niamh, open-mouthed and gleeful, carrying a sign that read in bold fuchsia, I AM NO ONE'S SUBJECT, even though (strictly speaking) Ireland made that point some time ago. Across the Atlantic, a wave of unrest and dissatisfaction is mounting. Online she sees Zach Papadopoulos, scruffy and jubilant in a tent on Wall Street, a Facebook post written by Molly McInerny on the ninety-nine per cent. All of it fills her with uncertainty, a sense of the world on a precipice.

As Niamh sticks a lumpy roll-up in her mouth, Viola thinks of the mangled pocket Bible Sebastian shreds for rolling paper. When did Orson start smoking again? Foul concoction, logically she knows it will kill her (remember: tar, arsenic, formaldehyde), but she is beginning to understand – the ugly smell, the ambient street lights in the narrow passage, Niamh's smile and the musicality of Rowan's voice make her feel as though she's living artfully, as though she's doing it right.

"No, I know him." Rowan is laughing about some campus legend, flicking a plastic lighter in front of Niamh's face. "He did legitimately try to steal, like, twenty candles from Corpus, for like, a séance. He's convinced his room is haunted by a dead ex-student."

"What a legend," Niamh says. "I mean, property is a construct."

"I love you," Rowan says. "They fined him two hundred pounds."

A light rain starts to fall, and the smokers huddle against the lip of the building. A snatch of music emerges from the open door, followed by a red-headed chorus girl, still wearing her costume headdress of goat horns and flowers.

"You all right?" the girl asks. People here are always asking that, though they never expect an answer other than *Yeah*, or the question repeated. It's the one thing that rankles here, the disingenuousness of it. *Why ask?*

"Can I bum one?" the red-headed girl begs Rowan, "I'll trade you for one of these prop ones." She holds up a packet of fakes they used on set. "I think they're full of rose petals."

"No, thanks. I'll stick with my death stick."

"Is that what you're calling it these days?" Niamh asks, cheekily inspecting the packet of fakes. Sugar Lilies, they are called, like they're going to dissolve in your mouth. Like they are not going to kill you.

"So, are you going then?" the red-head asks.

"Going where?" Niamh asks. "If you leave, they better not cut off my free wine."

Rowan waves a dismissive hand. "I'm not that desperate."

"Going where?" Viola asks.

"The Clayton. Orson Grey is staying there," the red-head announces.

"That's the goss," says Rowan.

Carefully, Viola had lined her eyes and brushed her lashes, bronzed and blended her cheeks. She is underdressed in the way an accidental ingenue would be underdressed, wearing her black college sweatshirt with St Sylvia's emblazoned over the breast, the small crest featuring an open book. Her tightest blackest jeans. The worst thing would be to look as though she was trying, as if she was after anything. It needs to feel organic, destiny.

"I don't find him attractive," Niamh says, exhaling. "Maybe it's his jaw, I don't know."

"His jaw!" Viola says in mock outrage.

"Or his chin or something. I don't know, something about it. His face." You can say that sort of thing about celebrities. Her dismissal is a shame and a relief.

"I heard he's a shagger," says Rowan.

"Really, Rowan, you can shame people for their weird chins, but not for sex," Niamh says.

"I always thought he had a nice face," Viola says.

"Oh my God, you want to lick his weird chin." Niamh places her non-smoking hand in Viola's pocket, and interlaces her fingers. "Fingers are freezing," she says.

"It's not that cold," Viola says.

"Well you're warm-blooded. You snow people. Or is it cold-blooded?" A pulse. A linger. Her phone is vibrating in the other pocket.

Sebastian
At Dad's. Where do we keep the flashlights?

"Is that your boyfriend?" Rowan asks. "Is it Orson Grey?"

"I thought you were my boyfriend, Rowan," Viola says, the wine hitting reckless. "You've seen me naked and everything."

"And wasn't it glorious."

Maybe she could get to like Rowan after all. Niamh holds out her cigarette and she realizes she has been staring at it unconsciously. Niamh wouldn't make a feature of it, that smoking isn't something Viola does all the time. Softly, gradually, that's her way. Like wading into a pool of water. It's tempting. But it's a distraction. *Stick to the plan*, rings a clear voice through the muddle of wine.

"I should go," Viola says.

"Home? Already?"

"No. Going to try to meet someone."

Niamh looks wounded. "But the wine."

"Go on, darling," Rowan advises. "Don't let Niamh bully you. She's probably jealous."

The moment yawns between them, the possibility of Niamh's attraction, the threat of a lust that could topple a friendship. Then it

138

dissipates with a cheeky wink, a kiss on the cheek, and Viola off into the dark.

She heads toward the Union Bar, the night slipping off her back. The evening is unusually warm for October, and students and townies are mingling more than usual, pubs spilling out into the street. Somewhere, distantly, someone is setting off fireworks. Outside, she wonders loosely whether she has watched too many films, devoured so many happy endings that she can no longer see them for what they are. She crosses the street and pushes open the heavy oak door into the glow of the bar.

The room is teeming with a different mix than she might have expected, fewer jackets, more skirts. Music playing and wine flowing and Orson Grey nowhere to be seen. Is there relief in this? Maybe it was foolish after all. What would she have said? *Hello, we met once when I was a child. Don't you recognize me?* Stupid, really.

Sebastian
power is out help

Viola
flashlights
where the phone basket used to be

He'll get it. Incredible that he manages to maintain the ignorance of a stranger in that house. Since the night he hit her, they speak only in short, functional bursts. She wonders how often he is going there, whether he is trying to tell her something else with the text. Whether he has found anything else.

"Viola!"

At the bar, her tutor, Doctor Maitland, is merrily sipping a bright pink cocktail. Viola sidles up as he gestures to the bartender.

"What can I get you?"

"Oh, really, I was just—"

"Nonsense. This one is called an 'Old Cigar Shop', beet and cinnamon vodka, really very unusual."

"Anything but that."

Maitland is a creature of his institution, with small, gopher-like features and a wardrobe that consists of a single tweed jacket and innumerable white-collared shirts.

He orders her a gin. "Where's your other half?"

Sebastian? "Niamh?"

"Who else?"

"I see. If Viola, Then Niamh."

"Apparently not."

"She's in – working on her extended essay titles."

"Well! Good for her. I had her pegged as a last-minute sort of girl." *You had that right.* "I assume yours are ready to go."

"Nearly," she says. She can do this now, she can focus. Shut out the bustle, think, again, about moral reasoning. *Impress him!* But she can't stop herself from asking: "Did you go to the Orson Grey talk just now?"

"Yes, lovely man, really. Off being swamped by adoring fans, I presume. Had a funny story about penguins."

"Really?"

"Yes, some trip to Antarctica. I've never seen any of his films, but now I think I just might."

Snowdrop. She's watched it three times, of course. Stark panoramas, tense, abrupt dialogue. He had been better outfitted for the cold than when they met. She glitters with second-hand stardust.

"Don't tell him, though," Maitland says. "I wouldn't want to embarrass him."

Viola laughs. "I'm sure he could handle it."

Sebastian
Thx. Dad getting desperate.
Farewell sweet world.

"You changed."

Orson Grey is sidling into the seat next to her, his face pink and half-lit by the wall sconces, angular cheek bones, full head of chestnut hair, green velvet jacket, hardly wearing the last fifteen years.

"Sorry?"

Surreal shift of the floor and ceiling. The bar has become a holo-gram of a bar, Orson Grey, his body in the seat next to her, his voice speaking only for her to hear. It's his smell she wasn't expecting to remember so viscerally, bitter and leafy like a tea.

"You were the runner earlier, weren't you? Kind of stared for a minute?"

"No. I mean, yes."

"Sorry, am I interrupting the two of you?" Orson gestures at Mait-land. Is it possible for a celebrity to interrupt? To be unwanted?

"No, no," Maitland says, chuckling at the insinuation. *Dear God.*

"I try not to presume," says Orson. "Particularly with all these geniuses running around. Who knows what you get up to?"

The collective stare of a group of girls in black tights bores into the back of Viola's head, and she is struck by the reality that this conversa-tion is happening, that he has approached her of all the women in the bar. A sword hangs over her head. "Do you want a drink?" she asks.

"Wouldn't say no."

Double malt, she guesses, slowly absorbing the reality of him, his forgotten third dimension. His accent – his real accent – still Scottish after years of shape-shifting.

"It was the neon," he says. "I thought you were going to a rave."

"Just helping small children cross the street."

"Ah," he says, smiling. *Funny, she's funny!* "A Samaritan."

"The Samaritan," Maitland says, leaning over the bar, nearly knock-ing Viola's drink, "is all about ethics versus morals. Having a good character rather than following rules."

"Is he your priest?" Orson asks.

"No, he's my . . ." she needs to get rid of Maitland, fast. "Professor, sorry to ask, but you don't happen to have a light?"

She turns back to Orson. "Smoke?"

Through the crowd again, drinks paid, aware that everyone is watching her, hating her, and she herself can hardly believe that she has bought his attention, that he is trailing her even now, whiskey in hand. That he is stepping out into the almost drizzle and closing the door. That somehow the two of them together is warding off the other students aching for his attention.

She hadn't intended to steal the prop cigarettes, but somehow they had entered her pocket. She offers him one and he laughs, recognizing them instantly.

"You're kidding."

"They aren't even mine," she says, blushing, seven again and ludicrous.

"Dear God. Put those away." He removes his own pack from a pocket, along with a silver-plated lighter. He offers her one. She accepts, as though she has done this a thousand times, her reserve liberated by the immortality of the moment, by his death-defying smile. The wind spins up the street and both of them turn to the wall, an instinctive, secretive arrangement. He lights up (hand brushing her hand) and she inhales her brother, her aunt Sadie, Niamh, poison, radicalism, Orson, all of it.

"So what's your name then, good Samaritan."

"Viola."

"Viola. Not too many Violas running about these days. Fan of Shakespeare?"

"I guess so." By most other measures, Shakespeare should appeal to her; the perfect plots and profundity, the sense of the universe and all humanity. The romance. But she cannot help carrying a grudge against him, as though he and her mother conspired in the choice of her name – too grandiose, too on the nose, burdened with unnecessary associations, with flagrant thespian pretention. The awful Viola-and-Sebastian of it all. She's never seen *Twelfth Night*.

He laughs. "That's lukewarm."

"I guess I just haven't seen very much."

"I'm impressed you've managed to avoid it." Oddly familiar and fluid, their conversation, oddly easy to approach him with the innocence of a seven-year-old. "I thought you might be American. I don't know any English person who would dare to be quite so fluorescent."

Sebastian
Burning your books for warmth sorry

Sebastian. Even five minutes ago, she could have texted him about it. Wouldn't have, but could have. He would never have believed her, they might have laughed. But now it wouldn't feel right. Any past understanding of Orson has given way to a living, breathing person.

"That your boyfriend?" he asks.

"No," she says, pocketing the glowing phone. *Where is this going?* "I have to admit something."

"Go on, then."

Here's the moment, now, declaring itself: *Disclose!* She always thought she would need to mention her mother, that this would be the key to his attention. But he's looking at her like a fully formed thing, a woman whose origin is irrelevant. Perhaps it is irrelevant! How far she's come from the country of her mother.

"I didn't come to your talk."

"Well, I appreciate your honesty. It was considerate of you to stay away, to be honest. The neon would have been very distracting."

"Well, in that case, you're welcome."

"You didn't miss much anyways," he says. "It was very dull."

"I'm sure it wasn't."

"That's kind," he says. "But I assure you, talking about yourself is exceedingly dull."

The door swings open and a group of students she recognizes as Union people pass by them. "You all right, Orson?" one of them asks, clapping him boldly on the shoulder as they pass by.

"Stupid question," he mutters. "So repressed. Never ask a question you don't want the answer to."

Exactly! Standing in his glow induces a pleasant melting sensation, an awakening to a new kind of tenderness. A new quality of being alive.

"Well," Viola asks. "Are you all right?"

"Right now?" He smiles, playing at really considering the question, at taking stock. "Yeah, I'm just fine, thanks."

"When did you start smoking again?" The question slips out softly, an admission of a one-sided intimacy.

"I never stopped smoking," he says, furrowing. "You, on the other hand, have never smoked a cigarette in your life."

She reddens. Is she so transparent? Was it the Sugar Lilies? Or something about how she's doing it, clutching the cigarette between her second and third finger, like she's seen in the movies? He is looking directly at her for the first time since they began talking, a look that threatens to become more than a look.

"I'm worried I'm going to say something rude, now," he says. "They've been plying me with drinks."

"It's our highest value currency, students," she says. "You should be honored."

"I'm honored, yes," he murmurs, his eyes swimming. "No, I was going to comment on your hair. You were hiding it, before, you had it all up. I haven't seen that much hair in a decade at least."

Her mother's hair. Unruly, impossible to coerce, but lustrous, rippling around her face, cascading down her back. She realizes, looking at his face, all question marks, that through some combination of humor and beauty, knowing and not knowing, she has enchanted him. That the night is hers.

"Sorry," she says. "I didn't realize I needed to disclose, about my hair."

"I can understand it would be impractical. You know, running with all of that."

"Certainly."

The problem with Orson is that she has grown familiar with the scripted version of him, the one-woman man, pining after and occasionally dying for the singular object of his affections. Has she been naive to dream of romance with someone who has been described as a 'notorious bon vivant' in *Vanity Fair*? Even now, as he is extending his fingers into her hair with the expertise of someone who has encountered curls before, who knows not to manhandle them or pat them inanely, but to entwine his fingers inside and clutch, she wonders whether she should disclose to him that no one has ever touched her hair like this before. Whether it would make a difference. Whether it would guarantee her any greater chance of forever, or at least not just a single night.

"Sorry," he says. "Don't let me get carried away. There are spies everywhere." He isn't wrong. Only a couple of tables away the editor of *The Tab* is watching them ravenously, waiting for a story to unfold. "I do feel out of sorts in this town. Like everyone's brains are whirring twenty times faster than mine. Though maybe that's the scotch."

"I'm sure it's the scotch," she says, and it's clear this particular arrow of kindness strikes his heart.

"I should probably get out of here. You students all get a bit funny after midnight. But I owe you a drink," he says. "You're welcome to come for a nightcap if you like. The hotel bar has these great nuts. Spicy. More-ish."

She understands the offer. She has read the script. In ordinary circumstances, she has heard, the game is to be withholding, to make yourself desirable through unavailability. But these are not ordinary circumstances.

Sebastian
Resorting to cannibalism

Orson catches the name that flashes up on her phone, and something

145

sparks in him, some glimmer of recognition. Viola. Sebastian. *Does he remember?* Is she going to be forced into it here, disclosing the fact of herself? *Fuck.* No time to find out. Behind her the door is swinging open and Maitland is stumbling out into the street.

"I should probably make sure he gets home," she says, fearing the rapid shift of parameters, not wanting to know where she stands. "But it has really been nice to meet you."

Before he can reply, she is turning and greeting again her professor, guiding him away toward the dim lights of the taxi rank. Whether Orson waits and watches her or pinballs off into the hungry harem, she will never know. It doesn't matter. There is nothing more precious than the fact that it might have happened, nothing more important than leaving while the moment is still perfect.

1989

One thirty in the afternoon, get it on – quickly! Before the school bus comes back and the streets are full again with the ricochet of children, before your boss opens the door to the break room and says, *bit late for lunch*. Try not to fumble with the remote (whichever one is it these days), or get caught by the dark reflection of yourself in the dead screen. Hurry, the world is springing to life, the familiar synthesizer: This is *Life and Times!* Dissolve; feel your own problems grow trivial against the melodrama, against the height of what a human can feel.

Here they come, just as you knew they would, those known and beautiful faces of Cedardale. That bartender, in particular, has really become one to watch, ever since the love triangle and now his strange moody drives out of town that he claims not to remember. He's filled out, too, turned into quite the dish. Even now as he is pouring a drink for Margie Ludlow, there is a new potential about him, as though he might hit someone. You wonder whether something might happen between the two of them, and didn't you read about it last week in *Soap Opera Digest*? Yes, make no mistake, something is going on.

```
                    MARGIE
     You really haven't been yourself lately, Joe.


                     JOE
                How do you mean?
```

```
                      MARGIE
I don't know. You seem like something's on your mind.


                       JOE
   Nothing's on my mind, all right? Stop fishing.
     Nothing's going to come of it, Margie.
```

"Cut!"

"Tell them I dropped an earring," Susie whispers, and ducks behind the bar to vomit into a small trash can.

"Can you see it?" Orson says, for anyone who might be listening. "Did it maybe go under?"

Most people are disappearing into the labyrinth of sets, setting up for the next tape, but Marion from make-up is watching, pursing her lips. Below him, Susie is wiping her mouth with a roll of paper towel, clearing her throat and saying "Got it!" Marion hums and waves slightly to Orson before floating off as well.

Susan groans, pulls herself up on the counter, Orson passes her a bottle of water.

"It's worse in the afternoons," she says.

"At least you're done for today."

"I might have to do that pick-up."

"They won't get to it."

"They might."

He takes in her pale face, the sour smell on her breath. "I'll get rid of that," he says, pointing to the bag full of sick.

"No, I can. My mess."

"My bar," he says, looking around the set that has hardly changed since he started filming almost three years ago. And hasn't he made it his own? Outside the thick stained-glass door, a neon sign reading Joe's. Inside, the chairs stacked up on the tables where he left them at the end of the scene. How many times has he stacked those chairs, has he swept these floors? In this corner he broke up a fight, in that one,

148

consoled the matriarch after her third divorce. *The wisdom of youth*, Rip used to say, winking at him, but Orson is hardly so young as he was then.

He takes the bin out of Susie's hand, ties up the bag and strides through the tangle of equipment rolling to its next destination and people calling for a bit of tape or powder, pushes out through the exit, and chucks it into one of the industrial waste bins in the back lot. He has time for a quick smoke before his next take and thinks, as he often does, how like life this all is, how you only get one shot at things.

All the work he's done behind the scenes is starting to pay off. Just think: three years of putting it in with Flowers, of listening to him talk about his ex-girlfriend and the guy who backed into his car and looking with him through the headshots of blonde, barely-of-age extras. Even for all that, the idea for the secret admirer was all Susie, who sweet-talked Rip into trying it out. *Fans want to see more of him*, she said, and it turns out she was right. Finally, Orson has his own storyline. Finally, he's been offered an actual contract, promoted from a recurring day player. He's been told more than once he's part of the family, which makes him feel grateful as well as neglectful, because isn't he missing his niece and nephew growing up, and the cold highland winters?

When he comes back in, he catches Susie on the way back to her dressing room, looking like she is going to collapse. "Suze," he whispers. "Sooner or later."

Susie looks at him with her eyes full of something he has never felt, something he has hardly had to perform and isn't sure he could. "They'll fire me."

"They won't."

"Mark will fire me out of spite."

A new assistant director hurries by with a clipboard, asks them where to find one of the sets. "By the train station," they answer in unison. Everyone knows how to find the train station.

It had shocked him when Susie told him last week, her eyes shining.

She was making him dinner, their Thursday ritual. *I have to tell you something,* she said, and he felt the bottom drop out of the universe. Not that he had thought it impossible. He knew about pregnant women, twice watched his sister transform into a supernatural creature and back into a mortal. But this is different. Susie is a friend – perhaps his best friend. He relies on her. He'd felt almost betrayed, as though she'd begun a journey she could not take him on, and embarrassed. He should be happy for her.

"What do you think is going to happen if you wait?" he says.

"I don't know. Maybe they won't notice?" she pauses, expecting him to laugh. He doesn't. "I just need time to think."

"Well, time isn't on your side."

"I can't lose this," she says, and he's not sure whether she's referring to the job or the thing inside her. She is looking at him, pleading and he knows this much; she hates having to ask for help.

"OK," he says, a plan coming together in his mind. "Let's see what we can do."

Marion is the first person he tells. The first thing he learned on set is you should never underestimate Make-up and Costumes. If you want to be liked, let them have their way with you; they know how to whisper a quiet word where it counts. It's obvious Marion knows something is up. She's been both lingering and avoiding him, insisting on small unnecessary touch-ups between takes but not saying much. *Maybe she believes what the magazines are saying about me and Susie,* he thinks. *Or maybe she likes me.*

"Hiya, Marion," he says, popping into the make-up room. Twenty people are buzzing in and out, but Marion looks only at him.

She runs her fingers through her auburn fringe. "Hi."

"Can I talk to you for a sec?"

She moves to him like he is the most important person in the universe, steps out into the corridor and half closes the door.

"I like your nails," he starts.

"Oh," she says shyly, wiggling her fingers. "Thanks."

"They're like disco balls."

"I chipped one," she says, grimacing as though he would give a fuck. *Focus, be polite.*

"Shoot," he says. "Listen." Her eyes grow wide as he describes the situation, asks for her help, her discretion.

"It's not—"

"Marion, obviously it's not mine." He rolls his eyes, socks her lightly in the upper arm.

"I'll talk to the girls," she says, adding almost gleefully. "We'll make sure she's not in anything too tight."

Rip is next. "Give her an illness," Orson suggests. "Bed rest or something. Or just put me in scenes with her, I'll help her cover it."

Rip sighs heavily. "Buddy, why are you getting involved?"

"She says she needs time."

"Flowers is going to be so pissed."

"Flowers doesn't need to find out."

"Are you in love with her?"

"No!" Of course he loves her, but he isn't *in love* with her. "Jesus, Rip. It's just. She brings everyone up, you know?"

Rip nods. He knows. "We could always send her into a coma."

For several weeks, it seems to be working. Winter comes and with it, baggy coats. The costume department makes the most of her bloating breasts, cleverly adapts a seam here and there. As more accommodations need to be made, Orson delicately slips the word around set: an AD, a cameraman. Close-ups, large props in front of her. Rip gives Margie some shift-work at the bar – that keeps her hidden. But when even the child actor who plays the matriarch's coddled daughter approaches Orson to say "Guess what . . .?" he knows her time is running short. Everyone knows except Flowers.

It's late and Susan's feet are pounding. For months she has kept her mouth shut, and the army of hidden helpers is enough to overwhelm her. Rip promised to send Margie on some kind of vacation. *Somewhere warm*, she requested. Rehab can be warm, he winked. It's nice to think they'll both come back transformed. It will be easy enough to let it all flow from her, all of the sadness of saying goodbye. *You're going to start smoking,* Orson joked. *Everyone does at rehab.* With all of them behind her, masking her belly and rewriting her plotlines, it feels almost possible it will work out. She'll be back. She will give birth and keep her job and Al will see the light and they will live happily ever after in Hollywood.

As if on queue, the phone rings. "Hi, Susie Q," her husband says.

"Hi, Doc."

On the dressing table is the latest bouquet: roses and lilacs, lavender and eucalyptus. Al sends them weekly, bursting with pride and wonder and maybe also fear. To avoid flying, Susan is sub-letting a small studio apartment in Sun Valley, and they are both aching. This is the longest she's ever been away from him.

"How was today?"

"I threw up again."

"Suze, it's been twenty weeks."

"I know."

Twins, the doctor told her last week. She had gone to the appointment on her own, and she could sense the nurse wondering how she'd got herself into this mess.

"OK, we'll go together next week," says Al. *Thank God.* He's coming for spring break, driving across the country – he says it's not because of his growing fear of airplanes. He'll enjoy the journey, he says. It won't be a moment too soon. Al always seems to know what questions to ask at the hospital. What to be concerned about.

"We can ask them the genders."

"Don't you want to be surprised?"

"I guess." Her heart is aching for at least one girl. To bring a woman into this limitless planet. She is struck with a small wave of nausea. *Hello there,* she thinks familiarly. *My awful, wonderful secret.*

"I've been thinking more about names," says Al. "How about Lawrence?"

"Of Arabia?"

"No, after my dad."

"Huh."

"What?"

"No, it's just. Surprising, that's all."

"It might make my mom happy."

"Is that the factor?"

"No, it's just. It would be nice." *Nice for whom?* Al always seemed afraid of his father. Afraid of becoming him, afraid of disappointing him. It wasn't a legacy Susan much wanted to carry on.

"I was thinking more Hollywood. Brigitte, Marlon."

"Mm. Something from Shakespeare?"

Susan laughs. "That would make your mom happy. Me pretending to be highbrow."

"What is that supposed to mean."

The phone hung silent.

"Let's just stay open. It will come."

When he hangs up, she pulls off her oversized shirt, holds her hands onto her sore breasts. She's so tired she could cry.

A knock at the door. Costumes, no doubt, coming to collect the many layers she wore today to hide her belly. Baggy dresses, a shapeless coat. They are miracle workers. She brought them all coffees today and little chocolates from the patisserie near her apartment. It's the least she could do.

"Just a minute," she says, but the door opens anyway and there is Mark, taking in the half-naked swell of her, the slow understanding of her betrayal hardening into an unforgiving rock.

Flowers' office is full of heavy objects, solid glass paperweights, a heavy silver bowl, a photograph of the child that he gets to see every other weekend. On the wall are framed posters and playbills and letters from fans. He stands with his back to her, looking out of the small window, occupying the space with a rare grip over time. They are always rushing here, fielding daily catastrophes minor and major, adapting, abandoning storylines that other soaps are copying, writing people in and out and changing the wardrobe or the lines. Stillness is precious – which is to say, expensive. So, you better make good use of it.

"Have you done something new in here, Mark? The wallpaper or something?"

An odd serenity has descended over Susan, an almost giddiness. Whatever happens next, there is no more hiding. She stands, one hand on his long, leather Chesterfield, the site of rare, precious naps and several rumored fucks. She has never been alone in here with him.

"Sit," Flowers says, and though she would rather not, the tone doesn't leave much choice. She sits.

"I know you're upset. I should have talked to you."

Flowers removes his tinted glasses, wipes them with his pocket square. She is aware of movement outside the room, the chatter of people packing up for the day, making evening plans, light gossip. The office is thick with bergamot cologne, with his silence. *Men are always trying to figure out what to do with her, aren't they?* She can still remember that look on Bourke's face – was it six years ago now? What a child she was! How foolish, thinking she had the world to lose. She had nothing – no credit to her name, no tools more sophisticated than self-sabotage, no respect other than her own. She had *wanted* Bourke to give up on her, hadn't she? To admit she was too big for him? Like Bridget Bishop, she had been prepared for the very worst.

Well look at you now. Everything to lose. And maybe just enough savvy to save herself. She shifts on the sofa, aware of her stomach, his resentment of it. *Think of something,* Margie hisses at the back of her mind. *I don't want to die.*

"Listen, I know you think this is bad. But I really think there might be an opportunity here. I mean, you always say characters are verbs, right? And Margie, well, she's due for a bit of reinvention, isn't she? If we made a feature of it, we could do all kinds of storylines – I mean, the paternity question alone . . ."

The words coming out of her mouth are hasty and hare-brained, a true Margie maneuver, but she is willing to do anything (*anything*) now to keep him from closing the door on her. Because outside she can hear Orson laughing with someone, his high-pitched cackle reserved for only truly funny and slightly naughty comments, and it's enough to make her cry. This is her family. Every day, they show up, prepared to be vulnerable and brave, determined never to let each other down. They can read you with a single glance, will keep you level with an Aspirin or a coffee or a quiet word. Most of them, she'd trust with her life.

Mark still isn't looking at her. She knows she's nothing to him, replaceable as a shoelace. But still, she is talking, almost as though she expects this to be a scene from the show.

```
                         MARGIE
Whatever it takes, boss. I'll do it for free if you'll
    just let me come back. We can even use the babies,
       if we need, for filming. Did I mention it's twins?
```

If Rip were writing the scene, Margie would be compelling. Her wheedling would move mountains. Mark would scratch his head and say something like: *This just might work.* Or maybe, appealing to Margie's regular currency: *You can keep the job if you fuck me.*

Would she? Now, in the interest of keeping her options open, when her whole world feels like it's on the line? She can feel the coiled springs under the cushions of the couch, the bodies which have surely succumbed here, before, to the desperate need to please. He is crossing the floor slowly in the direction of his desk, and she is trying to envision whether it could be just another role, because as Susan, she cannot do it. Her husband is fixed in her mind. But surrendering Margie is not an option. Mark leans against the desk and looks at her squarely, his eyes running cold over the shape of her.

She looks at him with all of Margie's desperation and he looks back at her like a used tissue.

"Listen, Susie. I like you. But if you don't look the part, you don't have the right to play it. Contractually, we can do what we want."

What he's trying to say is no one wants to sleep with a pregnant girl.

"But what I'm saying is—"

"This conversation is over."

Susan is descending from the sublet and dropping the keys in the mailbox and folding into Al's arms. She breathes him in, the unfamiliar way he smells after a month without her, and they rock together as people pass around them, a stone in a stream.

"Miss me?" he asks.

She nods into his shoulder. He has driven across the country to get her. He places both hands on her stomach (his stomach) and looks at her with a wide-open face.

"You want to go home?"

She presses her cheek into his cheek, the stubble where a beard won't grow. She shakes her head against his head, her nose wiping against him. *No.* She doesn't want to go anywhere.

With her suitcase in the trunk of the car, they buy tickets to the Los Angeles aquarium. He takes her hand and leads her through the towering tanks.

"The other night," he says, "they were showing something about the origins of life on PBS."

"Trust you to watch PBS while I'm away."

"Hey, they have good stuff on there."

"Lifelong learner. See, you act so above it all, but I told you, you'd love having a TV."

"I was never above it all."

"I'm just teasing. What did it say?" She rests her cheek on his shoulder, the softness of his shirt, the hardness of his muscle underneath. His glasses are reflecting the blue of the water.

"There are these vents in the floor of the ocean where magma hits the seawater. And they think that's where life began"

"Huh," she says. "That makes sense."

"Does it?"

"Yeah. You're seawater, and I'm magma."

He pinches the flesh on her elbow and she wrinkles her nose at him. They pause to make way for a young mother and her small, beautiful daughter who is babbling, pointing, peering up through thick eyelashes as a shark coasts through the tank. The mother lifts the child, who places tiny hands against both of their mouths, in a moment where words can hold no meaning.

"Do you think children look at the water and remember the womb?" he asks.

"Maybe." It always amazes her, how these thoughts float into his mind. "I mean, do you remember it or is it just something you know? Deep inside you, do you know that someone carried you?"

"Probably. It's why we have to be nice to my mother."

"I am nice to your mother."

"I never said you weren't."

Al and Susan watch as the shark drifts past, breathing in silent synchronicity. Her heart slows, lost in her own overpowering future, the proximity to danger, the serenity of his arms wrapping around her chest, swaying her back and forth.

"I want our children to be deep sea divers," he says. "I want them to identify twenty new species of fish and discover long-forgotten wrecks."

"I just want them to have everything," she says, squeezing his hand. "Everything they want."

2010

Viola never gets mail. So it is unusual when she discovers a postcard (still life, fruit, a jug) resting in her letterbox.

To: Viola with the fake cigarettes
c/o St Sylvia's College, Cambridge

Ring me, it says with a number.

In the last week, she has re-watched – twice – a period drama in which Orson plays a brooding artist/farmhand who is sent to war and makes obsessive drawings of a local heiress. By the time he comes back from the bloody battle scenes (layered obviously with pastoral reveries and provincial longing), his memory of his beloved has been so warped that he mistakes her for her sister, who turns out to have been in love with him all along. Long moody shots of the Yorkshire Dales. Birds taking off as the sun rises. His face, screwed up and intent: this is how she has kept him alive.

She phones him from the wildflower garden outside of the library.

"Hello," she says. "It's Viola."

"Ah, hello! I wasn't sure you'd call."

Of course she was going to call. "I'm sorry," she says, "for abandoning you so abruptly."

"Well, that's just it. The thing is that I really hate to be in debt and I still owe you a drink. I was hoping you might come with me to a . . . thing I have to do this Saturday. London thing."

"A thing?"

"It's for charity. You like charity, right? You're a fundamentally good person?"

"I'd hope so."

"I can't imagine you doing anything truly awful. But then again, I'm a terrible judge of character."

Surely it is the only reason he is speaking to her, the only reason she has stuck in his memory one week later, when he has returned to wherever it is he goes, surrounded by beautiful anointed people. He must have figured it out: the resemblance to her mother, the name. Would it spoil things to mention it? To project a dead woman's judgment onto the situation?

"So you'll come, then?"

Inside the library, she can see the table she shares with Niamh, the stack of books by her own empty seat, all selected with the intention of reading them, or at least flipping decisively to the relevant section and pulling several key quotes to use in her extended essay proposals, which are drawing frighteningly close. It is strange, isn't it, that she says yes without hesitation, that were he any other anonymous forty-year-old man, she would never agree to come meet him. But this is Orson Grey. Quite possibly the love of her life. She can afford a Saturday. She knows more or less the ingredients for her essay: propositions, representations, relationships.

"Saturday. I'll get you a hotel. You can take the train?"

Across the garden, two women have entered, tourists, taking pictures and commenting unsubtly about whether or not the quad featured as a location on some TV show. They bend over, enchanted by the bees suckling at the last nectar in the red blossoms of Autumn Sage.

"I can get the train."

One of them takes out her phone to photograph the stone library, and as Viola hangs up, she finds herself caught in the snap. Her mind dislocates and she is cardboard, a stock figure in someone else's romance. There is an unpleasantness in the objectification: of her, of a place that, however ethereal, has become real to her – a home. A porter rounding the courtyard calls out: "Members of the college only, ladies. Didn't you see the sign?"

They slink away, leaving Viola feeling slimy. She'd had a similar sensation when, a few days after meeting Orson, she caved and texted Sebastian. Somehow, she wanted it to be a peace offering, an appeal to Sebastian's twisted intrigue. A way to break the frost without apologizing.

Sebastian
Seriously?? Did you ask him anything?

Viola
What do you mean?

Sebastian
About mom?

Viola
It didn't really come up.

The conversation flattened her in the same way, magic rendered cheap and two-dimensional. No: she wants Orson to be human. She wants him to be hers. It's why she left out the details – the scotch, cigarettes, fingers running through her hair. She won't mention London. Sebastian would have expectations. His own agenda. Discussing it wouldn't fix anything between them. The last thing she needs is for him to entertain Niamh's suggestion: *he wants to sleep with you.*

"What if he doesn't?"

"Who wouldn't want to sleep with you, Viola? You're luscious."

Someone who knew me as a child. Someone who knew my mother. Delicious, anxious, wriggling thought. Her desire is a saber cutting through the confused unknowns: *what would it be like to sleep with him? What would it be like to sleep with any man?* When did her virginity become a burden? It's not that she has anything against sex in the abstract, just that it must happen in the right way, with the right person. It must mean something.

She moans. "What do you wear in London?"

"Jesus, Viola, if you don't sleep with him, I will. Rowan is going to die."

Adrenaline rush, sifting through the clothes that she had stuffed into two suitcases, entirely insufficient for the occasion. She goes out and buys two dresses that look more expensive than they are: a floral print bandeau, a strappy black thing. In a fit of chaotic anticipation, she throws into a bag a stain-remover pen, breath mints, make-up bag, Kleenex, extra hair ties, bobby pins, safety pins, tampons, then takes it all out again, because there's no romance in overengineering. In her small purse, she brings only a tube of lipstick called Rouge Noir.

"Honestly, if you wind up in the *Mail*," Niamh says. "You best not leave me alone with Maitland."

"I'd fear for his life."

The train deposits her at Liverpool Street in ninety fleeting minutes during which she fails to absorb a single word of *The Conquest of Happiness*. London is a cacophony of bodies, noise, and discarded coffee cups. The sky feels impenetrable, an illusion created by the hemming in of the horizon, the glassy eyes of the buildings. Viola has never understood the appeal of cities, the true crime peril and low-grade dehumanization, everyone looking at you like an obstacle. Recently, walking through the common room, she caught a segment about a serial killer who strangled women and left them in abandoned alleys, in garbage bins, on riverbanks. The images stuck with her: police tape and blue lights, the low-resolution faces of victims contained in white, square frames, their eyes already haunted by the tragedy hovering over them. As though their futures were predetermined, and it was the sadness of this knowledge – rather than the horrific uncaught perpetrator – that killed them. Still: maybe she just hasn't figured it out. Maybe the metropolis will open up to her. People fall in love here, don't they?

Dad
Have fun. Go find Nelson's column.
Be careful. Love you. Dad

Just a normal trip to the city, that's all she mentioned. You can't tell everybody everything. She follows the line on her phone south from Liverpool Street, through coughing taxi ranks, down Threadneedle Street to the river. The Millennium Bridge spindles against the sky. Buildings she recognizes but cannot name hover to the east. A light rain spits or doesn't against the side of her face. The world is awash with gray – gray is the sky, the glass, the metal of it all, gray is the river roiling fat beneath her, gray are the squat little boats that chug off to the west and the people's faces bent back against too-thin hoods. A gust of wind wrenches a man's umbrella up into the sky, and it too turns gray and disappears – into the water or the air, no one could say. Orson is standing at the end of the bridge.

Tentatively she holds up a hand. He holds up a hand. Everything peripheral – all the mess of it and the noise – disappears down a cinematic tunnel, the world closing in on the two of them, great and fated lovers: Cathy and Heathcliff, Rhett and Scarlett, Tony and Maria. As he crosses towards her, she tries to detect in his gait the same urgency that she feels.

"Hi," she says, her heart tugging, her lips and face and hair damp in what she hopes is Austen-esque.

"Why are you soaking?" he cries, kissing her cheek. "You should have taken a taxi. I would have paid."

"The walk was shorter, apparently. You know, normally people pick somewhere inside to meet."

"The problem is that, inside, people try to talk to me." He is wearing rain-fogged glasses, which he wipes on his shirt. "Well, anyway, do you want to dry off? Do you want to drop off your things?"

"It's fine," she says. "Where are we going?"

The thatched, reconstructed Globe Theatre crouches on the south bank, fitting neither with the looming, industrial Tate or the ballistic Gherkin.

"I thought this would be educational for you."

"Educational?"

"Well, you said you hadn't seen very much."

"Oh no."

"Don't worry, I'm not going to force you to sit through *Cymbeline* or anything."

"You said this was a charity thing."

"It is! Come on then, do you want a drink?" Swiftly, he steers her into an innocuous-looking entrance that descends into a mezzanine under the Globe. She trusts him implicitly, like one would trust a president, following him through a series of stairwells and into a dressing room, in which they find a woman with long blonde hair and red glasses.

"Who is this?" the woman asks in a way that implies Viola is not the first *this* she has been introduced to.

"This is Viola. Jen, would you get us something from the bar please? A nice red, not too dry, not too fruity."

"A Goldilocks red."

"You're an angel."

Jen looks at Viola coolly. "He isn't always this picky."

"That isn't fair. I'm a fairly discerning person."

Jen smiles indulgently and steps out of the room.

"I'm sorry we can't go anywhere normal around here," he says. "It's just such a hassle."

"It's fine," Viola says. "The weather is better down here."

"I like you," he says. "You like a glass half full, don't you?"

"Maybe I'm too idealistic."

"Well, that's just the tonic. Hollywood makes you cynical." He drums his fingers on the table. "Admittedly, London isn't Southern California weather-wise. The thing is, I'm always being asked to go on stage here. No one in California would dream of asking a movie actor to perform on stage. It's just embarrassing, really, for most people. And most of the time I tell them to fuck off, or Jen tells them to fuck off, but it's just hard to tell a charity for childhood diabetes to fuck off more than twice. It just starts to feel like you don't care about childhood diabetes, which of course you might not feel any personal connection toward, but the kids really are sweet and they're always sending photos of them, and if there's something that you can do – something that should be easy, that should be your stock and trade – then, well, you want to do it. You want to be able to do some-thing aside from swanning around and spending money and talking to pretty girls outside of pubs."

His foot is tapping restlessly on the ground, and it occurs to Viola that even though he is twenty years older than her, he too might be nervous.

"I don't understand why it would be different on stage than film," Viola says. "Isn't it all just acting?"

"Oh, there you're wrong. Completely different. For one, if you fuck up on film, you can just do it again. Doesn't matter. Take two. As many takes as you want to get it perfect. If you fuck up on stage though, that's it. You've blown your shot. Terrifying really."

Jen returns with a bottle of red wine and a bowl full of mixed nuts covered in a thin dust of cumin and cinnamon.

"They're the ones from the hotel!" he said. "Jen figured it out for me, where to get them, she's extremely clever like that. I thought it was just a crime that you didn't get to try them."

"A lot of phone calls went into those nuts," Jen mutters. "So please, do enjoy them."

"Jen is just sour because she has an allergy, aren't you, Jen?"

Jen turns to a stack of papers in the corner.

"So, sorry," Viola begins, trying to ignore Jen who is trying very hard not to look wounded. "But what is this?"

Orson sighs, pours out the wine. "It's a *Midsummer Night's Dream*-themed charity fundraiser. For orphans I think? Or a refugee crisis? Jen, did you write the speech?"

"What do you think I'm working on?"

"I have to read a monologue. Oberon, something about oxlips and nodding violet. It's embarrassing really, I haven't even memorized it, that's the kind of shit film actor I am. Learn my lines right before the scene. They've printed it for me, haven't they, Jen?"

"Yes."

"So that's all it is. And then it will be free booze and wealthy, well-intentioned people signing big checks. And it would just be so great. For me. If you could just whisper idealistic things in the corner. Especially about how I stack up against all of these very serious Royal Shakespeare people, I just don't really hold a candle, and I'm very embarrassed."

"Don't be silly," says Viola. "Of course you'll be fine."

"There, see, perfect. Just like that. Anyway, I thought you could be my nodding violet, or whatever. My talisman."

"If that's what you need." His gaze, holding hers, is full of an inescapable past. Viola is certain now that he knows, that the fact of it approaching barometric; they are too familiar with each other.

Jen, having had enough, gets up and leaves the room without a word.

"Is she okay?"

"Oh, sure. Just a bit moody," he says. "Insecurities aside, if I didn't take you to Shakespeare, I never would have forgiven myself."

It's coming up now, hot and inescapable – the fact throbbing between them.

"I'm sorry, I just – do you remember my – do you remember Susan Bliss?"

"Of course, I do."

A long moment, the atmosphere thick with something, an end or a beginning, she can't tell. She slides a hand across the table, touches one of his electric fingers. When he looks at her again, he looks older, furrowed with a need she cannot identify. The back of his hand reaches across, strokes the inside of her arm.

"Do you remember me?" she asks.

He shakes his head back and forth – noncommittal. "You've changed a bit," he says, a smile cracking through the seriousness of it all. "I'm sorry I've got so old."

"Don't. You haven't changed at all."

His hand swirls her hair as he leans toward her, pushing gently at the back of her neck until his lips brush against her forehead. If he hesitates for a moment as she bends her cheek to him, she hopes it is because he is leaving behind the child and her mother, both long gone anyways, and surrendering himself to the woman here, now, who has come so far and waited so long for him to arrive.

1990

Kelp, Samphire, Gecko, Lime Rickey. Oh Pistachio, Picnic. Killarney. Frosted Emerald. Pickle. Susan knows it has to be green, but has never really considered the sheer range, how each one might make the room feel. Even now, as the light shifts over the various patches of paint on the stripped walls of the bedroom that will belong to her children, she cannot tell which shade she prefers. The wall looks like America from above. Like a journey to another life.

"What if you did four different colors?" Sadie suggests. "Or stripes?"

An autumn breeze catches the opened window, and both sisters turn toward it. To Susan, the view still feels surreal. The old house, the new town. Her body, transforming daily, her appetite for spice. Twice a week, Al drives to Fortune Palace to pick up noodles drenched in chili oil, plastic jugs of hot-and-sour soup. He takes such joy in caring for her and it fills her with gratitude, an almost-peace about being here. But life still feels like it's happening somewhere else.

"You could always just leave it like this," Sadie says. "You know, let them gravitate toward whichever green they prefer. Get in touch with their inner greens. Maybe you could just let them crawl around the house and decide which room they want. You've got enough space."

Sadie won't stop bringing it up, the size of the house, the well-to-do area. It doesn't change the fact that it's a fixer-upper. That they have to start thinking now – somehow – about school districts, planning permissions. Or at least Al thinks they have to think about these things. They belong to a category that Susan has never considered before and still has not fully engaged with. All she can focus on is making the

167

house her own: filling it with her music, making a phenomenal mess in the kitchen, taking up space in all the ways Hollywood hotels did not allow.

"Do you remember when Mom painted the whole house red after Dad left?" Sadie asks.

Of course she remembers. The story is so stale with retelling it doesn't matter anymore whether or not it happened the way they tell it; what matters is the cadence and the stiff character assessments that it produces. *It was like being inside an intestine.* Someone said it once and nothing had been funnier. But the more it was repeated, the sadder it sounded. *And then we had to wallpaper over everything . . . But Mom always used to say . . .* Susan allows the conversation to traverse the dry, familiar riverbeds, to review the same, unchanged people. Their mother's cirrhosis (worsening), their father's absence (continued, unsurprising). Sometimes now with her sister, she feels their relationship is no more than a residue. As though they are only pantomiming how they used to be with each other before some invisible line was crossed. It's the loneliest feeling.

"It could be worse," Sadie says. "You could be waiting tables and living with your mom."

"Oh stop," Susie says. "You could do anything you wanted, if you worked for it."

"Well, I can't dance."

"Oh, Sadie."

Sadie has been frustrated for two years, ever since her knee injury. She's been putting weight on as well, but that's not something Susan can bring up lightly. It's strange, the unspeakable sense of their universes pulling apart. *It won't be that way with the twins,* she thinks. Underground rivers will run between them, currents carrying them in the same direction. They are beginning together, and together they will encounter the world.

"Look," Susan says. "You just need to get creative. Limitations are key to innovation."

"I wasn't looking for advice."

Susan rolls her eyes at her sister, chokes back the words *attitude is altitude*. She really does believe in it, making your own luck. Sadie reaches out and peels a small roll of green paint out of Susan's hair.

"It's more that I feel like I'm supposed to want more than what I have. Like I'm weird because I don't have, like, a dream, like you."

"You're not weird," Susan murmurs, pulling her sister close. "Okay, you are weird, but only in ways that I know about."

"Oh shit," Sadie says, pulling back, giggling, holding up green hands. "Shit."

Two green handprints wave from the back of Susan's white t-shirt. A moan turns into a laugh, the playful struggle for revenge.

"What's going on up there?"

Sadie looks at her sister, giggles calming to sighs. "I should go."

"You don't want Chinese?"

"It's fine."

The kitchen air is thick with barbecue ribs and juicy dumplings. Susan watches her sister and husband exchange curt pleasantries. It's a shame they don't get along. But you can't make people like each other. You can't will them to be anyone other than who they are.

"Hello beautiful," Al says. His face is tired contentment. He has been working late hours, taken on new lectures. He holds two square hands against her lower back underneath Sadie's prints and she can feel the weight that she has been carrying release into the warmth of him.

"God, that feels good."

As he decants the hot-and-sour soup from plastic jugs into bowls, he tells her about his day, the papers he has to mark this evening and—

"Oh." Her chair is wet, maybe with soup, maybe with urine, maybe she is pissing, *No, they need to go*, right now, there's no more time!

Her body, cut open and numb, flooding with the soft gorgeous smell of the tiny body alive on her breastbone, her daughter's pinched, perfect

169

face, her lips, her nose, everything that she has yet to be. They breathe together, her impossible fingers clutching at Susan's dressing gown. The new word *mom*, applied to herself. A soft, insipid word – not enough, not remotely, to capture the conquering flood of everything between herself and this little person.

Al, in the corner, is holding her son. *One of each.* Susan looks at him for an endless moment, and he gazes back, his face soft with gratitude.

Twelfth Night? he had suggested in the early hours. *Confusion and a happy ending?* She hasn't seen the play, but in the end it felt like nothing, giving him this – she knows the tumult and theatrics of these children are hers. Everything she thought she knew about the earth is upended. Each breath, each heartbeat is its own reason. Each clench of little fingers, each twitch of the mouth. She doesn't want to miss a second of this life.

"Hi," she says as the little eyes flutter open, green and unfocused, looking at but not seeing her face. The bare, damp top of Viola's head rolls back as she opens her mouth and screams.

2011

Viola leans naked against the bathroom door, avoiding the mirror. On the other side is a real, slowly exhaling man, a man who comes and goes and remembers her birthday but forgets her middle name, who leans his head to the side and listens to her opinions on matters of varying importance, who keeps most but not all of his promises.

"Everything okay?"

Orson is everything she wants. Over the last year, their relationship has grown in the eaves of their lives, in a handful of stolen moments during the breaks in his filming schedule and her term time. They have met in London's private corners, sharing drinks, tentative brushes, occasionally – when they know they are alone – a kiss. He touches her like he cannot resist her, like he ought to resist. He disappears into taxis. Until now, time has frustrated them, refusing to amount to anything, to give them certainty and space. The world detains him for long, unpredictable months. But he sends her small intimacies, her phone blinking out the thrill of him like a lighthouse.

O
saw a crow on set today kill a pigeon
sorry is that disgusting
i had to tell someone

Viola
you didn't intervene?
I thought you were a hero
disappointed x

O
too fast. too evil. I am but human
shite weather have to extend a day filming
sorry
means sat is off
i really wanted to see you

Viola
sorry for you
and me
but I understand

O
how is school
are you a genius yet

Viola
yes
ask me anything

O
how did the universe begin
no
what shampoo do you use
oh god sorry what a creep
i just want to know what that smell is

Viola
coconut and rosehip
weirdo
;)

O
am I a horrible old man

Viola
no, you're a very nice old man
benign
like a

O
I didn't know roses had hips

Viola
pigeon

O
jesus
does that make you the crow in this analogy
are you going to eat my heart out

Viola
yes x

His bathroom gives little away. Slate and silver, a powerful, pendulous shower head. A few jars in the corner: Marine Collagen, Wrinkle Corrector, an expensive-looking deodorant. Outside is December: colored light displays switching on and local vendors shutting for the evening.

This is mad, he said on the phone last month.

What, just generally?

No, well yes, but no, I had a specific madness to suggest . . . She imagined his trailer somewhere in northern Iceland, his windows glowing into the starry abyss. She imagined him lying on his small bed, shirtless perhaps, his face shiny from make-up remover. Were the remains of dinner on an abandoned tray, or had he eaten with others: the gorgeous co-star, the clever production crew? Who else was attending to his needs? On the phone, he shapeshifts, becomes younger versions of himself, characters from decades ago.

Go on, mad man.

His calls had become frequent, and she understood there was little else to do. For a moment, the phone cut out and when it came back in, he was saying – *it's just too weird now, with their boyfriends or girlfriends all trying to get you presents, being all Ho-Ho-Ho, you just feel like a bit of a spectacle, and I'd rather just do something quiet anyway.*

Sorry, your niece and nephew?

Oh, did you miss that?

Sorry, I—

Ach, God. Do you want to come for Christmas?

She closed her eyes and allowed his voice to become the only moving thing in the universe.

There is nothing I want more.

She said it because it was true. Because it overwhelms her – God, each morning she is hit fresh with need. The whole world has taken him on as a permanent undertone: the music on the radio, the earth under her feet. Is love a persistent wondering? *What will he think, say, feel? How will he--? Has he ever--? When, when, when?*

They still have not slept together.

Do you think your family will mind? he asked. *Do you have, you know, Christmas stuff?*

I think they'll get it.

Is that a twin thing, you just get each other? Do you have freaky twin thoughts?

About blood elevators in old hotels? Yes.

He laughed hard, then said: *I always felt like my family was a bit of a weird appendage, even when I missed them terribly and was fucking homesick. They just never felt more important than the whole great adventure, you know, the whole spectrum of what you could do with a life. And they never really understood what I was trying to do until I had done it.*

I get that, she said. *Your world was so different to anything they'd ever known.*

Exactly, he said.

He was trying to empathize, to make them alike – two people without a need for the worlds they had left. But she cannot reciprocate his vulnerability. She cannot reveal to him her baggage. He has all the choice in the world, but for her, he is singular. She has to be perfect for him. It's why he had not known to ask: Do you miss your brother? Do you regret fighting? Do you wish you could tell him about us?

After a minute, she asked: *Do you think everyone in Hollywood feels that way about their families? Like they're less important than the rest of it?*

No. Definitely not everyone.

The next month throbbed with the anticipation of it, a giddiness she tried to hide from Orson but could not hide from Niamh, who insisted on referring to the whole thing as sex-mas. For all her teasing, Niamh was fantastically discreet. In public, she only ever alluded to Orson as Viola's "elderly paramour"; most people assumed she was sleeping with a married man. She was surprised by how little she cared.

When she called her father to say she wasn't coming home, she blamed her studies; it was a currency he had to respect. He reassured her he would spend the day with Tillie and her family, and Sebastian would spend it with Sadie. Still, it was hard to ignore the disappointment in his voice. She could live with it, as long as he didn't suspect anything. Not that she wanted to lie to him – only, oh how could she explain any of it in a way he could understand? Maybe it would only last a moment. Maybe her degree would end and she would go home and never hear from Orson again. Or maybe she would spend every Christmas with him for the rest of time.

O
don't get me any presents
you are my present

                                Viola
                            come on
                     a little mistletoe?

O
you are so cute
but I'm serious
commit to naughty Christmas
I'm only getting you coal

Viola
I'm getting you lingerie
satin or lace?

She had taken the long walk north from the station, trying to slow the anticipation of the threshold, of what their need would become in private. She is still unused to this part of town, to any London that people actually live in. She tried playing a song on her headphones, but found it unlistenable against the pounding of her heart. Gradually, the houses began settling back from the road, cloaking themselves in sturdier hedges, the motorbikes roaring up the high street puttering farther and farther away.

The problem arose when he opened the door, vibrating and human, his body calling her body into being. *Come in*, he said, taking her hand, *I missed you.* She had entered his large clean house and he had taken her through to the back (away from the windows). The cold expanse of it jarred against the warmth of him.

Is it what you expected? he asked, and she said, *It's smaller,* which made him laugh, but wasn't true.

She was aware that they had not kissed, aware of his awareness. He seemed nervous, more nervous than he had ever been in public, decanting boxes and boxes of Chinese food from a paper bag. *I realized I didn't know what you eat*, he said. *Do you eat?*

No, I just photosynthesize. She stood on the other side of the kitchen island, allowing him to serve her.

I suspected as much.

But seeing as it's Naughty Christmas, I'll indulge, she said and though her stomach was swimming, she placed a dumpling onto her plate. Orson stuck a spoon into a carton of rice and ate a heap of it, plain.

God, just, thank God, Viola.

For rice?

No—

He bent himself over the kitchen island and sighed, and she

ventured a hand to the top of his head. His hair was damp, and he exhaled for a long moment, allowing her to massage his scalp.

I was just thinking how nice it is that you're not going to go around telling everyone you know that I eat heaps of plain rice.

I might.

You won't.

I won't. You can be yourself.

When he lifted his face it was very close to hers, and she looked at the peaks of his mouth, his thin nose, the lines tracing down to his stubble. *Thank you*, he said. *I will.*

A small plastic tree with fake snow on the branches sat on the table, a tag still wrapped around its base. While they ate, his foot found hers, pawed at the toe of her boot.

Can I offer you a tour? he asked when they had finished, handing her a very large whiskey and leading her through his living room strewn with scripts and half-read books and a couple of expensive-looking paintings. *This is where I spend most of my time.* He allowed her to thumb through his detritus and point at photographs and ask *is that your sister*, and say *she is very beautiful.* Above them was a shelf lined with statuettes of gold and glass engraved with his name.

Then, on the sideboard in a small silver frame, she saw it: a photograph of her own mother. Greyish around the edges with the quality of a disposable camera. Susan was sitting at a simple wooden table, laughing hard, head thrown back, one hand almost obscuring her face. Wearing a low-cut blouse. Was it the same blouse from the tabloid? Viola could not remember. It had disturbed her, just a few years ago, the photo. She couldn't bear the thought of anyone seeing it. *And now?*

Orson noticed her noticing, waited for her like he expected her to say something. But all Viola could think was how the woman in the picture appeared to be everything she did not feel. Uninhibited. A natural. *Was that an illusion?* She felt stuck, unable to read the joy on her mother's familiar, unknowable face. Will it disappoint him, her inability to remember? She bit back a thousand stupid, unaskable questions: *Are we alike? Would she have wanted –? Did you love her?*

What was she laughing at? she finally mustered, and he thought about it for a long moment before saying sadly: *I can't remember.* And then: *Probably some funny shit you pulled. She was always going on about you two.* When she could not respond to this, he added: *Or more likely me. Because I'm fucking hilarious.* Viola laughed a little and he said: *Let's cut to the end of the tour.*

O
I've been working better
since I met you
it's odd to explain

Viola
how so?

O
I don't know
I felt like I'd lost touch with people
like I didn't know how it felt to care
very much about anything
like characters do

Viola
well, let me reassure you
having watched every single film you have made
you understand people perfectly
if anything, too well
maybe that's what makes you feel lonely
because you feel like they don't understand
you back

Upstairs, he sat her on his bed and unzipped her boots, then sat on the floor looking up at her.

This is so crazy, he said. *I've just really wanted to be close to you.*

She pulled up her shirt and he climbed to his knees and placed his hands on either side of her stomach which twisted sick with wanting something too much. *I just need a minute*, she said, forcing a smile, scampering into the en suite, where she has now taken off the rest of her clothes and is trying to come to terms with the fact of herself.

She turns on the sink, exhales, braves the mirror. Her face is flushed, her hair too big. She twists it around, ties it back tight and high on her head, hates it, lets it down again. Her small breasts, her articulated ribcage. How many hours of running have fought against excess? *Will he find her unwomanly? Will her body know what to do?* She thinks of the whiskey abandoned downstairs, feels overexposed. Has she been blinded by his easy familiarity? Is that something he can affect with anyone?

More than once she has asked herself why he has chosen her. Has told herself, hopefully, that it is because she is beautiful to him, because she can make him laugh, because she can soothe him when his work is too much. That her heart is enough. That her mind is enough. But perhaps Susan is the only reason she has held his attention. It is possible, when he looks at her, he is looking for a woman she has never known.

She emerges, backlit and Orson can see her heart is racing too. His phone is in his hand, stupid, a nervous tic, and he thrusts it back toward the sideboard.

"Jesus," he says under his breath.

If you could only see her, bare hip against doorframe, the bounty of her curls parting over pert handfuls, you'd be dumbstruck too. He'll never get used to it, the sight of a naked girl. But this time he's in too deep.

"This is going to be embarrassing for me." He throws a hand on his stomach. "They made me pack it on for this one."

"Stop it," she says. "You look the same as you always have."

He knew the moment he saw her; he was doomed. Susie but not Susie. Stunning, funny, clever. Vibrating with the same absence he has carried all these years. It takes nothing, a smile, the way she tilts her head back, her laugh for God's sake, and he's twenty-seven again, the last version of himself that he can truly recognize. He'd forgotten that tenderness, that level of concern and interest in anyone. He'd struggled to feel it in decades. She became immediately singular. Immediately necessary.

Christ, what would Susie think?

"I didn't mean to make you nervous," she says.

"Imagine such a thing," he says.

"I can."

He shifts back on the bed and they gaze unblinking into each other's eyes, overwhelmed by the unlikelihood of it all. He'd worried it would be too much: that in the moment he would be unable to separate them, that he would mistake what he was doing as a perverse kind of displacement instead of – well, an act of discovery. But it was wasted concern. She is so specifically, strikingly herself.

Tentatively, she moves from the doorway and places herself next to him, and suddenly it all feels so serious. It's possible she's never been serious before. God knows he's a selfish prick to pursue this, but she wants him too, right? Even the ancient state of him? He only wants to take care of her.

"Viola," he says. "Look, we need to take this slowly."

"I know."

"No getting hurt."

She's not a child, he reminds himself, but maybe it doesn't make a difference, really. You never know what kind of effect you're having on people. What kind of ideas they might have about you. So often he feels people just want to please him, like he has a hold over them he never asked for.

"Can you just tell me before we do this . . . If there's anything I should know. I mean, anyone else." She looks embarrassed and adds, "So that I can kill them, I mean."

Oh Viola. He shuts his eyes. It's crushing, the thought of her reading them, all those tatty articles calling him a womanizer, speculating on the thinnest gossip. Is she willing to think that? To fear him?

Or does she just know what it's like to be abandoned?

"I swear," he says. "It's only you."

She reaches her hand to his face, his lip, and moves to him saying, "Good," and slowly allows him to trace his finger over the patch of vitiligo on her rib cage, charting the perfect map of her skin.

1991

Susan is giving her body to other people. Happily, generously, despite the depletion. She offers herself to an unending cycle of tiny mouths, to the fingers that want to grab her hair and pull *hard,* to the cries in the night. All of it is worth it for her daughter's shy smile, her son's loose, infectious laugh. To see them touching each other's faces, babbling back and forth with great seriousness, known and unknown to her. Theirs is a world that demands her completely, that makes her feel not like a new character, but like she is borderless. She is simply matter and limbs and voice that exists in service to them. They move so quickly between need and satisfaction, terror and wonder. It hardly leaves time to think about what she has lost.

But she allows herself this: for a half-hour every day, she watches her show. She gives over to a world that does not involve her children, nostalgia and cold comfort. In her exhaustion, the grandiose stories sweep her away. Scenes she never saw shock and delight her; moments that felt frantic and disjointed while filming appear smooth and satisfying. The six-month delay between filming and airing allows her to observe herself like never before. The woman on the screen is uncanny. Margie is another person, drifting in and out of her consciousness. Lines are remembered entirely, or half-remembered, or completely forgotten. Her son breastfeeds as she watches herself throw back a martini. As Margie covers up a bruise under her eye, her daughter claws at her face. Did she film these scenes, or was it someone else, a not-mother that she used to be? After a while, she began to enjoy the collapse of it all – the before and after; the fervid, fearless Margie and soft, aching Susan; Orson and Ali and Richard and Glen and Nancy; her babbling, beautiful babies and this house and California – all of it coexisting for thirty blessed minutes. It feels like coming home to herself.

Then one day Margie is gone. No one in Cedardale can find her; it is rumored that she fled to Argentina with cash and secrets. That she may have been murdered. *Is that the best you could do?* she thinks bitterly toward Flowers. Eventually, people stop mentioning her. The town, vacant of herself, becomes strange, as mysterious to Susan as to any other fan. It is like witnessing a world in which she has died. The other characters' lives twist onwards.

She misses them every day.

Orson, more than all of them. How he improves with every episode! His timing funnier, his face more handsome, his scenes more moving. He can make her belly-laugh even when her body is drained from lifting and feeding and burping and swaying. *He's going to be famous,* she thinks, and the thought makes her feel small and sad, because she won't be with him when it happens. *I should give him a call.*

"Come back," Orson says. His voice is surreal comfort. "No one has forgotten you."

Her children are both sleeping, hands touching each other, nine months old.

How?

They need her milk, her arms, her voice singing and playing, her face making faces they can mirror, her pushing them in the fresh afternoon air, her mantra to them: *You can be anyone you want to be.* But doesn't it ring hollow against the new narrowness of her world? Isn't it her duty to show them; to astonish them with her own powers of transformation, to demonstrate that it is possible to do all things, be all things?

"What about Flowers?"

"I'll talk to him."

In Orson's voice is a new authority, a certainty of his position. He has become indispensable.

She knows from the flutter in her chest, the familiar intoxicating hope, that if the call comes, she is in great danger of saying yes.

"I can't bring them."

"Why not?"

Why not? She looks at the soft, folded faces of her children.

"Come on, Susie. Resurrection is always possible."

2011

"You think the world is going to end when you lose your sister, but the truth is, it doesn't."

Sebastian watches Aunt Sadie bite into a free burger – her post-shift perk. On a Wednesday night, Sully's American Bar and Grille is a dead zone. The televisions blaring out Red Sox games are hung so high up that the five remaining customers have to crane their heads back in order to gape at the leaps and dives of their familiar saints: Jacoby, Beltre, Big Papi. Their faith is unwavering.

"Jesus, Sadie, she's not dead," he says. Though it kind of feels like she is.

It's hard to believe Lola is still gone. Even after he moved out and they more or less stopped speaking to each other, he always sensed her proximity. At least he could imagine where she was or what she was doing at any given time. Now he has no map of her terrain. Online she is tagged in photographs with so many strangers, and it overwhelms him, her belonging to these fairy-tale people.

He looks again at the message on his phone, written in a manner that he might have mistaken for stream-of-consciousness if he had not known Lola, who hasn't texted him about anything in six months, who analyses everything to the point of death.

Lola
Yo yo
Hope everything is good with you !
I have a favour to ask . . .

Would you mind (pretty please)
going to my room and sending me
. . . my driver's license

He had almost laughed at the labor of it. The U in favor (as if to emphasize that she has become English-and-therefore-superior), the parentheses, even the space before the exclamation point, as though it were an afterthought rather than an immaculate calculation. She would have stared at this for hours. Still, it feels nice to be the one who is needed. Always it used to be him: asking Lola to help with his homework or forge their father's signature. Asking Lola to trust him with anything. *Why on earth does she want her license? She hates driving.*

A few months ago, she texted about Orson Grey. He thought it might lead to something else, but it was nothing. *Is it worth it, even pretending we can be friends?* Still, the silence is its own kind of exhaustion. Maybe she wants an excuse to talk to me, he thinks. Maybe she feels bad.

Sebastian
Yo yo
Looking to mow some people down
on the wrong side of the road?

He returns to his father's house every few months, slipping inside and grabbing a thing or two. Gathering information. Tillie is there all the time now. On one visit, the power went out. He'd had to text Viola then – the idea of being alone in the dark with the she-devil filled him with no small anxiety. He avoids mealtimes and any of his father's attempts to engage. Recently, Al asked: *Want to go fishing next weekend?* They hadn't gone fishing since he was a kid. He claimed he was busy. Come on – the trip was a trap, an excuse to wheedle information out of him, to press judgment upon him. He only felt a bit guilty.

Lola
I ACTUALLY need it for ID thanks
Shouldn't you want to invest in me
becoming a degenerate ;)

The reply is rapid, her relief almost palpable. The thought of Lola drinking, misbehaving, fills him with hope and melancholy. *He is missing out on her life.*

"Why don't you sneak me a beer, Sadie?"

"You're nuts, kid, I'm not losing my job. I'll pay for your burger though."

He hesitates for a moment, because it's a fair offer, because he's saving up for a new car, taking on extra shifts at CVS, because he knows she likes his company while she's working. But he checks himself. He flips his card onto the table.

"No chance."

She picks it up and waggles it. "You better not ditch me as soon as you've got your new wheels."

"I'd never ditch you. I'll just stop asking you to tow me around everywhere."

To: Dad
i have to come by later
dont wait up

"Do you mind stopping by Dad's on the way back?"

She raises an eyebrow. "Really?"

"Sorry," he says. It's out of the way.

"The things I do for you," she moans. She's teasing, mostly. She's been driving him around quite happily for two years now. "How does he seem, your dad?"

"The same."

"Still with that woman?"

"Tillie? Yeah."

"That's a shame."

"You'd say that either way."

She tries to repress a grin, but can't help herself. Sadie collects misery the way some people collect stamps. They trade in bad news – as long as it isn't theirs. "I wish your dad the best," she says.

"And I wish for nuclear winter."

Sadie sips her beer, looks contemplative. "You know, I had a friend of mine whose dog died a couple years ago."

"Sorry to hear it."

Sadie shrugs. "Doesn't matter to me, wasn't my dog. But she really loved that animal, a big Newfoundland, loved it more than anyone else in her family. Tied at the hip. It was like losing a limb, she said. A couple years later, she got the tiniest white dog, so delicate you could break it with your shoe."

"What are you saying?"

"Not much. Just that it's hard to repeat things in life, you know?"

His mother would have hated Tillie. No one but Sebastian seems to care about this fact. And Sadie, he supposes. When it comes to his mother, she is his most reliable source, even if she is prone to exaggeration.

A manager sticks his head out of the kitchen and says Sadie's name in a slow, even tone. She turns, nods, reaches out to gather up glasses and dirty plates. It is odd not being able to help. At Sadie's house, he is always helping. Lola always did all that stuff at their dad's house: putting things away, vacuuming. Now the bar shape-shifts into a set of things to be done. He can see it more easily, perhaps, because for Sadie the effort is heavy.

Dad
Sure. Drive Safe.

Last week a program came up on TV about a man who discovered that he had a hundred and fifty siblings. His father was a sperm donor.

They all met up and touched each other's faces and commented on each other's earlobes, hand gestures. Then the producers brought the father in and some of them cried and then the father cried, and the camera was right up in his face, capturing his wrinkles and regret. He had the same earlobes as well.

When she emerges, he says: "Hey Sadie, I was wondering. Did you ever visit my mom in California?"

"No. She was always so busy." The note of resentment is almost too light to detect. Quickly she follows with, "I wish I had."

It's important, isn't it? Knowing where you come from? You have to be able to explain yourself. You have to have the facts. Even if they aren't always what you hope for.

"Do you think she – you know. Do you think there was ever anyone else?"

Sadie's face clouds over. She blinks three times. She does not look at her nephew. There is a wobbling inside him. Sometimes he forgets that she was actually there. That they are not both engaging with limitless hypotheticals, the same amount of blank space.

"You really think she wouldn't have told me?"

At his father's house, Sadie's car shuddering outside, Sebastian closes the door quietly. He assesses the scene. Awake or asleep? Upstairs or downstairs? Despite his estrangement, he misses the house. The people who aren't in it now.

He isn't expecting to find Tillie alone in the kitchen.

The Martha Stewart monstrosity is tucked in the corner of the countertop, pale pink manicured fingers holding a copy of a book that Lola had been reading a few summers ago when she was still obsessed with the concept of France. The cover has a woman's face on it with painted lips and eyes full of a desire that he can't imagine Tillie could ever comprehend. Sebastian is startled at first by the sadness of the scene, Tillie's attempt to connect with a person so far beyond her. But then he realizes he is dealing with a rival scavenger.

"I said he didn't have to wait up."

"He's not waiting up. I'm not either. Just wasn't tired."

Sebastian scuffs the wooden floor beams. "I just need some things."

Tillie turns, puts the kettle on as if everything is normal, as if she is supposed to be here, in his kitchen, at midnight. "That's fine. Tea?"

Something inside him is bubbling, unresolved. "I'm not staying."

"No one is making you stay. How was your day?"

"Fine."

He can't help but notice, on the small kitchen table, a stack of catalogues that he hasn't seen before in the house; glossy prints of nuclear families clad in plaid and laughing as dumb puppies jump around their folded knees. They are all sitting that way, even the fathers, which cannot possibly be comfortable. Criss-cross applesauce. He imagines cutting out all the Stepford Wife faces from the pages for his latest project.

"You can take those if you want," Tillie offers. "I brought them over, but I don't need them."

It is astonishing how pale and thin her lips are when she isn't wearing any lipstick. He isn't used to seeing her like this, incomplete, or at least not for public consumption.

"No thanks," he says. He can't figure out how, but it's a trap. Tillie shrugs. She doesn't look hurt by it. She pours the hot water into an old pink mug with a faded flower pattern on it that his mother used to use.

In an episode of *Life and Times* last week, they cast a woman to play his mother's character in a flashback. She looked like her, or at least, they had done her hair in the same way. It was awful. Sadie had to turn it off.

"If you change your mind about staying," Tillie says, "your bed is made up."

He doesn't answer. His phone buzzes against his leg. He slinks back into the hallway, and around the corner to Lola's room.

Lola
You should be asleep

Perhaps she's right. It's late, it's already tomorrow where she is. She sends a few photographs from England: ancient courtyards, long lavish tables.

Sebastian
I'm raiding your room

How did she decide what to take and what to leave behind? Here are some of his t-shirts that she used to sleep in, the good nail clippers. A small, lacquered jewelry box full of baby teeth. He senses disturbance, Tillie's meddling. A photo of Lola smiling at the pond by their grandmother's house, the two of them, sitting in the open trunk of his car: he is looking at her and she is looking at the camera – or rather, their father standing behind it.

Maybe he has been too stubborn. Maybe truth is less important than keeping the peace. Were they ever as happy as this? Or did happiness just always look like fighting? He tucks the frame into his bag.

Lola
Criminal
Did I leave my chapstick next to the bed

Sebastian
Don't they have chapstick in England

Lola
It's Carmex
Heavy duty
The good shit

He finds it, pockets it.

Sebastian
Mine now

He has to move if he wants to salvage things. You never know what his father might get rid of, what Tillie might get her hands on. In her bedside table, right where she said, is the license. Tick. Underneath it is a folder marked SCIENCE. Odd, he thinks. An odd place for science. Inside, a parcel of photographs.

Their mother naked. Her familiar, unfamiliar body, its smell and sound, her laugh, her everything.

Holy shit.

A complicated feeling: she was beautiful.

A more complicated feeling: Lola hid these. And all this time, she acted like he was insane.

He doesn't owe her shit.

Sebastian
Couldn't find it, sorry

When he gets back to Sadie's, he lights a joint and spreads the photos of the two of them and his mother's nudes and Lola's license out across the floor. Then, the scissors seem to be cutting on their own. On black cardboard, he pastes what is left. *This is what it feels like to be the one who stays*, he thinks. From the floor, his mother squints up at him, freed at last from her paper prison. She opens her mouth wide and laughs, unbearably loud, unbearably gone.

1991

"You told him what?"

Susan's husband looks perplexed. Since his promotion to Associate Professor, he's been roped into more department meetings, fewer late-night feeds. And now he is sitting on the edge of the bathtub, the sleeves of his shirt rolled up over his elbows, absently cruising a small plastic motorboat around Sebastian.

"I told Mark I want to go back to the show."

Orson was true to his word. The call had come, begrudgingly, from Flowers, saying he was open to discussing it. He was a practical man, and the ratings had dipped since Susie's hiatus. She knew, the moment he rang, she wanted it.

"But . . . You seem so happy—"

"I am happy," she says. Her hands are massaging suds into Viola's head, molding the nap of her hair into a mohawk. How can she explain? Happiness has washed diffusely over these last nine months. But now it is concentrating into intent. "It's just, I'm ready to get back to my life, you know? And this is the chance."

She lifts Viola up and swaddles her into a towel and rubs her tummy and pats between her legs and under her armpits. She presses her cheek into her daughter's cheek. Al is allowing Sebastian to claw at his finger, to hit the water with the flat of his palm so that it flies up onto his shirt.

"Well, how would that work?"

"I could bring them with me."

"And what about me?"

He sounds stung, like she's reduced him to an afterthought. Which might have been true when her heart jumped into her throat at the sound of Mark Flowers' voice. But all afternoon, she has been thinking of little more than how to present this to him. How to make it a shared adventure, an opportunity to unify their world.

"Well. I was hoping . . . You could come too."

The last time they discussed this, it seemed impossible. Academia appeared to her an endless succession of hurdles. But now she can see that it need not be so. *It is only his fear of the unknown that is stopping him*, she tells herself, resolving to be gentle and positive.

"You're suggesting I quit?"

"You could get a transfer."

"You think it's that simple?"

"I never thought it would be simple, I only thought . . ."

As Al lifts Sebastian out of the tub, their son starts to wail and piss into the water. Not all men are good with babies, but Al never complains. He changes their diapers and wipes their noses and spends Sunday afternoons putting together car seats. And now he is swaddling and applying baby powder and clapping his son onto his shoulder. They carry the children into the bedroom with its soft orange lamp, diaper them, place them together in the crib. She reads them a story about some meddlesome kittens and Al leans against the wall listening. *This is the best part of my day*, he told her recently, and she feels almost apologetic that she has taken something from him in this moment, a sense of total peace.

Gradually, the twins settle and curl toward each other, and he follows her quietly into the hall.

"In this plan of yours," he says, "who would take care of them all day?"

"We could bring a nanny. Sadie will do it."

"With all due respect, I wouldn't trust your sister with a pet rock."

Heat rises to her face. She follows him step by step down the stairs and does not say that Sadie has been beyond helpful recently. Susan has always loved this man for his simple offerings, for things he gave freely because they were easy to give. But now that she needs something difficult, he has hardened himself. Perhaps she has dashed some hope she didn't realize he was holding: that she had reached a point of completion. That she would never want for anything else.

They move to the kitchen, where he makes a cup of tea. In the bright light, his profile is smooth, plump with the hours of sleep, all the nourishment his mind is getting from his young, brilliant students, who are also sleeping for eight to ten hours, who are capable of adult conversation. With sudden fervor, she resents him. When did her desires, which have always felt so simple – to work! to live! – become selfish?

"Okay then," she says. "Why don't we just leave them with you? You can breastfeed them, right?"

"Susie."

"Or here's another idea, why don't we each take one? It will be like a science experiment."

"Susie."

"Or we could each take *half of each*. Very biblical."

"Christ's sake, Susie, don't be hysterical."

"The only question is *which half.*"

He clears his throat in a way that she hates, a deep hacking sound. How can anyone clear their throat at a time like this? It is as though he can't understand the stakes of the conversation; she is talking about her life.

"Look at me," she commands.

She can feel his mind at work, trying to find some logic, some solution that will bend things to his favor.

"I can see you're bored," he says. "I understand that." He puts a hand on her back and leads her to the living room. She can't be too loud in here. The children are overhead. He sits on the couch and asks: "I just want to know where this is coming from."

She sits at the far end, resisting the tranquilizer of his voice. "I don't want our children to look at me and think I'm a nobody."

195

"How could they possibly think that, Susie?"

"Because I gave up everything for them. For us."

In spite of herself, the anger is leaking away. He opens his arms and calls for her to crawl into him, and she caves to the ease of it. For a minute she lies with her head on his chest, opening to his rise and fall, diffusing in the old familiar ways.

He will never leave her.

"Look. I know you *think* the only thing you will ever love is acting. I know it's wonderful for you. But you know – and I know – this job could be snatched away at any moment. And then whose salary do we need to rely on? I don't want the kids growing up feeling lost or unsafe. Feeling like they don't know where home is."

She sits back away from him, covers her face with her hand. *Oh God*, she thinks. *He is going to make me choose.* Here with them or there, alone. She hates him, she hates his logic, she hates his concern for the children, hates that her desires are extraneous to the world that he is continuing to depict as the only world—

"Suze, I've been making some big sacrifices to get ahead. Frankly, people respect me now in the department. I can't just throw that away. And nowhere, nowhere is going to pay me better. So, please. Please. For me. I just know if you put your mind to it, there will be all kinds of things you can do around here. You just have to be open to them."

He is reaching for her hand and tucking her hair behind her ear, and she feels the force of his belief in this world where she can be happy and small. She's so tired, and her arms are so sore from carrying the twins.

Stand up for yourself, Margie says. *Fight.*

She lifts her face.

"Al, I have been open. I have been so open that sometimes, I stop feeling myself entirely. But I am telling you this is what I want. And whether you like it or not, I'm going."

Her husband pulls back, speechless. Their house, their accoutrements scattered over the floor, their children murmuring static through the monitor. And yet somehow, she is insisting on herself as a separate being.

Al stands up. His face is caving into childish frustration. It is awful to stop herself from comforting him, to hold herself hard and apart while he becomes fourteen again and unable to stop a woman from leaving his house. Here is the boy who awoke to find himself sisterless, denied the power to bargain, stripped of any choice. *He is not a child, though,* she reminds herself. *He is only choosing to be hurt. He could choose me instead.*

"Do what you want, Susie," he says. "But don't pretend it's for the kids."

In the end, he will see he is wrong. For them, for herself, she will not give up on her life.

2012

On a hot June morning, Al boards a flight to see his daughter.

In the three years of her degree, she never suggested he visit. Always, Al had interpreted this as characteristically kind; in the years since Susan died, his fear of flying had developed physical symptoms. On an unfortunate family trip to Yellowstone, he'd retched so violently on the plane that they'd returned over three miserable days in an aging rental car. It was easy to believe the shroud over Viola's English life was a by-product of her thoughtfulness, her self-sufficiency. Though the distance was at times painful, he could understand her desire to pursue something authentic. Wasn't their New England just a facsimile of this truer, older one? Here she might find originals of all the towns that surrounded their own; primary sources and ideas that had bastardized into Americana. But when she failed to come home for Christmas, he began to worry.

If this was the beginning of a disappearing act, she was carrying it out in a typically Viola-esque way. No drama, no grand pronouncements. Only quiet, competent intent. Perhaps she was not running toward something, but away from it. Perhaps the something was him.

Don't catastrophize, Tillie said. *Kids make decisions that have nothing to do with you.*

But how could it not be about him? Given space to reflect on his shortcomings, Viola might find a thousand reasons to desert him. He had failed to hold the family together. All his efforts to shield them from the world had only resulted in its implosion. And the wreckage revealed his repeated lies, his parental deficiencies. By now she must

198

have seen through all the falsehoods and fake presents, through his stuffed and insufficient Susan.

It would be nice to have someone else to blame. But it was hard to see beyond the common factor; Al had been left behind too many times to blame anyone but himself. His only defense is that he lacked the language, the sophistication, to talk about Susan in the way she deserved. And for a long time, he was still angry.

Go see her, Tillie said. *You're not doomed to repeat things in life.*

So, on their monthly video call, he said:

I'm coming for your graduation.

Really? Are you sure?

The gratitude in her voice cracked him open. Another future appeared suddenly possible; Viola would come home and the world would be unified – his daughter sitting on the sofa reading and Tillie doing her Sudoku and Sebastian crashing about in the kitchen. He determined to do whatever it took to make it real.

"Dad!"

Here she is, waiting on the train platform under a close, uniform sky. Is she taller? Thinner? Something about her face – more make-up. It's colder here and he feels underdressed in his short sleeve polo. She gathers him off the platform, asking about his journey, new intonations transforming her questions. *How did he find the flight? Did he manage?* He wonders whether she is losing herself or finding herself.

Insistently, she carries his suitcase, which rattles and bumps down cobbled streets. His lodgings are separate from her lodgings. How far he has come to stay so far away from her, at an inn across town from her college that she insists is the best. He walks more slowly than her natural pace, not because he is tired, but because he would rather the seconds didn't pass so quickly.

"So, how does it feel?" he asks. "That it's all ending?"

"Odd. It feels like it ended a while ago and we're just lingering before something else begins," she says, adding with a smile, "not necessarily in a bad way."

She talks him through the schedule for tomorrow, the ceremony, a restaurant she has booked for lunch. They pass a group of her peers, and fondly she promises to catch up with them later. When they have gone, she tells him all of their names with great significance. He forgets them almost instantly. He cannot help it – his mind ascribes no importance to them. How fleeting were his own college friend-ships? In years to come, these rounded fleshy people with surnames and specific opinions and obscure tastes will become no more than archetypes in her mind, outlines of fortunes that may or may not arrive.

At a creaking backstreet pub, they order beer-battered fish. Al's appetite is warping with his sense of time, hours and days collapsing into years. He eats ravenously.

"How is Sebastian?" Viola asks.

"Good. I think. It's hard to say." He smiles at her and she raises an eyebrow knowingly. "He's been coming home a bit. It still feels like he's avoiding me."

"I see."

"You know, I think when you come home, it will really help him."

Viola's forehead twists into a knot. She chews slowly. "So," she says. "About that."

She tells him she has been accepted onto a master's program in London. That she has found some funding and it would be a shame not to take the opportunity.

"You sound unsure about it."

"No, it makes sense."

"Did you look at other programs? You know, if you came to Har-vard, we could get your tuition waived—"

"I'm also seeing someone."

Someone behind him opens the door and a gust of cold air moves a napkin across the table. A part of his brain is still reminding him to search for the London program when he's back in his room tonight, to check the ranking and the reviews of the professors, the safety of the campus area. And another part has stopped moving entirely, is fixated on the daughter who has become an unknowable woman.

"Is he a student?"

"No, he's older."

So this is the change he felt in her – love! An image forms of this older man, some English boy in his twenties, gone to the city for work. What would it take to steal her heart? He feels sick with the realization that Viola is as old as Susan was when they met. How little they knew about the world then, how useless were all other choices when they had found each other.

"Is it serious?"

She laughs a little bit and says: "It's not, you know, a terminal illness."

Viola holds his gaze. There is her determination, a stubbornness entirely different from his own, unafraid of lighting out in the dark. The familiarity crushes him. But he battles the instinct to argue, to drive her away as he drove Susie away, underestimating her desires.

"Am I going to meet him?"

She shakes her head. "He'd like to, but it won't work out. Next time."

The mysterious older man. A person already moving into his life, settling into a sense of what is required of him. Al never wanted Viola to be determined by someone else's dreams. But hadn't he been six years older than Susie? Hadn't he wanted to shape her?

"I hope he treats you well," he says.

"Oh, he does," she smiles. On her plate is most of her fish and a fistful of uneaten chips.

"You gonna finish that?"

"Can't. Stuffed."

The next day he watches her graduate, allowing the musical Latin to wash over him as a man confers magic upon her, transforms her from one thing into another. She emerges afterwards robed and beaming, and they take photographs together. The sun is shining, and as they walk through town, young people are pushing boats down the river and laughing, and the world is good but not his.

"Could you see yourself living here?" she asks. Her eyes are bright and sparkling.

No sense in putting her out. He smiles benignly. "Maybe," he says. "You certainly seem happy here."

She beams. "I really am."

He will give her the gift of her departure, even though he is breaking inside – it is his only hope. If he lets her go freely, then freely she may return.

The next day, he is gone.

1991

They would never understand: it was love of them that made Susan close the door. Love of them that sent her out into the snowy night, up above the thin black rip of the tarmac into tomorrow's California. The worst part was the thud of the lock, clicking into place with her on the wrong side. She was walking away from the wail of their great and immediate need for her.

The aircraft shudders against a cloud. Dawn breaks on another shore. By the time Susan disembarks, her back is aching, feet pressing against the sides of her shoes. No one told her about that, how her feet would never be the same size again. She slips into a pair of flip flops as she steps out into the cool city. It's a nice time of year, the concrete no longer holding heat. She stretches herself out, peers around.

Eventually she sees him, a man leaning against a tall pillar in a crisp black t-shirt, holding her name. His caterpillar eyebrows furrow as he searches, then release when he spots her, his gaze traveling over her unswollen stomach.

"There she is," Orson says and all of it floods over her, the memory of herself as a beautiful creature, wanted and good and desirable, the relief of coming home.

"God I've missed you," she says, and in an instant they both know that the words contain too much.

The brown, diamond-patterned carpet, the brown striped Travelodge duvet. *It's not so bad*, she tells herself. She told Al she was staying at the Hilton. She didn't want him thinking of her in a place like this.

He would think she couldn't take care of herself. She deposited the savings into an account at California Federal Bank under the name Susan Byrne. *Just in case*, she told herself. The secret filled her with a luscious guilt, as though she were playing a private game with him and surprised them both with an outlandish move.

It didn't need to mean anything, if she didn't want it to. If she really felt bad, she could always buy him a nice Christmas present.

Everyone's going out later, Orson told her. *If you're interested.*

Her mind is too full of her children. *Did they fall asleep easily or wake in fits and starts?* Little Viola is always having nightmares these days. They say it's normal for one-year-olds. Susan always lobbies for her to come and sleep between them, but Al is firm. She won't learn that way, he says.

Naked, she crawls into the sheets, like she used to after she and Al first moved in together. Naked had been a revelation of textures, the reassurance of his warm, freckled back expanding and contracting in the deep of the night. Always, it made her feel so free. But here the sheets are stiff and starchy and rub raw on her breasts. She is swollen with the need to express, but cannot bear the thought of her milk pouring down the drain. She left them as many bottles as she could, showed Al how to prepare the formula. Her brain counts the sets of clean clothes and packs of diapers. Is it enough?

Stop, she tells herself. *Nothing you can do now.*

Five minutes. Ten minutes. Even in the dark, Susan knows where the remote is, the distance from her outstretched arm to the base of the bedside lamp. Nothing but light from the television, blue-yellow images diffusing onto all of her pale skin. Bosnia again, cameras almost pornographically close to the faces of sobbing mothers, grim-faced fathers, amputees, broken, bloody families. The footage is running, shaking, blasted by the explosions that are rocking a city called Sarajevo, a city she had never heard of until a few months ago. Everyone speaks its name now with concern and a sense of inevitability. On the program, another mother is handing over her child to a man in a blue helmet who is going to carry it across the border. *It is the only thing I can do,* she is saying, and the woman is crying and Susan is crying, and the child is screaming, and then gone.

She could hear them babbling today, in the background, when she called to say she'd arrived.

"It's Mom on the phone," Al had said, muffled and distant. "Where's Grandma?"

"Grandma's still there?"

Susan hates the way his mother talks to them, as though they are wrong by default. As though it's her duty to introduce them, quickly, to the stiff propriety of adulthood. It's not right; wonder should be prolonged for as long as possible. *Be quiet,* Melinda tells them, *stop making a mess.* His mother cares little whether they can understand or comply. She is concerned with their behavior, the outer layers of them, not the people they are becoming. Not the miracle of their existence.

"Don't start," he said.

"I'm just saying—"

"I'm serious, Susan."

She knows that he is overwhelmed, that he is staring down a week of reasoning with the unreasonable. He lacks the intuitive strategies for keeping them occupied, for calming one while handling the other. He does not want her opinions on top of her absence.

"Where did you put the kitten book?"

"It should be in the usual place."

"What's the usual place?"

"The drawer, just under the lamp."

I've unsteadied him, she thought, listening to him rummage around the house. Everything between them was dislocated.

"I can't find it."

"Haven't you memorized it?"

"There once were three mischievous kittens. And they had fur coats. And they all decided to go the hell to bed, the end."

He was trying to land the joke, but both of them could hear his frustration and neither knew what to say. She had made him feel unwanted and there would be no fixing it other than the old contrition. It irritated her. *I don't even love him*, she thought, and the thought was so frightening that she shut it away in a box. If it was true, she didn't want it to be true.

When she turns off the television, the room regains its composition. The far window, the innards of her suitcase strewn across the spare bed, the sad wooden desk clutching tomorrow's script. A loneliness wells up inside her.

Exhale. Let yourself imagine it. The children, here, a small house in Montebello, orange trees in the back garden. Bath time and bedtime every night, their slippery bodies, contagious giggles, the sleepy weight of them. A man.

When she reaches out for the phone, a soft, familiar voice answers. "Are you awake?" she asks. "Can we go for a drive?"

2012

Orson is driving far on the arm of the Cape, past the shingled settlements that cluster around penny candy shops, the sunny habitat of an endangered species.

He's hardly touched this coast since that night, Susie's funeral. Mostly he remembers a great distance between himself and everyone else. He remembers thinking about leaving America entirely, going home and working on an oil rig or God knows what, anything not to be around those people, their unbearable conversations about the next series, the next big thing. But then came this serious little version of Susie like a sign, telling him to get on with it. And here she is now, sitting next to him, bare feet up on the dashboard, eyes hidden behind big sunglasses. He still can't get over it.

"So how does it feel?" he asks. "Being here."

She wrinkles her nose. "It's strange."

"Has it changed?"

"No. I don't know. Maybe just me."

I love you. When she said it the first time, it fucking terrified him. If the world found out, if they ruined her, he would never be able to forgive himself. The age gap, Susie, how many vile headlines have tormented his imagination? *Like Mother Like Daughter*, *He's got a Type!* How could it be worth it? Happily, they have burrowed into their private world. But it cannot last forever.

"Was the flight okay?" he asks.

"Dreamy. Thanks. Yours?"

"Well, there was this very cute girl two rows behind me."

"Did you get her number?"

"I was too shy."

Separate arrivals at the airport, separate seats. He paid, obviously, for the ticket, business class and all. But he was whisked away to the private lounge, didn't see her till touchdown. She suggested that the secrecy of it all might be sexy, but it just made him feel like an ass. This summer she has hardly left his bed.

"Poor Niamh. Is she going to mourn your absence this week?"

"She already complains I'm never there."

He purses his lips. "I do want to meet her. And see your girly little flat."

"There is nothing to see. When you're gone, I live in squalor."

And when he's not? Her life has attached to his. Everything else – the projects and paychecks and gossip and bullshit – disappears when he closes the door behind the familiar sound of her laugh, the strength of her embrace. It was jarring, to realize how lonely he had been before, consumed with the project of himself. So many relationships had only ever felt incidental, part of the endless pursuit of the next thing. So many exes craved the publicity, in a way that alienated real feeling. He'd begun to think it was just his nature, that isolation. But God, how good it feels to throw himself into caring for something – someone else.

Please God, let it last, he thinks.

On the radio, a program is playing about the upcoming elections, the heightening rhetoric. "I swear, you people are going to have a civil war," he says.

"Good," Viola laughs. "I've always wanted to invest in a bunker."

"I think we'd thrive in a bunker."

"You wouldn't. No limelight in a bunker."

"I'm sure we could get some installed."

"I wouldn't put it past you."

"Shit—"

The traffic slows abruptly and the nose of his car almost kisses the ass of the truck in front of him. For a moment they are face-to-face with two bumper stickers: *Always Look on the Bright Side of Life!* and *Where's the Birth Certificate?*

"Some people are just stupid," she says.

"No," he says. "They're just experts in seeing what they want to see."

He can feel it simmering in this country, a willful ignorance. You can hear it in the laugh track, in everything the dream factory promises. There's always something darker on the other side of the curtain.

"Enough politics," she says. "Dinner. I'm thinking mussels. White wine. Garlic. Butter."

"Talk dirty to me."

Viola twists the radio to a familiar channel, hums mindlessly to a song he doesn't know. How easy she seems here! How . . . herself! At times he worries whether in the momentum of the two of them, she is alienating herself from her own desires. Constantly, she anticipates his arrivals, his moods, will cancel plans without a thought if he suggests she come around. *She's so young*, he reminds himself, drums his fingers on the steering wheel. Maybe it's okay. Or maybe he's making it worse. The master's thing, for example – it's only a bid to extend their time together, just another thing to achieve. It doesn't animate her. By hiding herself away with him, is she leaving herself unresolved?

It's why he chose this place: a refuge only a few hours from her childhood home. Here, she can have the upper hand. Show him, maybe, what and who she loves. He feels compelled to give her everything Susie would have wanted her to have. Confidence. Beauty. Love. Hasn't she given him these things? It feels like carrying through with something.

"Do you want to see anybody while we're here?"

"Not particularly," she says. "Thank you."

The way Susie used to talk about Al, Orson always imagined him as tough: stubborn and old-fashioned, set in his ways. But at the funeral, he'd been surprised by how disoriented he seemed, a man without a mooring. He must have pulled it together, done all right to produce somebody like Viola. She speaks about him fondly, and it makes him feel guilty for taking her away from him. For encouraging Susan to do the same.

"Well, let me know if you change your mind."

"I don't need to turn our sexy getaway into a family reunion, do you?"

She reaches a hand across to his thigh, recalling the completeness of the two of them, and in a world where everybody wants something from him, God it's good to know she requires nothing but himself. When they get to the house, the first thing they will need to test is the bed.

Tucked deep into Wellfleet pine forest the refuge reveals itself: svelte, modernist. Its long windows expose Cape Cod in the way that it was intended to be exposed – rustic and wild. Were it not so hidden, you would inevitably peer inside and wonder: *Who lives there?* In the open-plan heart, there is nowhere to hide. As Orson peels off her dress and kisses the tender skin of her stomach and clutches at her hair in needy fistfuls, she never loses awareness of this exposure. The potential to be seen. When he stands to unbutton his jeans, she pulls down the wide, translucent window shade.

They have been so careful. She will be careful her whole life if that's what it takes. Now that she has something to lose, she has become consumed by the fear of losing it. How many ways the world might snatch him away from her! Distortion or demonization or death. The only purpose she feels is this: being with him, loving him. She is lost in it.

After, she sends a photograph of the living room to Niamh, who responds instantly.

Niamh
Fuck off

Slowly, she is coming to understand Orson's wealth, or at least the implications of it. It moves with subtlety, fluidity. It has no interest in putting its name on buildings. Rather, it is a vehicle of freedom. If her father painted wealth as a pattern of behavior (summers in the Vineyard, winters in Maine), for Orson it is limitless horizons. Innumerable are his sun-drenched islands, his private white sand beaches.

We're going to your neck of the woods, he said. *Show me your natural habitat.*

He has been itchy recently, she can tell. He keeps talking about wanting a break from performing, the endlessness of it, threatening to start a charity or buy a pub. She can feel him casting for something solid, a new project to throw himself into, something tangible and real. She knows he is hoping it is her.

Well, what do you want to see? she'd asked.

Niamh responds with a photograph of a giant wart on the bottom of a foot, which apparently belongs to her new on-again off-again boyfriend, a Swedish DJ named Matthias. *Thank God for Niamh.* Some people are getting so serious these days.

In the bathroom now, she pauses to examine her dead ends, runs a mascara brush over her lashes. On the back porch, Orson is singing to himself in the sweet, tuneful way he does when he thinks no one is listening. She steps out, barefoot, and he cracks open the bottle of airport Talisker, peers out onto the forest of locust-trees and kettle ponds. There is a perfection in nature, in life that doesn't need to question itself; the abundance its own justification. Cicadas cry impenetrably loud. She had forgotten that sound, nature like the roar of a jet.

"So," he says. "I have a surprise for you."

"You do?"

He nods, pushes up his sunglasses onto his forehead, his eyes dancing. "Go look in the closet in the living room."

"Is it a dead body?"

"Yep."

She smiles, moving nervously across the threshold. What could be in a closet? *A dress? A person? My brother?*

A cello. Beautiful curves, long, golden-brown neck, a waist that calls out to be held. The bow resting beside it.

"Oh my God."

"You're always saying you miss it. I thought it could be fun."

"I—"

She carries it forward into the living room, the familiar weight, the comfort of it between her legs. Presses her fingers over the strings, feeling for their tension.

"Do you like it?"

"It's . . . wow"

"Play me a tune."

"I don't know if I can."

Always, she has talked about her cello playing as a magical thing, a secret skill, her mode of artistic expression. Clumsily, she fits her fingers into G major, runs the bow over a slow arpeggio. She is aware of her desire to impress him, of his eyes and expectations.

"It's been a while."

"That's okay," he says.

Come on, remember, any song. The Bach: is it G? Then B or B minor? She fingers a few chords, isolated from each other, amounting to nothing. *When did this become a phantom register, a forgotten language?* Her loss would be agitating enough if he weren't witnessing it. He's going to think she has misrepresented herself, that he has gone to all this trouble only for her to disappoint him.

"I need music," she says.

"I can get something on my phone—"

"No, that won't—"

Her voice is sharp and unpleasant, childish. When she touches the bow to the strings, it squeaks. Her fingers form a chord, but the sound is harsh and wrong, and she begins to mutter to herself as she tries to tune it, humming pitches that she's not even sure are right. He sits patiently while she finds an app with sheet music, but it's making her nervous, his wanting something she's not sure she can give.

"I mean there's one I used to be able to play, I can't even remember what it's called, but . . ."

She begins, slowly calling forth a series of low notes, feeling the unpleasant softness of her finger pads, the loss of her strong calluses.

"The bridge is really high," she says.

"It sounds great."

A few more notes and then it is gone, the melody, the next note just gone. She is a vacuum.

"I don't know, I can't remember. It's just not there, I can't do it."

He looks at her, sad. She can see it in his face: he is less disappointed by her inability to play than by the way she is shutting down in front of him, erecting a barrier. She hates her own rising emotion at the fact that she has changed, that she has estranged herself from something she loved.

"Look, I was just trying to find something . . . Nice for you."

"I'll find something to play tomorrow," she says, tucking it back into the closet, knowing that she will not repeat the attempt. *I am a competent person*, she tells herself, banishing the clumsy, failing feeling, so alien to her image of herself. She never wants him to see her like that again.

Coffee, black and strong, a day yet to come. Orson in the kitchen, behind a stack of scripts, projects to consider.

"I thought we could go to the beach," she says. "Take some of your homework if you want."

"Or I could not," he says, and leans back and looks at her, probably trying to gauge whether she is the erratic child from yesterday or her sane and stable self. She wants to make up for it. To take charge. To demonstrate that she is a source of solutions, not problems, that she will never give him any reason to leave her.

"There's a sand bar near here. We used to go, sometimes with my

213

grandma, in the summer." When he smiles, satisfied by this, she kisses him, and packs a beach chair and a book, allows him to laugh at her and tell her that Hegel is not a beach read. *Come on now, better get a move on.* It is low tide. Focus on the tawny hairs that grow on his knuckles, the song he is humming under his breath, beware the mollusks and razor clams waiting to slice into the flesh of your foot. Spread your towel and put on your wide-brim hat and talk to him like a pin-up girl.

"You're going to have to leave me in a few years, you know," he says. The water behind them is rising on all sides. His hat is smaller, straw, casts a shadow over half of his face. "When I'm fifty. I'll be an old man."

"Well, I'll be thirty," she says. "So we'll both be old."

"Don't take the piss. You can only avoid these things for so long."

"I don't think it's been so long yet," she says.

She's not taking the piss. The thought of her twenties sliding away from her fills her with dread, the sense of becoming her mother in the only way that counts. She wonders if Orson has ever considered the possibility. *Don't think about it, how doomed it all is, how the moment is arriving where you are going to have to choose your life.*

"I don't know. Maybe I should kiss and make up with Jesus."

"That's the last thing he would want."

"You think he'd turn the other cheek?"

"Something like that."

"Your mom and I used to go to church together."

"Really?"

He nodded. "She told me that when she was a girl, she used to make up fake confessions. Because she hadn't ever done anything that bad. But she was afraid of having nothing to say."

"God, that's horrible." Horrible she felt like she had to perform. But also, in a twisted way, sweet. It's strange thinking about her mother as *Susan*, a mortal woman, someone's friend.

The waves kiss her toes, and she inches her towel further up the sand. When Orson mentions her mother, there is never pressure for her to add anything, not explicitly. But after last night, the slippage, she wants to give him something. Her own gift, a piece of the woman he knew. *Come on, think.* She grapples in her mind with a half-fledged thing.

"You know, I thought I remembered something the other day."

The memory is a blur. Her mother is not herself (or perhaps some truer version of herself, waiting inside to come out). Red wine, sharp and specific. Viola is outside, her legs covered in hungry red rash, tear-taste and streaky face. She had been hiding. "There was a man there," she says. "I couldn't get her attention. My legs itched so hard I thought they would fall off." Yes, her mother was shouting, red-faced, something about a pair of shoes. She describes it to him: the nausea at receiving more anger than a small body could bear, her mother pulling her arm, hard, into the car – the memory contains the feeling of a sore socket. *Don't tell anyone,* she kept saying. *Don't tell anyone.*

It disturbs them both, the warp of it.

"Are you sure that happened?" he asks.

"Maybe not."

Maybe not. Maybe just a scene from a film. Maybe multiple memories collapsed in an uncontrolled explosion. *Stop trying*, she tells herself. *You can't force it.*

"Why do you think you're so afraid of her?"

"I'm not afraid of her . . ."

But isn't she? How is it possible for a person to be both devoted and devious, known and unfathomable? To both love and abandon her family? Around them the water is coming up fast. A tall wave licks at the bottom of his towel, claws steadily toward the dunes.

"Are we going to get stranded?" she asks. She is trying to sound casual. She is too old to be anxious about something like this, but her heart will not stop hammering in her chest.

"I've ordered a shark to come and pick us up," he says, smiling. "Shuber. Very popular around here."

"Ha ha." The rising tide is constricting her windpipe.

"Viola, the reason I'm asking is that, you know, if we are to go public, she's liable to come up."

It would be very embarrassing if she stopped breathing. More embarrassing than getting caught in a rip tide, or eaten by a shark, to die from just thinking about the numerous ways that she could die. Have you seen bodies that have been in water? Pale and puffed up like porpoises. She is having trouble breathing now, and Orson is asking her if she is okay, and there is barely enough room to shake her head no. Her neck is white hot, and breath thin and gasping, he is pulling her to his chest, not understanding that she is going to die because she can't breathe, because she is mortified that she can't breathe, because the tide is rising, and at the bottom is her mother's body, rotting away; she is wearing a dress made out of seaweed and her hair is made out of seaweed and her eyes are giant barnacles and she is reaching out her arms and dragging her down.

1994

Her sister's house, a Thursday afternoon, the radio, kids rolling around on her lawn. Viola, in a blue dress, curls sprouting out of her head. Sebastian in green hand-me-down overalls from a friend of Sadie's, a little stain on the back of the pants.

In the kitchen, Sadie is pouring a glass of red. "You joining?"

"Just a splash," Susan says, because she's driving, but Sadie knows she wants it desperately. The travel is hurting her. Being away from her children is hurting her. Being with them – in such short, smothering bursts – needing to let Al have his own time, trying to undo everything his mother has done during the week, it hurts her. Three years of their faces rising and falling as she passes back and forth through the door. They have stopped running to greet her. Viola, a creature of ritual, wants only Daddy at bedtime.

Has she left it too late?

She rifles through Sadie's refrigerator, tops up sippy cups with watered down orange juice. Sadie has agreed to film Susan today, an audition for a major feature that her agent put her up for. *They'd be stupid not to want you*, Orson said. The director was a big Academy type and the way everyone talked about him intimidated her. Like there were right and wrong methods. But she liked the role: a young mother in a psychological horror film whose baby is kidnapped by her deranged neighbor. If she got it, it would be intense. It would mean she couldn't come back for some time.

They sit on the back patio as Sebastian explains to his sister why his blocks have to stack on top of hers, frustrated that his logic is

217

unconvincing. *You're not listening*, he says, with an exhausted emphasis that sounds like his father. They've tried to shield the children from their arguments, but maybe their hearing is improving. Or maybe they've got louder.

"Shall we just get this out of the way?" Susan asks, collecting the camcorder from her bag. "Maybe we could run it a bit first."

Sadie rolls her eyes. "Don't people get paid to do this for you now?"

"Not really. Please, it will be fun!"

Sadie relents and reads back the lines in the gravelly voice of a man. It keeps making Susan laugh. Susan's character is harsh, a woman on the verge of a breakdown, and her raised voice is agitating the children. Sebastian is pulling Viola's hair and she is screaming, which ruins at least two takes. Again, now with a different kind of frustration in her voice, the character growing dimensions, mastering her drunkenness. Harness the anger, the sense of loss, all the conflict she feels when she looks at her husband's face.

Don't tell anyone, the most difficult line, difficult not to look down at Viola, who keeps returning (so intent now!) pulling at her fingertips, picking up the ashtray on the table and asking what it is.

"Don't even need this out," Sadie says, placing it out of reach. "Gave up smoking for Lent."

"Shit," Susan says. "Lent!"

"It only started today. You could give up . . . coffee."

"Or like, everything in my life."

Sadie raises her eyebrows. She adjusts the pair of cheap black sunglasses over her nose, waits her out.

"I'm missing their birthday," Susan admits. Her voice wobbles, and it's strangely embarrassing, asking for strength from her sister. Laying all of her optimistic bullshit at the altar of a woman who has always been a realist.

"What? How come?"

On Saturday, Susan will be filming a scene in the rain. A climactic scene on a beach. No studio tricks will do. She thought she had more

218

time, but this low-pressure zone has come up from the South Pacific more quickly than anyone expected. And now she has been required to book a flight for first thing tomorrow. "It's not really a choice."

"Are you going to cancel the party?"

"I don't know. It's just insane, isn't it? The whole situation?"

"What did Al say?"

"Haven't told him."

Sadie's mouth is a thin line. The worst part is that, with Sadie, she doesn't need to explain why. Sadie, unlike Al, gets why it's important. Why it has to come first.

Often now she wonders how they ended up together. Why they believed, with all the divergence of their desires, a life between them could make sense. What naive chemical possessed them, what impossible blindness? This morning, watching him step in to re-explain to the children how to tie their shoelaces, it occurred to her that all the things she loves about him are the things that frustrate her most deeply. His closeness to the children, his desire to simplify the world, his instincts to protect them all. The way they look at him fills her with jealousy as much as adoration.

"You're going to collapse if you keep this up, Susie. You're going to make yourself sick."

Between them hover the shades of so many events she has missed over the last four years: first words and first steps and first beach days. The shades of future empty seats at plays and sports matches and birthday dinners and road trips if she doesn't just *do it*, just make her move.

"Susie, he needs to understand."

Her daughter has gone into the bushes and sat in poison ivy and Sebastian is pointing at the rash and screaming. Susan reaches, scoops her up, while Sadie runs upstairs – "I'm sure I have Calamine . . ." Trust her sister to have hung on to this bottle for fifteen years. But the pink liquid retains some effect as Susan rubs it into the backs of Viola's pudgy legs.

"Is that a magic potion?" Viola asks.

"Yes."

"Does it taste good?"

"No."

"Are you a witch?"

Her daughter looks up at her with her own eyes. *Has he told her this? That her mother is a witch?*

"No." Susan is firm.

Viola looks perplexed, blinks, tries again: "Are you a witch?"

Susan's resistance is melting. *What is so wrong, if it is only a game?* "No," she says weakly, wiping off her hands on the bathroom towel. *I am innocent of a witch.*

Viola traces fat fingers through the un-rubbed lotion on her legs.

"Please, Mom."

"You got me," Susan says, cracking, cackling, losing herself in the sweet giggly folds of her daughter's neck.

2012

"Right," Orson says. "Not the beach then."

They couldn't go today even if they wanted to. Viola hardly remembers getting home yesterday, the small coast guard boat that picked them up, helped her breathe. One of their rescuers had taken a photo of Orson, and already *People* is circulating a story about the "Damsel in Distress".

Orson launches a stream of profanity that startles even the birds. "Weasels," he spits. "Fucking shameless."

The article speculates on her identity (local girl? summer romance?). In the photo she looks bedraggled and weak, and of course it was her body that did this, that ruined their perfect isolation. Tenderly, he had carried her back to the house, stuck her in bed, made her large mugs of herbal tea.

"Come on, I'm fine."

"You're not fine, you had a panic attack."

The article goes on to talk about Orson's fall feature, the alleged sparks between him and his co-star. It turns her stomach. She hates that love is his trade; that he can produce it so easily for anyone.

She scrolls. The Orson Grey fan club is trying to identify her, posting all of the ridiculous things they would do to get him to rescue them.

i would turn into a giant trout if he would
hold me like that
i would sell my voice to an octopus sea witch
full ophelia vibez

"Stop reading that," he snaps. They look at each other gravely. He is growing long, ugly sideburns for a period piece he will start filming at the end of the fall. It's uncanny; his face no longer quite the face she fell in love with. "Sorry," he says. "But Vi, we need to be ahead of this."

"What do you mean?"

"They're going to be on the lookout. If we don't control the story, they're going to control it for us."

"Well, what if we don't give them anything to see?"

His face falls and this is the wrong suggestion.

"Come on, let's do something nice," she says, sitting up, touching his chest. It was her fault, and now it's her responsibility to fix this, to reconjure the magic of the two of them, a world without judgment. But they cannot go for a walk down Main Street. They cannot go to the beach or the ice cream shop.

"We could play some cards," she suggests. "We could play some music."

Orson places his head against the wall. "This was supposed to be about getting to know your places," he says. "We could go up and talk to your family. If that's the thing."

"It's not the thing."

But it is. One of so many things.

"Look, I don't know your dad. But I know he can be difficult."

"No, you don't know him," she snaps. What is he trying to say? It's unfair enough that he knows her mother – he cannot claim her father too.

"What I'm trying to say is, I don't think it's good for you. For us. All this hiding. I mean, it's been wonderful, being a grinch with you. But you've got your whole life, Viola. I mean you hardly see your friends. You hardly even run anymore. I feel like – I don't know. I'm just worried."

Outside, a robin is singing. Love, she has discovered, is entirely unlike film. In film, love is beset with external obstacles: good-looking rivals, warring families, natural disasters. Real love manufactures its own obstacles: needs, strains, arguments lost and unspoken. Orson taps his foot against the floor.

"You know," he says, "when your mom was pregnant, she didn't want to tell anyone at the studio."

Viola sighs and gathers herself. Imagines her mother, hiding her. "God. Why?"

"She thought she'd get fired."

"Wow. It's a jungle out there."

"It was mad. But she loved her work."

"I mean, they were going to find out, obviously, eventually."

"Don't you think that sounds familiar?"

She has never welcomed the future. Too inevitable. Too full of endings. "Yeah," she admits softly.

Is she too familiar? Even now, Viola feels dizzy, like she is falling into her. Does he take pleasure in it, their similarity? *Stay vigilant, don't lose sight of yourself.* Bleach your hair. Keep your edges sharp. Don't be shaped by denial.

"Why don't we go for a bike ride?" she suggests, a concession. No one will recognize them on the move.

The cycle path is an abandoned railway line that weaves through the forest in the center of the peninsula. The day is glorious and sunny, bright enough almost to evaporate the day before. They pass roller skaters, lawnmowers, women on horseback, families towing small, unwilling children.

Even though both she and Orson are wearing all black (sticking out like sore metropolitan thumbs), she notices the patches of sweat that grow on his lower back and under his armpits. She has always found his sweat surprising. She remembers the revelation of seeing it for the first time, realizing that she hadn't considered him capable of sweat. He rides with his face up, nodding at everyone they pass, inviting interaction, charmed by small-town pleasantries.

"Good morning!" he says in his cheerful brogue.

Shut up, she thinks. Surely some of these people recognize him. As he passes she can see them turning off to whisper to each other – *wasn't that . . .? . . . I heard he was here!* But somehow, more nervous-making is the idea of her own recognition, which, here in this place, is far from impossible. Aldwych people summer here.

She keeps her distance, at first purposefully, but before long she is falling quite far behind, her legs paddling hard on the rental that is slightly too large for her, the pedals annoyingly sticky, unable to find a gear that feels like the right amount of work. It's the kind of activity that should be effortless but somehow has created a tide of irritation. The bike is designed to look good, not to ride. She sits all too upright, annoyed by everything sacrificed for the sake of the picturesque.

There, up ahead, he has stopped. Waiting for her? She pedals harder, wind catching her body like a sail. *Oh no.* A man, slowing, pointing, clapping a thick hand on his back. She imagines the inevitable conversation: *I loved you in . . . would you mind? just a quick photo? for my daughter, she –*

But as Viola pedals slowly closer, Orson grips the man's elbow like an old comrade. He is older, the man, with watery eyes and a pouchy stomach. Fervently they are speaking about Los Angeles, the neighborhoods they have homes in, projects and restaurants and anecdotes and people.

"... and the funniest part was she was at that place where everything on the menu is just an attitude – you know that one – and she had fucking ordered 'the fortunate one'!" The man is dying with laughter, waving his hand at Viola, sputtering, "Sorry – please – pardon my language."

"Oh God, I've been rude. Mark, this is Viola," Orson says, wiping tears away, opening his palm to her.

"Hello, Viola," says Mark, pouchy eyes wandering over her. "Do you live in LA as well?"

For Viola, California still only exists in sunny scenes with convertibles and palm trees and sweeping coastline. There is nothing real about it to her. Even the love there is two-dimensional, waiting to get blown over by a big wind. "London," she says.

"Ah, London-town!" Mark says, naming a few places he loves that she has to go to. She nods and smiles. He carries himself like a person who was once attractive and hasn't yet figured out that he isn't any more.

"She's Susie's daughter," Orson says, as though it is some kind of explanation. As though it was prompted naturally by some invisible subtext, some question of *Why are you with this child?* "Remember Susie Byrne?"

"Oh—"

(she is gaining control of herself)

"Oh, of course – Susie, my God, what a darling, such a shame, and you look just like her, how could I not see it. Have you two . . ."

(processing, processing)

"Have you two kept in touch?"

He just said it. He did, he just put the fact of it right out there. Not *Viola, my partner.* Viola, the child of this woman we used to know. She feels sick, like somehow it's all been a set-up.

"You could say that," Orson says, oblivious. "Come, shall we go have a drink at our house? It's this gorgeous modernist thing . . ."

They walk quickly back to Mark's car, tossing their bikes in the oversized trunk. They have never before been in a car with another person, but without much discussion, Orson sits in the front seat, and Viola takes the back. When Mark turns on the radio, she can hardly follow, and Viola has the strange feeling of being underneath the conversation, like a child.

After three large whiskeys, Mark is describing in detail the recent removal of a kidney stone.

"They wanted me to rate my pain on a scale of one to ten."

"Christ, what did you say?"

"Eleven."

They find this hilarious in the way that only old men could find this hilarious. Dinnertime has come and gone, replaced by trail mix and cheese. Viola sips slowly, trying to stay sharp.

"It's not childbirth. It's not losing a limb."

"Well, it's the most painful thing I've ever felt."

"Well then the exercise is dumb," says Orson. "Pain isn't objective. If the most pain you've ever felt is breaking a toenail, and I've been stabbed with an ice pick, you can't compare that on a scale of one to ten."

"That's what they asked me to do," Mark says.

"It's such an American thing," Orson protests, "all this crap about 'How much does it hurt?' You all just want to feel good all of the time, don't you?"

"What's so wrong with feeling good all of the time?" Viola smiles.

"Nothing, if you want to live in Disneyland," Orson says, unexpectedly flippant. He shoots her a look and somehow they are talking about the cello, even now throbbing in the closet. They are talking about her mother. Is that how he perceives her irritation, her denial – as a desire to feel good? Is that what it is?

Turning to Mark, Orson adds: "Viola is a philosopher."

"Not an actor?" he asks. His eyes give her a wet, unpleasant feeling. "That's a shame."

"Did you ever think about it?" Orson asks.

"No, I . . ." Hadn't she? Ever? "I don't think I really did."

"Well, call me if you change your mind."

Orson inches closer to her on the couch, as if to say, *You should never call this man.* His fingers brush hers. "My point was, I'm sure she can enlighten us on the nature of pain."

She can't, really. She's a logician at heart, it's not her thing. But Niamh would certainly have something to say. It's the kind of existentialist minefield she loves to wander around in, waiting to get blown up by the possibility of none of it mattering. But Orson is looking at her expectantly, as though she ought to give them a joke or a sparkling witticism.

226

"Well," Viola says. "Pain is as much in the mind as it is in the body. When you hurt yourself, the pain is in a very specific part of your body. It's caused by an objective physical condition. But the way you experience it is private and subjective. So, there's a conflict there. Is it real or is it perceived?"

Orson looks disappointed by her assessment. Maybe she was too clinical. He bites his top lip with his famously crooked bottom teeth, a face she has never seen him pull in a film. Not that she can watch his films anymore. It's unnerving now, the way his work distorts her sense of who he really is.

"Real or perceived. She's too clever for me, Mark. Not sure I understand the difference. But either way, kidney stones, best avoided?"

The drink is surfacing something provocative in him. It is strange that she cannot ask what he wants from her. That the presence of this other person – the first real person other than Jen – is preventing her from saying: *Are you angry with me?*

"Remember that whole storyline, Mark, with One-Eye Stokes and the phantom eye?"

"Oh God. What was it again? A fork?"

"Can opener. Still not sure about those mechanics. But Vi, basically, he kept experiencing this pain where his eye used to be even though he hadn't had it for years. Very symbolic, naturally. But I don't know, could be fun to rewatch that, the three of us? Surely we could find it online?"

"Not sure I'm up for TV," she says.

Orson looks disappointed and turns, decisively changing the subject. "Where's your little lady?" he asks Mark. "I thought you were seeing that writer."

"Yeah, oh yeah. Ha ha. Still trying to work out if she's marriage material."

The conversation bends away from her into meaningless names and references, dealings that she has no currency in. The men take little notice when she puts the kettle on, fills a mug of green tea and steps out through the sliding doors onto the raised wooden porch.

From the other side of the long glass panel, the room becomes a muted sit-com set, the two of them on the couch, oblivious to the audience and the laugh track. She adds voices in her head: *Well, you see, Orson, the thing about Glendale . . .* Any moment now the main character will walk in and the audience will erupt into applause. Her mother, probably. That's who everyone really wants to see.

Or maybe Susan would have felt outside it too. Stood here looking up at the glimmer of the moon, her mind elsewhere. After all, she never lived out there, not fully. How many hours of her short life did she spend flying back and forth?

Why?

It was strange, now that she thinks about it, what Orson said about her father. *I know he can be difficult.* Had her mother said that? Or was it just a feeling Orson had?

Had it really been Al, all that time, holding her back?

1994

Why won't you make this easy? Al's wife is brandishing the receiver like a weapon. The holding jingle for the travel agency tinkles over the line.

"Suze, please. They have to understand."

But the only thing the producers on Susan's show seem to understand is the desperate need to churn out seven and a half episodes a week. And when one of the episodes calls for a dark and stormy night, everyone is expected to turn their lives upside down. It's absurd.

"Listen, Al, here's the thing. The people you work with are dead, okay? They don't mind if you show up late or – hell – if you don't show up at all. But there are people who are counting on me. And if I can't make it, well, then they'll start asking if I really want to be doing this."

He knows – she's told him before – about the room full of look-a-likes. They populate her nightmares: an army of almost-Susans, differing only by a beauty mark, by the size of their nose. For someone who seems to operate on such a high degree of faith in the universe, it surprises him how often her subconscious concerns itself with being replaced.

She tucks the phone into the crook of her neck, starts popping her fingers out of their sockets in that horrible way.

"I'm sure if you just said that it's important . . ."

"Al, here is a list of what's important: funerals, gunshot wounds, sudden violent illness. Nothing else will cut it."

Upstairs, the children are sleeping. Downstairs all the supplies for their two separate, simultaneous birthdays (astronauts for Viola, jungle for Sebastian), the giant cardboard space-ship Susan has painted,

229

stacks of deflated palm fronds, paper plates and small costumes. On the refrigerator, the recipes for two separate cakes. *How is he supposed to make this all happen without her?* And she dares to look at him as though she's powerless.

"You know, some people understand how difficult this is for me," she says.

"Really? Who is that? Sadie? What are you trying to say?"

Somehow over three years, they have normalized the coming and going, the unpredictable departures, the unsustainable distance. Somehow, the show has kept running and she has kept flying and performing and creating a parallel existence. He tries not to think about her world over there, all her needs he cannot fill that are surely being met by other people. Other men, perhaps. He's seen her handsome co-stars, listened as she told him stories about their antics, never given them any permanence in his mind.

"Just that you are willfully ignoring what I want."

Now she returns with a brazenness, like an animal rewilding. The more estranged she makes him feel, the more he needs her. He is desperate for the consistency with which she used to love him, their small, specific universe. As the jingle begins for the twentieth exasperating time, he feels himself bargaining. *Just this once. If she can stay, just for this. If she can bake these cakes. If we can get through tomorrow. If I can just get her to see the cost.*

"Viola asked about your show last week," he said. "She must have seen it at Sadie's. She wants to watch it."

"And what did you say?"

"I said it wasn't appropriate."

He didn't expect her to start crying – bending onto the countertop, face in her hand, jagged, exhausted inhales. Gently, he moves closer. *She's too tired to go*, he thinks, and it's a good thought, *she won't*.

"I mean, would you agree? They're just so young, Susie . . ."

He traces his fingertips down her back. She shudders, recoils.

"No, you're right. You're always fucking right. They shouldn't watch it. But I just hate it, Al, I hate it, I hate it, I can't fucking stand it. She wanted to see me."

"Susie, please stay for tomorrow. Just tomorrow."

When she turns, her face is flushed and firm.

"No."

He feels the bright, perilous urge to shake her. Instead, his foot connects with the painted cardboard box, the rocket launching and crashing into the leg of the table.

The jingle is playing on the receiver now down on the counter and she is saying words that he doesn't quite understand: *Your life has always come first* and *I'm losing them,* and *I don't want to do this anymore.*

All around him is the mess of her. Her scripts and magazines and trashy books and the peel of an orange that she ate earlier that she didn't throw away and her shoes in a heap by the door. Somehow, this conversation has metastasized, an expanding desperation – *she's just trying it out, just seeing how it sounds. She's tipsy from Sadie's house. She'll regret it.* He needs this, all these messy reminders that he has created a family, that his wife continues to find something in him worth coming home to.

"You don't mean that."

"I do mean it," she says. "Just watch."

A voice comes on at the other end of the phone, and she turns away from him to make arrangements.

"Go," she says. "I'm not coming up."

For hours, he doesn't sleep. His senses are electrified. He worries about the children. He worries about how to bake two cakes when he has never even baked one. He worries about how to explain where she has gone. He worries about what his mother will say or not say. He worries about the upcoming tenure review, and whether he will say all the right things, whether the students will say all the right things. He worries he will never hear her singing again. That she will write him in her mind as the asshole who tried to constrain her. That she will mistake his love for the opposite. If she left, would he chase her? Would she still want him? Would it all become a horrible bundle of lawyers and accusations? Is he meant to make some gesture now, go downstairs and prostrate himself? God, as long as she doesn't go in the dead of the night.

Eventually, he hears Susan creaking around, and the sound calms him, knowing she is near. He must drift off, because when he opens his eyes the sun is up and Viola is jumping on his bed. Downstairs they discover two birthday cards, handmade on construction paper. *I love you more than anything,* she has written to them both, and he wishes it were true.

2012

When Viola slides open the porch door again, Orson slips off to the bathroom. Mark Flowers – evidently sloshed – looks at her now with frank concern.

"You're sweet together," he says, "the two of you."

"Well, that's kind," she says, though she knows it has not been true tonight.

"He was sweet with your mom."

Hot, heat, tongue fattening. Don't respond. Don't bring her into this.

"You had a brother, yes?"

Dissonant, the phantom Sebastian conjured into this room where he could never be. Sebastian is so close. She feels unsteady.

"That's right."

"How is he?"

"Oh. He's well, thank you," she mumbles. "He's an artist now."

"Any good?" Mark asks. *Is this a trap?* Why should she be the arbiter of goodness? A good person would have called him sooner, perhaps after he won the magazine award last year. Or the thousand times she thought of him, wondered what he was doing, whether he would find something funny. When she felt lonely.

"It's hard to be objective," she admits.

Mark sits up as straight as he can now, rests his elbows on his knees and his pudgy face in his hands.

"Orson ever tell you he was so sick after your mom died?"

"No."

"Fever for weeks. Meningitis."

233

"He never said."

When did she become so unsure about so many things? Who her mother was or wasn't, or what she did, or what it makes her.

Don't ask a question you don't want an answer to.

Mark slumps back into his seat, gazes out at the endless darkness through the window. "Orson really loved her, you know."

No. Mark Flowers is not the person she wants to hear this from. If the horrible twilight fact is to emerge, to destroy her world, it should come from Orson.

Fuck Mark Flowers.

Orson comes back in and places a hand on the small of her back. "Bedtime I think."

As Orson bundles Mark off, she spreads herself across the bed and closes her eyes. The click of the door. Heat, weight, a nose burrowing into her ribs, wet, forgiving lips.

"I hate that guy," Orson says.

"Well, you could have fooled me."

"We all had to fake it. We needed him."

The click of a bulb, pink eyelids turn black, crickets loud outside the window. Is she imagining his breathing, heavier, tortured by something he cannot say?

He really loved her.

"Hey," comes his voice. "So, I've been debating if I should tell you this."

Breath stiff in her throat. "Yeah?"

He sighs for a long moment. "What you said the other day. Or thought you remembered. I don't want you to think she didn't care about you. She would hate for you to think that."

"Please just say it."

"She was going to leave him. Your dad. She wanted to bring you with her. I don't know if that's something you knew already, but I thought you might not, so I thought I should say it."

"Oh."

"Sorry. If that's weird."

In the half-light of the moon sliding under the shade, she wonders at the human capacity for blindness, at her own weak will for the truth.

How could he possibly know that?

If. If he was trying to tell her that early night, with the photograph of her laughing in his apartment. Horrible, hideous, intrusive if, buzzing like a gnat. *If, then.* If Sebastian was right all along. If it all fit into place, the tabloid article, Orson's embarrassment. The nude photographs. Do they have his gaze? Could she recognize it? If Orson slept with her mother, then what would that make her? Has she made a mistake, trusting an actor for all of these years?

This is the way it might have happened: her mother (drunk? borrow, here, the memory of red wine and raised voices) arriving at Orson's apartment. He, bewildered, but easily flattered. Maybe they regretted it. But maybe it happened again and again. They would have buried it, tried to keep it from permeating her other life. Her father may never have known. Was it a fling? Or was it love?

Maybe someone else can ask.

Viola
Do you want to come visit?

If she could just hear him say: *that never happened.* She'd believe him, wouldn't she? It would be enough. It would make it all bearable, anything the tabloids threw at them, she would be ready.

And if it did happen?

Well, it's a risk she's willing to take.

1994

Orson has never been a particularly good Catholic, but homesickness has him going to St Robert Bellarmine with Susie on Sundays. They sit in the strangely modern building, which feels familiar and foreign to both of them, the neo-classical façade, the long white nave, the chandeliers strung from the ceiling like disco balls, all of it like a movie set, each angle hosting a different scene. But the lull of Father Patrick's voice, even if Orson doesn't believe in it anymore, is soothing. If not home, it's at least a place he understands. Susie has it too, the homesickness, along with the guilt that she confesses constantly – to him as well as Father Patrick – of leaving her kids behind, of not raising them in the faith. Privately, but with little shame or remorse, he confesses his own sins: the girl in the green bra at the Century Lounge, the singer in that band at Café Largo. He can't tell Susie about these; it's become too strange to talk about that sort of thing anymore.

One afternoon, after church, she asks if he wants to go for a drive. "A joy ride," she calls it, but lately she's seemed more desperate than joyful. They crawl down the freeway toward Pasadena, Susan talking fast, excitable, almost manic.

"I told Sebastian I was investigating a heist," she said. "He liked that. Turn left up here."

"He must think you're incredible."

"Why is it so easy to lie to them?"

"It's not a lie, it's a game. You're giving them a story they can digest."

"They're both so obsessive," she says. "Viola will just keep asking you something until she gets the answer she wants. Is it dinner, is it dinner, is it dinner?"

"Sounds like you've had some early dinners."

"It's worse when I call and she asks if I'm coming home tonight. Right, go right."

"They'll grow out of it," Orson says, though he has no experience in this. "It's the age."

She directs him to a cluster of low houses, and into the drive of a modest condominium with a FOR RENT sign out front. Susie jumps out, peering over at the house like it's the most beautiful thing she's ever laid eyes on.

"What do you think? It's only a sublet, but it'll give me some time to buy everything they need."

"Holy Mary, Susie B. Did your man see the light, then?"

"I'm doing this without him," she says.

Shit. All those years of complaining, and she's finally doing it. *What kind of bastard wouldn't move out here with her?* Anyone could see how much she needed this. Still, the poor fuck had a nasty shock coming to him. Watchful tears rim her eyelids, and she reaches for the sunglasses on top of her head.

"You're sure this is a good idea?"

"Well, if it's not, it's too late now. Come on inside."

She leads him. The house is full of someone else's family, their smells, their furniture, their children in framed school photos on the wall behind the door. One bedroom has a vague Disney theme. Simple, sedate. Plenty of light. As she steps in the room, she is still talking about the children, how the bunk beds will be perfect. She seems so much older to him, the problems in her life so much more real.

As she walks down the narrow hallway she hovers in the doorframe of the master bedroom, and he is suddenly aware of how quiet it is in here with the carpeting and the low ceilings, how different it feels to being in his lonely bachelor apartment.

"So, I guess the thing is to figure out schools around here. You know, because they're starting next year. And that will make it easier, I think, for filming and all that. Kids make friends pretty quickly at this age, right? They'll adjust?"

When she pushes up her sunglasses, her eyes are searching him for something solid, some level of certainty that he could not possibly contain. God, what can he say? The whole house feels like a set, like they are about to do a scene in here. Like she wants him to be a character.

Like an audition.

"I guess I wouldn't know, Suze. I've never known a thing about kids."

It would be unkind to let her believe anything else. To conflate him with her desire for a happier life.

She nods, and places her sunglasses back over her eyes, moves her mouth to one side. *She's just scared*, he tells himself. *She's just worried about being alone.*

"God help me," she says quietly.

"Fuck God, I'll help you," he says. "Anything you need, Susie."

But she knows as well as he does: anything has a limit.

2012

Swipe down the illuminated screen of your phone to get a sense of his work: aerobics girls set against celestial clouds, retro nudes with marigolds flowering from orifices, a long, tanned leg becoming a nuclear missile. It's not bad, kind of interesting, and you think you understand the project more or less. The eighties are in again, the new flavor of nostalgia. Maybe it's political – after all, dissatisfaction is in the air. But there's something in his stuff that makes you feel good, magic superimposed onto ordinary lives. Maybe you'll buy one. Not now, because who has time for that, but at some later moment. The followers are increasing, so maybe you'll consider, if he becomes a bit bigger.

Art is a commitment.

That's what Sebastian tells himself as he plunges into Sadie's attic for his ritual trawl through the stacks of magazines and report cards and class photos and Christmas cards from decades ago. Paper dolls. Nancy Reagan. Michael Jackson. Leather. Sex. Whitesnake. A photo of his grandmother. Glamour and grunge. Unlivable, sure, but when you think of it as time travel, you can forget the chaos, all the space it is taking up in their lives. After all, this was once his mother's house.

Score. *TIME* magazine, Brooke Shields, those eyebrows, that hair. He swipes it and stumbles back down the stairs to the bedroom that has become his studio, unmade bed pushed to the corner, clippings organized into neat Tupperware boxes, a large piece of paper taped to the wall, sticky brushes and a small armada of Elmer's glue bottles at varying stages of emptiness, translucent skeins wisping off orange beaks. This is his largest project to date: a giant mosaic of his mother's face composed of everything she might have encountered in her life, things that he supposes would have made her feel something. Faces of people from her work, faces of celebrities, Barbie dolls, hair products, fast cars, sunsets, Meatloaf. Lola. Sadie. Himself. It's amazing what you find when you take apart a face.

Scissors travel over glossy paper in a severance that has come to feel like prayer. He is beginning to realize that no masterpiece – no magic clue – will clarify her, will clarify his existence within his family. His mother's giant, half-finished face looks down at him with a single green eye. He has been working off of one of the nudes – she is covering her breasts, turning away slightly from the camera, her ribs articulated. A scar on her stomach. *Was that from him? Or another surgery?* He drifts his hands over the scraps that he has organized in a spectrum: varying shades of blush and deeper pinks which will become the cheeks, and a mountain of dark brown: coffee cups and grizzly bears and leather jackets. *What to leave in, what to take out.* The process used to feel like detective work, like he was getting closer to a kind of truth, but now has started to feel like deconstruction. The choice is overwhelming. He's been stubborn really, never asking his father about his archival work, even if he can imagine the excruciating answer (*there's content and context, and really it's as much about understanding historical value as anything . . .*). He sighs, steps back, examines the blank spaces of her face. Like it or not, Al was also a part of her life. He is beginning to feel stupid about avoiding him. About everything he used to believe. Nobody is getting any younger. Prompted by Tillie, undoubtedly, Al has begun to send encouraging messages about the work Sebastian posts. It's embarrassing really. But also, kind of sweet.

He takes his phone out of his back pocket, snaps, uploads a photo: *WIP.* He used to fantasize, when he started this account, that someone would see his work, someone like Orson Grey, and recognize a familiarity, and claim him. Stupid, now, he can see. As an artist, you have to train yourself to see what is real, not what you want to be real. He is trying to evolve. Still, the most rewarding thing remains the reactions; everyone sees something different in his work.

Lola
Do you want to come visit?

The text from last night eyes him, marked red for unread, a zit demanding to be popped. *Fuck.*

He understands she is doing more school, endless degrees. Avoiding the real world. No point in telling her that. There are lots of things he doesn't tell her. Like about trying LSD or what girls he sleeps with. He assumes she doesn't sleep with anyone; she's a nerd after all, and not the one-night stand type. She'd have told him about anyone serious, wouldn't she?

Are you close? someone asked him recently. Are you close to your own heart, to the insides of your pockets? He wasn't sure how to answer. She will never not be a part of him. But she doesn't come back for Christmas anymore. He does not know what she eats for dinner on lazy weeknights, or what music she listens to, or whether her friends are good people, or how she feels about her life.

Seb
Wish I could afford it $$$

The truth is, having sold a few works, he's doing better than ever, cash-wise. But it would be painful, wouldn't it, to hope that this time she might change? Probably she's only interested now that his art is getting a bit of attention. Maybe he's finally worth her time.

As the sun dips at last below the house across the road, he goes to the kitchen, peels the dried glue off his fingernails, runs his hands under soapy water for a while.

"Ready?" Sadie asks.

"Let's do it."

On the side table by the television is a folder full of papers that he is going to help her understand. Since Sully's laid her off after her knee injury, money has been thin. Someone has to figure out how to get her on benefits. Sebastian cracks open some beers and begins dissecting the impenetrable language.

"OK, you'll need to fill your name here." He's figuring it out as he goes along. Why isn't this the kind of stuff they teach you in school? How many years did he spend pretending not to use his calculator for long division?

"What do I put for this?" she asks.

"I don't know. Maybe non-workplace related injury?" That sounds right. More convincing than "Slipped in Stop and Shop. Took down a tower of greeting cards." For a week after, he kept saying: *My Condolences.* Objectively it was both hilarious and not at all a laughing matter.

"Lola texted me," he says.

"Really!"

"She wants me to visit."

"Aw, that's so great."

"I don't think I'm going."

"Are you kidding me, Sebastian?" Sadie stares at him. "I can't even say what I would do for one more day with my sister."

> Seb
> you know what
> screw it
> lets go

*

To promote Al's new book, *Colonial Worldviews and Imperial America,* the college museum has invited him to curate an exhibit, and Tillie has come. The book made a splash in certain circles, and the show is at least likely to interest the geriatric alumni who donate to the institution. It's the sort of thing Susie would have peered around, not bothering to read the meticulously written (and occasionally witty) captions, focusing on the glitzier (if less historically interesting) pieces, making him laugh, asking questions that she thought were stupid but were actually brilliant.

God, he still misses her.

But here is Tillie, quietly, thoughtfully engaging, nodding in a way that acknowledges his work. Pausing in front of a shrunken head, acquired (stolen? gifted? obtained through deceit?) by the East India Marine Society. People come just to see it, a novelty, grotesque and unimaginable. It annoys him, sometimes, that most people view the quotidian as disposable, unworthy of record. That it is the dramatic, the rarefied, that gives shape to our imaginings of the past. But the fact is: the head supports the rest of the exhibit. And so, it feels justified. Still, he cannot think about it as ever having been a real person, someone who loved and belonged. It would precipitate an unraveling.

"Does it bother you," he asks Tillie in a low voice, "that sort of thing?"

Tillie thinks about this seriously before saying: "Of course. But you can't write off everything with a problematic history."

She's right. He'd be out of a job if the public were to reject wholesale the country's checkered past. For who could bear to look at the treasures of imperialism if they were thinking about the costs?

He hovers for a moment, rereads his caption. He had thought it sensitive, at the time that he wrote it.

The EIMS received the head of an embalmed Māori Chieftain as a donation from William Dana. Out of respect, it was displayed under a veil.

It's obvious now that it is insufficient. That the perspective is wrong. That he has framed it as an object when it had once been a thing with a soul. That it deserves not a caption but an elegy.

When they've finished their circuit and polished off a few glasses of cheap prosecco, they head around the corner to one of Al's mainstays, a dimly lit Chinese joint with white tablecloths and fried things on metal trays. Over time, Tillie has learned to push him, gently, artfully, toward the limits of his comfort zone. Nearer to, but never quite over the line. Mostly, he appreciates it.

"Crab Rangoon?"

"Is it. What? Cream cheese?"

"I think you'll like them." She smiles. That's generally enough to get him to commit. "So I was thinking. I mean, I can't help but be aware. It's almost fifteen years."

He looks desperately for a waiter. "Yeah."

"Do you want to do something for it?" she suggests. "Maybe for the kids?"

Yes? Maybe. *What could it be?* He hums, non-committal.

He knows he is guilty of simplification, that Susan, in the ocean of his mind, has lost any sharp edges, is pearl-round and gleaming. That she has become unlike herself. But how can he let go of the ways in which she was, truly, perfect?

"I wish I could have spent more time with her," Tillie says.

The day that Susan and Tillie met at Dan's engagement was a painful day. Not that he remembers the specifics. Rod said something horrible, Susan was late. They came home to a mutilated mouse. None of that matters. The only thing that matters is Tillie's kindness. That for a brief moment, they brushed against each other, laughed about some nothing. That her presence made a difference.

"I felt sorry for her. She was never really comfortable around us. Not that I was always comfortable either, it's just. I was a native."

"Susan was comfortable anywhere," he asserts.

"Well, it just seemed to me that she felt she had to try quite hard. Almost like we expected her to perform."

He'd never thought about it that way. His wife's charisma had always seemed – to him – effortless. At least before she was sick. It was only then that he could recognize the cost.

"You know, for a while, we all kept expecting you to move to the West Coast."

"You did?"

"Yeah. Given she was in California so much."

Dumplings arrive. Tillie stabs into them, slices open their slick skins. Al can't find his appetite. It was strange, the phrase "a year to live", when really, they meant "a year to die". It's hard to make the most of time that is running out. In the mornings, Al felt a sense of having cheated death if he could breathe in the hazy smell of her, half-lidded, for ten, fifteen sweet minutes before waking fully to the hourglass.

"So, do you want to talk to the kids about doing something?" Tillie asks. "Some kind of memorial?"

Even though he has been speaking with his children more, he knows them less; who they are and what they want. They text him un-descriptive and largely functional messages, asking for a particular recipe or the name of somebody they might have seen on the street. They have lost interest in him. And why not? Children all become disillusioned with their parents.

"Could you do anything with Sebastian's old piece?" Tillie asks.

Over the last several years, Tillie has been excavating Viola's room with the delicacy of an archaeologist. She has been converting it, tact-fully, into a small study. A place to do her watercolors and Sudoku puzzles. It's a benign intent and has his blessing. A few months ago, she uncovered Sebastian's early collage under Viola's bed and they laughed about her first visit to the house. He had marveled at her, unfazed by the haunting.

He was obviously talented even then, she said. *Your daughter must have seen it.*

Leave it to Viola to save the work. As if she knew he might need it at a later date. Tillie reapplied glue to pieces that were dried and peeling. Superior restoration work. All of it made him feel idiotic for ever having feared her reaction.

It has taken Tillie to show him how to see his son. He knows, now, how to talk about what Sebastian is doing. Tillie has given him language: inventive, exploratory, composite. He is beginning to see his similarities with Sebastian: a love of sifting through ancient things, clarifying their purpose, rescuing them from obscurity. *Is it too late to rescue something between them?* When she gets up to use the bathroom, he takes out his new phone, his fingers still clumsy against the screen, the too-small letters.

Al
How are you doing Seb?
Having dinner in Boston
Nice sunset tonight.

For a flickering moment, after he threw the tapes into the ravine that night, he had considered jumping after them. Perhaps his children had been the only thing standing between himself and that great doorway. *I should thank them*, he thinks, *for needing me then.*

Dawn is a thin red strip slicing through the leafy North London skyline, waking Viola from the space between Orson's shoulder blades, the back of her hand arching toward a headboard that he selected years ago with the Armenian supermodel. Orson is breathing gently. It's when he's sleeping that she notices his age the most, the soft folds of his face beginning to betray him, his slack jaw and wrinkled elbows.

It is early enough that nothing else exists beyond the carpeted south-facing bedroom. She is not thinking about the shoot that Orson is leaving for later, nor the maddening coursework that she is ignoring, nor her brother arriving that afternoon. Not the paparazzi who may or may not be camped outside. Not the unknown, inaccessible layers of Orson's past, or the person he is when he is not with her.

You're a prisoner to your own success, she tells him sometimes.

It's true, he says. *That's the problem, when you belong to everybody.*

His hand drifts back to catch her thigh, and he breathes: "Don't be awake."

"I can't help it," she says. "I'm savoring this."

"Okay fine," he says, turning and wrapping himself around her ribs, brushing under her rumpled silk top, his eyes still shut with sleep and his hot breath – somehow both pleasant and unbearable – in her face. "I'll let you be awake. But you are making scran."

"You are the worst," she says, by which she means, *I love you.* "What is there?"

"Sausages, eggs. Half of a tomato – no, a full tomato."

"As much as a full tomato."

"Times are hard around here, Viola," he mumbles, pressing his nose into her stomach, and she thinks unpleasantly that it will be hard to make time for the gym this week, with her brother here.

"Bread?"

For a minute she thinks he may have fallen back asleep. "No bread," he says.

"I'll get delivered."

"Faster if we just run out."

"Please."

Sebastian
Bawt tickets 🀫

he had texted, and her heart burst alive. The fact is rushing in – *My God, he's coming. Here. To see me.* To see her life, the truth of it, with all his brother-ness and stubbornness and conspiracy.

"You have that face," he says.

"What face?"

"Your worried face. I'm only gone a few days."

"It's not that."

"Your brother?"

247

"It's going to be fine."

"I thought you were excited."

"I am," she says, which is a part of the truth, and slips away, calling back. "Order the bread!"

The stainless-steel refrigerator opens with a satisfying pop, offering its insides. She loves cooking in his house, making use of Orson's otherwise neglected kitchen, knowing that every few days Marina will scrub all the mess away. Sometimes the house feels like the set of a sit-com, where everything gets reset at the start of each episode. Too easy to be real.

Sweet, meaty aromas twist from the oven, oily vegetables caramelizing, wafting (she hopes) to the bedroom, an incantation to stay, to let this moment – this Before – stretch forever. Sizzle, flip, taste, salt. Search: what to do with visitors in London. Bookmark a few results. Mozart is playing on Radio 3, a chamber piece she could once name. Eggs crack onto a pan, hands behind her, lips on the back of her ear.

"Scran."

"Two seconds!" She can feel him watching her hungrily as she plates, cracks pepper and tosses fat sea salt flakes on top. "Greedy," she says, grinning.

He shovels and groans with pleasure. She cooks almost as well as her father now. Maybe as well as her mother too.

"What does today entail?" he asks.

"Home." *Real life,* as she thinks of the flat she shares with Niamh south of the river. A world where she doesn't need to check if anyone is following her or listening in to her conversations. Where she disappears into her research, a mind without a body. Where Orson doesn't exist. The dissonance is making her insane.

"How is Niamh?"

"Busy." In the winter Niamh is going back to Dublin to teach. The obvious solution, under any other circumstance, would be to come here. But to be obvious is to be in danger.

It can't go on.

"And your brother?"

"We'll see, won't we."

A hum of traffic rises from the street. On the countertop, a speckled ladybug flicks to the granite surface. Orson cups a hand around it, lets it crawl onto his thumb.

Yes. This is worth all the excruciation of asking the difficult question. If he can be this, for her, forever. He blows lightly on the beetle's wings, and it takes flight.

"I remember your mom said, when your brother was little, he would always ask her where she was going, and she would start lying to him and saying things like the moon or a pirate ship."

The bell rings and Viola lingers in the safety of the kitchen, allowing Orson to cross to the door, peek through the spyhole, and then, plausibly alone, retrieve a loaf of fresh bread.

"I can't wait for you to meet him."

When the door to Lola's flat opens, she looks like a photograph of herself that has been washed out by years of sunlight. Sebastian is shocked to find the color dyed out of her hair, skin luminous pale, wafer thin and manicured in stiff, fashionable jeans. She crosses the threshold and throws her arms around him, the familiar smell of her sweat mingling with something new: floral and expensive.

"Did you find it okay?"

"More or less." It had taken several long, branching tunnels to get here from the plane. He imagines himself for a moment as she must see him: towering and lanky with long hair tied up in a dark, greasy bun. Travel itches his skin.

Her roommate (pixie cut, purple lips) doesn't introduce herself but hugs him as well. He has seen enough photos of her to know who she is, but avoids saying or even thinking her name because of all the consonants. Neem? Nyam? "I knew you guys looked alike," she says, "but it's kind of amazing, you have the same . . . hand gestures."

"What do you need?" Lola asks.

"A shower," he says. *A drink*, he thinks.

Easily, she slips back into the role of anticipating his needs. A towel, a coffee. Turn the left handle, not the right handle; the hot and cold are backwards. She has made up a bed for herself on the couch, insists that he take hers. When she closes the door behind her, it is an odd feeling to be alone (naked) in her room, and he feels somehow unsteady to be here on her good graces. He assesses the space. There are no clothes that are not cut to her shape, no boxers or beard oils. It's a relief.

When he is changed, they step out together under the low London sky, walk down a street lined with open-faced brick buildings, women with shopping bags, old men stepping slowly onto lofty red buses, languages he has never heard before being shouted by young boys on the streets, everyone slouching under the release of a Saturday night. He wonders, with her new, anemic hair, if people can still tell that the two of them are the same.

"Are you jet-lagged?" she asks.

"Not really."

"Are you hungry?"

"I mean, sure," he says, though he feels an odd detachment from all of his senses. The outside air or perhaps their presence on the street (in public) has snapped him into the reality of the situation; he is here, he is walking next to her, they are walking together with all of the life shared and unshared between them. She strides up the street with the slight mania of a tour guide, pointing out obvious things to him. *The architecture around here is very mixed*, and *this park is really nice*.

He's not sure what he expected from London, but it wasn't this. The houses have a plain unpretentiousness about them. The streets are no more remarkable than streets anywhere, punctuated by occasional plastic bags and dog shit. The people look like people anywhere, except maybe better dressed. In short, he likes it more than he expected to; instinctively, he feels deeply at ease. Perhaps more so even than Lola, who won't stop apologizing for things that have nothing to do with her. *Sorry, they've been doing this construction for months now* and *the sirens are really loud here.*

"It's cool," he says. The place she takes him is light-filled and sanitized and full of white people. It serves sandwiches with vegan mozzarella and a sauce that he has never heard of. "Go-chu-jang," he reads.

"It's spicy," Lola says proudly. "It's Korean." But she orders a smoothie. Green Machine. *Machine.* How can a smoothie be a machine? *Who comes up with this stuff?* When she speaks to the waiter, her vowels move forward in her mouth. It is strange to hear her voice, how different it sounds here.

"So!" she says, as though they are just beginning. She smiles at him.

"I still can't get over your hair," he says.

"Do you like it?" she asks. She bites her lip and wrinkles her nose, bug-eyed, an old familiar face.

"Dad texted. Asked me to check up on you."

She smiles, then frowns. "What does that mean?"

"Check your vital signs, make sure you're eating your vegetables." He gestures to the Green Machine. "Looks like that isn't a problem."

It strikes him deeply how unknown her life is to him. How old they both are in person. *Soon she'll be Mom's age*, he thinks, *when the cancer must have started.* The worry hardens.

"Sorry I'll have to work a bit this week. My course doesn't really understand the concept of time off."

"It's cool," he says. "We can still do stuff."

"Definitely," she says, lighting up. "My evenings are totally free."

"Not shagging anyone then?" He says it in a Dick Van Dyke voice to make it clear it is a joke, but Viola doesn't laugh. For a moment, she looks quite serious, as though she might say something import-ant, but then a cloud crosses her face and she fixates intently on the empty bottom of her Green Machine. The café moves around them. How have they forgotten how to speak to each other? He should have remembered her sensitivity around these things. For a minute they search quietly for anything else to talk about until his food arrives sizzling and succulent and they can comment safely, idly on the freshness, on the quality of the space.

Niamh's room is dimly lit, and Sebastian can tell by the way that the mirrors are placed that she likes to watch herself during sex. He is running his fingers over the plastic keys of the portable keyboard that is certainly the most expensive item in the room. Unless she has some jewelry or something. She doesn't seem like the type to own expensive jewelry.

"So what, are you the cool twin?"

He attempts but fails to pull off a grin, takes another hit of the joint he packed. "It's legal in Colorado now," he says, as though that is a sufficient answer. He has never enjoyed that type of comparative question.

They had been quiet on the walk home, and he had the sense that he had disappointed her somehow. Lola had gone straight to bed, and Sebastian and Niamh tiptoed around her huddled form on the living room couch. *Strange question,* he had asked. *But can I smoke in your room?* Lola has never liked the smell.

"Still, it's a bold move, drug smuggler. What if I was like, a cop or something?"

"You don't look like a cop."

"Well, that's just prejudice, isn't it?" Niamh reaches for the joint and takes a slow, meditative slurp. "I think I would make a fantastic cop."

"Really?"

"Well, I rate my own judgment about people."

"OK," he asks Niamh. "What do you think about me?"

"I think you care very much."

"I do care." The thoughts in his mind are beginning to separate, like Christmas lights strung together with long bits of wire. Like the Christmas lights hanging from Niamh's ceiling. "Caring is my downfall."

"Most artists are very caring," she says. "That's been my experience, anyway."

"That's good. I was under the impression that most artists were narcissists."

"Sorry, I should say most good artists."

"Thanks."

Niamh adjusts her feet, and he notices for the first time that her toenails are painted blue. He plays another few notes on the keyboard.

Sebastian feels full of a story about a late summer's day when, driving around looking for something to do, he and Lola had stumbled upon a nature reserve, spent the afternoon following a trail to an ostensible summit, scrambling over fallen oak branches and white birches. They had tired before they reached any sort of vista and, resting on a large, rotting pine log, decided to build a fortress. With great gusto they assembled a sort of wigwam, dragging broken branches across the leafy forest floor. Lola did the structural work while Sebastian focused on artisanal touches: a pinecone chandelier, an arrangement of needles that read 'NO BEARS', which for some reason had been hysterical. *We'll come back*, Lola had said with every intention, but they didn't. Or perhaps more accurately, they couldn't. No matter how many times they tried to find the forest again, they could not remember what turn they had taken to get there.

"Brains are funny."

"Well, that hit quick," she laughs. "What do you mean?"

Sebastian strikes the bottom key, holds the note. "Humans are bad," he says. "At giving other people space to be complicated."

When Sebastian wakes up late the next morning, Lola is already gone. She has written a list of places he might want to visit: splendid green parks and botanical gardens, meandering canals and homes of literary notables.

But Niamh says: "You strike me as more of a Camden guy," and so he takes his loaded Pentax uptown to capture Life. It is almost overwhelming, the deluge of punk, the sheer number of faces, piercings, cleavages, and navels. Small-town faces can be studied, known,

253

captured in contours and wrinkles. These faces blur, transient, gone before they arrive. The city teems with unknowable lives, graffiti doodling under ancient bridges like ivy. He buys hot dumplings at a market. He sets up his tripod outside a hotel, shoots the people coming in and out as though they are all celebrities, as though they are all being caught in an act.

In the evening, he returns flushed and fulsome with market treats. A cut of soft, aged cheese, bottles of ale labeled with vivid samurai cartoons. It gives him great joy, and it's the least he could offer. Niamh and Lola bustle back and forth over dinner.

"How was your day?" Niamh asks.

"Good," he says. "I saw Trafalgar Square."

"That big phallic column?"

"I saw it."

"Every city has one," says Lola.

"Damn patriarchy," says Niamh.

Lola fills the pot with water, Niamh turns on the electric hob. Niamh is peeling carrots and Lola is chopping them. "Can I do anything?" he asks.

"You could put on some music," Lola says.

"You could open a bottle of wine."

The sun has set, and it's dark inside the third-floor apartment. Sebastian finds the small, shitty portable speaker and sticks his phone into it and out comes the soulful, acoustic album that he's had on repeat for the last week. He opens the wine and pours some glasses, which they clink, and then the girls return to their preparations – handing and washing and swaying slightly as Niamh sings the high harmonies despite not knowing the words, and the smell of softening, buttery onions fills the room. He listens to the swinging female rhythm of the two of them chattering, gossiping about people they knew at university, moaning about the mundane passage of their days, and wonders whether this was something she had needed. Whether his boyishness had taken up too much space. He has an urge to ask the kind of question you would ask a stranger: *Was it hard for you, being the only girl? Was it hard we never saw it?* But it isn't worth complicating the happiness of a night like this.

"How's Dad?" she asks. They are on the couch watching a British panel show, faces that she finds familiar now. They have drunk the samurai ale.

"The same."

"Have you decided to stop hating Tillie yet?"

"She's not so bad," he admits.

"I never thought she was bad," Lola says.

"You were around more."

"Well, you're around more now."

"Only technically."

"What, like in body rather than spirit?"

"Yes, I'm a zombie. I'm patient zero." She laughs at this. "No, I just mean, I don't see them much."

"Well, you should fix that."

"It would help if you were around. I'm too argumentative."

On the panel show, one of the comedians is doing an impression of the Queen.

"Would you ever move here?" Lola asks. "I mean, obviously, I'd need to buy a bigger couch."

He smiles. It's the kind of thing he was hoping she would ask. "I don't know. I'd need to find a British wife or something."

"Niamh could help. Though I guess she isn't technically British. European."

Lola places a pillow on her lap, kicks a foot out against his thigh, loose tonight, happy. Her phone buzzes and she glances at it quickly before shoving it under her leg. She ate a lot of dinner, which he takes as a good sign, even if it was only soup.

"You sure you don't want to trade tonight?" he offers, patting the couch. "You'll sleep better."

She shakes her head and smiles. "I'm enjoying my weird dreams."

"Gross."

Lola laughs. "Had one about Mom."

"Yeah?"

"In the dream, she kept knocking on my door, like she was trying to tell me a secret." Lola smiles, as though she thinks it's ridiculous, as though it's unimportant what their mother might want. "Psychoanalyze that."

They are dancing on the lip of something.

"Do you ever think about going to California?" he asks.

She tilts her head back to meet his gaze, eyes sparkling. "All the time," she says softly.

His eyes drift back to the television screen, watch the talking heads react to a loud, incessant buzzer.

"I'm seeing someone," she says. "I want you to meet him."

The next night, they are taking a train to the north of the city, hustling out at a busy station and pushing past Turkish greengrocers and hairdressers and espresso bars that slip down familiar side streets. She sets a fast pace, afraid of herself. Afraid of her changing mind.

"Tell me about him," he asks. "What do I need to know."

"You know him."

"I do?" Sebastian folds up at the thought, as though she has presented him with a riddle. "I don't know anyone here."

Hurriedly, she leads him closer, organizing her own execution. Is it too late to turn around now? To go back to the flat, to make a cup of tea with Niamh and watch something mindless on TV, or to go to the library and disappear into a world without consequence? When they open the door and Sebastian sees what she has done in the face of all of his evidence, will it be the end of her?

"Hugh Grant?" he laughs, looking at the houses that are growing taller and whiter as the road inclines sharply. "Winston Churchill?"

She is doing this for both of them.

"It's Orson Grey."

The door opens on Sebastian's shocked face, and there he is, the love of her life, ushering them in and offering them drinks. *Tea or something stronger?*

"I can't tell you how great it is to meet you," Orson is saying. His hand sweeps tenderly through her hair. She extracts herself briskly. Her brother is moving through the room, unreadable. He is examining the dusty record player in the living room, his eyes trained on the black disc going around and around, playing an upbeat jazz trumpet. *Say something.* Orson is behind her, lighting candles, bending to lift something out of the oven, some kind of puff pastry hors d'oeuvres. *Say something, Sebastian.* But he says nothing, looking only at the record, imprinted with a sound from the distant past, and Viola feels her breath quickening, applies desperate focus to the back of a discarded packet, pronouncing with great emphasis: "*Mini-gougères au fromage, fantastique!*"

Sebastian turns and she braces. A smashed glass? A piece of his mind? She has envisioned a thousand permutations of his anger.

But no. For an instant, his face is crumpled. He looks at her without recognition, and she feels a vanishing of herself. How bizarre she must appear to him: the foreign world she has placed herself in, the firmness of Orson's life, his age, the majesty of his presence, all of it surrounds her like a fortress. *God, I'm still your Lola*, she thinks. But in an instant he has gathered himself and approaches Orson, taking his hand, pulling his left arm around his shoulder.

"Make us a drink, Joe, why don't ya?" he says.

Orson beams as though he is twenty years old, as though he has been given another chance to play his favorite part. From inside a lesser-touched cabinet, he retrieves an old silver cocktail shaker.

Sebastian asks: "Is that from the show?" He handles it like a holy relic and applauds when Orson shakes it, launching into a thousand questions that Viola never thought to ask.

"How did you film that scene . . ."

"When my mom went to rehab, was that when . . ."

257

"What was it like with the guy who played . . ."

His eyes are wide and lit up with a genuine curiosity, not a flicker of anger. Viola is unmoored. She reaches for the merlot.

I had mistaken you, she thinks, *for a fixed point.*

She gulps quickly. The room is slipping into a merry nostalgia: Orson is animated, jumping around the kitchen at the excitement of reliving it all, the simpler time, before fame and secrecy and expectation. Everything she expected to feel – all the relief of her life coming together – is absent. What she feels is an old, petty envy.

Her mother has always belonged to her brother.

"Here, Viola, you be Susan," Orson says, taking the trash bag out of the bin and cheating her away from Sebastian to cover up her stomach. "And that was you both in there, imagine it!" Orson rubs his chin and they do imagine it, the thought expanding in the room, and Viola wonders what she is lacking, that she has never been able to give him this kind of lightness.

"You've been holding out on me, Lola," Sebastian says. He is smiling, but his eyes are full of lost time.

"Well, you know. I wasn't sure what you'd think." *Ask. Say it out loud.*

"How long has this – have you . . .?"

"A little while."

"Since you told me you met? What, three years?"

"Not quite. Two and a bit."

"It's been hard, you know," Orson says, "I'm away . . ."

"And I was studying . . ."

"Right." Sebastian examines them. Her fingers find Orson's. "And you haven't told anybody else?"

"Well, Niamh."

"Ah, okay. Wow. Didn't pick her for a secret-keeper." He grins, cheeky. "Bet I could make loads of money if I were to rat you guys out."

"Only if we go halves," says Orson.

"Don't," says Viola.

"No? Okay. She's the boss around here." Orson's eyes are dancing, clicking with Sebastian's. He's enjoying it, this new dynamic, someone else who knows her. When Sebastian excuses himself to go to the bathroom, he looks at her and smiles.

"What?"

"You okay?"

"Yeah, I'm okay—"

"You don't need to be nervous, I like him."

"That's what makes me nervous."

How much longer can it last, this happy charade? Surely none of them can sit in it much longer. Maybe even now, her brother is scouring the house for evidence, preparing his great reveal. Orson is glowing at her, fitting his fingers against hers. Was it worth it, allowing him this sparkling, unsustainable moment?

"You've wanted this for a while, haven't you," she says, trying to keep the sadness from infecting her voice. "You've been tired of just me."

"Not tired of it. Just. This is a really good step, Viola. I'm proud of you."

She feels sick. When Sebastian re-emerges, Orson brightens toward him, begins to ask about his art, and Sebastian is digging out his phone and the two of them are looking over it. She can't really see and is trying to gather what it is from across the table. Her brother is using his fingers like a pincer, moving in and out of something, explaining: "I actually found these photographs of her in Lola's room – just another thing she was hiding from me I guess – but Mom's face in them was wonderful, so I used that as a base . . ."

The photographs. The nude photographs. The smoking gun – is this the test? Does Orson recognize, does he remember? Here is her mother's body, that ancient horror, is no one else mortified at the sight of it? Oh God, what has she invited! But no, not a beat of knowing.

259

The actor gives nothing away. Orson is only complimenting Sebastian's eye and his instinct, and Sebastian is moving forward to other artworks.

"It's like a stained-glass technique," Orson says. "So clever. Saint Susie. Tell me what you remember."

Slowly, Viola takes a bite of a mini-gougère and feels sick to her stomach. It occurs to her with deep, horrible certainty: her brother is not going to ask.

"Small things," Sebastian is saying. "I remember her coming home. Bath time. She used to let us brush out her hair. Sometimes we would pray before bed."

"Really? She was always going on about how your father didn't like that sort of thing."

"Well, I remember it anyway."

"He's got a better memory than me, Orson, it's really not very fair."

She can hear the boldness in her voice. A moment is arriving that she will not be able to return from. My God, if she can just know, then it will be over, the doubting. She can move on. One way or the other.

"We used to talk about you at home, Orson," she says. She pours herself another, fuller glass of wine. "Growing up."

"Really. Good things, I hope."

"You know, Sebastian has this theory that you slept with my mom." She leans on it like a punchline, like it's absurd. No one is laughing.

"Right."

"Or at least he used to be obsessed with it."

"And where did this come from?"

"Some tabloid."

A long moment. She never expected it to sound so ridiculous out loud. She looks to her brother: *Well?*

But Orson is looking only at her. "And is that something you think?"

"Obviously not."

"But you were putting off telling me about it."

"I was just a teenager," Sebastian says quickly. "You know. It was all a part of trying to imagine her life. Just. Abstract."

Orson nods solemnly, his eyes unmoving.

"Well, lest there be any doubt, that never happened." He pauses for her response, but she cannot speak. "Capiche?" he says.

Embarrassment flares through her body, her cheeks, and when at last he looks away, he does not look at her again. Conversation meanders loosely through the end of their drinks, and then Orson suggests he should be getting to bed, that he is off again in the early morning. When they leave, he stiffens against the brush of her hand.

1994

Susan has packed bags for the twins, a week's worth of clothes, tooth-brushes and a few key toys: picture books, Sebastian's blanket. Hidden them in the trunk of her car. It will be a long drive, but they can stop off in Chicago for a night. She will take them first thing in the morning, when Al leaves for work. He won't hear if they put up a fuss. He won't be able to stop her.

"Mom, where is Silky?"

"I'm sure it will turn up, sweet one."

"I looked, I can't find it."

"Come on, buddy," says Al. "Let's check where you might have left it."

This is deranged, she thinks as she watches her husband tenderly turning over pillows on both children's beds, looking for Sebastian's blanket. She should have grabbed it last, she should have known better, and now she's drawn attention to what she's doing. Al prepares to check the laundry basket and she says *I think it's in the dryer,* and *I'll bring it to you when you're sleeping* and her husband is scooping up their little boy.

How can she possibly take them without letting him say goodbye?

When she had come home last Saturday, he looked almost shocked to see her. The house was messier than usual, the children's toys everywhere in multiple rooms, pots piling up in the sink. He was wearing the t-shirt he wore when all of the others were in the wash.

"I thought I was going to have to come out and get you," he said.

"Well, I've saved you the trip."

Nothing had felt right since the day she took Orson to the sublet. It was stupid, expecting him to react any other way, to throw himself into her life. Their friendship only works if both of them are unattached, if they can play at being children themselves and unresponsible. She would be as lonely there as ever. *It will take some time to get used to*, she thought, but maybe she'd never get used to it. Maybe nowhere would ever feel as warm as this house: full of her comfortable things, the smell of her children, her husband. Is it insane to tell herself she does not want this life?

One week – why not give them all one week that felt normal, that felt right? A parting gift? It would be the performance of a lifetime. When it was over, she would need to run without looking back.

She threw herself into the act. So deeply at times, it all became muddled. In the afternoons, she lay on the floor with the children, watching them put marker caps on their fingernails and practice counting. She sank nervous energy into the project of replacing all the fixtures, the doorknobs and cabinet handles and shower heads. Al was tentative, gentle, dropping the children at daycare, applauding her handiwork and taste, bringing back sweet treats from the city. With each morning she awoke next to him, his hand or face finding her shoulder, she felt herself shedding toughness, all the Los Angeles layers required to stay safe, to stay focused. Margie's voice grew quieter.

Now, waiting in the hallway while the children brush their teeth, she remembers the first night she and Al slept here. In the late afternoon, Al had carried her across the threshold, swept her up the stairs, pointed at the empty rooms and filled them with imaginary furniture. Dinner tables and wine racks and record players and children. Children hanging off the banister and running through the back yard. Al looked at her in the way he always looked at her, as a woman who could transform all this empty space.

Hadn't she? Here is the proof, scampering into bed, both of the twins kissing her on the cheek, their happiness excruciating. Now that she has set herself in motion, she just needs it to be done, as soon as it can be. When Al goes downstairs to make a cup of tea, she goes back to their bedroom, reaching as quietly as she can for the heels she keeps on the top shelf of the wardrobe, stuffing them into a duffel bag, her heart pounding loud—

"Silky is not in the dryer."

"No?"

Al is by the door, holding a cup of tea. He is wearing no shirt, only his glasses and his long pajama pants. "Don't do this," he says.

"Do what?"

For all her theatrical credentials, she cannot hide from him. He is looking at the bag in her hand, the shoe in the other, the failed naiveté on her face. Whatever they are, they are not strangers to each other.

"Susan, if you go, if you take them—"

"Al, I've already decided—"

"I know this has not been easy. And yes, probably, my stuff has come first—"

"We're going tomorrow, first thing. It's—"

"But I swear, I know you. I know that you want all of it, every form of happiness, and that you just won't feel satisfied until you get it. And you're going to break both of us in the process, you'll see. And I always thought – we said we never wanted this, the brokenness we came from, just – your dad, my sister, that feeling of never being complete or happy, of people quitting on us. I don't want to quit on you. I don't want you to quit on me. Can't we – I mean, Christ, Susie, I love you."

She moans – frustration and longing. No, she doesn't want it, the brokenness, she doesn't want them to inherit it, to blame her for not making it work. But God, what will it cost! He is moving and his arms are wrapping around her so that hers do not need to move and he kisses her perfect face, and by the time the sun rises they are lying back in the same bed that they bought together so many years ago, the floor a mess of their clothes, yielding to each other in the only way that they can: the rough entanglement of hair in fingers, the clasping of flesh, the flattening of hip against hip and will against will.

They have to know she always loved them, that she chose them above all else.

2012

When she is sure Sebastian is asleep, Viola calls Orson. When he doesn't pick up, she calls him again.

"I'm sorry," she says. She feels, once again, like a child – the game of adulthood, of control, is shattered.

"Viola." His voice is unornamented now. He is not the characters in his movies, the man inflated with the dreams of a little girl. "You don't trust me."

"I do," she starts. "In fact, I really think we should do this now. Talk to a publicist. I just want everything out in the open. It was Sebastian—"

"I don't think you understand." She listens to him breathing for a moment, her heart in her chest. "You let yourself think the worst of me. And you went on thinking it for some time."

"I never thought—"

"Of course you did. When you asked, wasn't a part of you afraid of what you'd hear?"

He exhales heavily through his nose.

"Let me tell you something. You turn everything into this great soap opera drama, in spite of yourself."

"Wait—"

"But here's the thing: most of life, and most of what passes between real people is just mundane. It's not great loves or hatreds or violence. Your mother and I took care of each other. It doesn't mean we fucked. I loved her, but I can't pretend that I understood her whole life, or even the choices she made on a day-to-day basis. There were times when she was cowardly and times where she was phenomenally brave. She wasn't

265

one thing, there was nothing absolute about her. And I think you want to simplify her, to make her this cartoon baddie who cheated and abandoned you and lived this sinful life so that you can console yourself. Convince yourself that you're better than her. More worthy of love or less susceptible to death or whatever it is for you. Like you're in competition with her and terrified of losing. I think you find it easier to hate her – to write her off – than to deal with who she really was. And I feel sorry for you. What you miss is an absence. What I miss is a person. You're never going to know her, not really. Especially if you don't know how to ask."

"Orson." Her voice cracks.

"I really want what's best for you, Viola. And I said nobody was going to get hurt."

"Please, can I just see you?"

The walls of the room have not changed, but she is standing in a blown-up building. Her purpose is hanging like loose cable and—

"I'm going to miss you, Viola. Always."

The phone is dead.

After a moment, breath. Sharp, gulping breath, breath taking place in a new world, a world that refuses to contain Orson Grey. She looks around the room for evidence of him, anything solid, but all her proof is unraveling. No one can tell her it was real, that the world *was*, that Orson existed for her and loved her and had terrible taste in music and looked great on a bicycle and could be kind and wrong and gentle and distant and hers?

It's stupid, and it's her own fault. She searches and finds the dull, useless truth; the only person she wants to speak to is the mother that she was just beginning to know.

From the living room, murmurings. It doesn't sound good.

When Viola first mentioned Orson, Sebastian assumed it was trivial, a brush, that she had oversold it even then. What an idiot he had thought her, not to have asked him more. Why didn't she tell him then, what it was becoming? Was she afraid of his judgment? Is that who he is?

The living room goes quiet, and then there is some shuffling and the door cracks open.

"You okay?"

"Just looking for something," she says. But she only hovers over her darkened desk, the light on her phone barely moving.

"Couch okay?"

"I'll be honest," she says. "It's not the one."

He flops open the duvet on one side of him. "There's room. Don't be weird."

In the dark, he cannot see her face, but he can hear how fraught her breath is. When she crawls in next to him, he can feel her exhaustion.

In a small voice directed mostly into the mattress, she says: "I don't know what I am doing."

"He loves you a lot," Sebastian says.

"I know," she says, high and breakable.

"He's a good person. But he really is just a person."

Meeting Orson was like meeting any old guy. Like shining a bright light upon a shadowy corner that he had long presumed to be full of intrigue, and revealing it as a series of ordinary things. Clearly Orson loved their mother in his own way. She had been a friend to him. Clearly he loves Lola – regardless of the strangeness of tonight and whatever he said on that call. It had been a joy to spend an evening moving through his memories. The disappointment is hard to articulate. There was nothing Orson knew beyond anyone else about the workings of his mother's mind: not what she wanted or who she loved. All he really held were a few brief moments, and the lingering sense of how she made him feel.

Sebastian places a hand on her back, chucks her a pillow.

"It'll be okay."

"Maybe."

"No, it will."

1995

In the waiting room are two women who look like her. Susan studies their faces. One has a longer nose, one is younger. They both look nervous and she tells herself: you'll be okay. She looks up to the ceiling, counts the tiles, tries to hang on to a sense of control.

When she walks in, a man (older, moustache) is busying himself with some papers. Would you mind taking your clothes off? She's done this before, it's nothing to her, remember Al, the first time, how unthinking? But hasn't her body changed, become more vulnerable, less her own? Slowly, she folds up her shirt, facing the wall, buying herself time before she has to face him.

The words do not make sense coming out of the doctor's mouth. They are words for another woman. They do not apply to her, to the organ that grew her children. Quite far advanced, normally a compliment, something she never was in school. We'll have to act fast.

Her husband in the waiting room. There had been so much blood they thought – could it have been possible? – she had been pregnant again, she had lost it. The flood had made her nauseous, and she had vomited too. None of it made any sense, and more than that, the pain, the ruined pants, blood still caked in the fault lines of her palms. She has been asked a question and realizes she is supposed to give an answer, but nothing is entering other than the surreal way the clock on the wall is still moving, hands still falling steadily forward.

She nods, and Al's body is around her, her face in his chest, both of them moving with heavy, frightened sobs. *Where are the children? Safe, fine, with his mother. It's not real*, she says. *You're going to be okay*, he says. *We're going to fight this.*

What is next? The dismantling of her broken pieces, the removal of rot? Only yesterday she had opened a sweet potato, peeled the perfect orange exterior, and chopped in to find that the core was liquid and wrong. None of it is fair. Her husband's attention, his mind connects perfectly with hers for a moment and even in the terror they pass strength between them. They reach inside each other to find something solid. They hold each other's gaze like it's the only safe place to look.

When they arrive home, she can't get out of the car. Her insides are still so cramped up with failure, with the exodus, and she cannot face them. So Al brings the children to the car, straps them into their car seats. He is talking about practical things, about whether or not they are going to McDonalds or Friendly's for takeaway. He is acting with a numbness she never before understood as a strength. She can hardly look at their beautiful, beaming faces – she cannot break in front of them. She cannot let them watch her go to pieces. Look! How much time have you wasted?

They ask to listen to the Disney CD and Al humors them even though the songs make him insane, and the two of them look out the windshield and try not to cry while the kids scream Hakuna Matata at the top of their lungs. Susan places her hand on her husband's hand and tries to catch her breath.

I have this, she thinks. *Thank God I have this.*

When they get home, Al takes the kids into their room, and she calls Mark Flowers. "I can't do this anymore," she says. "You have to kill me."

2012

In a quiet thicket of Regent's Park, a sign advertises tonight's outdoor entertainment: *Twelfth Night.*

"Oh look, a nice trash can for me to hide in."

"I'm not forcing you to go."

"You absolutely are."

It's a quintessential London experience, Viola had told Sebastian in the affectless voice that was the only one she could muster. *I thought it would be nice.*

Somehow it seemed important that they went together. It felt like they had been avoiding it their entire lives. She had bought the tickets before he came, in a gesture that she had written off as a generous surprise, a thank-you-for-coming gift. But she can see now in his squeamishness about the whole thing (here! in this languid, gorgeous everyone park!) that it had only been something that *she* wanted. Perhaps the idea had been a way of managing her anxiety about the visit, of what to do with him. But it will be nice, just sitting next to him in silence for a while. Letting the story go by.

"Lola, you are sad, and if this is going to make you feel better, than this is what we'll do."

"It will make me feel better."

"I can't promise I'm going to like it."

"You are entitled to not like it."

"Am I entitled to think it's pretentious bullshit?"

"Sure."

"And that their accents are stupid?"

"Don't push it."

The set is lush, and thickened by a dense soundscape of crickets, tropical birds. In the general settling, a small band begins to play. Breathing next to her is her brother, and she can feel the quieting of his mind as he looks around the amphitheater at all the people coming in, little children and a woman in a wheelchair and some too-loud Americans and a pair of German girls. She can see him unfurling in this rough assembly of people just here to listen to a story about a boy named Sebastian and a girl named Viola. Gradually it grows quiet, and a woman trundles up to stage.

Here she is: herself but not herself. Mannish, commanding, wide-faced and broad-shouldered. Her voice is a surprise, all delicacy and enchantment:

"What country, friends, is this?"

She slips into the spell. *A memory.* Thick red curtains, the ceiling painted with a false sky, people talking and then silent and dark, the stage lighting up. *What country, friends, is this?* Her mother's voice: *that's you,* attention directed toward sentences she couldn't understand, her mother's voice explaining the motions, the turmoil, the mistakes. Cold ice cream on her tongue. Just the two of them. Bliss.

1995

Her daughter's perfect tiny features, hers for the evening, the lights coming down. Imprinting something that might matter. She needs this time. When she looks at her children, Susan is overcome by how quickly they are growing, how far they have to go. Her love for them arrives fiercely in strange moments, a desire to pin them down, to suspend them in time. To suspend herself. She knows she is unnatural with them now, that at times she spills over, that it isn't fair. And so tonight, she is only trying to create some normalcy. To escape. Just her daughter and her.

They settle into their seats. Her daughter is wearing a black velvet dress and tights, tiny patent leather shoes. When the play begins, she tries to lose herself but instead just feels lost. Disconnected.

She wonders now whether she had been wrong to capitulate about the names. It's a silly show, really. Predictable, clean. Everyone just ends up with who they are supposed to. It all passes by in a laugh. None of them really see each other at all. But to be honest, she can hardly focus because she is so smitten with the rapture on her daughter's face, watching her fall in love with the lights and the drama. *What's in a name?* The magic of being in this space together. *She will remember this forever.* Nothing else matters.

"Did you like it?" she asks as they walk back to the train station in the dark. It's well past Lola's bedtime, and her daughter is picking at her tights, overtired, her skin itchy.

"Yes," she says seriously, nodding her head. Trying to stay awake. To act older than she is. "Did you like it?"

"Not really," she says, because there's no need to lie. "But I loved getting to go with you."

2012

The air is cooling off the backs of her knees. Languid orange clouds streak the sky. Viola watches The Viola draw her rapier, declare herself "no fighter". She prays to God, she makes a dick joke. The Sebastian is a goofy-looking boy poorly disguising a heavy Manc accent, but sweet and compelling. Every time her brother laughs, it is a gift. Viola can feel her mind at work, keeping up with the plot and the meter and chasing a memory she did not know she had.

"How have you made division of yourself?" The Antonio asks.

Her brother's hand finds hers, a soft magic. The perfect sense of falling apart and coming together. Well, almost perfect. It finishes with a bitterness she cannot quite swallow. There are no parents in Illyria, only revelry and pleasure and youth. Lovers who misunderstand each other, who want each other to be different. They see each other only for their disguises, they objectify each other. The humor fails to mask the undercurrent of unnecessary pain. The refused space to grieve. The audience is applauding, the cast is returning to bow and receive.

"Did you enjoy it?" she asks her brother as the crowds file out.

"Can I be honest?"

"You can be honest."

"It was crap."

"You think?"

"Yeah, complete bullshit."

"Seriously?"

"Well, Sebastian was so . . . I mean, he was hardly there, wasn't he?"

"Yeah, true. It's not really his story, I think."

"No."

"He's there to solve a problem at the end, isn't he," she says.

"He's there to make Viola feel like she can be herself again. But it's not really about him."

"Right."

"And come on," he says. "Everybody takes their masks off and they still magically like each other? Ridiculous ending. Too many coincidences."

Viola thinks on this for a moment. "I think coincidences happen constantly, we just don't always see them. I mean, technically, you and I are a coincidence."

"I don't even think Shakespeare liked it," Sebastian says, waving the playbill. "Obviously he handed somebody the script and they were like 'what do you want to call it' and he was like 'whatever the fuck you want dude'."

"*Twelfth Night or What You Will.*"

"It's just crazy to me that it was Mom's favorite play and all."

Why had they thought it was her mother's favorite?

Their father told them so.

"No," Viola says. "It wasn't."

Then, as if an incantation, she describes a play, their mother beside her, the curtain going up, the look on her face as she studied the characters, the crowded train station and the sense of safety, of a protected moment, the small plastic cartons of ice cream.

"We brought some home for you," she says, the fact surprising her as it bubbles to the surface. "Chocolate, I think. It had melted."

All anyone has is a few brief moments. The lingering sense of how she made them feel.

Maybe that's enough.

In the morning, Viola leans by the front door as Sebastian pulls his suitcase out of her room and checks the bathroom for any traces of the last week.

"Don't go."

But he will, he has to. He looks at her with all the sad inevitability of adulthood, the impossibility of retreat into a house they can both call their own. And she will have to reckon with the wreckage, the number on her phone that she cannot text, the love that has gone.

"I'll see you soon?"

The memorial. Eight weeks.

She hugs him until he is too heavy to hold.

When the door clicks she is alone with the shadow world of her thoughts.

The play wasn't all terrible, was it? Surely it asks some questions of merit. Is love deluded? Can you walk away from grief? *I don't know,* she thinks. *I don't know.*

1996

"I just don't want them to think of me like this."

Susan is sitting on the edge of the bathtub, her feet arching, legs forming a table for her elbows, hands pressing up into her face. Her shirt is off and Al can see the mountain range of her spine. She's going under on Wednesday. *Hysterectomy, oophorectomy.* Why do we give the most horrible operations the most beautiful Greek words? *I don't care, take it all out,* she said.

"I'm not as convincing as you are," he says.

"You're doing great."

"Viola keeps asking me why I look so serious."

"Tell her that's just your face."

She flicks water at him. Smiles. Allows him to hold hope. Surgery, then chemo. And somehow, in between it all, a final trip to LA. She wants to say her goodbyes while she still looks like herself.

Oh the irony, that it has taken this to get what he wanted. And my God, it's beautiful to watch her walk around the yard, grateful for the outside space, the trees. To hear her packing snacks and lunches for the children in the morning, reading them bedtime stories at night. Together they refuse to acknowledge it, except when it will not be ignored. The house has taken on the smell of her again.

"You might not be able to walk for a few days," he says. "How are we going to explain that?"

"We'll just tell them I'm taking a few days of relaxation."

No point mentioning the other symptoms. The pain medication that will likely make her gassy and groggy and nauseous. The difficulty

277

urinating. The recovery will take as long as it takes. And then, she will get better.

With some effort, she lifts herself out of the bathtub. He bends to get the drain, holds out a towel for her to walk into.

"Ready?"

"Ready."

They will live each day in deluded hope. And when the dissonance threatens to sabotage everything, she will give him that look, the same look he saw in her eye in the dressing room that very first time, like she's about to go on stage and put on a hell of a show. And he thinks that, even if they are lying, they are being sincere.

He has never loved her more.

Susan stares out the window as marshes give way to tide pools. She likes volunteering as a chaperone for school trips. Now that she has stopped working – or nearly – she has more time than the other mothers with regular office jobs, and it gives her the chance to see Sebastian and Viola with other children, watch them socialize, study them. One last trip to LA and then it is done.

Now they are tiny marine biologists, listening underwhelmed as an elderly man explains about hermit crabs, damp worksheet papers flapping against the sea breeze.

"They fight, you know. They'll do anything for a bigger shell."

The other chaperones huddle together, observing, quietly comparing. Susan hangs back; she feels herself separate to these women who all play doubles at the tennis club on the weekends, whose husbands wear suits to work. She worries about the people their children will become.

Oh God, was it right, to stay? Will their world be bright enough here?

The sea expands to the ends of her senses. Al always says that it's a relief that the sea exists – something so unknowable that even a life's work can't plumb it.

It terrifies her.

Where did her children go? Susan blinks and realizes the fog is deepening around her, or at least the faces of the class are becoming more anonymous. It takes her a moment to spot Viola in her yellow mackintosh, studiously classifying animals and detailing her observations on the crabs: How many legs do they have? How fast can they run? Sebastian eludes her, his green coat dissolving into the others – is that him or one of the Dunning boys? She feels her breath shortening, tightness in her chest. She is shivering, she can see the goose bumps on her skin, but she feels terribly hot in her rain jacket. Where is Sebastian now?

The skies ring out with the cries of Susan's infant twins – or are they seagulls wailing against the northeasterly wind? She feels them again being pushed from her womb, sees them identical but marked by the arrhythmia of two tiny hearts fluttering at different paces, one tiny hand reaching faster for the rattle. How can she hold them both? How can she hold them at all?

Where is Viola now?

2012

Her new, unbearable reality hits in shockwaves. Orson's absence permeates her phone, her hands, her bed.

Every day she searches for his name. What is he doing, who is he with, how is he feeling. She gorges until she makes herself sick on it, all the promotional materials for his new movie, the publicity shots and glib interviews and threads of speculation and baseless opinion, and herself absent from all of it. As though she never existed. None of this will give her the rough bitten edges of his fingernails, or his late-night doubts, or his half-drunk coffee cups littered around the house or the heartbeat of his affection in her pocket.

hi little thing –
this made me think of you –
I didn't want to wake you but –
I'm feeling so bluuue without you –
love you too
really really
always

Is that all she gets from him? *Always?* What a pointless word. Dangerous, even.

She wanted more time. She was robbed of all the time she thought she would have, and it was—

Her fault.

And now Niamh is leaving, their flat a sea of cardboard, their life sorted into piles. Yours, Mine, Trash, Donate, Sell. People from the Internet keep coming out to trade crumpled bills for the stuff of their lives: lamps, placemats, the Botero. In all that time, Orson never came here. Because she wouldn't let him.

Viola gets off the couch as Matthias, Niamh's boyfriend, helps lift it outside and into someone's van. When he comes back in, Niamh kisses him.

"He's handy."

"That's why I'm keeping him."

It's pitiful watching the two of them, their all-encompassing happiness. Viola sits on the stained beige carpet and wraps herself in the blanket that she refused to pack.

"I'm going to be alone forever," she says.

"Oh stop."

"I'm fine with it. I'm going to die alone."

"Well, of course you're going to die alone. We all die alone. Honestly, I've been trying to tell you for years." Niamh rolls her eyes and Viola leans her face into her palms.

"I don't want to go home," she says.

"Why not?"

"My dad."

Somehow, she has come to blame him for everything that has happened with Orson. For who else had taught her denial as a survival skill? If she had not spent so long fearing the truth, there might be more to salvage. If her father had only acknowledged the reality of their childhood – that they were a family torn between separate dreams – she might have seen things differently. The unknown might not have terrified her so much. She doesn't want to go back to silence.

"If I had been a betting woman when I met you," Niamh says, "I'd have put this situation the other way around."

"What do you mean?"

"Me being the star-fucker and you becoming the boring nester."

"I'm not a star-fucker."

"Well, I'm afraid in the technical sense you are."

Another wave, her face stupid and hot. She pulls the blanket over her head and groans.

"Sorry, that's not helping, is it?"

"No, it's not."

"Come in my suitcase, you sad sack. Just until you figure things out."

Anything else feels like resistance. And Viola has no more energy to resist. She has no energy for anything. Reading is impossible. Reasoning is impossible. The Masters will not be completed. Of this she is certain.

They go.

1996

Even though she helped Rip write the scene (they had sat down together, gone through every line, every shot like clockwork), Susan cannot remember her lines. She always remembers her lines. But these do not want to come, do not bear being said. Elvis stumbled over lyrics that he couldn't bring himself to say. And she feels this: by saying the lines properly she will be saying goodbye to Margie. A part of her is not ready to let go.

She knows Margie like she knows her own bones – the invisible feel of them holding her up. She couldn't reduce her to an adjective, but she knows what she would or wouldn't say in any situation – God knows she's had to ad-lib enough when someone else has forgotten their lines. She knows what Margie's anger feels like, crystalline and animal, unlike her own muddled frustration. She knows how viciously she fights against fear, against perceived injury. She knows how Margie worships her own body, wields it like an expert. And here is Susan: chopping it to pieces.

Most of all, Susan knows Margie doesn't want to die. So thank God they've done it in this way, where she can't see it coming. It's like putting down an animal.

The final scene wasn't going to be cheap – Margie would be pleased about that, if she could have understood. They had to rent a special car just for filming the interior driving shots, operated by a stunt man who sits on the roof. Sitting behind the ineffective wheel is thrilling and terrifying. The stunt team have just filmed the barrel roll, gutted and cleaned the car, taking out all the gas and fluids. And now she is preparing herself to say goodbye.

"Quick and dramatic," she said to Orson, her face in pain with smiling.

"She died as she lived."

It's so strange to be with all of these people off set, the cameras rolling, characters walking around in the jeopardy of the real world. They've closed the streets filming, but that doesn't stop the blurring of it all.

"If I'm dead before it airs, can you make sure they show an In Memoriam?"

"Jesus, Susie."

"I'm just being realistic."

She tries to wink, but he's not in a mood for joking. Which is annoying, because what she could really use right now is a good joke. He's looking at her like he's trying to say something important, like he's trying to make every second count.

"Do you have a cigarette?" she asks.

"Yeah, actually."

Her stunt double is over flirting with Rip. *Good for Rip.* The girl is gorgeous. Marion comes by and fixes her make-up.

"I'm thinking blood here," she says, pointing to the top of Susan's head, looking at Orson like he has any idea where blood should be. He shrugs one shoulder, in his Orson way, not taking his eyes off her.

"Blood wherever you like, Marion."

Marion smiles, adjusts Susan's blouse, and busies off to massacre someone else. Orson lights her smoke. Looks out to the road again. That face. Her heart. The edge of the world. She wonders, after she dies, whether California will keep rising out of the water or fall back into the ocean. For a long time, she thought that she was living at the end of time, that everything would just continue on in its final per-fected state forever. But standing here feels like the opposite. Like the earth can't help but keep moving.

"Hey," he says. "You okay?"

She nods. She breathes in the smell of him. She'll give him his chance, now, to say what he needs to say. It's the nicest thing she can do.

"Orson," she asks. "Does any of this matter?"

"Of course it matters." He is looking at her fixed, scrambling for words. "It matters. Even if it's not us, even if it's not always good or meaningful, it helps people understand their lives. It matters that we show up for them day after day after day. It matters that we're here, that we spent this time together—"

"Susie, can we get you in place please—"

"Sure, sure." She looks at Orson. "Hold that thought."

She lies there heavy while around her are voices of people swapping out functional cars for busted up ones. She has been thrown from the vehicle through the windshield, and a props woman carefully places broken glass around her body. When she was little, she and Sadie used to outline each other with chalk on the sidewalk in front of their house. Her stomach is killing her, the surgery wounds have been so slow to heal.

ROLLING.

She tries not to breathe. Orson is screaming at her motionless body and she feels, in the vacuum of Margie, Susan leaking in. An untenable pride, at having begun this, at having finished it. At having nothing left to say.

When they cut the final shot, she walks away from the scene of her death, and into the waiting cab. Orson is looking around for her, distracted, as the car pulls away from their world. Don't look back, don't let yourself fall apart. She's learned this much: in real life, there's no such thing as a satisfying goodbye.

2012

They hit the Grand Social, the room pulsing with electricity, and Viola allows herself to be dragged through the tapestry of movement, fed pints of Guinness. Music splashes out of windows and voices call and heavy feet hit the ground and everywhere is senseless laughter, senseless joy.

She doesn't want it. She doesn't want to be wearing make-up or her best-fitting dress. She wants to be liquid, to sink into the ground. Dublin becomes a contemptuous purgatory. Somewhere she was meant to belong but never would.

"I'm going to say something you won't like, okay? Because I'm drunk. And I know this is going to sound stupid coming from the girl living with her monogamous whatever, but I am just begging you. You have to interrogate your own happiness. Sometimes I think you're so set on one image of love that you might be depriving yourself of everything it might be. Love is not just one thing."

"Okay," Viola says. "I will think about that."

They walk back across the Samuel Beckett Bridge, harp-like and impossibly suspended, a model of asymmetry. Her mother had come here to visit her relatives as a child, Sadie once said. How many cobblestones have changed in the interim? This bridge didn't exist, then, nor did any of the glassy buildings or fiber optic cables or rich Europeans in fancy glasses. *How did it feel to be here?* Did she love it or hate it or belong or wish she were somewhere else? What would she think of it now? What would she think of her child, here? It's all gone. No one, not even Orson, can tell her. *What you miss is an absence*, he said.

None of those feelings matter anymore, do they. *Nothing I feel matters much either*, she thinks.

Under the cold stars, they pass a homeless woman with sores on her face singing to a dog. Normally she would pass. It's a matter of safety, in the city, only seeing what you're supposed to see. But she can't, not tonight. She reaches into her purse and gives her all the money she has. She can't take it with her, anyway.

A thought flutters across her mind, freed at last from her own self-consciousness and the threat of Orson's feeling. Her mother, naked, was beautiful.

1996

"Okay," she says. "Are we going to do this?"

As he leads her up the stairs, she is surprised to find herself nervous. Conscious of her posture. As though this were their first time together.

"Is this okay?" he asks. In the far corner of the bedroom, he has used about a million thumbtacks to peg up a cheap black cloth along the top of the wall, carried up the stool that sits by the kitchen phone.

"Yeah," she says. "Yeah, it's perfect."

He sighs and looks at her. Looks away from her.

"We need to make this fun."

"Yeah."

"Sexy."

They are both becoming fluent in her body in ways they never expected to be. Its curves and crevices, its leaks and pains and weaknesses. Illness has become a new form of intimacy, a private language. Unsqueamishly, they speak to doctors about pus and surgical wounds and catheters. About how to bandage her. About how she will transform, scarred and bloated, requiring love in new ways.

But not now. Now is a farewell. A celebration.

"Do you want a drink?"

"Please."

Her shirt is a thin chemise thing, the bra a trickier negotiation. She loops around her neck a thin gold necklace that she stole from the costume department. When he re-enters with a thick glass of whiskey, he studies her.

"I'm not going to be good at this."

288

"Of course, you are."

"I have no artistic talent."

"You don't have to be that artistic to be a photographer. You just have to be . . . objective."

"Well, I don't even think I'm that."

She laughs. When she had proposed taking the photos, she had thought of them as a present to herself. A reminder of her immaculate youth – if she can even pretend to that. Her jeans, high-waisted, cover up the pale scar from her C-section and the fresh one from her hysterectomy. It occurs to her, though, that they are also a present for him. A way to remember her as she was, whatever happens.

"Sit, please, ma'am."

He flicks on the bedside lamp, and they take a few like that.

"There, sweep your hair to one side."

"I don't know if I can do that," she says, and she laughs, nervous. "There is a lot of it."

"Well, play with it then, or something."

She vamps. She pouts. She spends a long time looking to one side, lost in thoughts about how it will feel to lose her breasts. Whether she will feel like a child again. Whether the children will notice.

"Okay, now a bit less serious please. Try not to look like you're going to die."

He catches the stricken look. Pulls back. They watch each other for a long moment.

"Do you want to take off the jeans?"

Al has forgotten to shave today. His beard is starting to grow in salty, the sandy hairs on his head losing pigment. But his arms are as beautiful as ever. His eyes are soft. She takes off her jeans, stands in front of him, unmoving. Vulnerable. Powerful. He catches the gash across her abdomen.

He looks at her like he wants to kiss her. But he doesn't. Instead, he places down the camera and holds out his hands.

"I know," she says. "I know."

Love, she has realized, is not a feeling but a deed. It is the man waiting at home with her two children, who will change the sheets on the bed and count out her pills and remember her birthday, even after she's died. Who will watch her children grow up and bring home Christmas trees on the roof of the car and hold her hand until the final moments.

"Remember when you moved in with me?" he says.

"You didn't know how to cook."

"I still don't know how to cook."

"You've improved."

"I'm improving. And we took that ballroom dancing class?"

"The teacher was awful. But you were better than I thought you'd be."

"I did okay, didn't I? We learned the footwork. I learned how to do the . . . the hold."

"What's your point, buddy?"

"Just that." He stands back and picks up the camera again. Through the window, a cloud passes and the sun hits one side of her face hard, throws the other in shadow. "Just that I'm very lucky, Susie Q," he mumbles to himself.

This is real life, she thinks. It's loving the right person at the wrong time, it's incompatibility and doubt. It's the constant condition of misunderstanding, and the thousand ways people will prove you wrong.

2012

Sebastian
Any requests?
It's gonna be good vibes

He had texted last night, with a link to a playlist he had called Mom. Good vibes, what else could anyone want for a celebration of their death?

Viola
snacks

Sebastian
anything in particular

Viola
Cheese-Its?
I would kill for a Cheese-It.

Viola passes into Niamh's small kitchen, puts on the kettle, and leans over to feel the steam rising against her face, opening up her skin. The kettle burbles loudly and clicks, and she can hear Niamh stirring from her bedroom.

"Tea?" she calls.

"Yes, dear," Viola says. Milky for Viola, green with sugar for Niamh.

"Love you," Niamh calls.

Viola cracks open the door, holding the tea warm in her hands.

Niamh's room has a sweet, sleepy smell, and her clothes are strewn across the floor. Niamh gestures to the bedside table where Viola places the mug, and puts her head in her lap. "I feel like shit," she says.

"You smoked a lot."

Niamh nods. "I accept the consequences of my actions."

"It's snowing outside," Viola says.

Niamh gasps. "No. Why didn't you say?" It's much too early in the season for snow, but in an hour, after the tea and the cold shower have taken effect and clothes are bundled on, they catch a bus across town and walk, following the Liffey east to the sea until they reach a marina, a fleet of tall sailboats pointing stiff masts to the sky, thin white steeples. Flakes fall cozy and close. They share a set of headphones and Niamh sings along to Nina Simone, her voice low and strong, and Viola has the sense of being carried. They walk past old women dragging their shopping through the mounting snow, past abandoned plazas with weeds pulling up between heavy cement tiles. They walk until they come to a damp beach, surprisingly empty for its proximity to the city center. Viola thinks of the sand buried underneath the powder, of the cold blue.

Sebastian
Tillie has made snacks her thing
Borderline out of control
I'll tell her about the Cheese-Its
but you should be prepared to eat a million
Cheese-Its

Niamh Casey, goddess of Dublin Bay, lights a cigarette as fat flakes fall onto her neon orange beanie, onto her birthmark, somehow both otherworldly and belonging intensely to here, to this place, rooted and sure.

"What are you thinking about?" Viola asks.

"My mother," Niamh says. "And you."

"Sorry she's not well."

Niamh takes a drag. "I'm lucky I've had her as long as I have."

The water in the bay is profoundly still, as though it could hardly carry a ship anywhere. Thoughts of Susan surface with the sea foam, demanding nothing but offering nothing in return.

"You ready to see your dad, then?"

"I don't know. I just keep thinking. I used to feel so out of place as the only girl in the house. I spent so long trying to be like him. And it fucked me up."

Niamh nods. "I get it. But at least he was around. I used to really hate my dad."

"Sorry." She's being selfish again. Look at Niamh, look at what she has been through. "You're right."

"No, it's fine now. I think . . . I don't know. I just hope he found happiness. In the end I had a good life, with my mammy." She wrinkles her nose, deflecting her own sincerity. "You get the parents you get."

They turn back toward town, doubling back over their tracks. As they cross the street, nearly home, they pass a Tesco selling inflatable sleds and Niamh gets an idea. On a slow, south-bound train, they puff air into the plastic mouthpieces, other passengers looking at them strangely as they laugh loudly, the tubes ballooning in their arms.

When they arrive at Killiney Hill, the air is bracing and joyous, and all around them, children slide around on whatever they can find – lunch trays, shovels, garbage bin lids. Viola anticipates the bump, the jostle, the vertiginous drop. She is thinking of some half-fledged memory.

She wishes her mother could see this.

They climb to a good kick-off point, and the snow is still falling as they throw themselves forward and rip through the slush toward the Irish Sea.

"I missed this!" she shouts above the shrieks of happy children and the crashing wavelets and the expanse of the bay that feeds into the ocean, the cold dragging water out of her eyes.

I missed you.

Viola
no amount of Cheese-Its is too much
see you soon

In a matter of hours she is boarding. How many planes have made this journey before; planes carrying the Queen, planes carrying the Beatles, planes carrying bombs and drugs and priceless art. People running away from their lives, people running back toward them. When the wheels hit the tarmac, she can hardly believe she is here.

Tillie is picking Lola up at the airport. Tillie has done so much. There is a table of all kinds of drinks with all kinds of mixers. There are potato chips and tzatziki and guacamole, all of them emptied into little ceramic bowls of their own instead of sitting inside bags or store-bought plastic. There are one million Cheese-Its.

"Lola will be tired," Sebastian says to his father.

"She'll muddle through."

His father is wandering around, inspecting the family photo-graphs that Sebastian has hung. Sadie's newspaper clippings and childhood images and some of their own: twins clambering on Susan's chest, pulling at her hair. She is pulling a face, she is laughing. She is young and old and happy and miserable and exhausted and in love.

NEW TOPIC: SUSAN BLISS MEMORIAL PARTY
Posted by cutandpaste
You are all invited to join a celebration of the life
of Susan Bliss, who died fifteen years ago
on December 18, 1997. This will be an interactive,
expressive, joyful gathering of family, friends & fans.
Donations can be made to . . .
Directions to gallery . . .

*

Tillie had even helped him with the wording, checked his spelling. *I can't believe all these people still . . .* she started. He smiled because of course they do. Still. He has known them forever and yet he doesn't know them at all. He couldn't tell you their faces or even their real names, but he knows that LATfan4ever has three children who are all married and do not visit her, that burger_mama has been in love with a man for years who has never acknowledged her, that daytimemuse lives alone and makes show memorabilia (placemats, small sculptures) and sells it on Etsy. Probably none of them will come, but even if one of them does . . .

Somehow, this feels like the closest he can come to a real goodbye. And he knows he needs to say it. It occurred to him the other day, when he was working, that everything in her life, everything she loved, all of it was transient. Television shows like tissue paper. Stage performances that end when the curtain falls. And here he was trying to make monuments to her. If he considers – really considers – the lasting marks that people make upon the world, the buildings with men's names on them and the giant phallic statues and the landfills and landmines and highways and aerodromes from up above, most of them look like scars.

He is almost jittering as he finishes setting up the room. The centerpiece is interactive. Four boxes of scraps, painstakingly selected and cut, various shades and themes, magazines and family memories and everything discarded from every previous project, he brought all of it, let them choose. On the wall, a canvas with a rough outline in sharpie, and here are the glue sticks, maybe a thirty pack would do. Let them have at it.

"Good curation," his father says, looking at a photo of the four of them. They could never get one where all of them were smiling. But this one is close, his mother looking at something off camera, Sebastian mid-sentence. "Wonder where you get that from."

His father looks older. *I guess that's what happens when you see someone only once in a while.* They're exactly the same height, have been for a while, but it will always surprise Sebastian.

"I'm sorry, you know," Al says. He's still looking at the photograph. "I should have given you more credit. For your art I mean."

"It's fine, Dad."

"You could have gone to art school. You still could if you want."

Sebastian smiles. "I think I'm good, Dad."

He's been invited, recently, to a group show in Los Angeles. "A New Whole", it's called, which as a dyslexic person, he thinks is asking for many unwanted puns. But the group invited is cool, collage artists from around the country. He's buzzed, if he's honest. It's a bizarre feeling to be taken seriously. He's spent so long thinking of himself as the underdog. *More helpful than art school, in some ways*, he thinks.

His father puts a hand on his upper arm, squeezes it. Where is this new sincerity coming from? The room? Or maybe just Tillie, her soft influence. Either way, better not say too much. Don't spoil the moment.

There's a picture on the wall of his mom in the hospital, surrounded by cards. She's sitting up, waving. He had debated including it, but in the end, it would have felt wrong to leave it out. His father is looking at it now, the pain of it written on his face. Sebastian has never really thought about that year, what it must have done to his dad, having to care for her like that.

"I held it against you," Al says. "That you got to be with her."

Sebastian doesn't feel the need to forgive him for this. But he listens.

"I never asked. Did she say anything at the end?"

"No," Sebastian says. "Not really." And then, because he can see this answer is disappointing, he adds: "She asked what we were going to do tomorrow."

Al smiles. "And? What are you going to do tomorrow?"

"Remains to be seen."

What's next, if he isn't bumping up against this man? Or chasing a past that isn't his own? They smile at each other. The bell on the back of the door jingles and a small, frowning, middle-aged woman immaculately made up, is looking cautiously at them. "Is this . . .

Al moves to her, shakes her hand, says, "Welcome, please . . ." taking her coat and asking if he can get her some wine. Anxiously, she introduces herself as Marion. "I used to work on the show. With. I did make-up." She takes in the room, the boxes of scraps, dawn breaking on her face. "This is fun."

Then they all start arriving: a casting director, someone from props. Someone picked it up off the forum, forwarded it to the old crew. And then Sadie shows up with an old friend from Chicago named Bernie. The room gets loud and Sebastian turns up the music and is washed with the relief of having done something right for what feels like the first time in his life. Everything is in place except for Lola.

1996

It's getting hard. The medicine is making her feel out of control. At least she thinks it's the medicine. It could be any number of things, the situation, all the time alone. Who knows, really, what nightmare fear and pharmaceuticals might produce.

As it turns out, dying in real life is nothing like dying on screen. It could not fit into a sixty-minute episode. It is not a brief, dramatic moment, not a centrifuge for family catharsis. She does not look beautiful propped up on pillows, her hair tufty and unready, the scant remainder of her eyebrows hardly enough to convey the despair of it all. She wraps her head in scarves. When the children come into the room, she becomes a new character created just for them, a fortune teller, like the women in Salem who used to read people's palms. She tells them their futures:

You will have a wonderful day at school.
You will make a new friend today.
You are going to be very generous with your brother.
You have an old soul.
You will help your dad take out the trash, won't you?

Sebastian is engrossed by this act, asking a million questions, convinced she has all the answers. Viola absorbs each prognosis with skepticism, shaking her head. She knows something is wrong – they both do – just not what. They climb on her, study her intently, and run away again: exasperating, gorgeous creatures. Watching them is falling in love over and over and over.

But today is too hot for the act and the scarf. For months she has

298

struggled to regulate her temperature. Now she has closed the door and is sitting in bed looking distantly at the beads of condensation on the lemonade Al brought her, ancient and bald.

They finished the chemo last month. Next week is her results appointment. No one except Al seems optimistic. Aggressive, a word that should be reserved for sporting events and wild animals. Meta-static, a radio program in another dimension. Stage Four – the lot in the studio where they filmed cooking shows, which occasionally sent over extra choux buns. No one has used the T word yet. Not to her face. But she knows it's coming.

Al's positivity has been the one thing holding her together. He is unflagging. Even as he washes her in the shower when she can hardly lift her limbs and makes her food and takes limitless time off of work to bring her to appointments and keep her company, he has never indicated that this will be it. She needs his denial. It gets both of them through the day, through the distraction of not knowing what is going on inside her. It adds to her general irritation at not being able to do anything she wants to do. Physically, mentally, she is flagging. But she has to force herself to focus. To prepare – in case of the worst. She wants to write a letter to each of them. Something for later, some important day, in case she isn't there.

Dear Lola,
You should know that most of what you do in life
doesn't matter. All the petty disagreements and strains.
The rightness or wrongness of a decision.

That's not what she wants to say. Only it's all a bit of a fog; she is beginning to feel so small, trapped and invisible in the room, unimportant to anyone other than her family. Thank God she has her family. It's her own fault – she told everyone else not to come, it wasn't worth their precious time off. The show must go on and all that. Would it have been better for her to die with more people around?

In California, where she could feel the sun on her skin every day? If she had fought harder, sooner, if they'd had another month, another year. If they'd gone – oh what does it matter. You can't think about it. The point is, she stayed for him, for all of them, for their happiness. Maybe her friends all would have disappointed her anyway. Most people probably can't stand being around someone so close to the end, watching the slow fall of the curtain.

The only things that matter are love and sincerity.

Write it down, get it right. There's something she wants to say about the difference between sincerity and truth, but she can't quite remember it. She has to do it herself, as best she can, empty her brain before everything is lost. Because there is no character called Susan that Rip is going to write who is going to say the right things to them in the moment, who is going to appear at every necessary juncture of their lives and tell them to trust themselves or put away their pride or be brave. She looks at the scrap of paper, its worthless aphorisms, and thinks: *Oh my God. This is me.* All the other things she might say, the people she might be, none of them are real. This is, for better or worse, the life that she has made for herself, the people by her side. You make choices and then the show is over. No retakes. So she better be a professional.

They are supposed to go to the fair tonight. "If you're feeling good," Al said. Good comes in unpredictable waves. But God will she try. It's been so long since she last went to the fair. And never with them. She wants to see their faces as they eat cotton candy, and try and fail to win a prize, and stop at the top of the Ferris wheel. She wants to do everything with them – she wants to see them at eight and twelve and seventeen. She wants to see them fall in love and have children and make compromises and learn about life. She wants them to believe that life is beautiful. Now she worries that they will grow up angry and afraid, skeptical of beauty. But maybe that is better preparation for life anyways.

None of it is fair. None of it is easy.

A click.

"Don't—" she says, but not fast enough because the door is open and her daughter is standing and staring at her naked head. She walks so quietly, Lola, like a little ghost.

"I knew it!" she says. She looks like she could scream.

"Loli, please—"

Her daughter is checking behind her, like Sebastian might be right there, like she needs to report this to somebody.

"Come on, Lola, come here."

Lola's eyes are hard and untrusting, but she takes a step towards the bed. This child of exacting standards. *This is not how she wanted to tell her.* But in life, there are no retakes.

"Loli," she says. "Are you scared?"

Her daughter nods. She cannot look her in the eye. It is as though she has become a stranger. *Her body is so tired.*

"Come sit."

Tentatively her daughter finds the bed. She is studying the quilt, the diamond stitching. Her face is red and uncertain.

"I need to tell you something, Lola. Can you look at me?"

Her own eyes in a little face. There are a thousand things she wishes she could say, a thousand truths that might be possible. *I love you, you're so beautiful, you're going to have such a good time at the fair tonight.* None of them is the important truth though, the fact of what's happening.

"You know I'm sick, right?"

Her daughter nods. Still she is too far away.

"Here, come here, Loli."

She does not come.

"Viola."

Her daughter does not look at her face, but burrows into the side of her.

"I might not get better, my baby. My body isn't working very well."

301

She takes a deep breath and wonders how to say this. How to put mortality into words for a child.

"Are you going to die?" she asks. She looks at her directly, craving honesty, craving the truth. Her maddening, clever daughter.

"I don't know," she says. "We're doing everything we can, me and your dad. But I just don't know."

"Dad's doing everything he can?"

"We both are. But sweetie, if we can't fix it, I don't want you to blame anyone okay? It's nobody's fault." She takes her child's hands. "Let's make a memory together, right now. A happy memory. Let's make a wish."

"I don't want to remember this," Viola says. "I want to remember the future. When you're better."

"Well, if you do remember this, just remember I'll always love you. Love is the most important thing."

Her daughter closes her eyes. "La la la la la la la la."

"Viola."

"I'm not remembering this."

"Viola, please."

Her daughter looks at her very seriously and says: "Tell me when you're better. We can make a memory then."

Susan is getting desperate. "You're going to remember this whether or not you know it, Lola. It's going to be in there. I promise. You silly thing. You're going to remember when you least expect it."

And she tries to kiss her, but she is scrambling out of the room, shouting for her father.

When her husband arrives, Susan is lying on her side, too tired to cry. Too tired to go to the fair.

"They're never going to know me," she says. "Not really."

"Don't say that."

"It's true."

He is quiet for a minute. On the floor are the crumpled attempts

302

at notes, insufficient, incoherent. How to explain herself? How to give them all she wants to give? She feels disappointed in herself. Like so many things, she left this too late.

"They'll know people who loved you."

She pulls herself up and he lies next to her, lets her curl her head into his lap. He traces his finger around the outside of her ear. She closes her eyes.

Maybe that's enough.

2012

When you arrive, the gallery is full of strangers. A few people that you maybe knew in a past life, but all of them looking around in a curious state of wonder, running their fingers through scraps of paper, asking whether they can borrow a glue stick. Someone asks you if you'd like a drink and maybe you get chatting – *how did you know* and *isn't this a nice idea*. You don't have many anecdotes to share, or the ones you have are patchy now, have lost the rhythm they used to have, but you remember Susan Byrne, the warm feeling of spending time in her company. And when the daughter walks in, you can't help but stare for a moment – caught in the bright delusion of a miracle you didn't realize you still believed in.

Viola turns to a box of paper scraps. She thinks about her brother cutting all of it out, wonders what it was inside him that lit up so brightly when he felt her. Her hand passes over it like a defunct metal detector.

Another hand, on her back, a woman introducing herself.

"You're the spitting image," she says, and explains that she is a friend of Sebastian from some online forum. "I loved your mother," she begins, and explains how much she connected with her mother's character on *Life and Times*, how she helped her support a friend through addiction and recovery, how when Susan died, she cried alone in her house, she couldn't explain it to anyone.

Can she see it, all the empty space inside her where there ought to be a person and is nothing? A force in her wants to resist: to refuse to become a receptacle for all of the feeling in the room, all the old, homeless grief. But she says "Thank you" and holds it close to her, the woman's small offering, receives a mighty embrace.

Maybe it's all equally important, all the people who felt anything about you. That's the problem with belonging to everyone. But maybe it is the blessing too.

She gravitates to Sadie, who has lost weight, and also – it seems to Viola – height. She had always thought of her aunt as an overwhelming presence but now, it seems as though she has become a child again. She stands effortfully when Viola comes over.

"Sit, Sadie, you'll tire yourself out," Sebastian instructs.

They lower themselves onto some plastic chairs and Sadie begs for Viola's phone, her photos of Dublin.

Beautiful, Sadie says time after time. *Beautiful.* It was, they can agree, even in miniature captured on the phone of an unskilled photographer; clouds over the Liffey, a man papering up a poster, the sun setting on cobbled streets that have belonged to millions before and will belong to millions after.

"It doesn't really capture it," Viola says.

"Well, you can't do that," says Sadie.

Tentatively, her father approaches the two of them, and she rises to hug him, her body tense, resisting regression, refusing the teenage self who was so blinded by the gospel of Al. He turns, now, to Sadie, his old enemy. *Readying himself for combat,* Viola thinks, *using me as a shield.* But he only smiles shyly and says: "Nice to have this one home."

"Isn't it! Jesus, she looks like Susie."

"I know. More and more like Susie."

His sincerity catches her off guard. His white hair. They are both staring at her, and it's palpable how much they need to feel it. How desperate they are to say her name to one another.

"Your brain though," Sadie says.

"I don't know about that."

"I do. And thank God for that."

They both laugh a bit in discomfort and Viola hardly believes in it, the gentleness. Did it take them this long, just to grow up?

Al rubs the balding spot at the back of his head, turns to Sebastian. "Well, this kid has your creative streak."

On the wall, Sebastian is projecting some video, decades old, of their mother performing in a school play. They watch her for a little while, a woman of movement and joy. She's funny, she makes them laugh. She flubs a line. She is just a girl like any other girl. Viola takes in her corny gestures, meets her backstage as she giggles, as she receives flowers and blushes at praise for her performance. She introduces all of her castmates as though each one is a name they ought to remember. She is unapologetically herself.

The clip switches to an early family video. Her mother must be her own age, or near enough. Viola watches as she picks her up, a little girl, her feet dangling in the air, her curls downy on her tiny scalp, and they smile at each other the same smile, and she can hear her father's voice under the music that is playing saying: let's see a spin! and her mother is lifting her high in the air with strong arms and looking into her face and saying: look at you go!

"In some ways, it made it harder," he says. "Having had that time together. Feeling what it might have been like, to be a real family."

"We were always a real family."

Viola's anger is growing, alarming and righteous. It's his fault they didn't have more time with her. His fault that they grew up without the full picture. His fault that she doesn't remember her. But how can she hold all of this stupid, directionless rage when all she wants to do is slip back into the easy comfort of their relationship? What she wants is not to hurt him, but to tell him about her thesis and receive his praise, to go home and sit on the couch and watch detective shows. To cook for him. To talk to him like this, as two adults. To think about his time with her mother as a circumstance that arose between two people who probably loved and hated each other, who fought and made up and were similar and different. Who needed each other and didn't need each other. Here he is again on the screen, just a man, waving the camera away, not wanting to be seen.

"You know, I still feel sorry that I never asked her what she wanted. Afterwards, I mean, for the funeral. I had so much time and I just. It felt like asking would have made it come true."

Viola places a hand on her father's back.

The great sadness of her death had made it so easy to sweep away the smaller, more preventable sadnesses. She wonders if the greater tragedy was the one they might have affected.

"You were young," she says to him.

Her father holds her hand. *Maybe we are done, as a family, leaving things unsaid.* Or maybe this is just a moment in time.

"How is that mystery gentleman you were seeing?" he asks.

"It ended. Unfortunately."

"Sorry to hear that. Who was he?"

On the wall behind her is a cutout of *Soap Opera Digest*, Orson looking playfully into her mother's eyes. Her heart is wretched with him. Sebastian glances over, a snatch of their conversation caught in his face.

"Doesn't matter now," she says.

Al rubs his daughter's back. "Cheer up, sweetheart. The sea is full of fish."

Viola
I'm thinking of you.

Her brother's hand wraps over her shoulders, and both of them watch the video in silence. Around them the room is moving and people are talking about her, and not talking about her, spilling out into the street despite the cold, with plastic cups of wine. Her face, her mother's face, her brother wanting to be lifted. She looks to her father, and he is watching too, listening to some younger version of himself, and in the middle of all the guesses and imperfect memories, Sebastian has salvaged this: a brief and crystal love.

"Thank you," she says. He bends and hugs her around her neck, and then she pushes her way outside.

Someone has hung Christmas lights between the houses, and through the glass, looking back inside, Viola can see mingling in the dim, her father chattering to Sadie, Tillie refilling glasses and nodding her head at the woman from the forum. She begins to walk down the street to a small beachy point. A man pushes past on a bicycle. A woman carries something large and rectangular wrapped in thick brown paper. Where are they all going?

Where is she going?

At this time of night the beach is cold and empty, though still she can sense the ghosts of parents clamoring to catch the last rays of sun before the rhythm of school supplies and extracurriculars and report cards begins again, their children moving forward whether they like it or not, forcing them to reckon with the fact that they themselves are getting older, that they might one day be left alone and have to join some superfluous local committee just to keep busy, just to avoid reckoning with the smallness of their lives, the fact that they will, at some later point, die. All of them, everyone in the gallery and Orson and Niamh and her father and Sebastian, all of them will die. Still the seagulls cry and the waves crash relentlessly. Above her is a full moon.

Viola takes off her shoes and stands ankle deep in the water as it rushes around her, freezing, sinking into the soft sand. The beach is so much smaller than it used to be. She is listening more often now to all of the stories about the rising tides, the catastrophe waiting just around the corner. Ready or not. Overhead, a plane makes a wide loop, ripping gray across the sky.

Orson
thinking of you too.

1997

Dimly she is aware of the warmth of her child's body, her own weakness, her inability to hold him as tightly as she wants to. The room is out of focus, but sight no longer feels so important as smell and touch, the pleasant temperature of his skin, the clean smell of his head on her shoulder.

There is no more time. There will not be another autumn, another year to go to the fair, there will not be tomorrow and tomorrow. There is only this, her precious, stupid little life and the man that she chose and the children that she made. There behind her are all the hours of her experience, all the hours that counted and the hours she wasted, all of the TV ads and minutes spent waiting for trains and planes and sleeping in late and daydreaming. There is everything she missed and everything she has yet to miss.

The room takes on the sense of a departure lounge, the empty chairs at odd angles as though they are waiting for something to happen, as though they don't want to look directly at it.

Where are we going? she wants to ask, but her mouth is dry and not forming words. She cannot escape the pervasive feeling that she has forgotten something at home, that she doesn't know what she has forgotten, that there's something she has not done or said, something just on the tip of her mind. It's an awful itchy feeling. What was it? Wasn't there something that she was supposed to do? Take Sebastian to swim class? Put a spoon under her pillow? Watch her daughter fall in love? Outside, other planes are taking off, roaring into the blue. People are filtering in now, they've called the gate and the destination is just out of reach, she is checking her bag for her passport, her chap-stick, some piece of paper that will say everything she needs to know, a script maybe, that's the thing. She has forgotten her lines! Or maybe it's just that they haven't given them to her yet, maybe that's what she's waiting for. As the people around her start laughing and chattering and fading away she realizes, this isn't a departure. She has only just arrived. Of course, she can feel it now, the warmth hitting her skin, the sweet sense of somewhere new, of transforming – why didn't she notice before? That's it, she has only just arrived, here in California, to film her first episode of *Life and Times*. (Where is Al?) Oh it all makes sense now, why he couldn't be here, he's somewhere on the other side of the country, going to work. No – he's already at work. That's how time zones work. Yes, Al has been at work for three hours. Quietly shifting through old documents to find something interest-ing, or perhaps writing a caption on an old broken piece of ship that they will mount to the wall. She clutches her Styrofoam coffee, and the early-morning ballet begins around her: cameras sliding into place, make-up artists dashing powder onto actors reading and rereading their lines, the sense of an orchestra tuning up.

She steps forward to speak.

2013

It is morning in Los Angeles. The sky is blue, cloudless. Outside of LAX, a light breeze stiffens against concrete. A driver is waiting on the curb with the trunk open, sunglasses wide over his nose. He is holding a sign that reads BLISS. Sebastian and Viola step out of the automatic door, bags in hand, into the beginning of a dream.

"Can I get that for you, ma'am?" the driver asks. He is wearing a cap low on his forehead, smiling broadly under thick eyebrows. The thin film of an accent.

"Thanks," Lola says.

His sister is happy, nervous. Ready for something. But he isn't sure what.

The sliding door behind them swishes open with another flurry of passengers, all checking their phones for their taxis, checking that they know where they are going. They are loud and distracted, all kinds of America tumbling onto the pavement, looking for magic and money and the promise of a life not yet lived.

"So. What can I show you?" Orson asks.

"Everything," Sebastian says.

I owe a great deal to my early readers, for your time and your thoughtful notes, and for telling me it was good before it really was: Sophie Vipond, David Watson, Brita Lee, Dave Martin, Jen Kapila, Vic Hadley, Ros Purcell, Katie Jenkins, Lucy Bulmer, Benedetta Mancusi, Jean Kaimakliotis, Melissa Twigg, Mark Richardson, Rachel Colley, and Sarah Bell. To Eilidh Brooker for Scottish dialect consulting. To everyone who fed me and swam with me in the reservoir and tolerated my moods, especially Katy Papineau, Jo Estrin, and Flo Perry, for long chats about the art and impossibility of ever spending the hours in your day correctly, this is for you. Charlotte Dillon, I still have a screenshot of the text you sent to tell me you thought it was good. You matter more than I can say.

Acknowledgements to Shakespeare, obviously, and the 1980's cast of *Days of Our Lives*. James Lindgren's article "'That Every Mariner May Possess the History of the World': A Cabinet for the East India Marine Society of Salem" inspired Al's exhibition, and is a superb piece of historiography. Gratitude to all the staff of Luminary Bakery – it was better that you never quite fixed the Wi-Fi.

And of course, to my family, who gave me such little drama about embarking on this book. Lauren and Keith, thank you for your dogged encouragement and for talking me up even when I wasn't all that much. To my parents: for coming to see me in every school play, even the bad ones, and for nurturing my love of words in every form. Caroline, if I have learned anything about being a sibling, it was from you. I love you. And to Miles, for everything, especially the day at the Banya, it's all for you *amore*.

Acknowledgements

To the remarkable Felicity Blunt and Rosie Pierce: you read a single page in the voice of Susan Bliss and believed in her. Thank you for your toughness, your fierce intelligence, and your unflagging faith. I needed all of it. You have changed my life. To my sparkling US agent, Rebecca Gradinger, what a dream to have you by my side. To Tanja Goossens, my translation agent, who read this book before giving birth to her own twins: Susan would be proud. To Lisa Babalis, for a deep read at a critical juncture, your notes felt like therapy. Allison Defrees, you were the first person to tell me: "You are a writer," and it mattered. Emma Walker, thank you for helping me get over the finish line. To everyone at Curtis Brown Creative, especially: Jennifer Kerslake, Jake Arnott and Suzannah Dunn. You improve the entire ecology, and I hope you know it.

Jo Thompson, my UK editor: this story is far greater for your love of Al and concern for Viola. How you managed to give yourself to this book in a moment of your own family grief will forever astound me. Every character (and author!) deserves a friend like you. To Carina Guiterman, my US editor: when you first told me your hopes for this book, I thought I'd just forgotten about American exuberance. But no, you meant it all! Your ambition blows me away. Thank you both for all the care you've taken with these relationships. You're a hell of a team.

To everyone at Borough and Simon & Schuster: truly I am lucky to be yours. Special thanks to Francine Brody for copyediting.